ZEPHYR Volume 1

Warren Hately

It's 2013 on the eastern seaboard of the United States. The place is Atlantic City: a sweeping longitudinal metropolis rebuilt following widespread devastation in 1984. Superhumans are not only real, they're human. All too human, as Nietzsche would say.

"… like superheroes in the world of American Psycho …"
@wereviking

For more about Zephyr or its author, visit **warrenhately.com** for musings about post-literary writing and Sturgeon's law – updated most weeks.

Contact the author at **wereviking @ hotmail.com**, follow **@wereviking** or find Zephyr on Facebook at www.facebook.com/Zephyrseries

Cover art by Alfredo Torres
@spacechipAT
redharvestportfolio.tumblr.com

Zephyr 1.1 "Bright Red Zee"

FOR A MAN with the power of six-hundred thousand light bulbs or whatever the fuck the advert says, I am feeling kinda wrecked as I stumble up the steps at Halogen, fingers clawing into Red Monolith's designer cloak as we make a show of laughing and clowning good-naturedly for the cameras. Actresses swirl around us like blowflies on a dead cow, minor grade, firm-bodied, their post-operative breasts stacked and racked as beautifully as the season's evening wear can hope to provide for, and it isn't like I am slapping them away. It's times like these – which means yeah, pretty much every time I stumble into Halogen or the Flyaway or Silver Tower, or sneak in through the back at Transit or Aubergine – that I think about Elisabeth. Funny how someone you love so much can seem like such a nuisance. I blame it on my inner child, knowing she would as well.

Inside, Darkstorm is talking to Lady Macbeth and I wonder what the hell a villainess is doing in here and whether I should kick up a stink, but actually I'm craning my head above the crowd wondering if Twilight has made a show. I see Black Honey talking to Demi Moore and Tony Sabato Jr, and Eric Clapton goes past and high fives me and then immediately makes a face aghast like he mistook me for someone else. I quickly turn my shoulder on Black Honey, knowing if she's here, her other low-level pals won't be far away.

I can't see Twilight anywhere, though the club is pretty packed and it seems like either the pounding music renders me instantly deaf or there's something else beneath it, the music and its accompanying vibrations somehow beneath us, subterranean and foul, and I brush past Lady Macbeth and she makes a face at me, baring her teeth, and I'm just thinking "fuck it" I might power up and slug her one and be done with it when Red Monolith appears, grabbing me by the wrist and pretty much ignoring the latent static charge he gets in return.

"Hey man," he grins in that stupid surfer voice of his. "Ease off the Lady, Zeph. Haven't you heard? The Lady turned."

I look again at the tall blonde, fairly graceful despite her age, and realize the snarling thing is her attempt at playing the coquette. She winks at me as I transfer my gaze with difficulty between her magnetic blue eyes and the dark sheen of Red Monolith's visor.

"What the fuck are you talking about?"

Lady Macbeth leans in and does this weird wiggly dance and starts talking like she's a stunt double for one of the bigger girls from the Supremes, which again, maybe I'm a little slow on the uptake, I realize eventually it's basically all just a performance for my benefit.

"Ain't you heard, Mr Zephyr? I'm turned," the old witch says.

"Turned?"

"Apparently Think-Tank fucked up," Monolith shrugs. "Get Lady to tell you about it."

I wince because even under the seven-foot-tall hero's red-and-black motorcycle helmet I can tell he's making wildly suggestive motions with his eyebrows, not to mention nudging me, and even if her brain molecules are still recovering from being re-organized by one of my old enemies, the Lady gets the drift and gives a look of discomfort, finding someone she knows in the crowd and departing. On reflex I turn to check out her ass and I have to concede she's in pretty good shape. The split-leg black evening gown helps. Lady Macbeth hails down Antonio Banderas like he's a taxi or something, but the sneaky bastard turns and pretty quickly opens his arms for the grope. It's not like she's a mass murderer or anything, so I guess it's fairly easy to forgive and forget. Especially for actors.

"Have you seen Twilight?"

"What's that?"

Red Monolith leans in and offers me the side of his head like I might speak right into his ear. Resisting the urge to pull off his helmet if not his head and throw it across the room, I calmly repeat myself more loudly.

"Oh no, I have no idea."

"OK."

"Beer?"

"Stoli," I reply.

I'm not going to the bar tonight after an incident the previous week that I can only remember in flashbacks. I also don't have any money. I could flash fry an automatic teller or yank one of the damn things out of the fucking wall, but for some reason I have not. Yet. I'm one of the good guys. It's a mantra for me. It's worked so far. It also helps me not forget.

The press and push of the crowd is a little sickening. The air's moist like we are in the presence of a giant fourth-dimensional armpit, though I know the smell, if I'm not imagining it, comes mostly from the carpeted floor. I've been here in the daytime – woken up in a corner, in fact – and it's not one of the prettiest sights.

I retain the curious conviction that if I keep looking long enough I might find Twilight, so I move along under the awning beneath the DJ booth and nod hello to the guy from Ned and Stacy and one of the Ramones and a girl called Constance who I saved once from a burning tenement, which she has used ever since as her excuse to get into exclusive clubs like these. It is possible that after saving her, Constance gave me a blowjob, but since I was out of my skull on horse tranquilizers at the time I can't really recall. She says hi, does a little wave. I pull my hard face, eyes far away as I shoulder past her like a man with an important engagement – like I have to return some videos or something.

*

RED MONOLITH FINDS me lurking like a sex offender beside the doors to the girls' toilets. He passes me the cold bottle and I drink half the thing straight off, knowing there's no way in hell my constitution will allow me to do something as unhelpful as get drunk. Tired as I am, thanks to a police station siege, an overturned fuel carrier, a weakened bridge in Old Brooklyn, and two separate corner store hold-ups today, I can practically feel the little bubbles of sweet liquor pounced on by my hyper-charged enzymes and converted immediately into latent energy, incorporated into the living battery that is my endocrine system – "recruited to the cause," as I sometimes think about it.

I don't like to think about it that way, I just do.

I upend my bottle and when Monolith asks "Another?" I nod and he laughs, producing a second Stoli with a flourish from under his legionnaire's cape.

"Oh so that's why you wear that thing? Are you sure Calvin approves?"

"No, man. Come on Zephyr, you know I just wanna be like you."

I take a quick glance to see if he's joking and of course he is.

"Like me?" I motion obliquely. The leather bodysuit fits like the proverbial glove, a bright red zee like a lightning bolt in the middle of my chest descending to the buckle. "I gave up that spandex shit years ago."

"I liked your old costume man, seriously," Red Monolith says.

I frown because now I think he's being honest. Yet I know if I give in to it, the joke'll still be on me somehow. I glance away and take in his helmeted head two or three times and wonder suddenly how the hell it is I am able to read his expression given his face is covered by a ballistic carbon shield.

"You know the Red Monolith and the old Zephyr, man, we were like color co-ordinated," he says.

"My costume was red and white," I answer. "You're red and black . . . and you've got those yellow panels."

Monolith motions under his armpits. The actor who used to be known as Tom Cruise walks past holding hands with Richard Gere. A dreadlocked kid raises an eyebrow at us and I make a spark leap from my finger so that he goes away. Fucking drug dealers – never around when we need one, and pulling Uzis on us when we do. On a good day I might bust him. On a better day I'd find he was carrying something that might actually get me high.

"I'm thinking about gettin' rid of the yellow panels, man," Monolith says, bringing me back to the dingy reality of the club at its zenith.

"Really? Man, you should." I try not to sound so earnest, but it comes out of me in a rush like I've spent every waking hour chewing nails over Red Monolith's costume, so I give up completely, hoping he'll read my reaction as irony as I add, "I've been wanting to say something for ages, but I didn't know how to bring it up."

"Zephyr, man," Monolith answers earnestly. "We're friends, aren't we? You saved me from Doctor Octopus, remember?"

"Doctor Octopus is a comic book character. I've told you that a hundred times. It was Doctor Nefarious, OK?"

"Nefarious, OK," Monolith half-chants to himself. "Then why did he have those mechanical arms?"

"I don't know." I sigh, swearing beneath my breath and looking away.

Drew Barrymore and her girlfriend emerge from the toilets and I know they're big fans so I hide as quick as I can, leaving Red Monolith's bulk as a distraction. Then, sipping my Stoli, I scan the room again wondering if Twilight has arrived while Monolith was talking shit. There's no sign, no trace. I flex my fingers and a crackle of static emanates across the room, one in five girls feeling a gentle shock, nipples hardening, hair standing up on arms. Demi Moore looks my way and I shake my head, and Black Honey, her new costume or at least her outfit for the night made of shiny PVC instead of the usual black leather, glares at me like she could make something of it. We both know her heightened agility and acrobatics won't mean shit the day I decide to cram thirty thousand volts of lightning up her ass. I do the sparking eyes thing, which even I have to admit looks extra cool with the domino mask, and Honey quickly looks away. I notice David Hasselhoff and the moment he sees me he flinches like a beaten dog and scurries out of sight – as well he should.

The guy comes out of nowhere, all Clark Kent with his slicked black hair, lantern jaw and wire-frame glasses. He has the nerdy dress code down pat too. I can't imagine how he even got in here.

"Uh, Mr Zephyr?"

"I know it's hard when you're dealing with someone with one name, but it's just Zephyr, kid," and I throw off the hand he tries put on my arm.

"I've got to speak to you."

I look over my shoulder and I can't see Twilight anywhere and I'm thinking that if he's stayed home, maybe he made the right call. I should be at home too, but if I was Twilight, with a sixteen-bedroom mansion on an island far away, I'd definitely skip Halogen if there was something better on offer.

"I'm not buying, sorry."

I turn my back on the kid and start away and I am totally unprepared for him to grab me by the shoulder and try to turn me around. I resist the urge to flash-fry his balls and whirl back, my practiced badass look made supreme in the leather bodysuit, all the static in the air congealing in my hair which is already standing up.

"Get your fucking hands off me."

"But, I . . . need to speak to a hero."

The young guy's face is kind of lame and he's as embarrassed as I am, knowing he nearly said the line from that song. I gesture around.

"The club's full of 'em. Knock yourself out."

And I know he's going to tell me that there's no-one like me, that Paragon and Stiletto and Black Honey and even Red Monolith can't match the legendary Zephyr, and he's right, but suddenly I just don't want to be there unless I can be drunk, and I can't be drunk because it's years since I even tried, playing skal with two cases of mixers and pissing like a racehorse as a result. So I just walk. The kid follows. I'm calling him a kid because he's so clean shaven, but I'm thirty-five and in superhero years that makes me his grandpa. And he can follow all he likes because the moment I hit the chain and Leonardo inclines his shiny black head at me and parts the rope, I do the crouch thing and disappear with a whoosh into the sky.

Zephyr 1.2 "Going Walkies"

THE SKY IS a grey curtain like a cataract across the stars. Thanks to me. Free-floating eight-hundred storeys above the tarmac chaos below, there's nothing like it for fleeing your troubles – and I should know. The heavens are a frequent refuge of mine, even if the irony stinks. I can't get any closer to heaven than the rest of you.

The cityscape is like a science fiction artist's wet dream, at least by the light of the three-quarter moon. Superheroes have sure left their mark on this city and given the government more than a few excuses to redecorate, but the botched Kirlian Invasion of '84 destroyed so much of New York's infrastructure the city as it was known could never be the same again. With the millions already quarantined and evacuated for fear of contact with our aggressive spectral invaders, a major, once-in-a-century rebuilding effort seemed so logical even Congress couldn't say no. Thus Atlantic City – the world's great megalopolis and magnetic north for every costumed loony in creation – was born.

The architects wanted to include Manhattan instead of leaving it in ruins, the tunnels choked with the dead unable to get through the gridlock on that fateful first day when the skies rained an army of living light beams clad in powered armor. The president himself convinced the architects to make their mark on destiny regardless, gathering a team of designers with a budget never seen in the history of modern development. Legend also has it an inner cabal of architects, in the face of such a vast rebuild, watched Fritz Lang's *Metropolis* no less than twenty times and tried to raise Frank Lloyd-Wright with a Ouija board with mixed success.

Astoria where I grew up as a child still exists, though no one calls it that any more. Likewise bits and pieces of the old cities here and there. In the Bronx, there's The Bubble: a twelve-block radius of rundown tenements and historic brownstones preserved by the superhero Infinity at the moment of his death. People can still come and go from the force field-protected museum piece. Infinity was one of Captain Atom's successors from the 70s New Breed team. It was just light he was trying to keep out, given that's what the Kirlians were made from. Hence the dome looks like a giant black half-marble, especially on a night like this, and I'm just close enough to be able to make it out, dopplered in architecture with the new

Planetarium, the needle of the Silver Tower begging for my attention close by.

The mayor of this vast domain is Roland Pykes. Good old gutless Roland – or at least his PA Alison Kirkness – knows how to irritate me better than almost anyone, and that includes Phantasmagor, Crescendo, Think-Tank and the Ill Centurion combined. You'd think I'd get used to it, being a hero on call, but that's not really one of my virtues.

If I was able to answer my new Blackberry as quickly as my old phone, I wouldn't have half the problems I do, but the damned thing comes with *It's Raining Men* as the ringtone and I haven't figured out how to change it yet. I'd get Tessa to do it for me, my darling technopath – that's a joke, she's normal, I hope for her sake – except the whole secret identity thing would be kind of hard to explain while she's fiddling with Zephyr's red lightning bolt-emblazoned cell phone. Kind of a giveaway.

The phone is sponsored by Enercom and slips into the back of my hidden belt compartment, nestled there right along with a brace of condoms, an emergency cigarette, a phial of special painkillers, and usually the idea is to have a $100 bill except I spent mine when Tess needed money for the school excursion I'd forgotten to pay last week.

"Mr Pykes," I respond in my best gravelled voice.

The reception is good even with all the turbulence I've created, shunting air molecules around creating a narrow storm-front.

"Hi Zephyr, this is Alison Kirkness here."

"You're up late, Ali."

"Still getting things together for this ceremony tomorrow morning." The reply is as taut as those long legs of hers. "Mayor Pykes asked me to give you a ring and, uh, you know, just make sure we're all on the same page still?"

"Ceremony?"

I run through a mental catalogue – the closest thing I have for a diary. Elisabeth is in the downtown office, Tessa has school by quarter-to-nine, I promised to clean cat puke (not ours) out of my wife's car. No ceremonies leap to mind and I'm paranoid enough to believe the mayor's office could be messing with my brain. I spent a month once convinced I was a sexual abuse survivor named Valerie (thanks Mentor), so I've learnt to keep a skeptical view of reality.

"The Hermes Foundation ceremony?" Miss Kirkness prompts.

"Hermes Foundation? The porn guys?"

"That's the Eros Foundation, I think you'll find."

"Look, I'm sorry Ali," I reply and only just manage to mean it, "but I don't remember any mention of a ceremony."

"Well it's not like you have a regular mailing address we can send you the invitation. We have to rely on your memory instead."

"Sounds like that's a pain for you," I mutter.

No reply.

"Well, sorry to keep you in a job, Miss Kirkness. Just tell me the when and where and I'll make it."

"The civic centre at ten," she says, tired and doubtful.

"OK."

"OK."

She hangs up.

I'm floating in a foggy cloudbank. With my eyes closed, I put away the cell by touch alone, enjoying the sensation of wet static as it rolls across me with the air. It doesn't matter about the leather all but insulating my physical shell. The extra senses tied in to my special abilities are alive and well, tickled, in a metaphysical sense at least, by the surrounding saturation.

"Just a little more. . . ."

I flex my fists. *KABOOM* – and thunder rolls away to either side.

I give a chuckle, knowing the city dwellers will be turning in their beds or glancing out windows at the unexpected weather. More than a few will blame me. The garbage men always like a good rain so I lay it on for them. Soon the shower is falling away from me, the impression like hundreds of thousands of tiny parachutists going past falling to their doom. My face and hair are slick. So is the leather. I'm tired still, on some level, but the effort to keep myself aloft is minimal and the clouds shield me from the city and some kind of haven is what I find myself craving right now.

I should be home, asleep, perhaps even making love to my wife. Possibly both. Tessa sleeps soundly in the flat's second bedroom, the soft whine of her laptop always a strangely reassuring sound in the dark.

I conduct the storm like it was an orchestra, flinging my hands wildly and grinning, hair just long enough to be in my eyes when it's not standing characteristically upright. A peal of thunder rings like the bells of Hell and then a stroke of lightning shudders through the night, my very own electric violin quartet.

Eventually the music stops. Fades. The clouds dissipate under their own will, depleted, drifting back towards the Atlantic.

And somewhere in the city it sounds like a building turns over in its sleep, like an uncanny echo of the thunder from before. I drop altitude on instinct and pretty soon pass below the dispersing cover and see a mushroom cloud of brown dust emanating from halfway across downtown.

Without really thinking about it, I am down and swooping across the city, a black shadow flitting between the taller skyscrapers. The lights that way are still on. Dust roils down the street and now car alarms and others are going off. It's just after midnight and by rights I should still be at Halogen or maybe partying on at De Lux. I said I would meet Robert Downey there, I suddenly remember.

It seems like now I have an excuse.

*

WHAT I SEE is a building walking towards me.

It's the Federal National Bank, Jane Street branch, where I have banked a dozen times or so while in the neighborhood they call Eisenhower these days. It's a five-storey brownstone full to the brim with offices, just a handful of lights somehow still on, while down below multiple pairs of gigantic earthy legs propel the building ponderously forward.

I don't know whether to call them legs or tentacles, but clearly this is nothing alive, or not alive in any real sense because I can see churned-up bricks and slabs of concrete and electrical wiring and broken tarmac and random assortments of trash swirling through the huge vats of moving earth supporting the building as it lists wonkily from side to side as it comes down the street. There's a crater somewhere in the background where the bank used to sit and now for some reason it's going walkies.

For a few seconds I just watch. There's nothing like gathering your thoughts and not getting too stupid with adrenaline. A moment's foresight is like a thousand hours of hindsight, my old tutor Hawkwind used to say, often before beating the crap out of me.

As I'm watching the building lurch down the street – and it's going pretty slowly and the noises it's making aren't pretty – the first cop car slides to an awkward halt throwing parti-colored light over everything. The strobe reflects off something in one of the upper floor windows and I glimpse the figure of a man before he darts away from the glass.

The vibrations and structural damage to the bank alone create a nightmare. Pieces of masonry and drainpipes and marble cladding fall from the upper levels like chunky rain, and all at once, most of the windows in the place shatter outwards, glass sparkling like a waterfall of sharpness as it showers down and crunches beneath the myriad stamping stumps moving the bank ever along.

More movement catches my eye. The woman is blue and wears a black leotard and a black ponytail juts from the back of her head without moving in the least. She comes from some height, probably off one of the neighboring roof-tops, and there's a moment of inertia when she hits the ground, landing in a crouch, before her own particular physical properties kick in and she's propelled up and powerfully forward into the air and through an empty second-floor window.

Her name is Vulcana and I still owe her thirty bucks.

I see her again about ten seconds later when she flies backwards through one of the last windows with glass still in it, so yeah, in a sense, uh, somewhat rectifying that situation, and since I was just about to go upstairs for a look-see anyway, up I zoom and catch the ungrateful bitch in my arms.

"Zephyr," she grunts.

It's not a question.

"Hey 'Cana, long time no see."

"I asked you to never call me that."

"Split infinitives," I tut.

At her hiss I add, "Sorry."

"Fuck," she aspirates prettily. "This city's got too many heroes."

I deposit her on the roof of a six-storey law firm down the street from the oncoming building. A few more police cruisers arrive, one of them managing to clip another as they haphazardly park. Cops scurry across the road like worker ants, shotguns and flak jackets and 9mm pea-shooters poised. One of them, a cop I recognize, glances up in the direction we've gone as Vulcana irritably shakes herself free of my helping hands.

"What are you doing here?"

"Me? I'm fighting –"

"I heard there was a wrap party for the new Meg Ryan film on 43rd."

"Baby, Meg Ryan hasn't made a film for –"

I catch myself on and stare miserably at the back of Vulcana's blue head. I'm not game to tell her that her vulcanized ponytail has snapped off until she reaches back a hand and swears.

"Not again. Jesus!"

"Short hair suits you."

After a moment to let her grieve, I ask, "So what have we got in there?"

Another figure lands on the rooftop and immediately chimes in, "That's just what I was gonna ask."

I look over sans friendliness as Nightwind walks matter-of-factly across the building's roof with a goofy smile on his otherwise grimly-masked face. I can't help registering my animosity and it's annoying to see Vulcana nod tiredly, but without any resistance to the imposter.

"What are you doing here?" I snap.

"Isn't that what she was just asking you?" Nightwind sneers. I can't help being surprised and he reminds me, "Super hearing, remember?"

"Super hearing my ass," I respond. "Dude, you are a fucking loser. Could you please stand aside so the real crime-fighters can deal with this?"

"Zephyr, what's your problem?" Vulcana snaps. "Do you always have to be so damned uppity?"

"Hey, let's leave the ancient history out of this, OK? At least we have a history. This guy's a fucking nobody."

"Hey," Vulcana says, her blue face dark in the night. "I've seen him on news reports like anyone else."

"He's never done anything!"

It's hard not to explode. This is a long-running frustration for me and only made worse by the fact I seem to be the only one onto

Nightwind's ruse. He has a cloak with some kind of thermal fan under it that lets him glide. His inventor dad or the uncle who molested him as a kid probably built it to keep him quiet. That and a few more gizmos are all his tricks, and I've never seen him once actually stop a crime. The best he can do is glide down to the footpath when the TV cameras turn up.

"Chill, dude," Nightwind says.

He reminds me so much of the smug handsome guys who were going off to college when I was repeating night school in the early years of my career as a fuckwad four-color masturbation fantasy that I almost punch his head in right then and there. At least he has the brains to back right the fuck off as Vulcana puts her hand on my arm. Thankfully for Nightwind, and unlike him, 'Cana has the heightened strength to actually hold me in place – for a moment, at least.

"Just forget about it, OK?" she yells into my face. "Like you said, there are bigger problems."

She points and my attention comes back just as the roof of the Federal Bank starts past us. I glance over the edge and see the police cars flattened and caked with mud and just generally fucked over in its wake.

*

WITHOUT FURTHER ADO I leap off the top of the current building and land on the roof of the bank. Although I can fly and shit, you'd think I would pretty quickly adjust to weird situations like the nausea-inducing way the bank roof seems to be rolling and buckling as the building advances down the street. But I don't. Almost immediately I fall over, harmlessly of course, but it gives me a good chance to appreciate the view down the street, the lights of twenty-odd cop cars and an equal number of cabs blinking and flickering as their drivers desperately try to reverse them out of the log-jam they've created. It's fortunate the bank moves slow enough that no-one has been caught underneath, though that's an assumption.

Fortunate for the guy within, anyway.

Fissures appear in the roof, but I'm not waiting for them to worsen. On the roof there's a pillbox with a door I'm powerfully hurling open and then an emergency-lit concrete stairwell. I can't quite work out how any lights are on, but then that's not really my main concern. Instead, I smash my way down the stairs, half-running, half-flying. A woman appears, disheveled, hair and blouse loose, spot-lit in the emergency lights like a cave-in survivor.

"What are you doing here?" I snarl.

She doesn't say anything at first, eyeing me up and down like a frightened rabbit.

"You're . . . you're Zephyr?"

"You'd better hope so, huh?"

"The bank manager is still inside, Jonas Severin."

"He's doing this?"

The woman looks at me like I'm deranged, eyes flicking from me to the false lure of escape above.

"No, it's some guy. I don't even think he knew we were here."

"yeah, what *were* you doing here?"

". . . working. . . ."

"Right."

I manage to push past her without making any promises and the hallway beyond the door is like the inside of a giant waste-paper basket. I'm reminded of that Monty Python skit about offices as pirate ships. There's not really any light now and it's cold inside, enough that my breath steams. I hold out my hand and create a strobe every few seconds to see the way, though that's pretty lazy since I can read the air pressure and use it like a kind of radar if I want (which, you know, most of the time I don't). I'm yelling out the bank manager's name though I know it's not the wisest course of action if I want any element of surprise. I've usually found saving people's lives and sneaking up on the bad guy are mutually exclusive activities, more's the pity.

The floor erupts in front of me. For almost three seconds I am in a hell made of equal parts earth and waste paper, with the odd filing cabinet thrown in. I imagine mob accountants have dreams like this. No horses' heads, though. What appears to be a gigantic fist flails about in front of me, the hole in the floor just wide enough for its wrist.

"Gigantor? Is that you?"

For a moment I'm choking with dread that it *is* Gigantor, even though I'm pretty sure he's still on ice out at White Nine. A moment later, I realize it's not a human hand, however large, since like the legs outside, it seem to be made from chunks of rubble and roiling masses of earth, and then I almost wish it was Gigantor, everyone's favorite English-challenged villain. At the sound of my voice, the fist becomes a hand and it turns towards me flattened out like an enormous radar dish.

At least it doesn't turn into a massive ear. That would just be plain creepy.

I charge up as it comes down, enveloping me, and just as the thing suffocates me like a premature burial I let loose, exploding in electrical fury, vaporizing the thing like a moth in one of those electric bug zappers. It leaves me grinning and sick with the familiar sensation of being momentarily between heartbeats. And then my inner wellness pours into the space left by such a major discharge as I absorb energy again from every movement, the lightest touch of the night breeze coming through the shattered windows across the jumble of office furniture, the friction of the leather costume on my joints, the very movement of the building itself.

I peer into the hole in the ground and there's another hole directly below it and then more office. I hear a man's voice, shrieking profoundly, a thousand times more likely to be our errant bank manager than the earth-controller – unless I have a total nutcase on my hands, which wouldn't be the first time. I levitate down through the cavity just in time to see a dark shape flit past me with the bank manager in her arms.

Vulcana.

Zephyr 1.3 "Days Of Yore"

WITH MY FAVORITE ex-teammate having pipped me again in the hostage-rescuing stakes, I figure that leaves me with the madman. I yell again, wordlessly this time, since he seemed pretty on top of his game when last I made a noise and this should make him come again. And I'm not wrong. Office dividers fly out of the path of a wall of dirt and boxes of photocopy paper and busted underground cables and suddenly second-hand computers. It's all I can do to jet out of the way as the mini-avalanche slams past.

In the vague hope I might be able to track my prey, I jog through the third floor of the bank offices in the wake of the debris, pebbles and grit leaving a path across the carpet like the skid mark of the world's biggest itchy-assed dog. Then I'm at the row of back windows, saw-toothed with glass now, looking out the back of the building like I'm in a slow-moving car, sienna'd automobiles trampled in the bank's wake.

There's a bunch of cops on the street corner so I jump down from the building and land in a pose in front of them. The policeman I'd seen before, Benjamin De Freitas, comes out of the crowd. I probably know a few hundred cops in the city by now, not that I actually remember all their names or anything, but they remember me and like to think the feeling's mutual. It's a good thing. I used to call cops "pigs" and a bunch of other names I've recently forgotten, but now I kinda feel like one of them, and I like to entertain the fantasy that *that* feeling's mutual. They go out with nothing but their badge and gun (oh and flak jackets, tear gas, pepper spray, those neat batons, yadda yadda yadda) and I have the power of six million light bulbs or whatever the fuck it is.

I don't know what I was trying to say there. Kinda drifted off sorry.

At least they get paid, which is what my wife keeps reminding me.

"Zephyr, what's the deal?" De Freitas asks, removing his cap and wiping dust from his forehead.

"I think my colleague's freed the bank manager –"

"What the fuck was the bank manager doing in there? It's past midnight."

"Well I'm just about to go back onto the roof and rescue his secretary, so maybe you'll get to ask your questions from someone who knows what's going on, officer. All I know is there's a person inside with earth-controlling powers. That's how come your bank's suddenly sprung legs and decided to go on a little holiday."

De Freitas nods grimly like that sort of explanation's just a walk in the park for him, though he *is* a beat cop in the world's biggest city, so perhaps it really is no surprise. He motions weakly across the street, drawing my attention to the first camera crew setting up for a shot. I notice Imogen Davies frantically brushing her hair and hurrying through her voice warm-up.

"You got time to explain that to them, Zeph?"

"I think I have to stop the bad guy first, right?"

I don't let him know I'm sorely tempted. The delectable Miss Davies is the new kid on NBN's graveyard shift and we haven't yet had the acquaintance.

"Well, it's not like it's in your contract," De Freitas says.

Me and the cops share a nice long laugh and I pat the officer on the shoulder and he stops laughing and looks vaguely disturbed, though the others don't seem to notice a thing wrong.

"Let me get back to you on this one."

I turn around as Nightwind comes down the rubble-strewn street with the bank manager in tow.

"What are you doing with him?"

"Hello?" the cloaked kid replies irritatingly. "Rescuing him?"

"I saw Vulcana carry him out of there. . . ."

"Yeah and she asked me to escort him to safety. Big deal, right?"

I'm just shaking my head as Nightwind actually says, "Oh goody, cameras," and moves off in the cute reporter's direction adjusting his cloak and cowl.

"Bastard."

I almost break the sound barrier on my way back to the bank roof. Sure enough, Mr Severin's mousy secretary crouches up near the air-conditioning, the so-called ground all around her crumbling with the disturbance to the building. Hovering, I offer her a hand, and then float back down to deposit the lady beside her employer, who already has a paramedic fitting him out for a blanket and hot chocolate and a valium suppository.

"Save some for me, alright?"

I wink at the cute young blonde medic and she gets all red faced, which you've gotta admit is kind of adorable. Very much a Minnesota farm girl, which is right up there in my top ten. Then I shoot back around the front of the building.

Yes I have a top ten. And yes it may contain more than ten items.

The bank marches inexorably on. Vulcana watches the front while walking steadily backwards keeping pace with it.

"What do you think?" I shout from overhead.

She glances up and shrugs, "Second floor, somewhere near the front."

"OK. Let me have a try."

There's not much left in the way of actual windows any more. I crouch and then fly in through one of the sagging frames and almost straight away spot the dude standing with his legs wide apart and his hands waving megalomaniacally, as these fucking guys tend to do. He doesn't have the decency to wear an actual costume. Instead, he wears these god-awful brown slacks, a Brooks Brothers t-shirt and a wrestling mask.

"Dude, give it up," I say loud and clear.

Earth-boy snaps his head in my direction. He's solidly built tending to heavy, though he's probably not as tall as me, which is a nice change. I'm a respectable five-eleven – a height frequently eclipsed in the superhero world.

"Man, go away, alright?"

"Go away?"

I make a show of clearing my ears and walk a few steps closer. As I drop my right hand, it fills with a nimbus of blue-white power.

The tough guy's stance reminds me of the captain on the deck of a ship and I almost laugh. The earth-controller drops his chin and repeats himself more sternly.

"Yes, go away."

I'm actually about to laugh when the whole world turns brown. Like a flushed turd, forces beyond my control vacate me from the building, and like, to continue the metaphor, down through the bowels of the bank I go, slamming and smashing through walls, floor and furniture beneath a gigantic tidal wave of torn up city street, until suddenly I hit something hard enough it doesn't want to give way. I'm crucified, bent backwards over the solid metal arch of the bank vault, and the crushing earth washes over and off me. I struggle for air. Battered but not bruised, I drop from the top of the recently exposed vault and onto what remains of the bank floor. There are massive gaps in the stone and wooden supports, the churning earth passing by beneath me. Whatever clever architecture once kept the vault concealed from prying eyes has now been reduced to so much kindling. The enormous circular door as well as its stainless steel chamber sit like an uncomfortable passenger in the bank's ship's hold.

Vulcana tumbles in thanks to her unusual body chemistry, unharmed after flinging herself curled in a ball through the bank's oncoming doors and doing the human pinball thing. She springs up straight and clasps me by the upper arm.

"Are you good?"

"Oh, now you give a shit?"

"Jesus, give it a rest, Zeph. I just saw you swallow a ton of dirt."

"I'm not a kid in a swimming pool, Connie."

"Don't call me by my fucking name, Zephyr!"

"Sorry," I mince. "Old habits die hard. I haven't seen you for . . . ages."

"I've been away," she concedes.

Exhausted of speech, we turn and regard the vault.

"Do you think this is what he wants?" she asks.

"Well, I don't know," I admit. "Why else do you hijack a bank?"

"Did he say anything to you?"

"Not a lot."

She turns away. "Calls himself the Terraformer."

"Terraformer?" I don't get it and just as well, because she's not about to explain.

"Maybe we can get him to leave the bank behind and just take the vault?"

"He needs the bank," I reply with rare insight. "Vault's metal. He's an earth-controller. . . ?" I shrug.

"Seems reasonable." Vulcana nods. "OK, plan B: we kick his ass."

I can't help but grin, and it almost feels like old times when Connie turns to me and holds out her arm like a lady and asks, "Fancy giving me a lift?"

*

WE DON'T EXACTLY catch the Terraformer napping, but he's distracted by flashes of light out the front of the bank.

At first I think the cops have called in the National Guard or something, and a whole platoon is taking pot-shots at the bank – and then I hear the harsh, amplified, mechanized voice that really takes me back to the old days.

"Stop the bank and come out with your hands up!"

"Jesus, it's Chamber," Vulcana says, voicing my thoughts precisely.

"Jeez, this really is getting like This Is Your Life or something."

The flashes of light are actually streams of densified laser coming from the rotating cannons on Chamber's forearms. I get a glimpse of the bulky former Sentinel hovering out the front of the bank, his torso that big characteristic metal box thing with the panel in the front, and that's all I have time for. Vulcana whispers in my ear for a "slingshot" and I sort of have to comply. It would be rude, otherwise, and sort of ruin the camaraderie of the moment, so grasping her opposite wrists and spinning around several times extremely fast, I hurl Connie at the distracted villain.

For a woman made of rubber, she hits him pretty hard. The moment the guy goes down, Vulcana starts pummeling him with her blue fists. The Terraformer gasps and shrieks and the bank grinds to a treacherous stop, the back catching up to the front in the worst way possible, the whole thing pitching forward on its axis, collapse imminent. Although I'm mildly worried about being buried alive, I'm not going to miss my shot to unload on our shit-eating villain, especially since Vulcana and I always had this neat understanding that, being rubber, she's mostly immune to my electrical powers. So I jog up and grab one of the Terraformer's flailing joggers and cram a few volts into him. He squeals appropriately, not quite reaching what I like to call "operatic".

"Jesus, I think you broke him," Vulcana says, standing as smoke comes gently off her, or maybe from him.

I don't say anything, though the idea of tires burning springs to mind. I don't think she has any sense of smell in her rubber form so I guess I can relax as long as the smoke dissipates. I look down at the guy on the ground and mostly out of irritation lean down and snatch off his mask. Of course I don't recognize the lightly-bearded blonde guy unconscious at my feet. He could be anyone, as long as you use the word "ratty" – a friend, a work colleague, an actor on TV, some guy at college, some twink on the Internet.

There is a sizzling noise and the brick wall in front of us basically vanishes. Chamber slowly hovers in and comes to a rest.

"Zephyr. Vulcana."

"Long time no see, Chambermaid. How's it hanging?"

"Um, fine?"

I laugh and wait for the wisecracks, but none come. The familiar mechanized voice of the man inside the powered suit clears its throat and says, "I think this building is probably going to collapse. You should consider coming out."

Then he leans down and picks up the unconscious Terraformer in his arms and retreats from the building.

"Is he allowed to do that?"

"It does seem like a . . . lapse in etiquette," Vulcana concedes.

It's not like we're going to do anything about it. There are cameras outside and the world's watching, or at least those who are still awake. I can hear a few choppers hovering outside getting footage for the inevitable voice-over. Vulcana and I make a few adjustments to out costumes and she fusses with what's left of her hair.

"I liked it short," I smile. "Remember when you had that bob? It was sexy."

"Jesus, Joe," she smiles tiredly, just a trace of genuine irritation. "When haven't I had a fucking bob?"

Holding hands like in days of yore, we jump from the second floor windows and into the camera lights.

Zephyr 1.4 "Spilling My Guts"

IT TAKES TWENTY minutes before I corner the new girl.

Imogen Davies resembles an Irish milk-maid with her long dark hair, dark blue eyes and fair skin, just a smattering of freckles across the bridge of her nose dark enough that I can see them by the streetlights once emergency services gets the power back up on the street. Possibly number one on my top ten, at least this week. Away from the camera crew and without her microphone she's just a teenager, nervous and adorable and I can't help falling into the smug, confident, all-powerful role she expects and will probably fantasize about later tonight. Or that's what I tell myself. She's new to the job, but is quick to remind me she's not fresh out of college, which isn't something I really want to hear with what I have in mind. But I reassure her it's the night news shift when all the cool stuff happens just as It's Raining Men starts emanating from my lower back, and if I look horrified, Imogen Davies looks completely gobsmacked. I make a pained face and mutter something about having to change that ringtone and then I back the hell out of there.

On the phone, it's my wife.

"Where are you?" She sounds sleepy. "It's 2am."

"Downtown, honey. Playing hero."

"Are you OK? Are you safe?"

These questions are rehearsed. I think the fear wore away long ago. I think she's forgotten I'm risking my life out here. I guess that's what I get for being too good at my job.

"Yeah. Yeah, I'm fine. A bank went on a rampage, nothing major."

"Oh." She's vaguely interested and I can hear her switch on the TV and mute the sound.

"It should be on NBN."

"They have a helicopter view . . . and an interview with Nightwind."

"That fucking. . . ."

I want to crush the phone, but the Enercom people were surprisingly firm when they had to replace the last one. It occurs to me I should get them to change the ringtone.

"Are you coming home soon?"

"It's my job, honey –"

"Your job doesn't pay the bills, Joey," Elisabeth says.

I shut my mouth and grind out my annoyance on my teeth.

"I'll be home soon," I hear myself eventually say. "Go back to bed, Beth."

NBN and the radio reporters have gone by the time I tuck the phone away and turn at the sound of the White Nine van arriving. "Van" isn't really the word. If the armor was just on the outside you would call it a tank, though it is that and so much, much more. Along with a crack squad of five SWAT officers, the enormous six-wheeled van disgorges technicians in coveralls and an honest-to-God scientist in a white coat. She's about sixty and appears to have a goatee, so I'm not that interested, though I do drift close enough to where Vulcana oversees them strapping Earth-boy to his stretcher, an awkward metal thing that slots into a cabinet within the van's insides.

"Is he still out?"

"Yeah, you zapped him good and proper."

Vulcana turns and acknowledges me with something akin to a smile.

"Well, you know, just wanted to make sure he was down for the count."

"I think I had it handled," she shrugs.

"Hmmm, where's Chamber?"

"Where does he ever go?" Vulcana asks. "I don't think we ever really settled that one."

"It was creepy, being absorbed into his chest like that whenever he teleports. I was never that comfortable with it."

As I say it, I know it seems like a moment's true confession and I guess it is. I sense rather than watch Vulcana regarding me for a long moment.

"Me too," she says slowly. "Still, we had to get around."

"I guess," I reply, thinking about our many trips shrinking down into the N-space void that filled Chamber's torso and reputedly fuelled his powered armor. I shiver. Connie's still watching me. How the fuck did we survive that and why were we so calm about it at the time? I blame the inevitable nihilism that accompanies any *fin de siecle*.

"I guess I'll see you tomorrow," she says.

Vulcana starts crouching to do her own "spring into the sky" trick, but I hold out a hand.

"Wait, what do you mean, 'tomorrow'?"

"The mayor's thing," she replies.

"Oh, that Eros Foundation . . . uh . . . thing?"

"Yeah. It's kind of a get-together of the old gang. I'll see you there, OK?"

I'm still grappling with this concept when Vulcana does her trick and flings herself into the night with the vague noise of a tire being depressed. I'm left surrounded by the technicians for the prison van and cops and a few late-night spectators and a few TV stringers filming the scene for additional footage "just in case" before they go back to their soy frappuccinos and file their reports. There doesn't seem to be anything else for me to do except I don't really want to go home.

Nightwind appears out of the shadows, but I still refuse to believe it's due to any "ability" he might possess. I secretly imagine luring him to a rooftop and teaching him to fly. He grins as he comes across the buckled street to me. The smug cut of his mouth is all I can see below his goggle mask.

"How do you think they're gonna get rid of this building? It's kinda in the way, don't you think?"

"Man, I could care less. . . ."

"Do you wanna get a drink? I hear Chloe Severigny's at De Lux."

"It's Sevigny, man. And no I don't *wanna*. Sheesh. If maybe I needed a fucking *blowjob* then I would go to De Lux to see Chloe *Sevigny* thanks very much, Ass-wind."

"Wow, you're such a jerk, it actually hurts," the other guy responds.

"You want to start a slugfest, motherfucker?"

"A slugfest? What the hell does that mean?"

"That's when two masks go at it and wreck a few city blocks," I snap.

"Christ, you're wasted."

Nightwind then has the gall to turn his back on me and walk off. There's a few too many cops around for me to do something stupid so I turn away as well. I'm still thinking about my reply, but after a few moments, Nightwind is nowhere to be seen.

"This is such a pile of balls. I'm going home."

And I take to the air.

*

EXCEPT I DON'T go home. God knows, I know I should. My internal pedant, who I have pretty much strangled the fucking fuck out of my whole life, waggles the stumps of his fingers about my appointments in the morning, the thought of re-uniting with my other ex-Sentinels making my asshole completely tighten up, not to mention knowing I'm now past that time where I can actually get a full night's sleep anyway. It sucks, and the whole aftermath of the Terraformer thing just bums me out and I don't have any drugs that I can actually metabolize. I fly aimlessly over the city until I realize my unconscious has been nudging me towards the islands.

I hover over Twilight's pad. The tennis court and the twin swimming pools forming the yin-yang symbol are still lit up even though it's now well after 2am. I think Twilight normally likes guests to alight at the helipad, but for some reason it's not illuminated, so I descend among the spruce trees lining the edge of the cliff overlooking the sea.

There's a guy in a charcoal suit holding an Uzi and I crackle loudly, tracers of light running over my body as a courtesy to let him know I'm there. He recovers pretty admirably from being spooked, and then it's my turn to recover from being spooked as three more guys with laser sights on their various weapons emerge from the bushes nearby.

"You're Zepha?"

They're all Italian Americans, heavyset but well-built, their suits Armani or Louis Vuitton, cut-down versions of Twilight himself. Keeping it in the family, I guess. You can't really accuse the Mob of nepotism. That's the nature of the beast. These aren't Sicilians though, small, dark and murderous. Twilight told me where the family came from, but I'm never able to remember. They're northerners, anyway. I can only wave a hand as the sentries appear.

"Is the big guy around?"

The one who spoke before shakes his Rolex out from under his cuff and then looks at me.

"It's half-past two in the morning."

"Uh, so?"

"He's in the sanctum."

"OK."

I stand there a moment more feeling stupid, which is weird since if I was invading some villain's base I fancy I'd wipe the floor with these guys. Reminding myself of this, I clear my throat to avoid any imminent falsetto and ask them to tell Twilight I'm here. Reluctantly, one of the younger guards peels off from the others to do as asked.

The remaining trio escort me to the edge of the pool. There are a few deck chairs around, which seems odd given the cold night. There's nothing as tardy as wet towels or empty glasses to suggest the area's been recently used, nevertheless I get that sense. The water is heated, steam curling off it like a giant mug of warm milk. The goons don't waste the effort trying to make conversation and I don't bother either. Mafia and heroes don't normally mix. Or not normally, anyway.

"Zephyr."

Twilight mostly has the diction of a well-educated New Englander and if you didn't know his background, you at least wouldn't guess he was Italian mafia through and through. He looks more like a Greek god, which is to say he looks like the Anglo idea of such a god, something over six-and-a-half feet tall with a lantern jaw, dark blue eyes and impeccably groomed blonde hair tending ashen. He is possibly the best-looking man I've ever seen in my life and I don't mean that in a gay way. Twilight is the best of us, that's all. As a hero, he is perhaps the best. As for the rest of it, especially the mob thing, it all gets a little murky. Oh, and let's not mention the consorting with demons part.

He appears at the other end of the pool wearing a Chanel robe unbelted over his work costume, a dark grey bodysuit that imperceptibly turns black in the upper body, going into a high collar like a Star Trek uniform or something. Normally there are gloves, but these are removed, though the face mask remains in place, larger than the simple domino I wear. He's well turned out as always. The man's sheer physical presence conceals any signs of wear or tear or the lateness of the hour. In the body and shoulders he is enormous, possibly even deformed. I have to turn away after a moment because I feel like a midget or something compared to him. I'm in awe. It's embarrassing and gay.

"Hey, I thought I'd see you at Mechano's tonight, or Halogen."

"Is that where you were?"

He strolls down the edge of the pool and crouches to dip his fingers in the warm water before running them through his hair. Then we shake hands, mine with his other one and he grins, teeth practically sparkling.

"It's late, I'm sorry," says I.

Twilight keeps grinning though he turns and gestures for me to walk with him. There's no fence around his pool. Across a hundred yards of immaculate lawn the French doors at the rear of his enormous house are open and light spills from them suggesting warmth in the form of a large snifter of brandy if not a log fire. I note the path that wends away to the right, splitting off from the way back to the house and ending at a cold, grey-looking stone building, octagonal perhaps, and with a domed roof. Twilight's sanctorum. He steers me towards the house instead with a hand on my elbow.

"I'm Twilight," he says gently. "You know my time is the night."

I realize he's making a joke. "My time is the night" is the phrase his action figure repeats if you press the button in the middle of his back. At that moment I can't remember mine, but I remember the PA's face when I suggested, "How do you like your ass, deep fried or crispy?" After regaining her composure, she politely suggested mothers might not be so cool with their kids repeating that line.

Mothers! Reminds me I need to ring mine. Both of 'em.

In the end, I think my figurine phrase was "Electric, baby," I swear, in what sounds like Austin Powers' voice. I think it may have been a cost-cutting exercise.

I mutter something conciliatory to Twilight and thank him again for seeing me. You would never guess we were friends. I'm stammering something about how dead it was at Halogen, repressed memories of walking to school with my neighbor's dad coming back to me I guess because of mine and Twilight's height difference, and I vaguely wonder if this is what most women feel, always having to look up. If I had had a father of my own perhaps I would be better prepared or might feel otherwise. Emasculation isn't something I can feel growing on me.

"Zephyr, what's going on?" Twilight asks. "This isn't like you."

We pass indoors. The back room has a library, a rosewood grand piano, a drinks cabinet, a big slab of woodwork that conceals a widescreen TV though it is open now and gently playing a football game, Lions versus Jets. I always went for the Jets because that was Flash Gordon's team. Pity they're losing. Maybe they need another Flash, though they test pretty hard for supers these days.

"I'm just . . . I don't know. I'm a little down."

I shrug and try not to bob my head or do that Joe Pesci voice I always have to resist around Twilight, like I'm trying to get myself into trouble with the Cosa Nostra or something.

Twilight moves to the cabinet, dwarfing it, and nods for me to go on. I'm struck by the absurdity of the situation and once he hands me the expected snifter, I tip it up gratefully and indicate towards the outside bunker.

"Forget about me, anyway. Me and my mortal concerns. What's been shaking, Twilight?"

"Oh, it's been very quiet. . . ."

"It must've been. No adventures. . . ?"

"Actually no, just some . . . personal research."

"And uh, how are the family? You know, *the Family*, these days?"

"I think my uncle and I have finally come to an agreement," Twilight smiles. "You leave me alone and I won't interrupt your sordid little drug deals by summoning Dimensional Shamblers."

I laugh, though I have no idea of what he's referring to. I can only gather it's more of the mystical kook Twilight's usually mixed up in. Despite the heroic stature, he's more Dr Strange than Superman, as I sometimes like to put it. I did ask him once that, if he was a sorcerer, why he had superhuman strength, could fly and reflect bullets off his bare skin. The answer was a good one.

"Because I'm a sorcerer . . . and because I can."

I reflect on this as we sit down to drink. The brandy is warm, but that's about all it does for me. Not a problem for him. Twilight has that satisfied look on his face I've only seen on housewives trying to wean off chocolate and enjoying their failure.

"So what *has* been happening?" I ask.

"No," Twilight replies. "Tell me about you."

And he waves a hand and possibly says something, a spell or an oath or something, and then I'm spilling my guts like Woody

Allen, telling him things I didn't even realize I was thinking, about how I don't think I can balance my life and my secrets any more, that I feel trapped inside my own body, that my wife seems to want me dead and home feels like a jail, and that even though I would never want to take back the fateful day I was struck by lightning climbing the wind farm tower, I hope to dear God my daughter Tessa has the chance for an ordinary life.

"It's just such a pressure," I hear myself whine, vaguely aware the spell's effects are winding down. "I've had my powers twenty years next March and I sometimes feel like there's two of me, and I almost wish there was, it would be so much simpler, and so much kinder to my family."

Twilight sits back with his fingers steepled. I lean and wipe sweat from the back of my neck and exhale heavily.

"Whew, what the fuck was that?"

"Just a little trick I've been learning, Togamon's Tantric Expression. It normally only works on fairly simple minds, but I guess my magic is more powerful here in my home."

He smiles that elusive charismatic smile of his that convinces me to take no offence, though there's genuine chagrin there that he just slugged me with a mickey without even asking. Unless his family ties have done their research, he doesn't know my secret identity or too much about my private life. We're friends, yeah, but we're not exactly swapping spit.

"I might have an answer for you," he says eventually. "If you aren't put off by the solution being . . . esoteric? Leave it with me. I have to think, and consult my books."

I stand up because it might not sound like a dismissal, but I'm at once strangely keen to get out of there. In fact, I'm not quite sure why I've come. Perhaps it's the magic in the air or maybe just a little belated common sense. Beyond the French doors, a red laser sight sweeps over the hedgerows in the garden.

"Are you coming to this thing tomorrow?" I ask, shielding my eyes against light that seems too bright.

"The mayor's reception? No. They don't like people like me at City Hall."

"That's a shame, dude."

"Not really, as I think you'll find out."

"Hmmm," I nod. "OK."

"Just remember, Zephyr: I'm an *anti-hero*, OK?"

"Sure, Twilight. Sure. Why are you telling me this?"

I'm frowning at him and he seems to do the same himself.

"I'm not sure. Just . . . go home to your wife."

I nod and move out into the garden, and thence to home.

Zephyr 1.5 "A Guarded Sense Of Caution"

IT IS WARM in the apartment. The wall of white tiles in the bathroom slips gently back into place and I press down on it hard until I hear the magnets click and engage. I've already stripped in the narrow wall space, the best I get as far as secret bases go until we can afford somewhere bigger, and so I have a quick hot shower just because it seems the thing to do. From there to bed is a short journey, and a mercifully quick one.

There's all sorts of things I mean to do. Perhaps it is leftover sentimentality from my confessional with Twilight, but I want to watch my daughter sleeping and then hold my wife in the dark. I even want to give the cat a midnight dinner. I must be high, I reason, as I slip into the cold empty bed. I assume Elisabeth is passed out on the couch where she was watching TV. The moment my head hits the pillow and I only just realize I am alone, it's like I have fallen into a trap set by my mortal enemy, Mr Sleep (that's me being metaphoric again folks). My eyes lag shut – and then it's morning.

In fact it is quarter to ten. I leap up with a start, glad not to have fried the sheets as I sometimes do, and after securing my manly bits with a clean pair of boxers, I bust out of the bedroom and careen around the flat for a minute before ascertaining I'm the only one home.

On the bench in the kitchenette, Tessa has left me a note: "Mom said you worked late so I called Astrid's mom for a ride. Mom gave me the money for school so don't worry about that either. Could you still pick me up at three?"

She has forgotten to write any kisses on the note or sign her name. Instead, it is signed "Me," which seems slightly obnoxious, but very much her age. Fifteen years old and no longer her daddy's daughter. Or that's what I'm feeling.

The reality is I should be relieved. I can survive on five hours of sleep and I don't bother showering, going straight into the wall cavity and hurriedly dressing in my leathers again. An old white-and-red costume, complete with floor-length red cloak, gathers dust on a hanger. I can hear the phone ringing in the flat, but I ignore it.

I move to the tinted window and open it a crack and when the way seems clear I vault into the sky and the window pretty much swings back by itself. As I start to lag in mid-air, I push it, rocketing in an arc over the city, the traffic helicopter tipping in acknowledgement. At full speed it only takes me a few minutes to cross the city. I don't want the complaints that come with breaking the sound barrier, so I keep it to the low five hundreds.

Even though I'm not late, I feel late, descending with my shadow over City Hall insignificant compared to the hordes of people, cameras and news crews covering the steps and the wide marble courtyard fronting one of the city's most magnificent surviving Modernist buildings. There are a few costumes amid the front rows of the crowd, but these are interested onlookers like Paragon and Red Monolith who have been admitted to the front rather than invited. Since I was apparently never briefed on the details or else I've completely forgotten them, I don't have a clue in hell where I am supposed to be. I land on the roof and thumb the security code I was given years ago and I'm jogging down the stairwell when one of the mayor's secretaries whistles from an open doorway and I scuttle through into the oak-paneled interior of one of the city's plush meeting rooms, and suddenly I remember what Vulcana said.

The seven surviving members of the Sentinels stand on the other side of the room and my late arrival seems just too much like old times for it to be anything more than heavily ironic. I can only take my cue from how I handled it a million times in the past, laughing off the odd accusatory glare (Vulcana, Seeker, probably Chamber too, if he had a face), bemused smiles (Aquanaut, Miss Black), disinterest (Animal Boy) and worried anticipation (Lone Wolf). The mayor is there as well, along with his PA, the featureless Miss Kirkness, as well as a nerdy-looking guy in a tweed jacket carrying a large black electronic device. There's also a few cops in the chamber, but they're doing their best to look invisible, picking over the sandwich tray at the back of the set-up.

"Zephyr, you're late," Pykes says.

"Hey, chill, baby. When have I ever let you down?"

"Do you want me to get my diary, Mr Mayor?" Miss Kirkness asks.

I pout at the gibe and Roland Pykes, his security blanket and gold chains around his shoulders, gives an irritated gasp and gives up. I turn to acknowledge a few of my former teammates, though Chamber seems to be looking elsewhere and Lone Wolf, looking more like a homeless person than ever in his old trench coat and barefoot get-up, nervously avoids my eyes.

One of the secretaries fields a cell call and then sticks her head back into the room.

"They're ready for you, Mr Mayor."

Pykes turns to the guy in the jacket and asks, "Ready, Professor Prendergast?"

"As I'll ever be, I suppose, Mayor Pykes. Lead on."

They file past, followed almost immediately by Adrian's pet wolf. It must need to pee or something, presuming Adrian eventually managed to house train the damned thing. Seeker inclines her head at me, and Aquanaut gently punches my shoulder, and then I fall in beside Vulcana and Animal Boy, pretending for a moment to sniff the air around the once teenager.

"Jesus, Zephyr, get some new jokes, man," he says.

"Where have you been hiding, Tom? The zoo?"

"Actually I've been finishing college, I don't know if you've heard of the place?"

I eye him up and down a moment. He's still a weedy piece of work, but at least some of his old hyperactive energy has diminished. Shame the same can't be said for his Adam's apple.

"I guess you're old enough to shave now," I smirk. "What's that like when you turn into a Sabretooth? One big shaved puss –"

"Zephyr," Vulcana says and nudges me fairly hard in the ribs. "Is there something you were going to ask me?"

I cease my grinning and turn back to Connie. Since we're still in private she hasn't made the switch yet, which means I'm looking at a handsome brunette with a peaches and cream complexion, great boobs, and eyes that seem to see into the core of my Being. I also note she's sporting a fresh haircut, long at the front and shaved right to the nape of her neck.

"Nice 'do."

"Thanks. I had to pay an extra fifty for the first appointment."

"That sucks ass," I say, and then realize my sentiment's probably a little strong for something so mundane. I make the sheepish face that usually gets me out of that sort of thing and then gesture around.

"So what's all this then?"

"Professor Prendergast is donating his latest invention to the protection of the city," Vulcana replies in an unimpressed voice.

"Latest invention?"

"Yeah, the Hermes Foundation, you remember that?"

"If you say so."

"Hermes is the donation."

"The . . . Greek god?" I know I'm straining and the pain shows.

Vulcana gives me a nod, but I don't have a chance to ask any more. I still haven't found out what the hell the mayor thinks he is up to, assembling the Sentinels without discussing it with me first. First though, we troop down the last of the hall's main staircases and out through the foyer, following the rapidly-striding mayor and the diminutive scientist trying to keep up. Beyond the main doors there's the sort of crowd that has become a rarity these days. The day is overcast, the sky smeared with clouds the color of lead pencil. I check my mask and fix a rakish smile in place and then the cameras start flashing.

*

I AM ALARMED to finally understand Hermes is a fucking robot.

Me and robots don't exactly have the best history and this one is bigger than me and designed to resemble a buff super-warrior in an off-the-shoulder toga-cum-miniskirt kinda thing. His enormous silver head is styled with Classical curls. Beside me, Seeker mutters something about wondering where's the fig leaf and I laugh derisively as the mayor's ambitious speech overshoots his ability to deliver. I sense journalists in the crowd lying in wait to ask fresh questions about the latest scandal about his deputy's expense account, and like a good psychic, anticipate an adjournment so we can get together behind closed doors once the photo ops are over. As I have foreseen, so it comes to pass, and we're only fifteen minutes out the front of City Hall before the first raindrop falls.

Pykes stops mid-speech and turns back to me.

"Zephyr, can you do something about that?"

There's something I've never liked about the mayor and he knows it. I think he thinks it's his post-doctorate qualifications, his aid work in the Middle East, and his self-indulgent interest in paleontology. Actually it's his ruddy schoolboy complexion, the handsome-but-evil-Nazi-bad-guy scar running down one cheek, and his habit of consulting with no one before making big policy decisions – like assembling my defunct super-team without asking me, Zephyr, who's saved his worship's ass more than once.

With the city's entire media watching, the best I can come up with is a strained "Wh-at?" It's irritating that people still don't understand I can't control the weather. I can generate weather and make a stink when I'm up among the clouds, but simply magicking away a rain shower isn't in my vocabulary, so to speak.

Pykes simply hisses, "The rain," and turns back, beneficently smiling for the cameras as he resumes his speech about commitment to safety not just for the city, but the entire eastern seaboard, which is pretty much just saying the whole city.

"So, you gonna do somethin' about that, Zeph?" Seeker asks.

Those around me chuckle and I just sigh through my teeth, head shaking.

Five minutes later, we're corralled indoors, this time into one of the really really big meeting rooms, an impressive one on the first floor. Almost immediately, Lone Wolf's dog jumps up on the food table and starts chowing down on the buffet and Chamber reaches over with one of his big tensile-steel mitts and flicks the beast across the room.

I haven't seen Adrian this fired up in years.

"Don't ever touch Hero like that," he snarls, feet spread in a fighting stance and bo-stick upraised like a sword.

Chamber folds his arms over the metal trunk of his chest and says nothing. Perhaps because I have known him the longest and I always felt kinda bad about the circumstances of his leaving the team, I move across to Lone Wolf and try to smile.

"Hey Adrian, long time no see. How're you doing?"

"It's a long time? Yes, Zephyr," he replies softly, looking anywhere except into my eyes. "I haven't exactly been around."

I clear my throat and wonder why the hell I didn't just zero in on the free drinks.

"Yeah, so, how are you now? All . . . better?"

"I'm still in treatment, Zephyr, if you must know," he says.

Because he won't look at me, I can get a good look at him and how badly he's aged in the past five years. His hair and stubble are grey, his skin the complexion of a cadaver. Although there's still that suggestion of sinewy strength Lone Wolf always possessed, I can't help conclude something of the fight has gone out of the guy.

"Cool, yeah, OK, but are you like, OK?"

"Well . . . I am better than I have been . . . for a while."

"That's great," I say, leaping on any positivity. "Why's that?"

Adrian finally meets my eyes.

"I'm a lone wolf, Zephyr. I should've always been left alone."

Holding his fighting stick like a cane, Adrian whistles to his pet and then he strides from the big room without so much as looking back.

"I guess in hindsight he thought that was a pretty bad idea, coming here today," a cocky voice says to me from behind.

I turn and there's Aquanaut. We share a brotherly hug and I ruffle his slicked-back blue-black hair.

"Hey, Aquanaut, man, long time no see."

"Actually man it's 'Nautilus' these days. I've changed, uh, monikers."

"Oh." I pause and try and work out where I've heard the word Nautilus before and I can't place it. "That's cool. Any, uh, reason?"

"Oh not really, just the Aquanaut, I think it was a little difficult for some people. My agent thinks the Q and the two Us, and besides, it's a bit like, you know, *Aquaman*. Kinda gay."

"Well then, you were kinda gay for quite a few years there, Spock."

He laughs, but not without rubbing a thumb and forefinger over one of his gently pointed ears. His costume hasn't changed much, with sea green tights of fine metallic scales and a very minimalist singlet with a weird cross-shaped harness over the top.

"You're not in the city any longer?"

"No. I've been in California for the past two years, trying to get this pilot of mine made, and you know, generally just chasing waves and beating on the odd bad guy."

"Are there many, like, major villains over that way? I don't hear much about it on the TV," I say.

"No, not really. It's how I like it. This town's too creepy, man. It's like an idiots' circus, you know what I mean?"

"Uh, not sure I do, but then again I still live here, so. . . ."

"Yeah, sure, I didn't mean anything like *that*."

We both hum at the same time and look around – and that's about when Hermes comes over.

*

I COULDN'T TELL you how much he weighed. Judging by the sound, it is a hell of a lot. With roughly the same physical dimensions as Twilight except made from solid metal, with or without his platemail loincloth, Hermes cut an impressive figure. I wasn't buying the whole robot thing anyway and his impassive, immobile face doesn't help.

"Gentlemen," the robot says and inclines his head, offering a large hand. "It's a pleasure to meet you."

Nautilus and I just stare at him for a moment and Nautilus is probably even more open than me, moving slowly around the robot like the freakish example of modern art it is. Hermes' cloak is real cloth and Nautilus tugs at it. The hand remains open for all of three seconds.

"He's huge," the artist-formerly-known-as-Aquanaut says.

"He's sure that," I agree.

Hermes tilts his head slightly and I lift my eyes.

"How're you doing, robot?"

"My creator named me Hermes after the Greek god of messengers. I hope that's not . . . intimidating . . . for you."

"Intimidating?"

I look around. The professor is talking with Miss Black, who's flicking back her shoulder-length blonde hair almost like she's flirting with the old guy.

"How's he doing that?" I ask my former colleague.

"What?" Nautilus asks.

"The talking. I can't see the professor has any gadgets up his sleeve. Besides, he looks a little busy."

"Gentlemen," the robot responds in his most patient baritone, "I assure you there is no ventriloquism at play. I am the one talking to you."

I ponder this a moment. It seems kinda unlikely and I say as much. I'm surprised to hear frustration in the metallic echo of the robot's reply.

"Gentlemen, I assure you, I am very much the . . . the real deal."

"The 'real deal'," Nautilus laughs. "Fuck. Who programmed you, boy? Does the professor know jive too?"

"Jive?"

"You know, like 70s black people talk, not the dance," I feel compelled to explain.

"Gentlemen . . . Oh very well. . . ."

The robot walks away. I almost feel for him when his path immediately confronts him with the sandwich table, which obviously doesn't offer a lot of options for him. The robot's enormous hands conform to fists and he just stands there, his back to the small gathering as more and more people come in.

I'm still curious. I walk over to the professor and Miss Black and elbow my way into the conversation.

"So professor, what's the deal with Hermes? How do you make him talk?"

Prendergast obviously feels the need to back up his explanation with an account of early Newtonian physics and the work of the Russian Formalists. After a couple of nervous sidelong glances to Miss Black, who still looks rather fine, I must say, though in a slightly secretarial way, her customary flared black slacks and wide open-collared black shirt exposing both her delightful collarbones and wrists, I realize she's not going to interrupt because she's a knowledge junkie who's probably turned on by the balding egg-head. So I hold up my hands and actually use the phrase, "Whoa."

"I'm just trying to work out how you make him talk, doc."

The scientist actually tilts his head as he looks at me through thick spectacles. It's not the sort of look that would ever get me to take off my clothes. I ponder how he would look with a spark up his nose.

"'Make him talk'?" the professor repeats. "He talks for himself, Mr Zephyr."

"No, seriously. Come on. I know it's a trade secret, but we're all kinda curious."

"Hermes is a sixth generation self-replicating intellectual machine, Mr Zephyr. Don't be fooled by his rather . . . Adonisian exterior. He's essentially a new type of super-computer on a level far superior to anything the world's ever seen."

"If he's such a hot computer, how come you put him inside all that armor? Sounds to me like you could give Microsoft a run for their money if you went commercial."

"I'm not motivated by money, Mr Zephyr."

"It's just Zephyr."

"OK."

"So," I shrug, just making conversation now. "What *are* you motivated by then, professor?"

The scientist gets a faraway look as he says, "I want to stamp out tyranny, and the cruelty of men against men."

"Far out."

I think that's a shame because Hermes would look cool as a wrestler.

The old guy focuses on me again and says, "A colleague of mine by the name of Dr Martin Thurson recently went missing right in the heart of this great city of ours, Zephyr. When it really dawned on me that something like this could happen, I dedicated the Hermes project to the form you see now. I aim to find my colleague, sir, with Hermes' help. Any assistance you could offer would be greatly appreciated."

"Martin Thurson? OK," I reply. "I'll uh, you know, keep an ear to the ground."

The scientist nods and pats me on the shoulder and says it's much appreciated, and as he smiles encouragingly to Miss Black, who is watching me with a guarded sense of caution, I believe, there's a dramatic lull in the conversation I feel the urgent need to fill.

"So . . . what time do you think our old enemies will attack?"

The professor gasps and I check the time on my Blackberry, careful not to set off any buttons and Miss Black chuckles because at least she's familiar with my sense of humor. On the other hand, the professor looks like he needs a change of shorts.

"You can't be serious . . . and so calm about it?"

"Oh sure," I shrug. "It's pretty typical of big events like this. You know, all the city's top crime-fighters gathered under the one roof. I guess if it was Think-Tank or Overlord or someone, they might even try and steal your neat-o new computer boy over there."

The professor drops a few shades paler as he produces a square of handkerchief to dab his face.

"I'm not sure if Hermes is ready . . . I hope I haven't unveiled him too soon."

"The, uh . . . the mayor seemed to be saying Hermes was like, part of the police force now?" Miss Black says, speaking telepathically, and as usual, sounding like Daria.

"'Seconded'," Professor Prendergast slowly confirms.

"Cool," the former teen sorceress replies. "Any idea why the rest of us are here then?"

Zephyr 1.6 "Real Superhero Behavior"

VULCANA HAS OF course turned blue since we went public. Once I manage to get out of the threesome with Miss Black and the mad scientist, I can't help noticing her and Chamber arguing at the back of the room. Animal Boy is close by, watching and saying nothing, and it occurs to me a name upgrade might not be such a bad idea for him too.

"I can't believe you, Mike," Vulcana hisses as I move within earshot.

"Hey, what's the problem?" I ask.

"It's nothing," she snaps.

"Chamber says he can't remember Vulcana saving him from Infernus," Animal Boy offers.

"Ooh, so the cat hasn't lost his tongue after all," says I.

"Careful, Zephyr. You know cats love to scratch leather."

"That is a *really* faggy remark."

I turn to Chamber and eye him up and down.

"What gives? I remember when we tussled with Infernus. The irony that it was on Fire Island should be enough for anyone."

"It was a long time ago," Chamber quietly booms. "Sue me, OK?"

"Sue me?" I frown. I don't exactly remember those words being in ultra-stern Chamber's vocabulary. Next I expect him to call Vulcana "girlfriend".

"Jesus, this party blows. I don't know why I agreed to this. Step back."

We know what's coming next, but I can't help being a little patriarchal as I guide Vulcana away by the shoulders. She shrugs me off as the sliding double panel in Chamber's chest opens and what we could only ever describe as black light starts to pour out.

"Zephyr," a deep robot voice sounds behind me. "I feel I need to explain."

I turn and say Hermes' name at about the same moment Chamber appears to fold in on himself and disappear through the doorway in his own chest. We're all caught in the residual non-glow, but it's only a bit of N-dimensional energy wash and it's pretty harmless if you're not in direct contact, right?

"The professor was trying to tell me you can speak for yourself," I say to the robot.

Hermes says nothing. In fact, he stops moving completely.

"Hello?"

"Jesus, he looks kinda fried," Vulcana says.

Animal Boy turns into a mottled house cat and bounds away. Nautilus, sensing a commotion, comes over with his biggest shit-eating grin and rests his elbow on my shoulder.

"What blows?"

"This guy, I think," I say. "Mr Tin Can."

Hermes still isn't moving and I peer around for Professor Prendergast only to notice Senator Ivory Keenan and deputy mayor Anatolia Dufresne coming towards us. I don't have spider-sense or anything so convenient, but my eyes narrow as I turn back to Hermes just as he starts emitting a nearly silent, high-pitched shriek.

"Get down!"

Using super speed, I turn and collect the two female politicians in a clothesline hold, hammering across the room and basically throwing them through the double doorway to safety as there's a loud detonation behind. Now, mostly because that's where I wind up rather than any desire to shelter the pair with my body, when the commotion ceases, I snap about and off the two women and see Hermes standing in the same spot as before with ghostly smoke pouring from the palms of his giant hands. Vulcana and Nautilus are nowhere to be seen, and there's two big gaping holes in the floor where they were standing.

*

INSIDE THE RECEPTION room it's pandemonium.

The mayor and his staff and other dignitaries rush for the door and I have to wade against a human tide to even get back in there. It's the story of my life, going the wrong way when everyone else is running for safety. I should've gone to college and become an architect or a lawyer. I'm sure they still manage to get their kicks, even if it's only on the racketball court.

I mentally tick off the members of the team. Chamber and Lone Wolf have already skedaddled and I doubt they'll come back. Vulcana and Nautilus have freshly disappeared. Animal Boy's nowhere to be seen. That leaves Miss Black and Seeker.

"I'm here, Zephyr," Seeker yells.

I look across and note her hovering up near one of the corners of the roof, her milky white glow a signature move, long chestnut hair writhing perpetually on an invisible breeze like she's underwater or something. I hope her spiritual powers are as strong as ever, because when it comes to a slugfest and two of our other heavy-hitters are already down and out, I don't want to have to rely on Miss Black and her sorcerous "globes of power," no pun intended.

(We never really made a joke of that because she's quite flat-chested. Not that that sort of humor was ever really out-of-bounds, but let's face it, if anybody had globes of power it was Seeker. Not only has she got a serious rack, but they glow in the dark too).

It's good to have back-up, but where there was pandemonium before, suddenly it's just me, Seeker and Hermes standing in the big room.

Seeker and I exchange glances and I have to admit it's weird to be back in this situation. It's almost like I'd forgotten that for fourteen months about five years back, Zephyr didn't have to work solo. I'm not sure why I didn't enjoy it more or cut the others more slack. God knows, I'm no Nightwatchman, who seems to get off on his own stink. The idea of not being alone in all this has a certain appeal – or maybe I'm just getting soft?

Hermes snaps his head up. His eyes, such as they are, seem to track me as I inch into the room.

"Hey, buddy. What's going on?"

Hermes swiftly lifts his right hand and a spray of hot light hits me and I fly back and through the wall beside the double doors. As I'm pulling myself out of this, bits of plaster and chunks of wood falling around me, Seeker gives the robot a good dose of his own medicine. Her phosphorescent corona pours out along her arms, bathing the man-machine, who raises a forearm to cover his head but otherwise doesn't budge.

"I don't think it's working, Zephyr. He has no soul!"

I finally untangle myself and then it's time to get underhanded.

"Jesus! Haven't you learned that by now?"

It's hard to explain how I do it, but if you imagine my internal organs have more in common with a pop-up toaster than a human being then it's easier to believe I can concentrate and channel huge amounts of electricity through my body and out my hand and into our friend over there. Unlike Seeker's efforts, my powers seem to work just fine. The Tin Man judders and shakes and staggers backwards as I ease off the juice.

"Don't hurt him! Don't hurt him!"

I can't believe my ears and then I doubt my eyes as Professor Prendergast jumps up from beneath one of the catering trolleys with a black device in both hands. Seeker lands on the ground beside me poised for action and I shoot a glance as Hermes topples over backwards with smoke leaking from his chest.

"Please, please. . . ."

"You gotta be kidding me, doc. That's a dangerous robot you've got there."

"It's just a malfunction," Prendergast groans as he rushes over to Hermes like a fallen child. "I don't understand what happened!"

"I think he got a mouthful of N-dimensional radiation," I shrug, as you do.

"N-dimensional. . . ?"

I'm not quite prepared for the Professor to go quite so livid nor so foul-mouthed. He starts cursing everyone under the moon and wondering why he wasn't warned there might be an unsecured source of N-dimensional energy at the Hermes launch.

"I guess the mayor's not that *au fait* with Chamber's powered suit," Seeker shrugs.

I agree with everything she says except the French bits.

"Idiots," the professor continues. He presses some buttons, and robotically, Hermes climbs to his feet, though he stands unmoving thereafter.

"Obviously a stronger shielding device is going to be needed. . . ." the doc mutters to himself, adjusting knobs on his Walkman until Hermes straightens up and puts his arms out level.

With one more adjustment, Hermes' rocket boots ignite and he goes flying through the huge paneled window immediately behind him, changing course rapidly once he's in the air and arcing over the city and out of sight.

"I've activated Hermes' automatic homing system, which will take effect whenever he is seriously damaged. Obviously, there are a few adjustments to be made."

The professor looks around dryly and adjusts his tie.

"You can tell that fucking nincompoop mayor I will speak to him next week," the scientist says.

I'm still getting over the shock at his potty mouth, so Seeker stands in for me with a "Sure, professor," and Prendergast shuffles at a fair clip from the room.

"Well I knew something was going to happen," I tell her.

In the ensuing silence, Miss Black drops her invisibility and gently clears her throat.

*

PEOPLE SLOWLY START back into the smoky reception room. Among them is the mayor and straight away I march over and front him up. For the sake of appearances, I don't go grabbing him by the lapels like I'd like. Pykes and I have been here before. I keep my voice low, malevolent.

"What the hell were you thinking, Pykes? That damned robot could've gone berserk and levelled half the city."

"Really, Zephyr? With you here?"

"Drop it, Roland," I sneer. "That scientist's already left. How sure are you about him?"

"Look Zephyr, we're grateful to you that a crisis has been averted. We'd appreciate absolute discretion as far as dealing with the media goes."

"It's not gonna benefit anyone to go calling the press in," I lie wildly.

"Fortunately the Squadron saved the day, hmmm?"

"We were the *Sentinels*, Pyke. Now tell me what you were thinking, calling the old team together without even consulting me about it?"

"We *spoke* about this, Zephyr."

"Not that I recall," I reply, possibly getting even angrier. "Who do you think you are, trying to pull strings like that? You weren't even mayor then. God knows, Aaron Spelling wouldn't ever pull a trick like this."

Alison Kirkness keeps most of the people away, but Miss Black and Seeker are close enough to angle in for a listen. There's still no sign of the others.

"Zephyr," Pykes says, and he pitches his voice low and lets his eyes get all droopy with sentimentality. "This city needs you all. All of you. United."

"Don't you think there are better ways to get that result than just tricking us all into the same room together?"

It's Miss Black who speaks and I'm glad for her. It's nice to have another monkey flinging the brown stuff around for a change. Pykes is used to flipping me off and it's clear he's a little more lost for words taking it in the ass from a twenty-something girl magician.

"Well, I'm . . . We never meant. . . ."

"Some of us have higher responsibilities than a mere *city*, mayor," Seeker says, all the otherworldliness she can muster shining through in her haughty voice. I have to confess she makes a convincing sight with that hair of hers writhing slowly upwards.

"I'm . . . sorry," Pykes moans.

"Well there's a first."

I turn away and the mayor grabs my arm.

"Zephyr, please. Consider what I've said. We can talk about it again – under *proper* circumstances."

I relent, nodding.

"And please, the utmost discretion."

I look around. Senator Keenan inclines her head towards me with her mouth half full of pickle sandwich I'm pretty sure she salvaged off the floor.

"Good luck keeping it a secret in a city of forty million people, but sure, Roland. Just remember you owe me one . . . and no more surprises."

The mayor and his team disperse to shore up support among the other guests and Animal Boy limps in with Nautilus and Vulcana, both of whom look a little frayed.

"This is bullshit," Connie mutters.

"Why are you limping?" I ask Animal Boy.

". . . caught my foot on the way down."

"Jesus," I say. "Aqua – I mean, Nautilus, you OK, pal?"

"That fucking robot, man. Next time I see it I'm turning him into a waffle iron."

"Yeah," I laugh. "Well apparently he's a super-intelligent computer in a state-of-the-art military robot shell. I'm guessing he'd be tough to tackle if he had a brain in place. That N-dimensional energy seems like a bit of a . . . whaddayacallem? You know."

"An Achilles heel," Seeker says in monotone.

"Right."

I look at the others and there's a lull and someone in the background, a woman, starts laughing moronically, and I vaguely recognize her from an old morning television program. All eyes eventually return to the floor in the middle of our circle.

"Pykes wants us to reform."

"Man, that ain't ever gonna happen," Nautilus laughs too quickly and then, frowning, asks, "Right?"

"I've kinda . . . moved on," Miss Black says sheepishly.

"And I've got college," Animal Boy says.

"No offense dude, but I wasn't really thinking about you," I say.

"Really?" He frowns and looks torn between being incensed or actually upset.

"Zephyr's right, man," Nautilus says. "First sign of danger and you'd turn into a cat and high-tail it. What use is that?"

Animal Boy blushes and Vulcana growls at Nautilus.

"Hey, everyone's power has a part to play in a team."

"This from the lady who turns into *rubber*, for chrissakes," Nautilus barks.

If color could come to her cheeks, I'm sure it would. Instead, Vulcana slaps the ex-Aquanaut hard across the face and precisely because of her altered molecular state, Vulcana's hand bends as she slaps and it makes a loud and almost rude noise and it's so absurd Miss Black, Animal Boy and I burst into laughter with Nautilus only a moment behind. Vulcana, however, remains irritated.

"God, you lot were always so puerile. I can't believe I even entertained the idea."

Looking good in her high black boots and leotard, Vulcana waves half-heartedly and leaves the room.

"It wouldn't be the same without Vulcana. Sorry dudes. Love me or leave me, I'm out of here," Animal Boy says.

"You mean it wouldn't be the same without her to stick up for you. Take a hike then," Nautilus says.

"Feeling's mutual, creep," Animal Boy says and morphs into a dog and cocks his leg and sprays pee all over Nautilus's feet.

Nautilus jumps back and the dog, aka Animal Boy, bounds from the room.

"That's real superhero behavior," Miss Black mutters.

"When you make your decisions, I will be in touch," Seeker says, beginning to turn insubstantial.

"How are you going to know?" I ask the wind.

"She'll know," Miss Black sighs.

"I guess Chamber and Lone Wolf are out," I say eventually.

"I didn't think Adrian looked too good."

"Hmmm."

"I'll catch you dudes later," Nautilus says.

He slips me a business card and then jogs like a Superbowl champ from the room, issuing waves. Miss Black makes a pained face.

"Want this?" I hold up the card.

She snorts. "Hardly."

"How about this?" I offer her one of mine and she takes it pensively, chewing the inside of her cheek. "You wanna get a coffee or –"

"Actually, I've got to go. Thanks Zephyr."

I get a kiss on the cheek that makes me feel like a granddad and then I'm the only mask left in a room full of council employees and politicians. A janitor starts sweeping up plaster.

I slip from the room and text Salvador Doro: usual place, midday.

Zephyr 1.7 "Knowing When To Fold"

I LAND ON the roof of the Jenssen Building without a sound. Having extricated myself from the pomp and formality of the mayor's little shindig, my bladder aches, as do my ears from Senator Keenan's profuse thanks. I'm still not sure she was suggesting what I think she was suggesting when she slipped me her card. The fact she tried to put it in my back pocket herself is suspicious. And I don't have any back pockets.

I scout around in case Sal is early, which wouldn't be unusual. Instead, it's just me and the pigeons on the roof, so I start thinking about trying to change the ringtone on my phone and I scoot around behind the protruding back of the roof stairwell to take a leak.

For a moment I'm not quite sure what I'm seeing. Then what I first think is a corpse and then realize is a desiccated human being steps, disturbed, from possible hibernation behind the half-open janitor's cupboard at the back of the roof projection. Huge, nictitating brown eyes bat at me. I'm too stunned to notice the fist. It hits me with surprising strength and then the creature backflips, taking me in the chest with both feet on the way round. I go a good five yards and wind up hanging backwards over the edge of the building as I scramble back up one-handed, gobsmacked, this thing like a moss-colored, year-old cadaver with misty bits of cobweb or something drifting off it.

I can do no more than yell "Hey, wait!" before a long, weird, slightly unlikely-looking pair of insectile wings unfold from the figure's back, a pattern like an owl's eyes on them, and they're buzzing like a saw mill and he lifts up and away, over the edge of the building, disappearing, a moth-man, with no explanation.

I peer over the ledge dumbfounded, and I'm still there, kneeling, a little less awed and more contemplative when Salvador Doro comes puffing and cursing out the other side of the roof.

"Zephyr, Jesus, it's about time we found another place for this."

"You could be right."

Sal moves across the roof and it's only a minute or so before he's smoking. I accept the offer and marvel at the rank taste in my mouth, the sensation of my bronchioles scorching, the almost fizzingly palpable way my body goes into action repairing the damage. It's not hard being superhuman, just weird. Sal waves an envelope in my face.

"This better be on the money," he says.

"Hey, don't bat that fucking thing at me. I'm no crack whore."

I snatch the envelope and check there's five hundred inside along with the Chronicle's joke, a tax invoice, and I gut the package like a fish and tuck away the important bits. The rest becomes a crumpled ball, flash fried.

"So what's the story, morning glory?" Sal asks.

We have a special kind of relationship and he knows he's not up here for his good looks. He is, at least, a relief from the reporters too star-struck to remember what's off-the-record. A 35-year veteran of the boroughs, Sal Doro was writing about supers in this city back when Captain Atom left the army and Divine Grace was still a three-dollar girl who could only make a sparkle with saliva and a whole heap of elbow grease.

"Did you catch that show at City Hall yesterday?"

"The Hermes Foundation gig? One of the cadets went along. Marv got some photos of that shiny new robot. Impressive."

"I don't have to tell you this doesn't come back to me, right?"

"Sheesh. For the millionth time, Zephyr. . . ."

A guy's gotta pay the bills somehow, especially with my wife always ready to remind me that hero-ing isn't exactly an income. So I lay the scene out for Sal, the tussle with the robot, an inexplicable malfunction – no need to go putting sensitive information out there for the next jumped-up malefactor – and of course Zephyr gets a good mention. This time I'm generous: I concede Seeker, Vulcana and the old Aquanaut came up with the goods. The others don't rate a mention. Sal's smart enough to know there's an angle in this and asks me about the coincidence, every card-carrying member of the Sentinels in the same room. Then he raises an eyebrow and sits back to listen.

He's disappointed.

"You got another one of them envelopes in there?"

"Jesus, Zephyr," the hack coughs and flicks away the dead stub of his smoke. "I don't even know this is worth it, let alone paying for another."

"Worth it? You say that all the time, Sal, and then my quotes are on your front page, right beneath that photo byline the lino boys mocked up in the Stone Age when you still had your own teeth. Trust me, 'Robot rampage' might even be an easy fit. Tell the headline guys. All caps."

Sal quietens down to ask a few pertinent questions and I give him what I can, describing the professor and even throwing a few more names at him, this Dr Martin Thurson as well. Sal jots it all down in six-point type and offers me another cigarette which I decline.

"You hear what Nate Simon's been writing about you?"

"Like I've got time to read the Post. I hate broadsheets, you know that. Too damned hard to fold."

"Real cultured, you."

"So what does he say?"

"Jeez," Sal stands and makes a face, stretching his back in the obscene way only men coming on sixty and two-twenty pounds can manage. "Maybe I oughta let you read it for yourself."

"Spit it out, Sal."

"Well let's just say the words out on a certain fruity ringtone that makes people wonder whether Zephyr doesn't bat for the other club."

Blood, among other things, drains from my face.

"You're kidding me?"

"Look into these baby blues," he says, pulling down one vaginal lid.

"Shit. You know it's not true."

"Maybe I just ain't your type."

"It's this stupid phone. It's a default setting."

"You should get someone to look at it," Sal laughs, turning to go, waving with a folded up newspaper I didn't even notice him carrying. "Let me know if you wanna Sal Doro exclusive on why the Sentinels aren't reforming. I hear the mayor's been having hush-hush luncheons with half the city's masks."

I shake my head and let him go. Over time, my gaze turns. For home.

*

CALLING HOME IS overdue. Not my home, I mean the home I grew up in. They used to call it Astoria, before the whole area got wallpapered over as Pierce (carrying on the presidential thing, you know, for Franklin Pierce, 1853-1857 – I know it's not exactly the most memorable name, but unlike Cleveland and Washington, he didn't have a major city named after him already). The grey streets are much the same as they were when I was a troubled teen, unable to confide to anyone why I blew all the fuses in our semi-detached every time I had a wet dream. Or at least that's how I remember the area. Truth be told, the old town and I ain't exactly on best terms these days, though it's nothing to do with Max and George. Something about being a world-class, ball-busting badass superhero means you don't go back to the suburbs as often as reminiscence might otherwise dictate.

So, twenty-first century telemetry has to do the trick. In the wallspace again, I fire up Zephyr's iMac supercomputer and wonder how I managed to be conned into such a slackwire gizmo. The only thing I can download that runs on the damned thing is porn, but my guy in New Hampshire swore by it and so the Apple billionaires get another penny in the fountain thanks to some nameless schmuck who bought the thing outright one day, just walking in off the street with a wad of cash, the accompanying Tribune pay slip nothing but a smoky residue.

My guy – let's call him Niall, it's his name after all – runs the message board for me gratis ever since I saved his girlfriend from a flying car during a downtown slugfest with Crescendo. (See how naturally I managed to slip that word there into this, this whatever it is we're having, this conversation?) It was her first trip shopping in the big city on her lonesome. A cute little thing she was too, those tight little buns in my big hands as we flew to safety, the bad guy buried under rubble it took the city Works Dept three days to clear. Whew. Girls who look like Japanese animation aren't really my thing, but if you met Niall, well, you'd know how the rest of the stories goes if you can't guess already. Let it just be said the man does a fine line in sophisticated web artistry I'd frankly be too embarrassed to master myself.

There's not much happening on the Zephyr message boards. I put off the inevitable for as long as I can and then place the call, adjusting the webcam so it doesn't catch the old red-and-white get-up still moldering on its hook. Max and George were web-savvy before anyone even decided on a name for the Internet, so it doesn't surprise me when one of the dear old dykes picks up on the third ring.

Maxine already has the headset in place. She looks distracted for a second, gazing off-screen and giving me an unguarded look at the fine lines and wrinkles that come with the territory of being an ordinary schmuck. *Poor old bird* (imagine the English accent). The haircut is as fierce as it is trendy, undiminished by the natural steel wool color or the grey that seems to bleed into her cheeks. All the same, a genuine twinkle wipes twenty years off those bespectacled blue eyes that once melted hearts around the MIT Gender Studies Department water cooler. Or so she used to tell me. Georgia may have carried me to term, but it was Maxine who came through in the mothering stakes, as much as I would otherwise be tempted to call it an even race.

"Hi mom."

"Joseph," she smiles. "So nice to hear from you. I'll have to tell your mother all those things she said about you last night really were misplaced."

I chuckle. I never stopped pausing over that habit of them speaking about themselves in the third person. You blink and the fucking signifier's changed to the other one. Spivak pronouns be fucked. Other kids in the club had mums and godmothers, aunties, birth mothers, and craziest of all, one even had a dad (after the operation). In our family of three we just settled on mum and mom, Georgia with her Irish lilt, and Max with her ability to cut to the chase and otherwise read me like a book.

We shoot the shit for fifteen minutes. This is me assuaging guilt, so it's OK that I'm not big-upping myself. I've carried on a family tradition by never coming out to either of my parents. Though Maxine has always given me a knowing twinkle I couldn't shake, I figured if it was good enough for them to hide me and each other from their respective families until they were all safely in the ground, I can keep myself and Zephyr separate too. The only problem this leaves is me having to answer the occasional curly one about myself that hits on the issue of my life being a complete disaster if you don't have the fact of being an ass-whooping household name to fall back on. Quite apart from explaining how the fuck an ordinary Joe like me fills the day, being a work-from-home freelance writer and a practically unemployed one at that means I don't exactly glow in the "make mommy proud" stakes. Max has her own bodyweight in degrees, diplomas and honorary positions of merit. George is a published author of cringingly erotic fiction and a prolific visual artist to boot, though – and it sort of comes with the territory – while she's apparently mellowed out a heap since her student days, more often than not her pieces require a pretty spirited defense whenever they make it out into public. Some artists can get away with hand-making everyone their Christmas gifts. With some of the shit (and piss, and menstrual fluids) my mum has messed with over the years, you'd be begging Santa to go on the Naughty List once you got a delivery from her.

"We were a little worried about you, Joseph," Max lays it on me eventually. "Your mum ran into Beth last weekend and something she said made us wonder if there was cause for alarm? You know what we've always said about partners supporting each other."

I mumble something and the monologue continues. (Yes they really do speak with one mind sometimes. It's scary).

"What about dinner? It's been an age since we saw little Tessa. She's growing so fast. I know you're probably terrified about the prospect of her spending more time with her grandparents, but really, Joseph. . . ."

"Jesus, mom, give me a break."

"That's your inner teenager talking, Joey," Max replies sternly. "She must be what, almost fifteen? I'm not going to let anyone *seduce* her. God forbid she would grow up anything other than the 'normal' Elisabeth seems to so fervently want."

"Beth's got some pretty strong reasons for wanting her family normal sometimes. . . ."

"That sounds like something we could discuss over dinner one night this week. What do you say?"

Knowing when to fold, I nod reluctantly and we pencil it in. I'm no Sisyphus, but even I know when a chore's overdue.

Zephyr 1.8 "Between The Greetings And The Disconsolate Sighs"

ANOTHER NIGHT AND we're piling out of Mastodon's armored limo on the perennial red carpet at Mechano's. Doormen dressed as robots give me the creeps, but I'm with British hero Lionheart, Adam Sandler, and actors Jason Statham and Stanley Tucci, though I don't actually know which one is which, though one has an English accent and seems to be keeping Lionheart amused and that's all that matters because Mastodon and I are trying to show him a good time. He's been in the country a week on a film promotion for his new documentary on the evils of forgotten land mines, a passion he developed apparently after being intimate with a certain formerly alive British princess, not that he'll admit it, the cause like a torch he's carrying in her memory. I don't know why he bothers. He's plenty interested in the local variety of "tottie," so it's not like he's a monk.

Mastodon is an enormous, beyond barrel-chested one-time hero of the 70s who hasn't exactly gone to seed, but whose reputation was only enhanced by the news he'd married porn actress Ginger Lynn. He still gets around in the open fur-lined jacket, enormous side whiskers and the bull horns protruding from either side of his collar, but these days there's more white in his hair than black. I don't really care. I once saw him throw a taxi at a guy for wolf-whistling at a pair of underage girls. I like his style, plus I was quick enough to catch the cab and save everyone from an embarrassing lawsuit. If only he'd stop calling me "son," reflecting on battles with Dr Stingray and his Orbital Death Station, and remember I've saved the world once or twice on my own, things would be peachy keen.

Mastodon also has the best drugs. Almost a motto. I am sailing pretty close to the wind with a concoction the old man calls Lottery 99. He has connections to a private chemist and I know I saw him once, some years back, in police observation photos taken of Twilight's uncle, Mob boss Tony Azzurro.

As we emerge from the limo, Mastodon mutters something about "finding some bitches" and coincidentally the crowd of people who for some reason have nothing better to do than hang outside the club like lepers give a cheer and I, stupidly as it turns out, hold up my hands and grin. Jason Statham or Stanley Tucci elbows me and I turn to see a yellow cab disgorging four shabbily dressed Bohemians. It only occurs to me this is the rock band U2 when Bono walks up the steps past me, looks me up and down and nods, "G'day mate" in a fake Australian accent and gives a stoned laugh echoed by his bandmates. Me and Mastodon and the others filter into Mechano's like the rest is some kind of dream, and doormen and hat-check girls and bar staff effortlessly disappear in front of us as we proceed. Although I never have to pay anyway, it is slightly disturbing to see the actors we seem to have accumulated aren't at least being weighed for their value by the customary big men at the door.

Inside, it's like there's been a power failure. It's pitch black, the air so cold our breath comes out like from a dry ice machine, and for a moment I think I can smell sewage until I realize Courtney Love is standing in the foyer nervously juggling a baby it seems someone has unwisely passed her, the diaper full, her make-up a smear of red and black like some Norwegian goat metal band gone wrong.

"Zephyr," she moans like a zombie as we go past.

"I do not know this person," I say loudly just in case anyone's actually paying attention.

We round the bend and it seems like the Messiah has returned to earth. Amid the strobes, cameras flash, which seems weird because Mechano's has such a strict policy, yet Bono has his hands in the air and moves up some carpeted steps and I realize they are moving to our usual booth. Twilight, Darkstorm, even Red Monolith – none of them are there to stop it happening. The club owner is Mechano himself, a mutant nobody has really worked out whether his life depends on weird proto cyber-technology or if he just has a kink for wearing lots of metal. His polished bald head positively gleams in the light from rows of overhead monitors showing explosions and car chases and girls in vinyl giving lap dances and cars exploding from alleyways and leather-clad Japanese power pop bands pulling faces while women seemingly giving birth to fully-grown men.

Lagging behind Mastodon, we fall into a rut inches from the dance floor once we realize no one knows where to go. Lionheart bends over and throws up among the feet of some underage girls and they dance in it, oblivious, eyes closed like caught up in the Rapture.

There's already ketchup stains on the left side of the Brit hero's tawny-colored bodysuit, just shy of the heraldic lion-thing in maroon on the middle of his chest, and the matching briefs he wears over the top aren't as skin-tight as they probably were when he got up this morning. The strobe lights make my eyes tired even though today has been a total loaf. And when, minutes later, I spy Lady Macbeth slow-dancing with the Edge, frustration threatens to boil over.

We mingle near one end of the horseshoe-shaped bar. Red Monolith and – of all people – Miss Black stand with a guy in a pale blue-and-white bodysuit I don't recognize.

"Can you believe that shit?" I ask, thumb in the direction of the former villainess, but between the greetings and the disconsolate sighs, no one seems to take me up on my frustration.

I nod to Miss Black wearing her usual variation of the same elegant outfit, hair teased out a bit more and a diamond necklace around her high throat, and eventually my gaze settles on the guy in blue. He and Red Monolith talk half in sign language because of the music pulsing overhead, and one of Mechano's plate-armored waiters walks past us with a tray of drinks going in the direction of you-know-who.

"So who's this guy?" I ask the person on my left, realizing only as I turn that no one's there, Mastodon and Lionheart nowhere to be seen.

Jason Statham or Stanley Tucci says, "Where've you been? That's Sky Blue."

"Sky Blue? What sort of name is that?"

"He's the guy that saved that girl from that film," the actor replies.

"Oh." I want to say something about wishing someone had saved me from *Deuce Bigalow* as well, but it's just too fucking loud and I'm too annoyed to be bothered.

"And he was in *Starscene* this month," one of the two actors add. "I can't remember why."

It occurs to me it's been a while since I was in *Starscene* and I think about giving one of the reporters a call. Then I remember my ringtone and Nate Simon's column in the Atlantic City Post.

Fuck.

At that precise moment, Sky Blue leans across and asks, "Has anyone else been hassled out by that guy in glasses?"

I look at the spot not indicated by Sky Blue and recognize Clark Kent standing looking anxious. Every other head is turned in the opposite direction except for him, standing watching our little group, white teeth clamping his bottom lip, "stalker" written all over him.

"Yeah, I know that guy," I mutter.

I'm too tired for this shit.

"I'm going," I say, and physically push off from the bar.

Across the room, Mastodon and Lionheart sit in a booth with Cameron Diaz, Sheryl Crow, Ralph Lauren, Jack Black, Scarlett Johansson and the Edge.

As I'm leaving, I practically run into a skinny guy in an Armani overcoat, horn-rimmed glasses and suede pants, designer unknown, hair the color of an albino cat. Practically isn't actually the word since the other dude basically collides with my chest and it's only reflex that makes me snatch him by the upper arm so he doesn't fall over on rebound.

"Thanks," the guy yells in my ear. He has an Irish accent. "I'm a big fan of your work."

"Really? Thanks."

I barely slow. The guy holds out his hand. "Adam Clayton."

"Nice to meetcha," I throw back and then I'm gone.

Except not quite. Miss Black comes out the exit after me and calls out. We pause for the spectacle of mega-star Macaulay Culkin arriving in a white muscle car, the crowd surrounding Mechano's going nuts, the chiseled twenty-something still milking the success of his lead role as Achilles in *Troy*. I feel slightly ill to see Black Honey is Macaulay's date for the night, especially when I don't mind admitting he's one of my favorite actors. As the happy couple tread past, Black Honey's eyes find mine and she mouths, "Fuck you" very, very slowly and clearly.

I turn to Miss Black and tell her, "This is doing my head in."

"Being famous?"

"Are we famous?"

"Well I was reading about you in the Post yesterday," she says.

"Christ. I'm not gay," I stress.

"No shit," she replies, as I happen to be eyeing her boobs.

I make a noise to signal surrender. Miss Black shrugs and brushes back her hair.

"I wanted to ask you if you were serious about reforming the Sentinels?"

"I think the mayor thinks we're called the Squadron," I reply. "Why?"

"There's a bullet point in Sal Doro's piece last week about the robot malfunction," she says. "Man, I can't believe we can't keep anything a secret any more."

"I blame Animal Boy, personally," I say like turds wouldn't melt in my mouth.

"Gary?"

"Isn't his name Tom? Thomas?"

"No!" Miss Black laughs. "Jesus, Zephyr, how many years have you known him for? It's Gary . . . Gary Something-or-other."

"Long enough that he's not a boy any more, I guess?"

"Would you tell me, if you were thinking about it?"

I pause a moment, reflecting on what exactly we're talking about. I'm straight again, I also note with abject disappointment. Hand-in-hand with that comes wondering about the time. A revelation.

"Is this what Sal Doro thinks?"

"Quote, 'Is Zephyr reforming the Southside Sentinels? It's no coincidence the whole team from 2002 were at City Hall'."

"That schmuck." I feel owed five hundred dollars like it's a palpable thing, as conscious of it as I am of the hole in my ass.

Miss Black touches my arm lightly. "Zephyr?"

I smile, lifting a finger to brush across her cheek. I'm the hero again, at least for a moment.

"What's got you worried?"

She looks indecisively at the finger and refocuses her gaze on my eyes, eyebrows furrowing intently.

"It's been a quiet couple of years for me," she says. "I think I'm ready to take my career to the next level. I'm getting an agent."

"An agent?"

"Yeah. When I heard Aquanaut talking about it, I thought it sounded like a good idea."

"Since when does being a hero need an agent? Jesus," I sigh. "There's no end of bad guys to fight."

"It's a tough business," Miss Black shrugs.

The word *business* seems to resonate, and I think of my wife. It's only been a few days, but Miss Black hands me a card, still crisp from the printer.

"Just think about it, will you?"

Zephyr 1.9 "Older, Less Interesting, But Even More Essential"
IN THE WALLSPACE, once the window is secure, I switch on the light and fire up the computer on its small folding trolley. As the iMac goes through its start-up, I shuck out of my leathers and sniff my armpit and check my breath and squint into the small round wall mirror and then I put my Enercom phone and Miss Black's business card ("For all sorceries, great and small") on the pile of disorganized paraphernalia on the shelf unit built into the support struts at the back of my neighbors' wall. The piles of business cards, scrawled notes, spiked receipts and creased paperwork seem to stare back at me like a mistreated pet. Not for the first time, I imagine what it would be like to have a secretary, a personal assistant as they call them these days, but because of my talk with Miss Black I start seeing the idea in a new light.

An agent?

On the top of the pile is Senator Keenan's card and below is the one Nautilus gave me. Perhaps cleverly, the teal-colored rectangle only has the name of his agent, Saul Osler, a mobile number and an e-contact. I turn the card over a handful of times before snatching up my cell. It's just after one in the morning. On the computer, I move the mouse in the cramped space allowed and click on a link I have to Enercom's home page, and I hope I might be able to find some technical help because I can't find the card for the woman who signed off on the sponsorship deal, Karen Someone-or-other.

The call to Nautilus goes through to a machine and I leave a terse request for him to call me back, hitchingly reciting the Enercom number. I put the phone down and there comes a muted thumping on the bathroom wall letting me know Elisabeth is awake and knows I'm home. My phone problems will have to wait for another evening.

Thinking on Miss Black's comments again, I thumb the power down button on Zephyr central and tug the lever to release the secret door, not bothering with the spy-hole as usual. A vision from the Hell of the Irish clad in a dark lavender gown awaits.

*

"I THOUGHT YOU were coming home hours ago?" is the first thing she says.

Wearing just a pair of boxers and feeling the cold, I say nothing as I start the shower running, hoping the banging pipes won't wake Tess until Elisabeth tells me she's staying at Astrid's place.

"Again?"

"What of it? She's fourteen years old, Joseph. She doesn't have a wife to explain where she's spending all her time."

"God, you know where I've been. Out," I say – not my cleverest response.

Elisabeth nods. "I didn't see anything on the news."

"I'm touched that you even looked."

"Joseph," she says, and eyes me seriously for a moment until I cease all other movements and concentrate on her stern expression. "Don't talk to me as if I've stopped trying. One day I might, and you'll know about it then."

Elisabeth's parents were refugees from 70s Derry and there's still enough Northern Irish twang in her own voice that it reminds me of Bono and the other guy who shirt-fronted me at the nightclub and I go sullen, no real suitable reply, and shuck my shorts off and step into the shower which is too hot as usual. I rapidly spin the cold water tap and the handle comes off, so I repeat the move using slightly more care.

Elisabeth switches on the exhaust and steps from the room.

When I've crackled dry, I dress in jeans, a faded pair of trainers, a long-sleeve tee under a Jets shirt, and I grab my motorcycle jacket as I head for the door. Elisabeth sits on the bed like she's riding it side-saddle, a pool of light falling upon her from the tasteful reading lamps we recently installed. Her mouth opens in an O of surprise as I go for the front door and it's a pernicious but immature part of me that takes pleasure in it.

Down the all-night deli, I tinkle in through the glass doors and make a hotdog from the machine and take a napkin and eat while browsing through the newspapers and magazines. I take copies of the Post and *Starscene* and the last two Chronicles, since I don't know what day Sal's article appeared. Once the unmoderated buying begins, it's hard to know where to stop. Even *TV Week* does a line in supers gossip, and once I've got a *Who*, a *What's Weekly*, a *Give-Me-Five* and *CityLife*, even the teen magazines start looking reasonable. I belatedly realize I'm on the cover of a kids' magazine that is one part activities, one part comics, and three parts mindless drivel, with the caption "Could he be your father?" emblazoned underneath. I grab this one as well and head to the counter where the Uzbekistani teenager with a mohawk and lip ring nods coolly as he tallies up my spend.

I'm yearning for coffee and at the same time looking forward to sleep. I stumble and lose my hold on the magazines just inside the doorway to the flat and Elisabeth emerges, wild dark hair standing up, watching with quiet eyes as I clutch my purchases to my chest and push the dropped magazines along the floor with my foot and through to the coffee table in the lounge. The flatscreen is on mute, tuned to a news channel showing forest fires half a world away, and the city is dark and asleep outside the panel windows that line that wall of our apartment. A modular sofa starts beneath the windows and curls around the coffee nook, and I sit down, followed by Elisabeth, and start pawing through the Post.

"I need you to have a look at my phone."

"Your phone? You don't have a phone."

"Zephyr's phone," I clarify.

"What are you doing?"

"Reading."

"It's 2am."

"I know," I tell her. "I'm tired. I'll come to bed when I'm done."

"You don't want Tessa to see those magazines. . . ."

"I know," I reply.

Instead of disappearing, Elisabeth eventually comes and sits across from me. I briefly eye the long legs that disappear under her gown as she tucks them beneath herself. Her work cell sits on the ledge behind the sofas and she checks it for the time and sighs, tapping her fingers against the samsonite letting me know she wants a cigarette.

"Go on."

She laughs, more a purr than a laugh, and hunts down a cigarette and lights it, smoke spiraling slowly through the air.

"Explain yourself, Joe. This seems kinda nuts."

"I'm reading about Zephyr."

"You used to keep a scrapbook," she says.

"I used to be sixteen."

"We both used to be sixteen," Elisabeth says and I look up, wincing through the smoke at the face of the girl I fell in love with in high school and who has since grown older, less interesting, yet even more essential to my life. I nod.

"I have to treat Zephyr like a business. I'm thinking about . . . I'm not sure what I'm thinking about, but it's a change from the ground up."

"You're changing costumes again?"

"No."

I wait a good minute before saying, "Aquanaut has an agent. . . ."

"Bully for him."

"I think it's a good idea."

"And who's heard of Aquanaut? If I wasn't your wife – Zephyr's wife – I wouldn't know him from half the head-cases you've mentioned in the past seventeen years."

"He calls himself Nautilus now."

"Whatever. That's better than Aquanaut."

"I thought if I had an agent, a . . . PA, maybe even an office – even a virtual one – then this would be more like a job."

"A PA?"

"You've got one. And you're always reminding me this isn't a real job."

Elisabeth snorts contritely. "Don't hold it against me. I've been saying it for twenty years and it hasn't mattered yet. You don't have to have a real job, Joey. That's what you've got me for."

"I want more than just . . . just scamming money from reporters for stories," I say with a touch more anger than I expected.

A spark leaps from my eye to the glass window and vanishes.

"Is this about money?"

I drop my gaze to the table. I've opened *Starscene* to reveal photo after photo of figures in costumes mixing with film stars, musicians, famous directors, supermodels, the Dalai Lama, Robert Mugabe, Princess Mary of Denmark, King William, Giorgio Armani. Their masked, multi-colored heads grin out of the pages at me. Overleaf, there are stills from the latest Paris Hilton video leaked to the Internet. The headlines "Masked Ball" and "Superhero Gangbang" read garishly. I recognize Sky Blue grinning, naked except for his blue-and-white wrestler's mask, his lower torso pixelated, Paris leaning back into him with her eyes as droopy as ever. Paragon and Lionheart are also in the scene, masks intact. For a moment, the surreal idiocy of the whole thing overwhelms me and I flick back over the glossy pages with such haste they threaten to tear, and nearly invisible smoke curls off my fingers. When Elisabeth places her hand over mine, the page falls open to an image of U2 descending from the stairs of a plane painted the colors of the Pan-African flag, and the caption reads: Bono, the Edge, Larry Mullen, Adam Clayton. And I wonder what it feels like to be the guy in U2 no one knows.

"I don't care about Zephyr," Elisabeth quietly says, kissing the side of my brow. "I never did. Oh Joey, can you forgive me? I was a girl. It was so surreal, so amazing . . . but I moved on. You should've moved on too."

I try to say something and fail, realizing I have nothing in my lungs, so I take a breath so deep my chest shudders. I feel the urgent need to communicate, but I don't want to overdo it.

"The amazing becomes mundane so quickly, honey," Elisabeth continues. "I still love you. Do you believe that? You don't have to make Zephyr into a . . . franchise to please me. You need to do something for yourself . . . something other than beating up bad guys and waving to photographers."

I am feeling calm again. I turn slightly, but in the dark, between the shadows and the smoke, I can barely pick Elisabeth from the silhouette of the city.

"What would I do, huh?"

"Didn't you always want to go to college? Write? For real?"

I'm out of the room so quickly there's not even the chance to make a breeze. I slam the door to Tessa's room behind me and curl up fully clothed on her short bed, a banana print comforter across me. The paneled windows are veiled by thick velvet drapes, cut by a teenage hand and never hemmed. Somewhere close by, an ambulance starts up its siren and I close my eyes thoroughly sick of this madness.

Zephyr 1.10 "A Long Outstanding Pretend Enmity"

IT'S RAINING MEN starts up as I'm sitting in my boxers eating a bowl of Cap'n Crunch and browsing Wikipedia. I'm in the wallspace again. I snap my hand over the phone and answer extra quick because of the song.

It's Sal Doro.

"You owe me five hundred," I say.

"It's five hundred for a story. Have I run a story I didn't pay you for? I don't think so."

"I never said I was reforming the Sentinels, Sal."

"Zephyr, I connected the dots anyone else would when they read about your heavy metal friend Hermes. So I gave you the credit. You want me to make like it's Pykes's idea?"

I can't really refute that, so I say nothing.

"I've been digging around a little with that info you gave me," Sal continues. I hear a cigarette lit and after an intake of breath he adds, "Martin Hurson. Name ring any bells?"

"He's the scientist I told you about," I say. "That Professor Prendergast's pal."

"Right. No other bells?" When I say nothing, Sal says, "I have some paperwork on my desk right now that tells me your pal Prendergast and this Thurson fella are business partners."

"Is that . . . unusual?"

"Not at all. Prendergast's with Bell University, associate professor or something, but there's nothing unusual about having a research company, which he does, and nothing unusual about a few scientists with similar, uh, fields of . . . anyway, sheesh Zephyr, I have paperwork here telling me this egghead's company is the recipient of major funding from a shell company run by your friend and mine, Tony Azzurro."

"Tony Azzurro?" I say the name but I practically think, *Twilight's uncle.*

"Tony 'Toecutter' Azzurro. That's right."

"Weird."

"It gets weirder yet. Dr Martin Thurson went missing seven weeks ago. Last purchase on his credit card was an American Airlines flight to Newfoundland – which is home, by the way."

"How the hell do you know what he spent his –"

"He paid out the remaining three months of his lease in full, and I dare say he either told this Prendergast he was leaving or else he had a reason *not* to tell him. You *capiche*?"

"I think so."

"And then he went missing."

"Maybe that was his plan?" I say. "Maybe the rest was a ruse."

"Either he's missing or he's hiding then," and I can practically hear Sal shrug. "So what of it?"

"Hmmm, well it is sorta interesting, Sal."

"But it don't make you no five hundred bucks, I know. I'll call when I've got more. I thought maybe I could tickle your interest and see if you'd look into it from your end. Prendergast, the mayor, him meeting with all these supers, and then Prendergast kind of *building* him one, you know?"

Sal signs off with the whiff of more money firmly under my nose. What I might actually have to do to get it rather takes the edge off my hunger. Still moody with Elisabeth's words from the night before, I sit and fiddle with the phone for a while and finally manage to change the ringtone to something that just bleeps infuriatingly. I am almost happy. Then the phone rings again.

"Nautilus," I say, breathing slowly into the phone. "I thought we could meet up, have a drink, if you're still in town."

"Sure, Zee-man. There's a cast party for the new Die Hard movie at Transit tonight and you're invited."

"I am?"

"Sure, I'll get Saul to arrange it."

"OK," I say. "But I need to talk to you."

"Yeah?" He sounds afraid to ask. "Everything OK?"

"Yeah, I just need to talk."

"OK, just don't ask me to join the Sentinels, man, OK? I'm on the east coast now. I head back on Sunday."

"I'm not reforming the Sentinels, Aqua – uh, Nautilus, OK?"

"OK."

We ring off and I ease slowly back in my seat.

In the apartment beyond, the phone starts ringing. I sigh, grab my dirty bowl and coffee cup, and exit my fortress of solitude.

*

THE NEWS IS not what I expect to hear. If I wasn't the lovechild of a cantankerous old lesbian couple and conceived *in vitro* (or so the story goes), I'd almost be shocked. Instead, mere run-of-the-mill gut-wrenching surprise greets the announcement my daughter has been suspended from her school for "inappropriate relations" with a fellow student.

Since Elisabeth slaves away at her downtown law firm to ensure Tessa gets a head start in life by not being distracted by boys – it's an all-girl school, get it? – I can almost laugh at the irony as I quickly change into my Zephyr costume and fold a change of civvies into the flat panel pocket concealed beneath the costume's leather back.

Elisabeth was the girl every guy wanted at school. Too hard-nosed to be a cheerleader, she was Prom Queen on sex appeal alone. And I was her date. True, Darren Aronofsky was voted Prom King, but that didn't matter. I had something nobody else had. I was electric. And showing just how desperate I had been to impress young Elisabeth O'Shaughnessy, I proved it to her one afternoon way, way behind the football bleachers. Right where school property met the forest, in fact. And she was mine ever since.

For one – excuse me, fuck – electric moment, we were so close.

That we've been on separate paths since then seems as obvious an observation as it is trite. Beth is a long way from the ringleted high school beauty more impressed by a guy bench-pressing two thousand pounds and firing sparks from his eyes than someone with a talent based on something other than surviving a direct hit from lightning. Now she only gets that dreamy, faraway look in her eyes when she talks about her work, older colleagues, charity work, secondments to the United Nations, African aid camps, working pro bono for Medecins Sans Frontieres. . . . The list goes on and on.

If my little girl's gone girl crazy, you've got to think it's in the genes somewhere, passed down from Granny George. My mothers stressed pretty early on that my sperm donor wasn't one of their male friends, afraid, probably, I would grow up worrying I would turn out gay. When I was fifteen I reassured Max and George that I thought I was a lesbian too. The joke didn't go down too well.

But it does make me wonder about that other half of me. Scientists – well, Chamber, anyway, who has God-knows how many science degrees – once said people like me, struck by lightning and empowered ever after, were the "next step" in human evolution, just waiting for a metabolic catalyst to kickstart the process. Mutants like Mechano and any number of other freaks like Crosswind and his hangers-on who live under the bridge downtown, and those other degenerate fucks living out in the ruins of Manhattan, were the result of the human genome shaking its collective leg and coming up with freaky and universally useless variations, like a dress rehearsal for the world of tomorrow in which we're just born with our powers, as well as the expanded cosmic consciousness Chamber always believed will inevitably lead us to world peace. I think perhaps he read too many Julian May books. But this isn't a novel or even a comic book: there's nothing cool about being a mutant, born with corrugated skin or six sets of eyes or crab claws instead of labia. And though for many years I thought I was the smokingest shit because I could fly, channel electricity, give the weather a nudge, move super-fast, and flick away bullets, I can't help hoping Tessa has indeed got the queer gene – and takes after her grandmother instead of the more mysterious side of my family.

*

I HAVE TO go back in and make a sandwich or something before I take to the air because I'm starving and I learnt a long time ago not to go hyping up my metabolism on an empty stomach. World-pounding headaches result. So I'm standing there in the living room gobbling down Zephyr's patented triple jelly sandwich with extra jelly and the TV's on and I'm watching the new season of Phil Donahue's show. The guests are semiotician Nelson Mandela, some black academic trying to explain to middle America what the hell he does for a living; the actor formerly known as Tom Cruise, explaining why he abandoned his birth identity and is now totally committed to Richard Gere and how they are breaking the stigma of being Hollywood's first open sub-dom couple . . .

And Lady Macbeth.

I wouldn't normally watch such drivel except I have to finish my sandwich and then fly halfway across the city so I can attend a crisis meeting because my little girl's taken to munching rugs for a hobby. So I stand there like a robot, the jelly on stale rye, while Lady Macbeth breaks into tears as Phil explains to the audience how the former villainess wants to be known now as Jocelyn now she's reformed.

"Oh God, oh God. . . ." she blubbers.

A spark from my fingers, subtle and low grade, is enough to switch the television off without frying it. I stomp back through the secret door of white tiles and it's only a few seconds later that I'm jetting on a tight angle up into the sky.

The day is crisp, reminding me that autumn has full sway. The white streaks left by jetliners mark the ocean-blue sky like chalk marks on the wall of a child's bedroom. The city's hundred-odd skyscrapers are an uneven cluster like crystal shards reaching from the river mouth and the Atlantic beyond. Over a leaden grey ocean reflecting the distant clouds, a storm-front moves like an army, tactically deployed to lessen cheer and spoil Friday night barbecues.

As befits one of the world's greatest cities, the skies are not mine alone. Apart from the planes ascending and landing at the distant airport, I spot corporate helicopters lifting from the pads of at least three roof-tops. There is a guy on a hang-glider out over the bay. Another flying figure makes a brief appearance, the merest speck against the cerulean background. It is my custom to climb to a height and then re-orient myself towards my destination, heading straight down again rather than fly in a lazy arc over the town, but on this occasion it seems I've been spotted. I shouldn't be surprised. Most of the city rooftops bristle with antennae, satellite dishes and receivers. "We're in the Panopticon, baby," as Mastodon, not exactly a voracious reader, once slurred to me across a table festooned with bongs and cocaine-dirty glass.

The chopper is innocuous enough. No sleek black lines, non-reflective armor or curious rocket-shaped attachments. It doesn't look likely to transform into a Japanese robot anytime soon. I guess the gigantic yellow E! with the exclamation mark might be a deliberate clue.

In one of her more moronic deployments yet, Leeza hangs from the doorless cockpit with black plastic safety straps giving her a second boob job. Gravity and the wind factor suck eagerly at her face as she holds an enormous-headed microphone up like the prop it is. From the helicopter, her irate-cum-chatty voice booms.

"Ahoy there Zephyr, looking good!"

I wave a salute and dutifully hover a hundred yards away with a fake grin feeling like a circus clown about to get paid to get a blowjob. Leeza doesn't say anything for a moment. I guess the pilot or the producer is giving her instructions and the nose of the chopper comes about, slowly easing towards me. I swoop around the giant insect, the outside studded with cameras, and note an actual cameraman poised over Leeza's shoulder. Nearby roof cameras with telephoto lenses will provide the reverse feed later, the footage either sold to the entertainment show by freelance entrepreneurs or sourced ahead of time by the actual producers.

When the open door and I coincide once more, I give Leeza another wave.

"How're you going there, Leez?" I groan with just the right amount of zing. Hard to believe their producer once sent my fan club a letter addressed to me, criticizing me for "inadequate composure forbading close-ups" (sic). Just another reason to get an agent so I can learn more handy tips like those.

I grimace a smile and Leeza says something in her customarily flirty way and I respond with a quip about the air temperature up here that has her double-taking her nipples, which are standing up like chapel hat-pegs, as the old book says.

"Zephyr, what do you say to the buzz around town that you and your old teammates are planning a big announcement? Is there an exclusive you want to give our viewers?"

"I guess you've been reading that old hobo Sal's column in the Chronicle, Leeza, and like I told him, there's no substance to it."

I smile, imagining Doro's all-day-sucker face and his grin at our shared joke, a long outstanding pretend enmity. All the expression goes from Leeza's face and the voice booms back, "Hang on Zee, we're just checking the tape. Did you call Sal Doro a 'homo'?"

"No," I snap. "*Hobo*. You know, like a homeless guy? Though I guess that's not so cool either."

Leeza gives a trilling laugh and an effete wave and signals we're rolling again.

"Dana Ray puts you at Mechano's after the U2 show the other night and we have to ask – if you're not putting the team back together, what's between you and former teen sorceress and 2007 Penthouse Pet Miss Black?"

"What?"

"Are you an item?" Leeza positively squeals. "Do please tell us we can scorch that nasty rumor."

"Miss Black and I are just old friends, former teammates. . . ."

"Former friends as in 'just friends'?"

Leeza's voice halts, creating a pregnant pause quite hard to imagine hanging there almost eight hundred yards in the air beneath whirling rotor blades. My palms are prickling at the merest suggestion of closeted homosexuality. I reply without even thinking.

"Well, you know, 'been there, done that,' Leez."

The reporter erupts in duplicitous laughter and the helicopter moves off for a moment, the pilot shuttling around, adjusting for the change in breeze and then bringing it back while I continue to hover, uneasily aware I may have just committed a faux pas, throw in a little borderline defamation too, but not quite yet able to scrutinize the meaning.

"So it's just coincidence the city's seen Miss Black, Seeker, Vulcana, Gary Gray aka Animal Boy and Chamber all in the same fortnight?"

"It was for the mayor's sake we got together," I mumble, as much as one can when having a conversation with a helicopter.

"Is there some future news you want to tell us Zephyr?"

"I don't think so, Leeza."

"No thoughts about bringing the team back – or a new one?"

"Well, I enjoyed my time with the Sentinels even if you could say the experiment was a broken one."

I have no idea why I give her even that much information.

"The FBI are reporting your old nemesis – or one of them – The Tragedian, is coming up for psychiatric assessment after a possible radical new breakthrough treatment."

"Oh, they gave him a lobotomy, did they?"

Leeza laughs. She loves it. Truth is we don't get along. She told me she likes them dark and brooding, "like Nightwind". It's internationally-syndicated publicity all the same. For some reason I assume this is automatically a good thing, so I grin and let her come back to me.

"Any chance of a reconciliation?"

"With the Tragedian?" My response stumbles. "He . . . caused city-wide riots that left sixteen people dead. And that was just last time he was loose."

"I didn't hear you say no?"

"Um, no, Leeza."

The pilot makes a throat-cutting motion and the reporter does her thing with the rapid summary, the signing off, the business-like wave goodbye, and then the helicopter banks, descends, turns away, leaving me like any other ordinary guy who can hover half-a-mile above the street.

Traffic below is in gridlock. A pigeon passing through the turning rotor blades explodes in a fine grey mist. The roar of a nearby flight bound for Heathrow fills the world. I think again of Courtney Love standing in the club's foyer with a swaddled infant and am embarrassed that it only occurs to me now that I probably should've told someone at City Hall.

However, I am not a hero who dabbles in the family courts, even if maybe those people need superpowers more than anyone.

I am reminded of this fact only moments later as a red streak hurtles through the air towards me at just over the speed of sound.

Although I detect his arrival through my barometric powers, Thunderbird still manages to greet me with a full-force body-check that sends me spinning end over end until I can counter myself. A roiling nimbus of quasi-combustible energy surrounds the other super like a smoky glow as he hovers where he's halted, chest heaving, his heavy-lidded gaze settling on me like a stain.

"Don Azzurro wants to speak, so you're comin' with me."

Zephyr 1.11 "Ensuing Loyalties And Medieval Fealties"
TWILIGHT'S UNCLE ANTONIO is the head of the east coast syndicate. Although his nephew's dalliances with the occult – and his emergence as a bona fide super-being in his own right – was often a source of friction between the two of them during the years, I have it from Twilight that their relationship's now settled into an uneasy peace bordering truculent resentment. Again, as I understand it, the tension to a large part derives from Tony Azzurro's refusal to accept his brother's son does not have some manner of designs on taking over the family business, especially with the supernatural arsenal now at his disposal. Twilight's father was the former don and the business, with all its ensuing loyalties and medieval fealties, only fell to Tony the Toecutter because Twilight let it happen. He let it happen out of lack of interest, but Azzurro's seventh-generation Mafioso. Those people have a gene for paranoia hand-sculpted by natural selection.

All the same, Thunderbird – one of a handful of the syndicate's paid operatives – figures he's here to remind me Twilight's still family, as far as Tony Azzurro's concerned.

"I'm always happy to talk with Don Tony," I say with an inclination towards the distant ground, assuming the big guy is stashed away in an armor-plated limousine somewhere.

"Good," Thunderbird says.

"But I also have time to teach you some manners."

"Just come and try it, bitch," the other guy says.

There's something in his accent, Puerto Rican or Cuban, maybe. I've never heard him talk before.

I eye my imagined date with the wannabe Corleones down below and then Thunderbird. I genuinely have no qualms about taking on the city's number one enforcer for the syndicate, and that's why I guess I can let it drop.

"You'll keep. Take me to your dealer."

The rendezvous is not on a street corner and badgered into the back of a long black as I imagined. Tony Azzurro is much more wise to the surveillance possibilities of our fair city and awaits me on the roof of the Deluxe Continental Hotel. It's cold up there, even though the wind isn't up yet, and he's instantly recognizable among the dozen-or-so hoodlums the Cosa Nostra like to keep on hand for such eventualities. All the suits are Armani, which seems a little overdone to me. Talk about making the three-piece suit a uniform and they've gone and done it. Tony is a burly figure with the crew cut going silver at the sides, a grey Versace overcoat, Dior scarf and Colombian cigar completing his accoutrement. He also carries a walking stick with a mother-of-pearl handle and gilt grip. He leans on it more heavily than he wants to as I plop onto the roof sixty feet away at the edge of the venting ducts to ensure steam plays across our scene. The movie in my head just won't let up man, sorry.

"Mr Azzurro," I say. "It's been a long time since I had the pleasure."

"Zepha," he replies, stomping across, cigar in one corner of his mouth. "You know there's no pleasure in it. What have you done with my nephew?"

Fanboy as I am for Twilight, it's hard to adjust to thinking of him as anyone's nephew. I size the Toecutter up for a moment and the scowl adds authenticity to my genuine reaction.

"You need to explain what's going on. Twilight is a friend of mine."

"So I thought," tough guy Tony replies.

I wind my finger around, say, "The explanation?" and the Mafia hoods grow angsty, more than three of them pulling out their heaters. I keep my eyes on Azzurro and do the spark thing, one of the tendrils reaching smack across the roof and taking the gun from a trembling hand.

"Let's keep this nice, huh?"

"You was at the Island last week," the don says. "What gives? Last anyone knows you visited, my nephew disappeared into that pinball parlor of his and now there's a fucken mess and we ain't seen shit from Frankie since."

"Define 'mess'?"

"A big mess of red shit and light and shit," one of the neighboring goons says, apparently with approval.

"If by 'pinball parlor' you're meaning Twilight's inner sanctum, that's sacred space to him. I hope your men went in there for a good reason, Mr Azzurro."

I shrug, playing the mobster to the man himself.

"Twilight's a dangerous man. He walks in a dangerous world. You'd wanna know what you were doing before you go *upsetting* anything in there."

Azzurro sniffs and brusquely wipes at his nose. It's cold. The mist steams from us, air-conditioning or not.

"Maybe you need to have a look at it," he says.

"As a friend? Sure. Maybe I do."

The don nods. "Good." And he motions with his cigar as he turns and trudges off across the roof.

Thunderbird takes me by the upper arm and I frown, looking down, about to shake him free when I see my leather sleeve is coated in ice crystals – frost that would normally be impossible in such a short space of time, even in cold weather.

At about the same moment my apparent weight skyrockets from something around two-eighty and into the six or seven ton range. I'm lucky I don't fall through the roof. I am only just strong enough to turn my head and groan inwardly, played like a sucker as Gravitas and Frost emerge from concealment. The icy lady, as always, gives a cruel smile, lips blue with the cold she cannot feel. Gravitas has aided and abetted his costume with a thick fur-lined coat and aviator goggles, something between the Han Solo on Hoth action figure and Hugh Jackman's Wolverine musical.

The goons produce a steel trolley and I can hear a big chopper coming in to land. Right around that time a kind old man appears with a needle – a horse needle, in fact, to overcome my super-dense and thus extra-heavy flesh – and all Gravitas lets me do is groan.

*

ALTHOUGH MY ARM aches, it's the freezing cold that bites through the narcotic fug my Mafia friends create for me.

It's dark in the room and my wrists and ankles are shackled to the four cardinal directions. Although I'm still costumed, my leather pants are half down and a skeletal brunette rides the erection I'm frankly surprised I can maintain. Molecules of frost coat my uniform and float in the air like motes.

The woman grinds herself to a shuddering stop that returns no favors. In fact, I sense I've already made the donation as she slides noisily from my cold hardness, the silver highlights in her long loose hair a giveaway. It's dark in the room, though I am sure we're alone. My voice, when it emerges from the cavern of my mouth, croaks amid a locomotive cloud of steam.

"Frost . . . Proving you really can't get any, huh?"

The villainess purrs, blue lips black in the gloom as she steps into her PVC outfit and pulls up the arms, mesh over her small hard breasts, a black corset clipping into place. She flickers her hair loose of the catches before answering.

"I'm making a baby," she says.

I feel a trill of fear when I think about it. A few seconds tick by to allow me to ponder the enormity of this revelation.

"You're mad."

"Aw, Zephyr, I thought you'd be flattered. You think I'm asking any of these clowns?"

"It doesn't seem exactly . . . workplace chatter . . . around the water cooler."

Speaking of chatter, my teeth clack together as she carefully tucks me away, eyes locked on mine – I can't look back – and she refastens my belt, manner like the dominatrix she so much resembles, tugging hard until the loop's closed.

"I'm going to make a super-baby, Zephyr. A child like the world has never seen."

"You could've asked," I stutter.

"Really?" Her trilling laugh hurts my ears in the hard echoing confines of the room. "You might have said yes?"

"Maybe you should've asked one of the others. What about Thunderbird? He seems like he'd fit the bill."

Frost laughs like a crow. "You think I would do this with just anyone?"

"Speaking as the guy who's clock you just cleaned?"

She makes a face, glances at one corner of the room where I presume there's a door – I can't crane my neck that far – and then she adjusts her costume, producing a make-up mirror and doing the lippy-mouth thing for a few moments.

"I don't want any more children, Frost."

"How many do you have already?"

She tries to sound nonchalant, but I sense a deep, possibly morbid curiosity. I snap my mouth shut and there's the click of her high-heeled boots as she moves around the flagstone floor. Vinyl-encased fingers smooth back my hair, hard.

"Tell me," she hisses. "Do they have your powers? Do they do what you do?"

"Leave me alone, Frost," I growl in return. "I don't think old man Azzurro tied me up so you could use me as your private sperm bank."

"Do you have any idea how powerful the combination of frost and your storm-powers would be? Our children will be super-conductors, Zephyr."

"Get off me, you fucking madwoman."

All I can do is toss her back with an elbow, but it's enough. If she shows vulnerability in her confession, now Frost shores up her ego with another of those godawful laughs, head right back. Despite her pallor and size zero dress, she looks beautiful – and completely insane.

Light spills into the room as the door opens with the sound of a rifle-crack, ice breaking from hinges and frame as Tony Azzurro and a half-dozen goons stroll into the morgue-like chamber.

"He awake?"

"He is now," Frost says in her low, sardonic voice.

The Toecutter makes a motion and several of the young Italian guys move around the trolley and slowly reposition it. I no longer have Gravitas's powers affecting my mass yet the restraints, tungsten steel I am guessing, are good enough to keep me in place for now. The trolley starts moving up a ramp and we're through the door and out under the crepuscular sky, the irony of the actual frigging twilight lost on everybody as they wheel me, like I'm the madman, across from the estate's helipad, leaving the Neo-Classical stone maintenance shed and going up the garden path towards the main manor house and my friend's sacred laboratory.

The reddish glow to the air isn't the only thing that doesn't look right. Once I'm able to crane my head to peer between my feet, I can see a huge, slightly crooked disc of red energy enveloping Twilight's study. The surface of the void shows angry blood-red clouds moving slow as eels in a pond. The squat stone building is split in two by the presence of the disc. The front of the building with its studded oak door remains visible. The rear of the building is lost in shadow and red undercurrents.

When next I look around, Thunderbird and Gravitas stroll along with Frost and Tony Azzurro. Perhaps nearly twenty mooks in total have joined us. I have a fair idea what happens next and I rattle my chains, calling for the key.

"That shot the doc gave you should leave you a little weak," Thunderbird says. "Don't go gettin' any funny ideas, leather-boy."

There's a click, and when I look at my wrist, Frost is there, smiling, something intimate retained in her gaze.

"Trust me," she whispers.

It's perhaps the craziest suggestion I've heard so far.

Zephyr 1.12 "Cigarette Dots In The Dark"

IF THEY'D JUST told me Twilight was missing and his den was engulfed by eldritch forces, I would've been here at Mach 4. Instead, this whole charade has led to the east coast syndicate having a pretty good tie-in to my secret identity, while I'll be the one scrambling to explain if any blue-lipped, lightning-throwing teenagers turn up in a few years' time. God knows why, but I bet they'll be angry at *me*.

Gravitas, Thunderbird and Frost form an arc. Behind them, Tony Azzuro's bodyguards tote enough heavy ordnance to keep the Israeli economy healthy for a long time to come. True to their word, as I rub my wrists to help along my circulation, I feel shaky-legged from their chemist's poison. I need something to eat and a change of boxers, and I can already feel the headache coming on when I explain to Elisabeth why I wasn't there at Tessa's school.

I surreptitiously feel for the phone at the small of my back and Azzuro chuckles, tossing me the small dark object, like a hi-tech ladybird redesigned by Gieger, the Zephyr color scheme emblazoned on the back.

"You may wanna check the messages on that thing," the mobster laughs.

I look down and light up and see sixteen missed calls.

"Get on with it," Thunderbird growls.

I flex my fingers again, arthritic from the cold, and push open the sanctum's door.

Although I expected the red void would've penetrated within, I am surprised by the deathly glow and the palpable sense there's something extremely wrong with this picture. Twilight's study is hardly the alchemist's laboratory, with a widescreen TV and DVD player set up on a shelf containing dozens of occult books as well as a rack of burnt CDs, yet it's not just the enormous, complicated magical symbol inscribed in the marble floor that clues me in to the eldritch nature of my friend's home away from home.

The pulsing rift bisects the room over the middle of the huge floor symbol. It roils and boils like a witch's cauldron, only vertical instead of horizontal. Occasionally the surface bubbles and I wonder what might lurk within.

Clearly, I'm not going to get any answers without finding out.

Crossing over is like stepping through a light rain, except with me, I would prickle as my powers absorbed the friction of thousands of drops impacting my skin. There's no such feeling here. Instead, only the absence of light. I squint, stepping through, glad for the millionth time I can fly as the ground dips away from me and I plunge wholly into this new astral other-space, a black void lit up with a scene of such complete otherworldliness that I'm at a loss for long moments making sense of what I see.

Night's tarpaulin stretches dark, black and infinite against the backdrop of what might otherwise be a familiar scene. This is not the night sky I spent so many evenings watching, sitting in the branches of the tree in my moms' backyard over the years of my growing up. Between me and the perils of space are stretched strange and unusual constellations, and of course there is nothing like a ground to reassure me to the normalcy of the place.

First, like an enormous yellow intestine, a thick irregular membrane runs at an indeterminate distance from down into the deep, rising up past and beyond me, and stretching far into the upper heights of this weird universe. Several spheres, filled with light and yet less bright than the enormous sinew itself, are dotted across the tableau increasingly far away suspended in the nothingness. With nothing to compare anything to, it's hard to work out the scale until I begin drifting, drawing close enough to the yellowish membrane that I can see vague figures travelling within it, and more such conduits at weird angles off further in the deeps of this hollow realm.

I am outside the membrane. When I finally draw close, I can see muted forms of an alien nature traveling within. They move fast, their winged, clawed, proboscised forms unguessable as they flit by. The conduit itself is huge, though it feels so frail I could rip it with bare hands.

I don't have the chance.

The ushers come for me without warning. One moment I'm watching the membrane like a kid at his first adult movie, the next, large, winged, bloated creatures descend all around me, clawing and grabbing, everything suddenly airless. I let loose with a charge and the first of them floats off with smoke churning from its chest, and then I let the others pinion my arms and take me with them. I figure it's the most likely treatment the big wop himself received and thus it should be my conduit to a swift reunion.

It's hard to describe my courtiers, especially since we are so close. Their hides are like what I imagine a mangy wolf or a giant bat might be like, yet they are closer to half-man, half-giant flies, mandibles slavering, rows of compound eyes glittering like dark jewels in the glow of the distant globes I've already processed as "suns", though it soon turns out I am completely wrong, since the conduits all lead into them. Triple-jointed appendages ending in strong black knife-like claws hold me tight, and though I could resist more, I use the time to study these strange servitors instead. After a few barked questions I give up. If they speak English, or if they can speak at all, they don't seem to want it.

By unknown means we are propelled forward through the ether.

*

WE HEAD FOR one of the distant globes. There's more than just wings fuelling our propulsion and it's not long before the light source looms up close and I can see the sphere is really made of the same yellowy fabric as the membranes, though it is stretched over an infinite network of disjointed frames, energy within permeating the whole thing with a sickly jaundice like a low-res light globe or like a sun tuned to another channel. In various places there are openings like tent-flaps and we are through the nearest one before I can say Jesus H.P. Lovecraft.

Clearly, parts of the sphere-hive are not translucent, no pun intended. As we enter, it goes dark, and I am dragged along a tunnel, close-fitting like a stocking made of skin, nauseating and unnatural. My captors have either forgotten I'm alive or trust completely in my surrender. When we emerge from the passage into a large, irregular, weirdly-lit space, I go weak as otherworldly repulsion fills me.

Twilight is here. So is a large, porous, gigantic, slothful, multivalent creature that is at once all around Twilight as well as within him.

By this I mean it looks like my friend is getting double- or possibly triple-teamed. Pressed amid transparent flesh with the consistency of play-dough, Twilight is spread-eagled across one of the vast Being's many surfaces. His hands and feet have disappeared within its epithelial folds. Some kind of weird arrangement resembling a huge cock morphed into a gas mask has hold of Twilight's face. At the same time his pelvis has also been absorbed into the creature. From second to second, the genital constellation near Twilight's head seems to relax and the sorcerer-hero's head dips, mouth slack, but grinning with a beatific smile, drool – or God, I hope it's drool – pouring from within him. And then the thing refastens and there's a sound like a stomach pump for the soul.

This isn't good.

I flash fry the two fuckers holding me and turn and unleash hell on the two closest behind. Dozens of eye-like apertures open up in the weird beastie occupying the center of this grand, fleshy zero-g chamber and then my nausea acts up again as the whole orb in which we are held seems to rotate sharply. Twilight and his host now fill the ceiling above me like a pastry chef's nightmare, and two quick strobing discharges add a disgustingly sweet smoke to the air, followed shortly by Twilight's screams.

"He must be –"

I resist the urge for further voiceovers, rationalizing Twilight's responses without the help of boxed captions or fluffy white thought clouds. Although I'm wary of getting grabbed and force-fucked the same way, I swoop higher and get a hold of Twilight's midriff and try to pull him free. As expected, bland pseudopods instantly break from the nearby marbled surface and it's only super-speed that saves me. I turn and disintegrate the two feelers with more lightning bolts and again Twilight screams.

And then his eyes flick open.

The whole suffocating creature gives a wobble as Twilight shakes his head like a Doberman, eyes bulging, and a moment later he vomits out the end of the gag-like appendage. I swear I've never heard a sweeter sound than when he cries my name.

"Zephyr!"

He tugs violently at his embedded restraints without any success.

"This is a bit like that part in Pulp Fiction, except you're not black and there's no gimp."

"I don't remember any fucking muffin man scoring that role," Twilight gasps.

I lay my hand over one of his buried wrists and set down a short charge. It's enough to weaken the dough and Twilight pulls his hand free.

"Now," he yells in a deep baritone laced by panic, "uYuatil-el-Awahya, let's see what you're made of."

Twilight's hand is infused with a sea-green glow that burns as bright as a speck of some distant star. After a good grenade count, he makes a fist and stabs it right back into the underside of the enormous creature. I take my cue to zoom across the other side of the chamber as dozens of the weird bat-fly-dog-men come pouring through the previous aperture. The mystic entity apparently known as uYuatil-el-Awahya pulses and explodes, splashing the entire space with steaming hot porridge. We're lucky that when it hits the hordes coming in, they start sizzling and dissolving, tumbling towards the bottom of the spherical chamber like they are under the illusion of gravity where they splash down to merge with uYuatil's soupy remains.

Twilight, head-to-toe with the mess, swoops down and slaps me on the shoulder. He looks pained, though he's grinning.

"Let's get the fuck out of here."

"That was one helluva cumshot, baby."

Like something out of Star Wars, we pour on the speed down the twisting black corridor, emerging from the sphere-city just as a stream of conscious goop pours out after us. Twilight is slightly behind me, being the slower of the two and weakened from captivity, and he weaves away from last-ditch grasping pseudopods, eldritch energy flaring from his palms to make sizzling noises within the gigantic pissed-off matter seemingly in hot pursuit.

"What the hell is this thing?" I yell, adding a little sizzle to the recipe and withering a whole section of the creature's shaft so it resembles overcooked pancake.

"uYuatil-el-Awahya," Twilight says unhelpfully. "He's sort of a . . . mystic pen-pal of mine."

Twilight struggles with another mass of tendrils, this time flinging the mighty appendage away by main strength alone. With no further agreement necessary, we speed away from the weakened entity's remains.

"This way," Twilight says, correcting our course slightly, and sure enough the red portal appears in the middle distance.

"I know it's a cliché," I say, "but if that's a friend, I'd hate to see an enemy."

"It's his nature," Twilight replies philosophically. "He just bit off more than he could chew."

"I thought that was you," I reply.

"I'd appreciate it if this remained between you and me."

I return the serious sidelong look and nod.

"I owe you," Twilight says.

"That might not be how your uncle sees it."

*

BACK AT THE Playboy Mansion, Twilight does the arrogant nephew thing and refuses to talk to anyone except for me, at least until he's had a chance to clean the ectoplasmic scum off himself. Feeling more than just a little like the teacher's pet – and with the Mafioso hirelings no longer quite so sure about where they stand – I find a quiet spot near the fire and check my phone messages. Of the sixteen received, most feature increasingly irate calls from home.

I sigh, hanging my head, and think about what going home actually means.

Twilight emerges dressed the same way I saw him the previous week, costume on with the gloves and cloak removed, a robe over the top, hair tousled wet from the shower. He has a white towel, used, which he offers to me.

"I may have an answer to that problem we discussed," he says.

I dab at a few dried pieces of magical entity. They simply drop onto the carpet once the toweling breaks them free and from there dissolve without trace.

"Man, you look beat," I reply. "You sure you wanna talk about this now?"

"My research can get a little 'hands on,'" he says. "And there's no guarantees. If you're sure you want to solve the riddle of your split life, then I have an answer."

"You reminded me you were an anti-hero," I surprise myself answering him. "Why was that?"

Twilight grins, three-quarters the high school quarterback with just a hint of serial killer.

"As you just saw, 'consorting with demons' isn't just a catch-phrase. There's no black and white about anything, Zephyr. Not even magick. It all comes at a risk."

"Let me think about it then," I say. "You look like you could sleep for a week."

Twilight nods. His uncle approaches, Gravitas immediately behind, Thunderbird in the distance. Frost isn't allowed inside the house.

"Uncle," Twilight says. "I'm not sure I want to know how you treated my friend. Zephyr has shown you he can be trusted. I don't want him troubled again."

For all his bluster, Tony Azzurro looks embarrassed by Twilight's words. It can't be easy having a brat nephew with the looks of a living god and the power to match. Mustering his dignity, the Toecutter reaches inside his coat and produces a gold business card he passes to me.

"Any time," he says. "*Any time.* Got it?"

I study the card like it might come with instructions. It's a surreal moment and I lessen the effect because I can only nod.

"Sure."

And then the two head honchos disappear to discuss business.

Nautilus has left me a message somewhere in between Elisabeth asking if I was alright and latercalling me a sonofabitch. I phone his message service and confirm lunch at the Silver Tower, which is pretty much the only semi-secure space we supers can eat in public. There's a few more messages from the little people in my life, one from Sky Blue, though I don't know how he got my number, wanting to talk about me putting a team together, and there's a message from the Enercom PA discussing my next contractual appearance at the Motor City Expo next month.

I'm out in the yard and walking in the direction of the cliffs by this time, expensively upholstered sentries discernible as cigarette dots in the dark. The wind is buffeting from the east and it's all sweet gain as far as I'm concerned. Frost approaches from behind and it's only the tingle of a chill across the back of my nape that alerts me to her presence.

"Zephyr."

She looks lonely and thin, standing in her dark costume in the near total blackness, the moon hidden behind clouds and the radiance of the distant seaboard muffled by the pines and poplar running along the cliffs.

"Ah, my rapist. Fancy seeing you here," I say. "I wonder what the Toecutter will say when I tell him about your extra-curricular activities. Or do you have that sort of thing in your contract?"

"Oh Zephyr, you wouldn't do that?"

"If that's a question, then yes. Yes I would."

I turn my back and start walking and she lunges after me, an icy hand on my shoulder attempting but failing to spin me around.

"Zephyr, please, wait. We could make beautiful children. . . ."

"Are you out of your gourd?" I snap. "Lady, I don't fuck the enemy, OK?"

"I'm not the enemy, Zephyr."

"Last time I checked, you weren't exactly clobbering bad guys and saving the banks on their insurance bills like the rest of us."

"That doesn't make me evil," Frost replies.

"Whatever, Frost. I don't have time for this."

I'm thinking of Twilight's proposal and want to say yes, even though I don't have a clue what it means.

"I'm out of here."

I crouch and let loose, Frost thankfully unable to follow, and I arc over the city wrapping myself in clouds and trying to close my eyes, but there's no putting it off any longer.

I head for home.

Zephyr 1.13 (coda)

I'VE MISSED AT least two meals and I'm busting for a leak when I arrive back in the wallspace, but I have to wait in the shadows as the shower runs and one squint through the peephole confirms it's my daughter in the bathroom. We've showered together since she was a few days old and it's as normal as watching my own arm being cleaned to stand a moment and note how she has grown, pondering her weird, possibly off-balance lunge into womanhood, the thighs I know she fears will never become womanly, her grandmother's large breasts and beautiful ears, the muscles of her stomach and arms hardened from judo, a pair of overlapping love hearts tattooed just above the dark riot of pubic hair I try not to take in, all news to me, the snub nose, the bicycle-scarred knees, long tawny hair plastered wet across her supple back. There's no sign of mutations or manifestations. She's an ordinary girl who needs a fatherly response and instead, the red eyes and her lingering long after the soap has gone down the plughole tells me Elisabeth has been at her feral best.

I can't imagine what Beth's thinking and I realize I am genuinely afraid to find out. This is neither a good thing, nor a high point in our marriage.

Later, after draining my bladder, I slip into the passage and bang the front door shut and walk in, carrying hiking boots I've never even worn, the heat on and compensating for the slightly damp black t-shirt I now wear.

Elisabeth steps into the hallway and openly rolls her eyes at my charade.

"She's in her room."

"You wouldn't believe me if I told you what made me late."

"This isn't late, Joe," Beth replies. "Consider this early for the next crisis, OK?"

She slams the bedroom door and I hear the lock scratch into place. So I walk on, stopping at the next white door and gently tapping, head down. Even at average height I've got nine inches on my daughter. When the door opens a fraction, my eyes meet hers rimmed with tears, and even though she must've known it was me, she tries to press the door closed and I put my bare foot in the gap and am surprised to feel even the slightest suggestion of pain as she grows angry all of a sudden and puts her shoulder to the task.

"Tessa, for fuck's sake let me in," I squeal, easily pushing back the other way.

My daughter turns her back and walks to her bed and lies down, her back to me. She wears tartan pajama pants and an old Ministry t-shirt. I carefully close the door without another noise and hover, metaphorically at least, over the bed.

"Are you OK?"

"What do you care?" she snaps back and then blows her nose.

"I care, Tessa. Come on."

"You weren't even there," she yells, rounding on me, angrily tugging down her t-shirt and wiping furiously at eyes and mouth.

"Why weren't you there, dad?" she moans. "Why did you have to make *her* come?"

I sit on the bed and even though she's angry, Tessa drops her head on my shoulder and the tears come and I hesitate before finally putting a firm arm around her shoulders. I mumble something about it "being alright" and Tessa hisses that she hates her mother and I say nothing, feeling her pain, experiencing her emotions like it was a super-power in its own right.

*

IT IS JUST after noon. My cell phone is ringing for the third time in as many minutes. I stop again on my brief trip across the city, the roof of the Helides Building good enough.

"Zephyr? This is Captain Tegan O'Halloran from Commissioner Journey's office. How are you?"

O'Halloran sounds hard as tacks and just as sharp. I vaguely recall her as a formerly statuesque blonde grown tough as an old tree in service to the city. Although she heads up the public relations wing of the city's force, it's more forthrightness than charm working in her favor.

"Captain, I think we've met," I hazily reconstruct, police types always appreciating to know they are more than just empty shirts to the masks who nab most of their glory. "After the Think-Tank thing?"

"The Cohen Laboratories fiasco, that's right," she replies.

Fiasco. Huh, OK. On that occasion my erstwhile nemesis escaped from routine testing out at White Nine – the super-powered prison in the bay – summoned a back-up version of his mechanical alter-ego and proceeded to ransack a genetics lab in Old Town. If you can imagine a murderously insane lunatic from the waist up and a cross between a giant spider and a Sherman tank below, you have maybe half an idea of what destruction he could cause. I saved the day on my own, though Nightwind and Paragon were filmed in the vicinity.

"It's actually about White Nine," the older woman says. "I'm relaying a message there for you from Steven Zahn."

"Steven Zahn? I take it that's an inmate."

"That's right."

"You'll have to excuse me, captain. I'm not always . . . intimate with my prisoners' secret identity."

"I'm not sure there's anything secret about this one," O'Halloran says. "Steven Zahn is the man you helped capture when he was trying to . . . make off . . . with the Federal Bank."

"Oh," I ope. "The, uh, Terraformer?"

"You'd be telling me. Apparently he's emerged from his medically-induced coma quite rational. You'd know that putting them under for a time is pretty standard procedure for the carceral techs out there. Psych evaluation's showing high lucidity, a degree of reasonableness."

"So?"

"He wants to talk to you."

After a minute I capitulate and she regurgitates the details and then rings off like an ex-girlfriend, making some vague allusion to an inevitable future encounter we can't possibly predict. Feeling inexplicably moody, I stroll across the roof-top disturbing pigeons, watching choppers maneuver through the clear sky. A man in green spandex leaps from one building to the next, but I don't recognize him. The older, retired heroes like Mastodon and Hawkwind are in my thoughts, possibly thanks to the garish costume of the unidentified leaper. In my leather digs I'm the epitome of the new breed, even if I'm past veteran status myself.

My flight resumes. I'm keeping Senator Ivory Keenan waiting. It's a year since the Innsmouth Rail Disaster. I saved fourteen lives that day and nearly lost an arm. If ever I was a hero, it was on that day. A little girl, a Vietnamese immigrant, was saved by neurosurgeons thanks largely to my persistence. Ted Turner took out paid ads in three national papers hailing my efforts. And three months later, with dogged persistence and detective-work that would've made Batman proud, I uncovered proof that a truly sick mind was responsible for the derailment. A serial killer by any other name, I tracked down the creature who used to be a man, by then in the habit of calling himself the Smilodon. I don't think those who cheered could have stood witness to the end I gave him, there beneath the New Jersey Turnpike on an isthmus of trash only scavengers and the homeless ever venture across.

Today, the senator's office has requested I attend the memorial. Thankfully, I don't have to say anything, just raise my hand as usual. They know even our voices could give us away in this day and age. The media will be there in force, of course. I don't know what her chief-of-staff was trying to imply when he assured me there would be no other "costumed adventurers" present.

As long as Nightwind isn't laying the wreath, I'll be happy.

Zephyr 2.1 "The Good Courtesy To Be Dead"

SOME TIME LATER and it is only minutes until I'm meant to be at lunch with Nautilus (my old teammate Aquanaut) at the Silver Tower overlooking the bay. Instead, I am looking for batteries for the DVD remote as my sniffling daughter stands in the doorway in a nightshirt and socks, a scarf heightening the sick ward theatrics completely unselfconsciously.

As I proctor the couch, the phone rings. Driven by teenage instinct alone, Tessa hurries for it only to halt at a glimpse of the caller ID. Just in time to make an ass of myself, I lift my head and grunt for her to "answer the damn phone already".

"It's Astrid."

Her mother has banned all contact with the other girl. Tessa looks at me with her big cow eyes and I glance at the clock, guestimating not only how late I will be for lunch, but when her mother is due home. I, of course, promised to spend the day in. Tessa and I have already arranged a cover story if Elisabeth calls while I'm out. It's not like I could blame it on having to save innocent lives or anything.

"Ten minutes, Tess. You know what your mom would say."

Tessa hugs me and snatches the silent phone, calling her alleged girlfriend back and promptly disappearing into the bedroom. I'm smiling wryly because she reminds me so much of her grandmother Maxine today I'm almost inclined to drag her around there for a visit. It occurs to me that it was snowing last time we headed to the 'burbs. I still haven't set a time for dinner and wonder what Beth will say.

I slam the front door and double back through the bathroom and inside of a minute-and-a-half I am bursting from the side window and up and across the town.

The Silver Tower is hard to miss. When the east coast was largely flattened during the Kirlian Invasion of 1984, property developer, philanthropist and – as we call him – "super-friendly" technophile Amadeus Chancel proposed an ambitious project backed by many of the surviving supers at the time. The Kirlian Monument became forgotten as soon as the Chronicle dubbed the slender high-rise the Silver Tower. The only skyscraper of its kind on the whole eastern seaboard, the upper part of the needle hosts a function center, two prestigious restaurants, the home of Chancel's record label and a nightclub, eponymously named for the building itself. A security center and radar station backs up a dense cluster of sensor apparatuses feeding live to any number of local and national authorities, making the top of the tower an eye-in-the-sky for the government and anyone else concerned – like most of the city's "costumed adventurers" – with airborne threats.

For various astute reasons, Chancel also has a gentleman in his employ who goes by the call sign Stalemate. When the dignified black head of security is in the house, no-one within a quarter mile can employ their powers in anything except the most fundamental ways. Fortunately there's a big landing pad and an external elevator built three-quarters of the way up the spire, concealed by a fold in the organic-looking walls.

Here, at least, it is good to be known. The maître d' escorts me to the table overlooking the internal shrubbery, water feature trickling harmlessly into the koi-studded pool. Nautilus stares down like a benevolent uncle until I walk across the brushed concrete floor and then we meet in the middle of the room, shake hands and move to the bar. The city's movers and shakers wrestle with their feelings of inferiority as we stride manfully up into the carpeted area that rings the back of the restaurant, and Nautilus orders two beers and two shots and takes a stool and I lean on my elbow, aware of the hardbody waitress watching us like a hawk.

"To the Kirlians," Nautilus toasts, raising his slim European bottle.

I grin and return the gesture. "The Teslas were my favorite."

"Who were the other ones? Lichtensteins?"

"No," I say, "that's a European country. I think Chancel owns it. You're thinking about the Lichtenbergs."

"That's right," Nautilus snorts and nods. "Damned things."

"Before our time," I note, sipping the beer, something homoerotic in the gesture.

In the bar area, the wall is covered with framed photographs of the different Kirlian invaders in action – basically sentient light-waves inhabiting armored attack vehicles, brought to a messy end mostly thanks to the president's Star Spangled Squadron – but not before the east coast took a serious pounding. Still, it's funny how people move on. I was twelve years old at the time and it only increased my interest in masks. I don't know what it would've been like for me if I hadn't become one. Maybe I'd be one of those sad freaks like Nightwind, trying to get by in the shadows, living off the fame of others. One thing's for certain: I didn't have Chancel's money or Chamber's brain, so building myself a super-suit wasn't ever going to be an option.

Chancel's Chancellor armor looms over the proceedings, a discreet copper plaque reading "1996-1999". Amadeus is a better record producer than he was ever a hero.

I wave when the egg-headed motherfucker finally looks my way, but he looks distracted and returns to a fork-waving conversation with Jeb Bush and a guy who looks like a Nosferatu.

*

WE ORDER STEAKS and side salads and a bottle of red and I ease back in my chair, placing Nautilus's business card on the table in plain sight. I'm sure Stalemate is somewhere in the vicinity, but I don't know how his powers work that I couldn't let fly with a lightning bolt in here, yet I know my souped-up metabolism still won't let me get even the slightest bit tipsy. Nautilus is the same, so when the red comes we drain it off like it's no-one's business.

"So?"

"I've been thinking about when I saw you last."

"Man, that fucking robot." Nautilus scowls a grin.

"Yeah. Look, I wanted to speak to you about getting an agent."

"Really?"

"Yeah," I say more defensively than feels natural. "Why? Do you think I'm joking?"

"No man, not at all." Nautilus lifts his hands for peace. "I'm just surprised. I thought you were too cool for that shit."

"I'm not after the publicity," I say and feel like a liar, even though I mean it when I say it. "I want to get my game on board. It's not the 90s, you know? I feel like things would be better if I had someone helping manage my affairs."

I hold up my hand before he can say anything.

"Hear me out, man. I have to, you know, maintain the whole secret identity thing. But I think there are opportunities I haven't scoped, in all these years, just because it's too difficult, you know, to balance being me and, uh . . . being free?"

"Like?"

"Like . . . like my phone deal," I say, and briefly explain some of the complications involved in getting back to someone in the company when there's the whole identity verification stumbling block in the way.

"I guess I figured if I had an assistant, an associate manager or something, things could run way smoother."

"I could talk to Saul, I guess. . . ."

Nautilus looks unenthusiastic to say the least.

"Well fuck, man, you look like someone's trying to screw your puppy. I'm not trying to get in on what you've got going," I say. "I thought maybe your manager could suggest someone?"

Nautilus nods more soberly and clicks his webbed fingers.

"Pass me a couple of those business cards of yours."

*

I'M ON MY way home when the cell rings. Elisabeth and I have had a fiery argument about the Tessa situation and she nominated me to call the school and demand an appointment with the registrar to do something to salvage Tessa's place at the academy, and also her good name, whatever that means exactly, Elisabeth actually using the expression "the family name," reminding me of her mother who's at least had the good courtesy to be dead these last few years.

I don't bother with the caller ID and just answer. It's Red Monolith.

"Zephyr man, how are you?"

"Monolith," I say like the straight man in a buddy sitcom. "What's happening?"

"Where are you?"

"In the air," I reply. "Over the Commsec Tower."

"Man, we really could've used you today. Darkstorm and Sky Blue and Stiletto and me just got back from some fucked up alternate reality. Man, we almost got smoked. The people there, man, it's like New York never got toasted by the Kirlians, man. I think the world was ruled by winners of American Idol or something. It was hella weird."

I keep flying.

"Uh-huh. What were you doing there?"

"Uh, Darkstorm was like, following up those homeless dudes that've been disappearing down around the harbor? You heard about that?"

"Uh-huh."

"Well, they're still disappearin'. We didn't really get anywhere with that. He called me an' Stiletto up to help, but I think, you know, him and Stiletto kind of have that love-hate thing going so I think I was just there under false pretenses, you know what I mean, dude? It was like a bad Clive Owen film."

"Is there such a thing?"

"I only liked Shanghai Noon," Red Monolith says.

"I think you mean Owen Wilson, dude."

"Do I?"

"Man, *you* are a bad Owen Wilson film."

I groan and alight atop a tenement on the outskirts of what used to be called New Jersey. Red Monolith laughs as usual, like my almost-sick-of-you banter is a weird, backwards kind of compliment. He begs me to come over to Transit. They have a table. Sky Blue is buying everyone shots. It is about 3pm. I feel myself bristle.

"You never said how you ended up in this other place?"

"Oh, it's some old enemy of Stiletto's. Darkstalker? Dark Water? Dark Talker?"

"Darkwatcher," I say.

"Yeah. Anyway, between him and Darkstorm, I don't know, they cooked up a big cloud of blackness pretty bad. Darkstorm kind of explained it, but I think, you know, maybe he was talking out his ass. All that negative energy shunted us sideways instead of teleportin' around like Stormy normally does.

"It's cool though, we got back," he says.

"And Darkwatcher?"

Red Monolith inhales through his teeth.

"I don't know, man. Things weren't looking so hot for Darkwatcher last time I saw him. He leaves those portal-things behind, right? I got a look at the skyline, looked like a heap of crucifixions going on."

"Couldn't happen to a nicer fella."

I beg off the afternoon's entertainment and field a call from a reporter trying to get Mastodon's number which, in a pique, I refuse, and then I'm over the apartment once more. I trigger the window with my remote and shimmy in, unpacking my utility belt and putting batteries in the recharger for my handheld police scanner and dropping Nautilus's card on the desk beside the PC.

Beyond, the apartment is as quiet as a morgue. I call Tessa's school on Zephyr's mobile just to get a few more minutes before the inevitable confrontations, and eventually I manage to convince the registrar's secretary to make time for me in the morning. I sign off, crossing my fingers no citywide disasters intervene and thinking instead maybe that's exactly what I should pray for.

Zephyr 2.2 "Ridiculous Only In Hindsight"

ELISABETH WATCHES WITHOUT expression as I emerge from the bathroom trailed by the sound of flushing. For a moment I think she's simply not gonna speak, and then her eyes crinkle a little and she says, "I could almost make believe like you were in there the whole time."

"You can, if you want."

She has her shoes off and client files spread across the coffee table. The widescreen's on mute. Oprah interviews Paragon. Every time he laughs Oprah has to shield herself from the light coming off him. I grimace and sit so I don't have to watch.

"Did you ring the Academy?"

"I rang the Academy. I'll see old Mrs Wiselmann tomorrow."

"It's Weesleman," Elisabeth says.

"I'll see her tomorrow."

"I can't believe they had the nerve to send me an invoice for next term's fees today."

"Did they?" I ask. "I didn't see any mail this morning."

"The account comes to my office."

"Oh."

"If they're going to expel Tessa, I'm claiming back the rest of the term. You'll tell her that, won't you?"

"Are you sure *you* don't want to tell her that? You seem pretty angry."

"Joe," Elisabeth says, and does that thing where she drops her eyes until I stare, like an evil hypnotist's victim, directly into them with my own mouth shut.

"Mmm?"

"You have to get these people to see they've made a mistake."

"Have they?" I ask, which I know immediately is a bad idea, so I make it worse by trying to justify the comment. "It's just two good friends getting to know each other better, honey. Don't a lot of girls do this sort of thing?"

"In your dreams, Joe."

"Well, I'll just explain it's a bit of a family tradition. You know my moms."

"You'll do no such thing!" Elisabeth stands and immediately sits again. "Jesus, Joseph! Do you want to prejudice the school against her completely? You need to convince these people it's a mistake. *Their* mistake. And it is a mistake. Tessa's no such thing."

"Hmmm," I reply, nonplussed as I often am at times like these, perhaps my worst failing being to fail to get angry. Despondent, hopeless, yes. Fiery? No. There's something wrong with my wiring when it comes to my wife.

"What sort of thing?" I ask.

I am such a sucker for punishment.

"A *lesbian*, Joseph," she growls in frustration.

"Come on, babe. You're better than that."

"Hey, I don't care if she wants to date Willie Nelson, OK? I don't care if she's into girls or . . . flipping burgers . . . but I will *not* have those . . . *motherfuckers* . . . treat my daughter like a disease."

"Jesus, you're so sexy when you're angry. . . ."

"Joe! Now is not the fucking *time*, alright?"

Playful usually gets me everywhere, at least behind the mask, and I can't switch it off so I start crawling across the table, hedonistic, but careful not to scrunch the precious documents, saying, "I don't know about that, baby. It seems like the time to me."

Only it looks like Beth is playing for keeps. She stands up and away from the table, refusing to engage, leaving me like an idiot on all fours on the coffee table. At least I'm fully clothed this time. Normally at this point the table would break, so in a way I'm just kind of grateful when she simply walks away shaking her head and leaves me there.

I sit, forgetting about the TV, and see Paragon jumping up and down on Oprah's couch like a madman. He's gesturing and I realize Lady Macbeth aka Jocelyn is there hiding at one end of the couch. I can hear my phone – which is to say Zephyr's phone – ringing, which means I've forgotten to close the secret door to the wallspace yet again.

"Fuck."

Right about then Elisabeth screams.

I'm out of the chair so fast I actually make steam. Part of me is freaking. The other part, the backseat driver of my psyche, coldly calculates whether I'll get to play hero back into my wife's good books. I find her in the bedroom with its panoptic views.

Only this time the views aren't quite up to their usual. This is because the outside windows crawl with moths and a thousand other insects – bees, wasps, dragonflies, even crawling things like ants and silverfish. Beth hates bugs, among other things, including lesbians apparently, and I move up behind her with a reassuring hand on the back of her nape only to get slapped away.

My eyes track hers.

There are clouds of them wending their way over the city.

"Go and do your thing," she says, sickened, like her disgust includes me.

*

THE BUGS GATHER, or they seem to be gathering, in People's Plaza, the shoreline auditorium-cum-botanical gardens honoring the ruins of neighboring Manhattan. The silver cylinders and multi-shelfed monstrosities of the city's new business nightmare cast shadows ten blocks long over the water.

The sky ahead of me as I fly is overcast with insects. I clip the scanner to my belt and an earpiece feeds me a picture of the city descending into chaos. As the city's finest seem intent on repeating in astonished voices to each other over their radios, the worst thing about the storm of insects is that even the most genteel of the bugs are intent on biting the hell out of anyone they encounter. I'm fairly safe in my leather gear, but a butterfly, of all things, lands on my face and immediately sinks something sharp under my eye before I flatten it.

People in the streets are in crisis mode. Traffic stalls, half of downtown in gridlock, police cruisers with their bullhorns on full volume, frustrated by their inability to spread the word. I glimpse Red Monolith and Chamber in the distance, hanging like statues in the air over the city, rebroadcasting the public address system which booms instructions for people to act sensibly and stay indoors.

I head toward the plaza. The ground is furred with a carpet of creepy-crawlies. It's distressing to see a number of corpses among the insects, halfway to being picked clean by millipedes and flies and cockroaches already. As I descend, the huge swarm pours across my path and for a moment I'm blind, thankfully not psychotically disturbed by the sensation of hundreds of bugs filling my ears and nose. I can't imagine how Elisabeth would fare if she were here beside me.

I'm glad she and Tessa are at home, though suddenly I reflect on our argument and whether it is latent psychic ability or not, I tug my phone free of my belt pocket and, after exhibiting a mild electrical field that seems to deter all the bugs except for the moths and butterflies, I climb to a higher altitude where I can drop the EM cloak and actually get good enough reception to call.

Barking my question, it takes Elisabeth a moment to confirm my worst fear.

"Shit, how did you know? I thought she was in there studying."

"Why would a girl who's suspended from school waste her time studying?"

"She's fourteen, Joe. She's still going to have exams this year."

"She's fourteen, Beth," I bark back. "Do you think she's thinking about that?"

I snap the phone away. I'm Zephyr. It's my turn to be haughty and superior. Although People's Plaza seems to be holding court for the whole insect kingdom, there's no sign of a reason why. I buzz the crowd and then start for Astrid's house.

Despite the temptation to just do the sprint at a few times the speed of sound, civic duty or the pathetic looks of frustration on the cops' faces or perhaps the TV news choppers circling through the insect haze make me slow along the way across the boroughs to flip abandoned cars out of the way for the various emergency vehicles trying their best to power through the maze known as Atlantic City. Cops wave, beep horns, gesture cheerfully with unholstered sidearms as I do their work for them. Once clear of downtown, I accelerate and climb, buzzing Chamber hovering in mid-space with barely a "How ya doing?"

Tessa's plump pal is the only survivor of a pair of west coast stockbrokers relocated to the east after their previous trading company collapsed. Bankruptcy never looked so good as I angle in on the tower building that's become Astrid's prison since their very own personalized edition of Look Who's Coming To Dinner came down on them as well. Hard to believe someone, me, who thinks he's pretty close to his only child, couldn't see this happening. Worse to think her best friend in the world lives across town in such fancy digs and I don't know the actual apartment number.

*

WIPING INSECTS FROM my mouth, I punch a finger at the buzzer for Astrid's apartment manager. An elderly man in a blue suit comes to the glass doors and signs for me to desist. I get the drift: they're sticking to what the TV and radio stations are now advising constantly, which is to stay indoors and keep everything shut up tighter than a bug's butt. My fist clenches and crackles in frustration and the doorman's eyes widen and I try to make a sarcastic face to suggest that, yeah, right, I'm Zephyr, I'm hardly about to go kicking his door down. Problem is that's exactly what I want to do. It's only indecision that saves me as bugs swirl and whip in the surrounding air.

At first I think there's a storm coming in. Then I realize the street's gradually becoming more clear as the wind scours the bugs free from everything except the crevices in which some of them are managing to lurk. It's too complicated to gesture back at the doorman and I give up when the guy in the blue-and-white bodysuit lands in the middle of the street across from me.

"Hey, Zephyr, what's up? You're not trying to get under cover, are you?"

Sky Blue walks across the asphalt as unselfconsciously as George Michael in his old video clips, not in the slightest bit fazed by an outfit that will become so ridiculous only in hindsight. Sky Blue looks like a super-powered cyclist escaped from the Berlin Mardi Gras. The mask covers his entire head and reveals nothing but a clean-shaved chin and slightly pug nose. His eye holes are filtered and somehow shaped like a yin-yang symbol. I give belated acknowledgment with the jut of my jaw.

"That's some kind of joke, right?"

I come back at him quick because I don't really feel like feeding this turkey with the juicy details of my private life.

"Yeah, man. Of course."

"You don't know me well enough to joke, pal, so just shut your pie-hole."

"Jesus, you really are an asshole, aren't you?" he remarks.

"That's what they say, is it?"

Sky Blue holds his tongue at this point and before it can become a costumed freak convention, I do the crouch thing and jettison upward. Powder Blue follows, and next thing we alight on the top of the Helides Building. The statue of the Greek billionaire is covered in wasps and ants until Sky Blue touches down and a stark wind brushes the rooftop clear.

"So, wind powers, right?"

"Yeah. No weather control like yours, though."

I turn away. "I don't control the weather."

"What the hell do you think's going on?"

"Well, it's not normal." I know how lame this sounds so I follow up, "I'll call Twilight, see if there's anything on his supernatural radar."

"Could it be . . . mutants?" Sky Blue asks.

With my phone out, I pause long enough to give the guy a grimace like he just came down in the last insect-laden shower.

"Mutants? How? Name me a mutant who can do anything more severe than resemble, I don't know, an overcooked hot dog, and then we might consider it."

"There's Crosswind —"

I hold up a finger. "He's an anomaly."

The phone goes through to Twilight's voice mail, but he calls back almost immediately.

"Zephyr. You need a number for an exterminator?"

"This bug thing, is it on your, you know, radar?"

Twilight sounds groggy when he answers.

"It's . . . hard to tell. Hard to explain to you, too. It's like there's . . . magickal disturbance. It's been troubling me for a few weeks, actually."

"Is that how you got trapped —?"

"We don't talk about that," he snaps.

"OK. Well I'm downtown, if you have any bright ideas. See you later."

I slip the cell away and Sky Blue and I spend a long minute with our hands on hips, nodding seriously and grimacing down at the city below.

That's when we see him.

Striding down the middle of 81st Street, a shade over six-foot and shirtless despite the chilly day, the man has long dark hair well past his shoulders and seems to be wearing a cloth-of-gold robe and black silk pajama pants. I nod to Sky Blue, making sure he's got a good look.

"I'm going down."

"I'll be right behind you," the newcomer says.

Zephyr 2.3 "A Storm Of Thousands"

TOUCHING DOWN IN the middle of the street suddenly feels a lot like abandoning all tactical advantage. Time and again I remind myself not to do things like this. As Sky Blue alights behind me, I wonder I should've sent him down first, but then I have no idea if he really knows what he's doing. Could be another Nightwind, for all I know.

The guy in the silk PJs stops nonchalantly in the middle of the street. A few bugs crawl across his broad, naked chest, and there are butterflies like a little girl's fantasy as clips in his unbridled hair.

The eyes, though, look dead. His gold robe hangs off one shoulder and I can see tattoos peeking out from beneath the fabric. It's impossible to really say, but there's the sense the insect clouds are thicker around this guy and his deadpan demeanor reinforces that this doesn't bode well.

"I'm Zephyr," I say loudly, thumbing my chest.

"And I," the long-haired man replies in a voice Shakespearean actors would kill to possess, "am the Creeping Death."

Sky Blue breaks with protocol by coming alongside me and holds his palm out at the obvious madman.

"If you're the one behind this insect plague, you can stop it right there."

As if he has never seen his right hand before, the man lifts up his fingers and peers at them. Emotion fills his face for the first time, a sense of wonder, bemused marvel, as his fist is quickly covered in alighting insects, predominantly bees and wasps, that soon make a thick glove to his elbow.

"I think that about answers your question," I mutter.

Almost as an afterthought, the crazy man, this Creeping Death, flings his insect collection at us. It's misleading, since so few suddenly become a storm of thousands. I reflexively crouch and light up, wasps and flying ants and hornets and cabbage moths – all with carnivorous intents and purposes on my flesh – crackle and vanish in a whiff of unpleasant-smelling smoke.

Sky Blue's response is a vortex of wind that swirls the bugs and fliers around us like suds in a carwash, though I notice him hopping away scowling and barking, those few who snuck through digging in their pinching mandibles and giving it to him with all their tiny might.

As I straighten, I hearken to the sense of something bearing down on us, and I look up just in time to spot the robot, Hermes, seemingly even more silvery and polished than before, come down on Creeping Death with his enormous fists clutched together in a pile-driver blow that never lands. With the same sense of impending doom as myself, the long-haired crazy cranes his neck back, and as Hermes arrives, a solid dome comprised of insects materializes between attacker and target. It beggars credibility to think even a million close-packed bugs could do such a thing, but Hermes makes a faint metallic rebounding noise and vanishes through the front window of a fashion shop twenty yards away.

"At him!" I yell, and because I'm not feeling terribly charitable, the lightning bolt springing from my hand isn't a gentle one.

*

I'M PLEASED TO see Creeping Death buckle, crumpling backwards with a pall of blackened insect husks falling around him. They bounce in their hundreds on the concrete like a ton of burnt popcorn.

My senses crackle with the way Sky Blue's playing havoc with the air pressure, buffeting our target with wave after wave of compressed wind for unknown purpose, ignorant to my sensitivities or the way my own powers work. Across the street, the seven-foot form of Hermes emerges from the windowless shop-front, a woman's blouse stuck in the join between his shoulder and arm.

"Are you gonna behave yourself this time?" I call.

"Zephyr," the stentorian robot replies, "I need to explain. . . ."

"Not now you don't."

Creeping Death rolls over and stands. The gold robe is gone. He makes a fist and waves brutally and the sun's momentarily blacked out by insects. I've risen no more than a few feet off the ground before I am swamped in a tidal wave of chitinous life, hundreds of pounds of creepy-crawlies overwhelming my precious personal space and very nearly my lungs.

I make like a human bug zapper, which gets me a little leeway once again. Sky Blue isn't so fortunate, rolling around on the ground with his pretty costume in shreds, not the slightest sign of insulation or Kevlar to protect him. He bleeds from a thousand bites and will need medical evacuation if, as I suspect, half the insects are bees.

Yet Hermes is immune. He charges forward like the heavyweight he is, lumbering, not as smooth as I'd expect a state-of-the-art droid to be. I find I'm relieved, not that it humanizes him or anything. He and Creeping Death go into a tussle, a beard and sleeves of insects hanging from our opponent and seemingly lending him enormous strength. Although Hermes wins the slapping contest – Creeping Death rebounds off a parked SUV's windshield and goes over the top before righting himself on the pavement – our foe emerges with the upper hand as a new wave of insects sweep down the street, jostling parked cars and crumpling windows, basically collecting Hermes and sweeping him halfway down the block.

An armored limousine, jet black, appears at the other end of the street. Mastodon steps out in full costume, grins and waves to me, and Paragon and the self-styled "dark telepath" Nocturne emerge from the rear as well. No sign of Lady Macbeth, thank Christ. Mastodon does his signature stamp – we always teased him that he should've been known as The Bull – and in a couple of heartbeats swells in size from just over six foot to a little under nine, adding more than the expected amount of meat in the process. Giving an inchoate roar, Mastodon charges down the street and to avoid him needing an industrial-size tube of Tiger Balm, I lance another charge at Creeping Death, though it falls short at his feet.

The two men collide with a sound like hams fighting. Creeping Death knows he's in the shit now. Mastodon lands a few exquisite punches, and rather than wondering what the old dude is doing here, I wonder why he ever retired. He dodges a lazy right swing and clocks the insect freak's long jaw. I hover, thinking about whether I can safely rush Sky Blue to the paramedics. Hermes comes overhead, white-hot exhaust gushing from his boots. Paragon and Nocturne hang back, one glowing with his perpetual light bulb force-field, the other shrouded by her blue-black robes.

Nocturne's voice appears in mine and presumably all of our minds.

"I cannot get a thing from him," she says, rich Creole accent carried even by telepathy. "It's like I am not connecting with a human mind."

I point at Sky Blue and yell for Paragon to drag him to safety. Only a few bugs land in my mouth as I call. Mastodon suddenly hurtles through the air and the swirling cloud of bugs getting thicker and thicker with each instant. I'm staggered to see them manifest in a wave of force that slaps the already airborne veteran clear down the block, careening off the side of Astrid's parents' building and hitting a parked car that immediately starts up with its alarm.

Moving forward, the bug-storm becomes intense. Electricity flickering up my body sees me shedding insects like black dandruff on a scale unimaginable, yet seems to do little to the overall population. I shoot a glance at Hermes and he seems frozen to the spot, batting like a real person at the thousands of insects buzzing around him, his shiny armor splattered with more goo than an amateur porn queen.

So it falls to me to take the battle to our beetle-brained friend. Ladybirds and centipedes and earwigs carom off me as I swing a punch, but the vortex of insects around the madman is so intense it seems to thicken in anticipation to each blow, completely ruining my momentum even with my enhanced strength battling the tide. I try a few unpredictable attacks and Creeping Death, to give him the honor of the moniker, holds his hands out in front of himself like a kung fu master, eyes just slits, and every thrust and kick slows in the airborne tide of insects biting at me.

This goes on for a while. I'm batting blind. Eventually I punch a lightning bolt into his chest. A shield of flying ants and hornets materializes before my gesture and when the dust clears, the villain rises up over me, suspended, unbelievably, by several hundred pounds of insects clinging to his back, arms and legs, all seemingly working with one mind. Once I clue in to realizing it's not Sky Blue's wind powers sounding shrilly in my ears any more, I have to accept the air is filled with the sound of a million insect wings beating as one.

"Hermes, what the fuck is going on, man?" I bark.

"Insects have . . . filled my sensors. I am blind."

"Great. Nocturne, how's the Don?"

"Resuming consciousness," her liquid tones fill my mind.

"Any luck with our friend?"

"I hate to say it," she projects, "but his mind isn't dissimilar to the insects themselves. I can't . . . his thoughts shift too quickly, and they're too alien for me."

Creeping Death is true to his name: he's not exactly breaking the sound barrier as he lifts, turning vaguely in the direction of the People's Plaza.

Zephyr 2.4 "Like A Monarch of Antiquity"

"LET'S FOLLOW HIM for a bit," I tell Nocturne the moment I'm close enough to be heard without yelling.

I don't know how she keeps the bugs off her, but she does. Her perfume, perhaps – exquisite, but strong. I don't know if it's the cowl concealing half her face or not, but she's always been my favorite black female hero, even though she's flaked out on more than one occasion in the past and has a bad rep among some of the old guard for her moral panics. I know that's pretty damning, but she's got killer pins and looks all sexy and seventeenth century under that Little Red Riding Hood cowl. In my books, this more than makes up for leaving Grasshopper and Black Honey in the doo-doo every now and then.

Paragon drags Sky Blue into Mastodon's limo and they slam the doors and the car takes off for the nearest hospital as the owner himself comes limping towards us.

"Headache?"

Mastodon produces a tiny canister and shakes free a few pills, swallowing them with a grimace.

"That boy threw me good. I thought I was doin' well."

"You were," I reply. "The bug thing, his powers, seem out of all proportion."

"What's the plan?" the old man asks.

I scan around in case there's any late arrivals, but judging by the faint and not-so-distant alarms ringing around the place, plenty of the city's other supers have probably got their hands full already.

"First thing," I say. "Nocturne, honey, tell me you can keep a trace on this guy even if you can't get inside his head."

"That shouldn't be a problem," she says aloud.

"OK. I passed People's Plaza on the way over. There was a serious concentration of insects there. A few fatalities, too. He seems headed that way now. I say we try and scope it out, find out why."

"Sounds good."

From our position on the corner I look up. Lights inside the building reveal hundreds of spectators poised at windows. I keep looking up – Nocturne and Mastodon eye me nervously, like someone who's just slipped into a non-threatening epileptic seizure – until I spot a pair of girls on the fourteenth floor. Breathing a sigh of relief, I nod and turn back to the task at hand. A police cruiser slows at the intersection and a window rolls down. An Asian officer asks if we've got everything in hand and Mastodon snorts.

"OK, here we go."

I'm carrying my two offsiders, which slows me considerably as we climb a few hundred feet and fall into Creeping Death's wake. I remember images after Manhattan was destroyed and the skies, thick with ash, are eerily reminiscent here. Only now it is insects that dot the city's haze.

By the time we arrive at People's Plaza, weaving our way more or less in a straight line through the high-rises and ziggurats of the megalopolis, the entire city block is covered with a crawling carpet of insects. The amphitheater in the middle of the small park is just a black bowl towards which our target unerringly heads. Huge buildings surround the plaza and I note Grasshopper along with lesser-known heroes Falconer and Sun Man watching the spectacle from a safe distance.

"Ask Sun Man how many of these creatures he could cook?" I speak into Nocturne's ear more for the pleasure of it than any real need.

She replies to say the fire-wielding amateur couldn't do more than a few cubic yards at a time.

"Shame we didn't bring Hermes with us," I remark bitterly. "I could drop him on this fella from up here. Make a helluva splat."

Our self-styled insect king is lowered by his worshippers into the middle of the auditorium. The weird, extremely creepy sound of a hundred billion bugs cheering assails our ears and Nocturne starts to go faint like the sensation is many times worse at the psychic level. We drop to the sidewalk. There's a barricade of police cars covered in the living carpet, the closest few officers nearby guys I recognize. Detectives John Crane and Tiger Murphy hold the end of the line, Tiger cradling a shotgun against her svelte hip, and while they see me, there's not much likelihood of a reunion. I helped Nightwatchman haul ass last time we tussled, so the love-hate thing is a little lop-sided right now.

"I don't get this," Mastodon grunts.

"Just be glad I didn't drop you," I chuckle. "But what's to get? Maniacs get their designs on the city every few months. Not so many of them get this far, but still, what's to dig?"

"If he loves his bugs so much, why doesn't he go to Maine with 'em?"

"I don't know. He seems to like Atlantic City."

I check my knuckles and ball my fists.

"I'm going in."

*

AS FAR AS my normal senses are concerned, it's completely dark. My barometric sense screams silently as millions of insects pour like a living tide over me as I fly across the ground towards my target.

I can't remember there being anything like a throne in People's Plaza. It's hardly the Washington Monument. Therefore I assume the enormous seat is made now entirely out of bugs, and Creeping Death sits astride it like a monarch of antiquity, garbed now in a robe made from his tiny servants. I am Moses on speed, parting the black sea at just under Mach. The electricity coursing over my leathers is genocide for the villain's hordes.

We collide with a thunderclap. The throne collapses like an overflowing giant milkshake made of insects. After one solid hit to my jaw, I'm an octopus, my fists raining down from all directions. I don't feel quite hyped enough to go into Mach frenzy, compressing a two-minute flogging into one sonic boom-rattling second. But what I've got seems good enough – until a column of bugs vomits me thirty yards away, landing awkwardly on the edge of a marble walkway.

I roll off, cut loose with a blaze of white-hot power that vanishes a few thousand of them and causes our too-cool-for-school opponent to hit the ground like any regular Joe, no irony intended, pretensions at kingship momentarily forgotten. It gives me the peace at least to stand, and then a familiar figure drops from the sky and clasps my elbow.

"Zephyr."

It's Twilight.

"Hey," I pant. "Wondered where you've been."

"I think I have the solution for our friend," Twilight replies.

He holds up a small black object. It resembles a metal hoop, the kind of thing a Goth jewelry designer might make. The pulsing red cloud-patterned surface is familiar. Under my domino mask I do no more than raise an eyebrow and the blonde Adonis grunts a laugh.

"Yeah. I shrank it down, but I'm damned if I can get rid of it."

"Time to give ol' YouTube-bin-Laden a dose of the . . . bugs?"

"uYuatil-el-Awahya," Twilight chuckles. "You were going to say crabs, weren't you?"

We watch as Creeping Death stands and poses, glittering black chitinous robe swinging back, his hand out-thrust for another go. Twilight clears his throat and holds out the glowing red amulet in kind.

"By Ual, and Yog Sothoth, and He-Who-Cannot-Be-Named, and Y'Golonac – be gone you foul fiends!"

The amulet's aperture seems to swing open with a hissing roar. Insects in their thousands transform into the cone of darkness sucking into the palm of Twilight's hand.

I'm grinning like a loon. Creeping Death's expression goes from mad to worse, and I leap forward as his chirruping hordes abandon him, smacking him up the sides, across the jaw, blocking a weak attempt to grapple and twisting him around, leaving the ground for a second as we lock forearms – and then I ease back long enough to put my boot into the middle of his chest and *push*.

Like the evil robot doppelganger of some otherwise hapless male model, the interloper somersaults into the sucking cone and I am not sure whether I hope for the worst or cringe as he appears to disintegrate down into pieces small enough to fit through the magical crimson lens.

Although I hadn't kidded myself that we destroyed uYuatil-el-Awahya, I ponder for a moment what he/it will make of this offering.

The brightness of the victory seems to fill my eyes and I realize I'm clenching my teeth hard enough to need more work, my gums aching, the smile too manic to be maintained.

And then it's over.

Anti-climax be damned. I'm aching, exhausted, sore all over and panting like a fire station whore.

Eventually the euphoria dies away and the job becomes something like industrial carpet cleaning. Twilight patrols the plaza as our friends and hordes of cops and reporters descend on our position. For once I am happy enough for them to understand it was someone else who played the key role in the city's defense, even though Twilight himself eschews the attention and when I turn, halfway through an interview with Katie Couric that will run unedited at least six times in the next twelve hours, I realize the big man is nowhere to be seen.

As we wrap, Mastodon and the others are on their phones trying to make reservations for drinks, and Seeker arrives and keeps asking everyone, "What's happened?" I hear a voice in my thoughts that could only be Twilight with one of his I-don't-text-message spells.

I turn and regard the phantasm, Twilight's astral form that I know only I can see. It nods serenely, all part of the act, ethereal vagueness from the waist down.

"The portal was conjured in my quest to answer your question," Twilight says to me in an appropriately ghostly voice. "If you're ready to consider the answer, come to my sanctum at midnight tomorrow."

He rings off, blurring and disappearing on the wind like cigarette smoke, leaving me adrift amid the impending celebrations, only half able to grasp what it is I've asked him, and more than half-afraid to discover the answer for myself.

"Zephyr!"

Paragon looms in my face, cheesy farm-boy good looks exacerbated by the perpetual glow. His arm circle's Lady Macbeth's shoulders. Photographers rapidly turn the plaza into a light show and I'm reminded of Paragon on Oprah's couch.

"Did you get that fucking guy to a hospital or what?"

I bellow over the sound of helicopters touching down, a White Nine response team that can't really achieve diddly-squat prepared to burn a hundred thousand of taxpayers' hard-earned regardless.

Paragon nods earnestly, shelving his youthful enthusiasm for just a nanosecond. "Yeah, man, of course I did, Zephyr. Team effort, right?"

"And what did they say?"

"Who, man?"

"The doctors, dipshit."

"Oh man, he's gonna be out of it for a while, they said. He got stung like fifty-something times. Bees, wasps, you name it."

"OK."

"Are you coming to Transit? We've got a table."

I nod absent-mindedly. One more call to make.

*

ELISABETH HAS THE Range Rover and is on her way to collect our truant daughter from her . . . OK, her . . . OK, I don't know where she's going. I'm not sure 14-year-olds have lovers and they sure as hell don't have partners. Girlfriend, I guess, is a safe enough bet. Maybe not for Beth.

A second helicopter, another of the big twin-rotor jobs, descends from between the neighboring high-rises. The circular FBI crest is prominent on the doors and I can only sigh and note it's been a while since I had to deal with the so-called "Parahuman Wing" of the Federal Bureau of Investigations. As the agency ultimately responsible for White Nine, this show plays pretty much every time a supervillain is incarcerated. As Twilight once said, it's just a question of how fast we masks can get out of there before the pigs arrive.

By now the crowds are like well-wishers at the Superbowl. I barely register the cheers, the outstretched hands and improvised placards. My eyes glaze over the chiseled face, dark hair combed back and weak afternoon light already strained through the tall buildings reflecting off the rim of his glasses. Just another face in the crowd, even if he is calling my name with weirdly wry desperation.

While the blades still hack at the air, metal steps clatter out thrown by one of the FBI storm troopers. Vanguard and Synergy descend like a royal couple, though I have an inkling they are anything but close when away from prying eyes. Vanguard carries his helmet in the crook of his arm, knowing full well the resemblance to a medieval knight this promotes, his lank blonde hair plastered to his slightly too-small head, his expensive grin, the powered armor with its scalloped shoulders and knees giving him the dimensions of a star linebacker. At his side, Synergy is his opposite in so many ways: a tall woman with coffee-colored skin, a fall of beige ringlets, the smile of some Jamaican goddess, a woman's grey suit worn over her white lycra. There's a whiff of power around her you wouldn't attribute to an energy thief, yet the moment they've traversed half the crowd, I can practically feel her DNA tugging at mine.

"Zephyr!" Special Agent Synergy yells over the crowd noise and the chopper. "What did you take out this time?"

I wait a pause, long enough for them to get close so I don't have to yell. They're not accustomed to the fans, especially the ones with mp3 recorders and streaming video, and there's no need for the Internet to hear how little I know, even if that knowledge could still be a dangerous thing.

"Beats me," I tell her. "'Identifying the perp.' That's the term, isn't it? I think that's your thing."

Synergy laughs, a throaty sound that goes straight to my balls.

"Oh we identified the subject while we were in the air, Zephyr. Michael Damien Calloway, priors for possession, no other criminal record, no associates, no registered parahuman template."

I grunt. "So?"

"Would you describe the individual as a parahuman, Zephyr?"

"That's your term."

Vanguard bangs on the helmet, reducing his eyes to slits.

"You're not hindering a Federal investigation, I hope?"

"You hope, do you? Calls your impartiality into question, don't it, Vanny?"

"Don't *call* me that."

"Zephyr," Synergy says again, using my name to draw attention away from her team's weakest link. "Where's the perp?"

"He's, uh, gone." She's got me, on the wrong foot again. "It's sorta hard to explain."

"Try," Vanguard urges.

I prepare to spin my best bullshit yet.

Zephyr 2.5 "Party Like It's 1699"

THERE IS A crowd at Transit. We have a half-moon table towards the rear, a cityscape of bottles and martini glasses and brimming ashtrays and empty plates of nachos and complimentary tapas stacked haphazardly. Mastodon waves away the wait staff every time one of the girls gets close. He's wasted. I've had some coke, about six beers, a martini, something that was possibly a horse tranquilizer and some GHB, twice, so I'm feeling pretty even.

I'm with Red Monolith, his girlfriend, a new costume called Cusp, I have no idea what she does, along with Chamber, Miss Black, Stiletto and Darkstorm, as well as Paragon and his Lady Macbeth ("Call me Jocelyn, *please*"). Seeker left some time ago, frowning with her customary disapproval. It must be hard living half-in and half-out of her religion's afterworld. Monolith's girlfriend keeps playfully getting between us and trying to engage me in deep and meaningfuls, wherein my true intentions vis-à-vis reforming the Sentinels keeps coming up. Unfortunately for Monolith, I find I have a thing for girls with green hair and vinyl bodices, so I talk some shit to her for an hour-and-a-half, made especially easy after the horse pill and some cocktail I practically have poured down my throat. Also in Transit this evening are Billy Joel, Woody Allen and Suzanne Vega, Morrissey, Leonardo di Caprio, Rick Shroeder, Kurt Cameron, Scott Baio, Michel Foucault, Lars Ulrich and Dave Mustaine, Kurt Vonnegut and Andrea Dworkin. On the monitors over the crystalline bar, a video of burning Tibetan monks plays on looping slow-mo, the Transit logo fading in and out.

Things are progressing nicely. Cusp's hand keeps finding my inner thigh and I'm slightly lost in the fog of my own confused morals as I ponder how to balance my hard-on with my loyalty to Monolith, not to mention my wife.

It is night outside. I steal a few moments when my phone rings. It's Beth, returning a text from me. Tessa's home safe. "The city's in chaos out there," my wife says with an unusually disinterested voice. I explain I'm helping police with inquiries and going to have an after-work drink with the gang and for once she doesn't say anything, alarming of itself, my uprooted mind left to tie itself in knots within the silences she leaves. When I ring off, the phone lights up again and it's one of the agents Nautilus' guy has referred to me and I have to yell into the phone to be heard as the house band lights up and the woman agrees to call back in the morning, though I don't think I'll ever hear from her again and despite all my efforts to reach this point, for now I am relieved.

I switch to voicemail. I have forgotten about my appointment at the Academy in eleven hours.

At the bar, as I buy drinks with one of Sal Doro's crisp fifty dollar notes, I realize I am standing almost elbow-to-elbow with Robert Downey Jr, and for the first time in some time I feel self-conscious and vaguely ridiculous in my head-to-toe leather outfit even though Downey appears to be wearing a leotard over skin-tight medieval hose, flared boots, a redcoat's jacket and a feather boa. Only once does he even acknowledge my presence, leaning back after ordering a mineral water and refocusing on me with one eye before shaking his head and taking his change and walking away.

I would watch his departing back except there's a crash of glasses and much hilarity and when I glance back, knowing it's my table, two security guys are wrestling a masked man in a Baroque costume away from our table. It's Madrigal, a villain I've not heard of in quite a while. Last time we met, I pummeled him so hard he actually shat. Now he's squirming and screaming and his mask comes loose because he's crying, in frustration and for what other purpose I have no idea, a stream of drunk invective raining down on our table as Mastodon laughs so hard he slides under his seat and disappears. Paragon does the protective boyfriend thing and stands, clenching an incandescent fist, and I realize much of Madrigal's venom is aimed at Lady Macbeth, who sits embarrassed in her seat, lipstick blurred, surrounded by the good guys now as her former accomplice gets dragged kicking from the building. It's not exactly the showdown Madrigal might've expected, but tonight we are the kings and queens of Atlantic City and we're gonna party like it's 1699.

*

IT GETS LATER.

We stumble in as an enormous group to Silver Tower, flash guns going off like crazy, the saviors of the city today rather than its destroyers and so we'll be loved, like a pre-arrangement, a contract between the city and our tights. I'm not wearing tights any more. I ditched them for the leather get-up a few years ago. The leather feels good, so good, especially with Cusp pressing against me. The camera lights taste like tin-foil in my mouth, which is just a mild distraction.

I think possibly I have taken too much MDMA.

I'm probably the last one to notice we have been joined by the robot – and his creator. Dr Prendergast looks completely out of his element in the chic confines of the city's most exclusive club. It's normally $40 to get in, though Chancel waives our fees. It's good press. Young gods choose to party at the Tower. Amadeus even makes an appearance in his leonine smoking jacket and effete cigarillo, inquiring if Twilight is amongst us, vaguely disappointed when he isn't. Twilight has that dangerous allure that doesn't exactly go hand-in-hand with saving kittens and appearing on postcards to promote the preservation of the Jersey Ferry. I remind myself of Twilight's words: *I'm an* anti-hero*, OK?*

Also in the club: Julian Gaddafi, Paris Hilton, Denzel Washington, the Olsen Twins, Jackie Chan, Joey Wong and Yuen Biao, Axel Rose, Russell Crowe, Courtney Cox, Courtney Love (no baby this time), John Cusack, Scott Wolf, mutant basketballer Shaquille O'Neal, Maria Sharapova, the guy who played Avon in Blake's Seven, an Australian TV gardening expert, and a man who may or may not be the former villain Hunchback with new teeth, a tan, a facelift and different-colored eyes. We also see Black Honey and her goon squad of Portal, Falconer, Nightwind and Devil Betty, shooting evil glances and motioning furiously for Paragon to go over and speak to them. It turns out Sky Blue has been downgraded from critical at the hospital, but I think we're all too stoned to care, if we ever did.

After a few Stolis, it becomes obvious Professor Prendergast isn't here to party. I've barely spoken to Chamber all night. I'm disappointed his big contribution to the crisis was turning himself into a public address system. Prendergast keeps trying to get Chamber alone and I can hear him raising his voice over a dance remix of Godspeed! You Black Emperor's Slow Riot for New Kanada. The words "N-space" and "my robot's vulnerabilities" are all that's needed. For some reason, Chamber seems palpably confronted by the errant scientist and at something like 2am he storms out of the Tower, beyond range of Stalemate's invisible damper field, and disappears over the edge of the landing platform. I'm going to assume it isn't suicide.

Hermes stands out like a straight-edge punk at a gay orgy, watching everything that happens with an impenetrable stare, Neo-Classical visage unable to form even the rudiments of a human response. This is no coincidence. I gather he would be unable to experience emotions anyway, so the impression I have of his internal confusion or torment is just suckyness on my behalf and probably the drugs. He doesn't want a hug from me and when I send Cusp over, the whole crowd erupts in laughter at his inept response. She is well and truly in on the act and I find myself warming to her immensely, appreciation now well beyond her impeccable cleavage.

I fear Red Monolith has basically just relinquished his hold on Cusp because within an hour I am teetering on the edge of total unconsciousness, on my knees in the Tower's palatial women's toilets eating her pussy and trying not to fall over as she moans and the leather of my chest is slick with her juices and she's groaning and I am trying not to topple over and up close, her greenish pubic hair looks luminous in the fluorescent lights. She hitches her breath and cums and bursts out laughing and then returns the favor and my mind is far away, I can't get anywhere, thinking about Elisabeth alone in bed and wondering what it was exactly I agreed to when Twilight commenced upon his research.

For the first time in a long while I throw up and it feels like battery acid. Cusp wets my hair and strokes my brow and it feels so wrong and yet so high school that I can't resist, just lying there like a used inflatable sex toy after all the semen has dried, an embarrassing reminder that might normally be rectified with a hunting knife to then get stuffed into the crawlspace under the house.

Doc Prendergast is as drunk as a skunk and somebody has called a VTOL craft me, Cusp, Mastodon, Stiletto, Darkstorm and Falconer pile into, along with Hermes and his creator, while Red Monolith and Paragon come to blows in the corner of the club without any powers to back them up as the undercarriage doors snicker shut and the automatic pilot lifts us up from the Silver Tower and we hurry across the dawn sky, the city all smoke-colored domes and dully-glinting high-rises, a gigantic airship blinking with lights on the horizon as another transatlantic cruise comes to an end at the docks in Newark.

The aircraft is piloted by an earlier version of the same brand of artificial intelligence as Hermes, Professor Prendergast explains. I look around, but I can't see any more robots, and in tones bordering on the truculent the scientist explains the machine brain is *inside* the vehicle. Cusp is sitting in his lap and laughing like a drunk schoolgirl as his explanations maintain a stoic and didactic clip despite him being shitfaced, which I guess means the ship is his, and we cross the state as the sun comes up and touch down at a country mansion he says used to be a private school for gifted runaways until he bought it with the money he made from inventing the "show desktop" icon in Windows XP. I can't be entirely certain he is joking about this.

We tumble out of the aircraft and onto the lawn, breath steaming, and Prendergast's newly-awoken staff stagger around like broken robots to serve us coffee and croissants. Actually they are robots, eerie with their pink vinyl skins not perfectly maintained, their tiny sunken black eyes watching us in our tomfoolery.

Before we're all completely sober, Prendergast takes us on a tour of the mansion's basement, down to where he keeps all his toys. After he shows us the fourth or fifth ingenious high-tech device that targets parts of the brain to produce unnatural levels of animal passions – such as lust, Prendergast drily explains – most of us are snickering uncontrollably at the old pervert, and Darkstorm, completely shattered still, is making out with Stiletto, and Mastodon takes one of the ray guns and actually shoots them both with it. As the professor flips out. Darkstorm and Stiletto start ripping at each other's clothes and basically going for it like a pair of horny wolves. Cusp is leading me away by the hand with a wry grin, so I am spared the sight of the other two heroes doggy-styling, and it is two in the afternoon before I wake up in one of the manor rooms wrapped in a soggy sheet with only a pair of green silk bikini briefs to remind me what exactly happened.

And my cell phone starts ringing.

Zephyr 2.6 "Twilight's Secret Handshake"

I ARRIVE HOME to find my apartment is a war zone.

Tessa's crying and Elisabeth's face is a shocking mask of red and white, her cheeks flushing like only an Irishwoman's can, dark hair a curly mop pulled back tight from her taut face.

My daughter's tears go on and on and Beth exhales slowly, and into that lull, eyes me walking into the apartment with my things in the sports bag I have stashed at the gym around the corner for more years than I care to remember.

"Well, here he is at last," Elisabeth says. "Say his name enough times and maybe he'll appear."

As she walks from the room to the enclosed kitchen, she says, "Maybe you can talk some reason into her," far too dismissively for my liking.

I feel ill with guilt and nauseous with fatherly affection as Tessa goes into her room and swings the door incompletely shut. It's my cue to follow and yet I hesitate, moving close enough to have an eye on the kitchen where Elisabeth shakily pours herself a glass of whiskey neat.

"How about one for me?" I ask.

"When you've earned it."

"What the hell do you think I've been doing?" It's hard not to match her growl.

"Saving the city was yesterday, according to the news. I have no fucking idea what you've been doing today. It better not have anything to do with this."

From the kitchen, she hurls a magazine that falls open lazily, exposing itself before me with a page crammed with circle captions, a paparazzi snap of myself and Miss Black at Mechano's last week. My hitching breath and accelerating heart rate still themselves.

"That's just tabloid rubbish, babe. . . ."

"Just talk to Tess," Beth sighs and downs her glass with a grimace before switching on the TV and brushing past me, curling up resolutely on the couch.

On the flatscreen, an advertisement shows Vulcana lifting a car above her head and laughing as the wheels bounce away. The ads segue into the news, the naval blockade of South Africa, the Chinese AIDS epidemic, Finnish separatists bombing St Petersburg, strange obelisks found in the Australian outback, bodies missing from the city morgue, sightings of a so-called 'moth-man' around the plush new Pier 42 development, and a man with Siamese twin miniature poodles. . . .

So I turn back to the bedroom door.

My Enercom phone starts ringing in the gym bag and I ignore it with a mighty effort of will. Instead, I advance on Tessa's door like a weary patrol of marines at Iwo Jima. Through the crack, I see her sitting up, composed as she can be, her thick legs bare in her slobbing-around-the-house shorts and oversized Atlantic U t-shirt. She stares at the monitor of her laptop with determined remoteness, nothing showing but the screensaver of stars flying by. Gently, I rap on the door with my knuckles and manage not to break anything or give the light fitting an electric shock.

"Come in, dad."

I do so, moving across to the bed so that she's in front of me, back turned, the desk lamp creating a nimbus around her unruly and seasonably lavish auburn hair.

"What's going on?"

"Isn't it obvious?" she drawls, one hundred per cent teen.

"Not to me," I say. "I just got here."

"Yeah. Mum's been on about that too. We should leave her."

I snort a laugh. "Where would we go?"

"Anywhere."

"Mum pays the bills. . . ."

It occurs to me this line of comedy isn't something to be pursued. Tessa harrumphs. It's all quite serious to her.

"She can save herself a couple of thousand and give up trying to get me back into that fucking school. Astrid's folks are enrolling her at Greenwood Alternative. I could go there too, dad?"

She turns and looks at me, eyes blurry with tears darkened by the mascara I didn't know she wore. This is it, I think – the big push, the big hope, school with her little friend, girlfriend or whatever.

Beth would never stand for it.

"Honey, I know it says 'alternative,' but I think Greenwood costs about twice what the Academy does. . . ."

"Jesus, dad," my pride and joy snaps. "Spoken like a true bum."

"Thanks honey. You're reminding me why we stopped at one. . . ."

"It's not fair, dad –"

"Whoa," I say, and actually hold up my hand.

We've had an agreement about that particular line of debate for about eight years and Tessa knows fully well arguing the fairness of things is like trying to convince someone the sky is green.

She drops her eyes and pitches forward.

"Well fuck, it *isn't* fair, dad."

"You're probably right," I say with a sigh.

Tessa looks askance and there's a flash of amusement despite the tears, having me agree an unexpected surprise, and for some fluky reason, my break-through moment. Relating to her is one of the few things I've ever been able to pull off unassisted, it seems. How ironic for Beth and no wonder she resents it.

"What am I gonna do, dad?"

"Just give it time, babe," I reply. "What do you want to do? Leave home at fifteen?"

"I'm fourteen."

"I don't imagine you doing it *this* year," I retort.

Tess snickers.

"Is this for real?" I ask and make a complicated rotating finger motion, the universal sign language for exploratory teenage lesbianism.

"Well, I *think* so." She frowns, a pretty child, still so much a baby with her full cheeks and long lashes. "Is it . . . would it be so terrible?"

"Not to me."

"And mum?"

"It's the. . . ." I'm suddenly unsure of what I'm even going to say, so I plough on regardless, concerned less about being right than saying the right thing.

"It's not you, Tess, it's the world. Your mum cares, I'm sorry to say."

"And you don't?" she asks.

"I'm the bum, right?"

Tessa watches me closely for a long second and finally nods.

"If you say so, dad."

I later find a formal letter from the school regarding Tessa's expulsion.

The unpaid and forward-dated fees are not negotiable, it somehow argues convincingly.

*

THERE DOESN'T SEEM much point sticking around with Elisabeth shooting freezing looks. A glance into the gym bag shows Zephyr's phone has seven messages on it.

I slip through to the back room and fire up my PC, switching on the police scanner and quickly turning the volume down low. Proper soundproofing of my secret studio is one of those things we never really managed to get on the budget, and with my "cover" as a failed novelist and occasional baseball hack (I did get a piece in the New Yorker, once), the money's probably not about to materialize any time soon.

Unless I sort Zephyr out.

To this end, I wade through a number of calls from prospective agents whose eyes have obviously lit up at the prospect of representing Atlantic City's favorite son. That's how I try to think of myself, anyway, especially on low days. (Yeah, you wouldn't think it helps, but it does). With one hand on the computer keyboard I type names and numbers into a wordpad and then Google the findings, sifting through a few less fortunate contenders until I find a publicist named Hallory O'Hagan. She already represents a string of B-grade actors and minor celebrities including novelist Bret Easton Ellis and film-maker Alan Moore. Her webpage shows a cute button-nose redhead in a crème-colored business suit. This is not a good basis for a business decision, but she's hot.

I give Miss O'Hagan a call and arrange to meet at her offices in the morning, discretion being the better part of trying to conduct business in a public place. Although I note some of the other numbers down, truth is I hope to avoid any long and drawn-out process. This isn't new behavior on my account by any stretch. I'm already simultaneously thinking about lunch (it's almost 4.30pm) and my hours of missing sleep. The scanner informs me of a bank heist on the river, but I'm no sooner reaching reluctantly for my smelly leathers than I hear a radio code signifying a masked response and an over-excited identification of Hermes moments later suggests the officer must be new to Atlantic City.

I listen with professional curiosity as the codes relay the story as effectively and efficiently as any comic strip, with three of the robbers foiled on the spot while their leader, a costumed villain eventually identified as Ripper, battles it out against Hermes on the roof of the bank building.

I'm as astounded as ever that they even bother. It's a hard way to get rich. There are venture capitalists making twenty million in a morning, mum and dad investors losing life savings while trade corporations grow. God, think of the fossil fuel corporations, still pushing the diesel car as the most effective form of travel in a world where freaks of science like Chamber have perfected N-dimensional transport.

Hermes' response sounds as brutal as it is effective. The call goes out for paramedics and I figure that's one supervillain who's not going to be troubling the city for a while.

I discover yet more missed calls while I'm doodling with the cell phone, and finally someone picks up at the end of the first call and informs me I missed my appointment with prisoner S. Zahn at White Nine. Sarcastic comments about being busy saving the city from a biblical plague of locusts fall on deaf ears and I reschedule with a bored-sounding prison clerk for the following afternoon.

I can hardly wait.

*

BY EVENING, THE city is quiet. In the aftermath of Creeping Death's unsuccessful foray into super-crime, you can't buy a bug bomb in the local supermarket and people seem more concerned with staying home to lick their wounds than getting back into the megalopolis to party. The final count was six direct deaths from the insect plague and three more as a result of faults in air-conditioning and electrical cables after the incident. Although I assumed our perpetrator was sucked into Twilight's secret handshake, it turns out very fine tissue particles recovered from the scene suggest our play pal was vaporized on entry. It's a shame, because otherwise I had to hand it to Twilight, apart from the apparent homicide, it was a neat solution.

Bad luck the FBI don't think so. I have unreturned calls from Agent Synergy and a hankering for egg rolls from Li's in Chinatown.

In-between returning some videos in my secret identity and dinner en solo, I slip back into costume in an alleyway off the Chinatown High Street and alight at the base of the illuminated crane on Masters Tower to view the European-style reconstructed Old Town bordering where the Miskatonic pours into the sea.

Twilight is one of the few caller IDs programmed into the phone. I flick the set open at his call and gaze out at the lights of tankers plying the ocean as well as the latest in-bound zeppelin for Newark.

"Twilight. I just missed the sunset. What's up?"

"Calling you," he replies. "Think about my offer?"

"I have," I say. "Though I haven't quite finished yet. I'm a little hazy on what I agreed to."

"Agreed to?"

There comes the atypical Twilight laugh.

"Hmm, *little man*," he says, the endearment more a mannerism than the weird malapropism it seems, "I don't remember you *agreeing* to anything, yet. You were to consider it."

"'It'?"

"Um . . . the ultimate work-life balance," Twilight replies.

"And this is achieved . . . how?"

"It's a kind of magic," Twilight replies and laughs.

It occurs to me he might be high. I tell him to stop quoting Highlander.

"Tell me about this magic?"

"Zephyr, stop acting like a schoolgirl," Twilight replies. "You came over here bitching and moaning about how hard it is to be a hero and have a home-life too. Here's your chance. I don't see your two hands grasping for it."

"I'm not sure what you're offering, dude."

"A solution."

"That's what Hitler offered the Jews," I remark obliquely.

"Well, it'll be a gas, but not that kind."

We both let that one sit a moment.

"Let me think it over some more."

"Dude, get a grip, OK?"

"I'm gripping," I reply.

"OK. See you at De Lux tomorrow? I hear that scientist guy is a chemist as well."

"Prendergast?"

"That's the one."

"Hmm, super-drugs. I should've known. Seeya."

My phone blips as I hang it up and barely a split second after I have put it away, a shadow on my right displaces itself and I see a hood and black cloak, and thinking it is Nightwind, I do a flash-bulb with my left hand.

It reveals the Nightwatchman instead.

Zephyr 2.7 "Obscure Theoretical Principles"

"CHRIST, JEFF, YOU gave me a scare there," I swear.

"Jeff's not home," the black-clad figure replies, stepping calmly over a crane strut and moving slowly but steadily towards me.

"OK, who's this? Allison?"

The Nightwatchman stops a few yards away and stares hard, only the lower part of the skull-like face visible. And then he cracks a grin and yanks back the hood, the visor with the in-built night-vision lenses and other gizmos obscuring his identity to anyone who didn't already know him from school.

Jeffrey Rushbaum was the kid I would point at to distract the bullies when I was in junior high. A child of Orthodox Jews who quit Israel after a disagreement in a kibbutz left three people dead, Jeffrey moved schools when we were both fourteen. Imagine my surprise, ten or more years back, finding out I recognized my assailant when helping the boys in blue trying to nab the suspicious lone mask responsible for a string of violent street gang reprisals.

The eyewear makes the Nightwatchman look like an alien, sex predator and serial killer all rolled into one. And he *is* all those things, and more, the poor bastard. The face mask is just an external semiotic, a dark indicator of an even deeper blackness. Jeff shifts between three main personalities, but there are dozens of them in there, thanks to the unique curse of his powers.

"Once upon a time, can you believe I tried to limit how many people I absorbed?" he says aloud to me.

"You're reading my thoughts again."

"Just for a moment. It's passing," he replies.

"I can handle it."

"Yes, Zephyr, you can, can't you?"

The rictus grin returns. It's unpleasant. Oral hygiene isn't high on his list of priorities.

"Maybe I should add you to the mix, Joseph. Maybe you can help bring me into balance . . . as part of the overall cocktail, yes?"

"Is that what you're doing now?" I ask, and, so sue me, I step away.

The Nightwatchman turns his back and moves to the edge of the building again. He can't fly. You wouldn't guess it, the way he turns on a pin standing on the girders hundreds of yards above the street.

A spotlight plays across the city in search of a stage. Sirens warble past below and the horn of an incoming airship resounds out in the bay towards the ruins of Manhattan. Gulls, driven to the nocturnal by the city that never sleeps, whirl past like a dream of albino bats.

"Hmm," is all Jeff says. "Balance would be nice."

"When are you gonna make nice with the police?"

"When Commissioner Journey comes up here and kisses my ass."

I *tsk*. "Journey's not such a bad dude once you've met him."

Jeff turns and gives me such a look that even through the technogoggles I blush in the darkness. This is made worse knowing he can detect it on infrared.

"OK," I demur. "Your bodycount might make that a slight problem."

"So would yours, if anyone knew," he replies, almost mirthful.

"If they knew," I add warningly. "And I don't kill cops."

"My understanding is the cops return the courtesy. Not so for me."

This is too heavy for me. I let this be known with a casual snort.

"They ain't got you yet, as I understand it. Maybe you should go easy on 'em? It's not like they're powered."

"What, like I am?"

Nightwatchman strides back towards me like a black panther. You'd never guess he'd been the schoolyard wimp, let alone a ratty little Jewish one at that. He's more De Niro, with the pugnacious iron jaw, the bully at last instead of the other way round.

"You're the one with powers, Zephyr," he replies. "Don't go confusing the two of us. One of us is a hero and the other one's cursed."

I clear my throat. "Gee, is that the time?"

Jeff backs down and I relax my posture as well, though my threatened departure remains a reality.

"I think I prefer Allison."

"I'll tell her you called."

"OK. See you in the funny pages."

And again, I take to flight.

*

THE SCANNER TELLS me it's 3am and an alarm has gone off at the premises of Mys-tech Laboratories. According to the neat hundred-year plan of our architectural forefathers, most industrial development was shunted inland from the lower east coast, behind what once really was known as Atlantic City. Today, the area is known as Truman.

I should be turning in, except the hard partying since the end of the Creeping Death situation has left my body-clock in Mongolia. Besides, the word "home" doesn't really have the same warm feel it once did.

The high-tech end of Truman is all landscaped gardens and roll-on lawn behind razor-wire fences, low complexes of off-white buildings with tinted glass, polished chrome and the occasional wrought-iron sculpture dedicated to obscure theoretical principles.

There's only the little flashing blue light to indicate anything's amiss at Mys-tech. The connotations of the name don't exactly escape me as I sail under the radar, the gradual jingoisation of the whole world giving a healthy amount of skepticism as to the actual significance of everything and anything. I land on the crunchy grass and what I think at first's an automatic sprinkler pops its head up in the lawn twenty yards away. Instead, I'm scanned by a red laser beam, there's a brief moment of R2D2 talk, and then the thing disappears. The grass glistens with frost in the cold night air. My breath, at least for a moment, comes out in huge clouds.

Someone has melted a huge and perfect circle in the iron-shuttered automatic glass doors to the visitors' entrance. Down the main corridor past a scorched personnel desk, various fluorescent lights are on. As I follow through, I track patches of the linoleum melted in the shape of footprints, reminding me of someone I have encountered a number of times before. The air is warm and fuggy: another telltale giveaway.

It occurs to me I should probably ring someone, you know, call for back-up, but the scanner, now switched off, let me know the police were definitely on their way. My Enercom phone even has a special life-line button I've fortunately never had to use. I'm not about to start now. Instead, I plough further into the building, invigorated by the loud crashing noises deeper within.

I think I'm halfway towards the source of the distress when a head of black hair and a violet cat-suit pop out of an open doorway immediately to my right.

"Hey, I know you," a husky female voice says.

For some reason my brain goes into snappy comeback mode and I just don't see the haymaker coming. Next thing, I'm back about twenty yards down the hallway and Raveness, who I've read about but never met, steps in her full glory from the doorway.

Standing at about six-foot-two with a fall of wild, glossy black hair, the violet outfit suggests Raveness is just some sexy vamp, maybe a very tall sexy vamp. A criminal arrest sheet as long as my arm as well as possibly the state's only recent conviction for cannibalism tells a completely different story – a bit like the Versace cloak she's wearing.

Dusting myself off, I opt for a little of the time-honored superhero wisecracking in the hope it might draw Raveness's playmates out instead of letting them put their heads together. It's a stupid ploy, but I only do it because it works – most of the time.

"People often ask me," I say, grimacing and wiping plaster from my sleeves, "how come I ever get in close when I can hurl lightning bolts from a safe distance?"

Raveness wipes her palm along a line of saliva hanging from her jaw. Her heavy-lidded eyes give the impression of something eastern European, but maybe that's just me.

I throw a dose of electricity her way. The silly bitch blocks it with her arms and staggers back, teeth audibly clacking together. I hit the super-speed button, closing to a few yards in the space of a second, and once the rest of me arrives, I lay in with a dedicated combination of jabs and hooks that travel up the tall woman's ribs and end at her jaw. Raveness staggers through a shattered doorway and goes backwards over a pile of debris and office furniture.

I don't like hitting a lady, but fuck it.

One down. How many to go?

*

I'VE NO SOONER shaken the excess static from my fingertips than the hallway ahead fills with figures. At first, I expect it's Raveness's buddies come to whoop ass on her behalf. Instead, there's a strike-force of six dudes in black Kevlar and laminate armor, heads like praying mantises, their sidearms resembling some kid's weird experiments in black Lego rather than any weapon I've ever seen. I'm unsurprised to see pulsing, rippling purple energy hose out the end of the first few guns and I crash through the nearest plywood wall to escape the imagined effects.

I flounder through what's ostensibly an Ikea display for two or three seconds, sparks leaping from my shoulders and hands, and then I hit the fast forward button again. I can't accelerate time itself, just move super-quick by erasing all sources of friction and inertia in my path. That means while I can hit a guy twenty times in a second on a really good day, my brain's as slow as the next Joe (no pun intended) and I pretty much have to plan my combinations before I land them, otherwise they go nowhere. If there's something off in my calculations – and hell, it wouldn't be the first time – then the bad guys get the comical sight of Zephyr flailing at empty air while they whoop from the sidelines.

On this occasion, I come through the wall an estimated fifteen feet further down from where the goons are massing. I'm guessing they're security, though a known merc like Raveness suggests there's a high-tech player with an interest in whatever Mys-tech makes. My hunch is confirmed in favor of the former as I emerge from the wreckage to see six prostrate guys, two of them still twitching with little droplets of flame all around.

Infernus and I have tussled before – too many times before.

I figure he holds the record for escapes from White Nine, which is meant to be a serious Guantanamo Bay-style upgrade from the run-of-the-mill parahuman detention measures previously offered to America's finest bad guys. In his case, imagine a six-foot-three Afro-American linebacker, fire dancing across all his limbs, a helmet flared into two great horns and a red cloak no wider than a bath towel complementing his swirling silver bodysuit. What little I can see of the bad guy's skin is bright red. It's no trick of the light (or the flames). Infernus is seriously pissed about his proud African heritage being undermined by the same genetic lottery endowing his flame powers. And he knows how to channel that anger pretty well.

The master blaster is keeping good company. I don't recognize either of the two guys with him: a nondescript, stick-thin fella in a dark purple body stocking, chunky white combat boots, no gloves, a white domino mask not unlike my own, and a pugnacious sneer; the second figure is slope-shouldered and menacing, masked but with loose, sparse blonde hair hanging to his collar, black GPs and military fatigues with a black vest and military-style short-cut jacket over the top. The moment I look at the second guy my heart gives a lurch that can only be a taste of things to come.

"Infernus," I croak. "What gives?"

"Zephyr," the royal villain explodes a laugh that vanishes just as instantly as it appeared. "Never one to let sleeping dogs die."

"Sleeping dogs lie."

"I prefer it my way," he replies.

I duck the first jet of flames, but I lose all balance and stagger as I go into a defensive crouch, a feeling like vertigo flooding through me. I hit the corridor wall with my palm leaving a depression, and the stick insect in purple hits me with a spark of my very own flavor. The electricity seems to steady me and I grimace a grin, opening my palm and returning the favor. He disappears backwards quicker than a German civil rights protestor beneath a water cannon.

"You didn't introduce your friends," I remark.

"I figured they know you already, since you're always posing on TV."

"Not nice," I reply, leaping into a mid-air hover and spinning away from another controlled jet of Infernus's favorite super-heated plasma.

"Fuse you've already met," Infernus gestures behind him.

"And who's your other pal, Captain Seasick?"

Infernus grins in a way I know I'm not going to like. It's matched in a more animalistic way by the dude in black. I can't help wondering what's up with Infernus, a classic paranoid delusional, usually a class above hanging with convicted cannibals and an apparent rabies case. I don't know whether his offsider is going to sniff my balls, bark or speak when Infernus does it for him.

"I'm sure you won't forget Quietus."

In what seems like the longest heartbeat imaginable, Quietus teleports just behind me, hands on unnaturally long arms reaching up to clutch either side of my head and wrench me down to earth. Nothing seems to be normal – including my relationship to gravity – as I kick out and strike empty air and suddenly, sickeningly, get thrown haphazardly down the hall, bouncing off the walls and floor.

In so doing I pass Fuse, who thankfully seems down for the count. I've no more than asserted my ability to stand than Quietus teleports in again and my heart feels like it's going to explode, possibly taking the contents of my stomach with it. He lands a couple of good punches across my chin before my brain is able to discern right from left and I latch my hand on the villain's wrist and channel a few thousand volts. He doesn't even gasp, though he does at least go down in a satisfying crumple.

"You know I'd kick your ass on any normal day Zephyr, and with back-up, I'm gonna do it in style," Infernus bawls from twenty yards away.

"Your back-up's all unconscious, if you hadn't noticed."

"Not before taking you down a few notches, hardass."

"Oh, very Mao Tse-Tung of you," I growl back, not really sure what that means.

It doesn't matter because Infernus has a pretty short attention span and even the suggestion of a little verbal detour has him dropping his dukes and charging.

We exchange punches for a few seconds, taking out the last of the plasterboard sheeting and running on into the concrete-reinforced columns and laminated technical walls. He catches me napping long enough to cram my face through a length of plastic-covered brickwork and suddenly we're wrestling through a room with the characteristics of a giant filing cabinet, plastic containers of paperwork and God knows what else spilling around us. It doesn't take long for the whole place to start smoldering, thanks to the scorching heat Infernus gives off. I connect a fist to his chin and download a charge strong enough to blow him through an industrial door and out into what remains of the original corridor.

"Tell me who you're working for, Toby," I yell.

"Man, don't you fucken call me that!"

"Settle down, Toby. Your momma wouldn't want you to cuss so much."

If Infernus was able to look any angrier, he'd just explode. Although it's a little counter-productive to taunt bad guys with their secret identities, it's also pretty hard to resist. It's one of the few perks of being a good guy and keeping your nose clean that, generally speaking, that sort of information doesn't get on the public record. With over twelve appearances in the big house, Toby Ramon O'Shea aka Hot Spark a.k.a Infernus ain't so lucky.

We face off again, Infernus with his big mitts trickling flames, the overhead sprinkler system doing little to dampen the bad boy's enthusiasm.

"Tell me what the hell you're doing here," I say to him.

"Shut your fucken ass, Zephyr," Infernus replies in his best gangster voice.

I open my mouth, but Raveness roars in my ear, coming from nowhere, me and she going through the nearest wall, an external one as it turns out, and tumbling amid the broken bricks upon the complex's spongy, unreasonably well-irrigated lawn.

I manage to land one good punch to the underside of the bitch's jaw and then she wrestles me down again, gets an arm behind my back (my arm, my back) and amid the pain of that, Infernus rushes out and lands a disgustingly solid kick to the side of my head.

After that, well, suffice to say I was never happier to see the FBI than when they woke me up.

Zephyr 2.8 "Face Like A Weather Map"

THERE SEEMS TO be some sort of general agreement among the Parahuman and Powers Taskforce members that I am no longer needed at the scene. The lesser of my aches and bruises have departed along with the ambulances, most of an hour earlier, conveying Mys-tech's six unconscious employees to St Joan's. I'm left with a nagging headache and the knowledge that, yet again, I'm lucky I'm not dead. My neck feels like my head really was twisted all the way around and not just in the fantasies of certain FBI agents.

Once I'm done, Synergy, watched by Vanguard, keeps me back for the inevitable motherly moment. I can only sigh tersely under my breath. I know co-operation will save me a truckload more aggravation later on.

"You know, you haven't been returning our calls."

"Well, if they were *your* calls, things might've been different," I say.

"Don't be coy, Zephyr."

"I'm not tryin' to be."

"Or smug. I don't do smug."

"Well, I'm only interested in what you *do* do, so tell me more?"

"Zephyr, if you were half as smooth as you thought you were, I'd be twice as stupid as I know I'm not. You follow? Just tell me what you thought you were playing at, not returning our calls?"

I blink through that one and the threat of seizure slowly passes.

"Why are you calling me?"

"We thought you might be interested in the crime scene," Vanguard calls out like some weird uncle at a kids' football game, not really invited, but determined to take part.

He follows it up by actually walking into conversation range. In his multi-layered armor, he looks like an upright black lobster that somehow learned how to walk.

"Your dead insect guy," Vanguard continues. "We tried to call you from his apartment."

"And that's because . . . it was the scene of a crime?" I ask.

"You bet," Vanguard nods. He runs a gauntlet over his wispy blonde hair. "We just haven't worked out the crime yet."

"And you thought I could help . . . how?"

Synergy shrugs. She makes it look good enough it should be available in stores. A fall of light brown curls only highlight her darker face. Yeah, I'm kinda smitten.

"Just say we were interested in Zephyr's *unique perspective*, John," Synergy tells him.

"Yeah, something like that," Vanguard agrees.

"OK, so tell me about it. Or did I miss the boat?"

"Your Creeping Death had an interest in the occult. Tattoos, pentagrams, silver daggers, the whole thing," Synergy says. "There were cocoons all over the place. We figure the guy may have been an experimenter . . . turned out he was more successful than he knew."

"Successful?"

"We don't know anything else yet. Miss Black is looking into the mystical side for us," Synergy says.

"Miss Black?"

"Sure," Vanguard grins. "Haven't you heard? Little Annie's gone legit. She's one of us now."

"Don't taunt Zephyr about it, John," Synergy smiles. "He had his chance years ago, I hear. You turned it down, right?"

"I've got nothing against registration," I shrug. "I didn't freak out or go rogue when the Act came through in '97. I always said it wouldn't be enforceable. Still, I didn't feel too comfortable signing my life away to Uncle Sam just for a regular paycheck." I shrug. "Maybe that was my mistake. I didn't figure I'd still be hero-ing this many years down the line."

My comments cue Synergy to slip me another card. I lose interest once I realize there's no personal notes written 'pon it in an excited hand.

"Give us a call if you change your mind. The government could always use your experience," she says.

"And then we might be able to stop cleaning up your messes," her partner adds.

"Hey, you got one of 'em," I say and gesture, almost rudely. "Fuse or whatever his name is."

"Yeah," Synergy agrees and flips open her notebook. "Electrical controller, some power over machines, a known counter-insurgency nightmare. I imagine that's how they got in without the company's fast response squad bringing them down on the front lawn."

"They didn't look so hot to me," I remark.

"The guards? Yeah. Must follow up and check their gear is licensed."

"That's your Fuse-boy's work too," Vanguard says. "Paramedics reckon they were pretty badly electrocuted."

He holds up a big mitt unnecessarily.

"Don't worry, Zeph. No one's even suggesting it was you. Even you ain't that incompetent."

"Hey Vanguard, when I want shit from you, I'll squeeze your head, OK?" I snap back at him in record time. "Now put your fucking helmet on."

Synergy restrains her partner with the merest touch and they depart towards the helicarrier. I walk across the lawn, aching neck and jaw in hand, not quite ready to fly, the night air cool and fresh and surprising, coming across Truman from the bay. There are others still around in the night, though, and once I'm airborne I pass several of them, unguessed at figures, possibly even allies, caroming about in the night.

Go high enough and I know a glimpse of dawn wouldn't be far away. Instead, I turn for home and sleep, just another night with my bed left empty for me. Beth is under blankets in the lounge, snoring lightly, one of the old syndicated Captain Atom movies in grainy re-run on the flatscreen TV. I hesitate to rescue the remote from beneath my wife's pillow, so I fire a quick spark at the TV and head for the dark, first light not far away.

*

SLEEP DOESN'T LAST long. Elisabeth and Tess are off to see a family counsellor. Apparently I was advised of this several days ago. I can only make a pained face as I explain about my appointment with my agent, the charade based on me, the failed writer, for Tessa's benefit. My little girl adopts her understanding angel face. Beth is less receptive, face like a weather map and a cold front on the way. Not even I could turn that storm around. It's raining outside and she uses her scarf the way Shi'ite guerrillas have been known, disappearing into the lift with a paper shopping bag, a pair of $300 work shoes to be returned to the store.

I go into the den and review the day ahead as I brush my teeth and browse the news and gossip pages online. Sal Doro calls as I'm spitting up spearmint and straight away I know he means business.

"I hope you've got something for me, Zephyr."

"The bank's running a bit low. I could do with a top-up," I tell him.

"I think this one's for free," Sal replies. "I want to be distracted from this tale I've heard about the hottest green-haired heroine on the block and her quote unquote night of pleasure with her favorite man of mystery."

"Jesus, Sal," I reply aghast. "That's fucking blackmail."

"You've got something better for me though, right?"

Over the palpitations I nod, starting to outline last night's encounter only to have him cut me off.

"Let's meet. I need some new file photos."

"Ph-ph-photos are fucking extra, you creep."

"I'll bring a few twenties. See you at eleven?"

I direct him a little closer to noon and hang up, frustrated, also more than a little guilty at my infidelity as well as failing to give Cusp the follow-up call I'd promised. Of course, wondering how a hack like Sal Doro could've got word of the news, it's easy for me to ladle suspicion on everyone's favorite green-haired hottie as well.

Halfway to Hallory O'Hagan's office, a bureaucrat from White Nine calls to remind me about my rescheduled afternoon appointment with Stephen Zahn. As if someone as seemingly forgetful as I could be offended at such a simple reminder, I snap the phone closed haughtily and yell, "That's why I need a personal assistant" to the ether as I plough my way through it.

My interview with a vampiress awaits.

Her office is in a sun-shielded high-rise on the Jersey border, now just a vast terrain of silver-skinned architecture bifurcated by freeways and subway lines. The light-sensitive glass sheathing Hallory's building, like all the others, goes sepia in the approach to the sun's zenith. I try to make like a regular visitor and land on the sidewalk out the front of the squat edifice and make my way inside through the well-known route of entrance-foyer-elevator-reception.

The Puerto Rican girl behind the counter smiles through a row of braces as I prowl the area like a cat in heat, conspicuous in my leathers between block-mounted art photos showing the company's other clients. Although the presentation is good, they're mostly mid-range. Seeing fledgling stand-up Keanu Reeves on the books is almost enough to walk me out of there, except for the delectable Miss O'Hagan coming straight through the wide, you've-finally-made-it double door entrance to her private demesne.

"Hey," the redhead remarks in a faux conversational tone I find immediately appealing. "It's great to finally get to meet you, Zephyr. I've lived on the east coast eight years and can you believe I haven't met any color the whole time?"

My grin falters. "Color?"

"Ha, sorry," she says, pausing to straighten the lapel of her off-white power suit. "Just an industry term for you guys. You're not alone in seeking representation and I just want to say straight out to you that we're really super-pumped about establishing our new working relationship. We actioned a really unique list of key priorities this morning over group breakfast and everyone's super-keen to get this right."

"Really?"

"Hell yeah," Hallory says.

She gestures, so I flop on one of the burgundy couches in my best imitation male model slump. Miss O'Hagan sits perkily in the chair opposite, somehow not even managing to make an impression, giving me the sense of her firm ass hovering just microns above the fabric of the cushion. Neat trick. Something Sky Blue could manage, I figure.

We shoot the shit for a while. The agency has been approached by several lesser-grade identities seeking representation for their services. I have to clarify, trying to outline in bumbling terms that I'm after an agency that can meet not only PR needs, but provide contacts as a lifeline between me and the public. That I am also "super-keen," as she would put it, to maximize the opportunities for future revenue stemming from my incidental occupation as the city's foremost costumed adventurer is something, I stress casually, that also needs further investigation.

"So in other words you want us to help you establish some kind of dynamic connectivity between yourself and the people of the city that you know and love, while providing you with the chance to continue doing what you do best, to the mutual advantage of Atlantic City as well as yourself and your loved ones."

"And someone to take messages," I add.

"Sounds great, Zephyr. We would be totally thrilled to look into the possibilities," Hallory replies. "We already brainstormed a few options I wondered if you'd considered?"

"Uh, such as?"

"Lifestyle endorsement opportunities, synergetic branding, cross-marketing possibilities including a build-up campaign, maybe something big? You ran a team once, didn't you?"

"The Sentinels, yeah."

"Didn't I hear you were getting back?"

"Well that's, really, just a rumor. . . ."

She clucks her tongue and says, "And what about a comic?"

My eyes do the crackling thing and I stick out a hand.

"No way."

"Really? I thought that sort of thing –"

"Look, sorry, but no way. I've only just gotten over that whole thing with Grant Morrison. . . ."

She tilts her head like a particularly pretty android. "Explain?"

I try, but it's not pretty, and just as soon as I'm in too deep, wandering off on some tangent about the cherry-picking of conventional narrative, I try to back out of the explanation as gracefully as I can manage moments after I've begun, which isn't very well. It all ends with Miss O'Hagan staring at me like I've laid a turd on her carpet and declared myself a My Little Pony.

"Jesus. . . ." I clutch my head.

I'm ruining this, as was foretold in ancient times.

"Look, none of that's any problem," she says eventually. "We'll be able to chart numerous advantageous possibilities for making the Zephyr brand consumer-friendly and more high octane."

"*More* high octane?"

I give her the eyebrow, but she barely glimmers. Eyes on the money.

"OK," I relent. "I'd better go. I've got an appointment with an old enemy."

*

ON THE ROOFTOP once more, I'm relieved to see Sal's already waiting, picking at a pastrami on rye sitting on the brown paper bag it came in while the newshound smokes profusely from one of the grotesque cigarillos he often favors. He waves the ashen wand in my direction as I sit on the low brick riser with the gravity of a much bigger man.

"Get to it," the reporter says. "I'm in a hurry."

It's hard not to bridle at Sal's tone. The hook-nosed old hack coughs up a few lumps and spits them over the edge of the roof, a forecast of rain for one unlucky pedestrian. His dead brown eyes return to me and he dusts off his hands, impatience etched in every nicotine-stained line of his face.

This is a man who has been dealing one-on-one with costumed loonies since before even I suited up for the first time. Whatever allure they once held was gone. I know he sometimes wonders how he fell into this line of work, trailing egocentric freaks and one-trick wonderboys all over the coast when he went through grad school on the fumes of the inspiration from Watergate. I know this because of Sal's book in which I rate no less than sixteen mentions, most of them favorable. The old hack wouldn't have it any other way. To him I'm as obnoxious as the rest, but I have my uses. I'm not a hero when I'm here on the roof. I'm an informant. That even I know this is true puts a dampener on my day whenever we have to do this dance. So while I might be tempted to send a few volts through anyone else who spoke to me in a voice so short, on a whole other level, I sometimes wonder why I don't do something drastic to end his ongoing *schadenfreude*.

And then Sal reminds me. The crisp bills rustle as he produces his pocket Sony and glances up to check the position of the sun and the play of shadows.

"You've got time for this, though?" I ask.

I rotate my pointer finger unhelpfully. I'd like to stick it up the old prick's ass, regardless of the connotations, and watch that impassive Gallic demeanor dance on a few hundred ergs. But it ain't gonna happen.

"Sure, sure. Hurry up."

I grit my teeth and the flash goes off a few times. Sal only has to gesture and I change angles.

"Hover for me, baby."

I grunt under-breath and slowly rise from the roof. Sal judges unconsciously the angles like a true expert, clicks off a few more digital stills, and then his interest collapses. I have to remind myself I once wanted to be a journalist – and still kid myself I could be a writer. Writing what I know, that old chestnut, might not be such a good idea with my current mindset.

"The well's kinda drying up, Zeph. What've you got?"

I shrug. "The insect plague guy?"

"Go on."

"He's dead."

"No shit." Sal eyes me for a long second and produces another tiny cigar. "Still, you're not holding your hand up for that are you?"

"I don't think covering up infidelity with a murder charge would be clever, even for me," I reply.

"So you really are fucking that sweet thing? Man."

Sal hangs his head like most ordinary guys would, though he throws extra pathos into it somehow.

"I'm not admitting to shit. Likewise with the Insect King, or whatever you guys were calling him. 'Sources close to Parahuman Affairs told the Post the suspect would not be the subject of further investigation because it was believed he perished during the final moments of the confrontation'."

"You're not close to the FBI," Sal responds.

"You put it to them and I guarantee you it's on the money."

"Hmmm, OK. What else?"

"The Feebs have evidence of occult activity at the dead guy's brownstone. Again," I say, raising my hands before the interrogation can get underway, "you'll have to put it to them."

"Fucking hell, Zephyr."

"Angry I can't do all your work for you?"

Sal holds up his hands, envisaging a headline: "Zephyr gets green head."

I sigh and look away and a pigeon lands on the ledge nearby, gets a sense he's interrupted something private and flies off in a flutter. Sal snaps his fingers again.

"OK. What else?"

"*Else?*" I try and bring my voice back to a normal level. "Christ, Sal."

"I'm guessing you're a married man, Zephyr. Always have."

"Not for much longer," I can't resist muttering. "OK, how about Stiletto and Darkstorm?"

"What about 'em?"

"They're onto each other."

"Proof?"

"Sources?"

"Come on, Zeph," Sal says. "We're not E! We need to substantiate this information. If it pays out, then we all win."

He hands over the twenties for the new photos.

"Fuck it," I sigh. "Just quote me. An inadvertent slip. Zephyr was congratulating them on their help during the whole insect thing and said they made a lovely couple."

"I didn't see them at the crime scene?" Sal says.

"Oh, they were there. Fetching the drinks. Couldn't do without 'em."

"OK."

"Now tell me who snitched about Cusp?"

Sal snickers as he packs away his notepad.

"Gee, Zeph, you know I couldn't reveal my sources. . . ."

"Sal, I need to know."

We make eye contact like real human beings and the old goat falls for it. I sigh in relief as he peers over the edge of the bricks like the Press Council might be listening in.

"It's not the girl. I didn't know about Stiletto and Dark-wad. I guess they must've got together after you left Paragon that night, right?"

"Paragon?"

Sal coughs. "What about him?"

I stifle the reply and Sal gives a sick grin, real child porn material, and somewhere close by a siren starts up amid honking horns.

Business concluded like a back-alley blowjob, I start scoping the skyline for avenues of escape when Doro clears his throat and hands me a mini-DVD in its case.

"What's this?"

"Some stuff in there about Tony Azzurro you might take an interest in? Let me know what you turn up? Take some photos?"

"Photos?" I sigh and pocket the disc. "Fuck, Sal. How the hell have I got time to set up a camera for myself?"

"Never seemed like a problem for Spider-Man."

I grit my teeth in an effort to say nothing and Sal just laughs, loving life at my expense. If things could be as easy as the comics, maybe I wouldn't have a midnight appointment with Twilight.

"Fuck Spider-Man."

It's turning into a busy day.

Zephyr 2.9 "Some Weird, Perverse Foucauldian Metaphor"
THERE IS SOMETHING about being able to travel across the city at the speed of sound that can lend itself to impulsiveness. The Statue of Liberty remains like an incarnation of the ghost of some old battle-scarred warship, frozen in her metallic dignity overlooking the water where the New World no longer holds the promise of endless possibilities and even more than Han Solo could ever imagine. We one-time New Yorkers have retreated from that point. Sure it was the Kirlians who beat us back to the mainland, Manhattan being ground zero in their airborne offensive, but in the act of surrender there's been a sense, for some of us at least, that we did more than yield ground, but conceded some moral point when we left Manhattan to the gangs and the muties.

Sure, by "we" I don't really know who the fuck I am talking about since I was young enough at the time to be seriously considering what the term "bonk the baloney" might mean for my unsatisfied nocturnal urges. It's something cultural boffins like Mandela like to talk about a lot, though. Read: the city as collective unconscious, wasteland as signifier of disheartened American psyche, etcetera etcetera. Trite, I know, but these people have to justify their jobs, and the backstabbing in academia makes Caesar's Rome look like a kid's fucking birthday party.

One thing I know for sure is Manhattan's an irritatingly good hide-out for goons who know the everyday lawman's too busy and too cautious to go into those garbage-festooned canyons to bring them to justice. The mutant psychic known as Mentor does a pretty good job of halting their worst excesses, and there's rumors the Atlantic City Council has a secret supply deal to keep the freaks sweet. All I know is every second or third time I wander into old helmet-head's airspace he likes to give me a mental tap on the shoulder.

Today's no different.

After devouring two Wimpy burgers perched on the old lady's crown, I'm set to make the afternoon appointment at White Nine when that creepy feeling overtakes me. Nothing could be as freaky as Mentor himself, but if psychic presence could be said to carry overtones, Mentor leaves a very specific kind of skid mark in the mind.

"I can feel you trying to get your fingers under the edges, Mentor," I swear through gritted teeth. "What do you want?"

"Ah, Zephyr," the thought comes, that pederastic hesitation over the fricative leaving me in no doubt as to who I'm talking to as I can virtually see the self-styled King of the Mutants steeple his unnaturally long fingers together. "I thought it was you passing by. Long time and a very long see, I fear. You've been staying away."

"For good reason," says I. "I have a life. You know, sunlight, clean air, hotdogs in the park, pennies in the fountain, riding bicycles through Central Park, girls in short shorts? Remember any of that?"

"Central Park is a gothic ruin," Mentor's typically erudite tone responds, emanating from somewhere within the devastation of old Manhattan. "You know Freakasaurus and his Sideshow Peeps have made that their killing fields?"

"I'm talking about the *new* Central Park, you anus," I reply.

My voice is caught in the wind travelling around up high, but I know it won't make any difference to this particular transmission. Telepathy's not a power I've often wished I had. It's Mentor's only concession to a useful existence, since the rare mutation that threw up his grandmaster level mental powers also reduced his body to a near-useless pulpy mess he animates by sheer will alone.

"You know, commissioned in 1984, first plantings in '86, open to the public, what was it, the Atlantic City Fair of 1989?"

"You know your history, Zephyr," the old chap replies. "And I know mine."

"And never the twain shall meet. Tell me what you want, Mentor old pal. I've got to meet a man about a horse."

There's a brief twinge as Mentor tries to ride that thought back down into my cerebellum: a move I know from history would give him ranging access to my memory banks, and if I really lost control, total mastery over my body. It would only take a few seconds to transform me into one of those mindless drones that form the bulk of his Manhattan army. Fortunately for me, I've been here before, and a quick selection of deliberate and shocking disconnected images throws the telepath off long enough to lose the trail. It's a good thing Mentor's desire to overthrow humanity only comes every five or six years. God help us the time he gets it right.

"Zephyr, don't go," he pleads quickly. "Please. Come to Manhattan. There are matters we must discuss."

"I'm not coming anywhere near you, pal," I think more than speak.

"I will swear to any truce you demand. Your visit is . . . imperative . . . and would be for both our gain."

The slippery thought tones try and inflect the message with every suggestive trick in the book.

"Both our gain? Better tell me now or it's no deal, Mental-man."

"It's to do with our mutual friend Think-Tank."

"*Mutual* friend? That guy is a pain in the ass and you know it."

"Well," Mentor responds hesitantly, "at least *mutual* remains correct. He is proving to be a . . . problem for myself as well."

"You want me to come to you for this?"

"You would not be mistreated. You have it on my honor."

I snort, but that's enough posturing for today. Truth is the headcase has me intrigued. Think-Tank is one dangerous motherfucker I would like to put away for good, if not drown in the Miskatonic.

"Alright," I say, "but another day. There's too much on now."

"Your humble servant awaits. . . ."

"Great," I reply, jetting high enough into the atmosphere I begin passing light planes. "Now get the fuck out of my head."

Within moments I pass out of range and do not receive the mutant's chosen response.

*

SITTING IN THE middle of the river, there's really two prisons on Riker's Island. The original prison has agglomerated wards and sections slowly since it was bought from an old Dutchman in the 1800s, and these days has facilities to deal with over twenty thousand inmates. There are playing grounds and recreational canola fields for the nearer-to-rehabilitation inmates separating the hard prison from White Nine, which from the air, as I'm approaching it, looks more like an observatory than the world's most impressive solution to the parahuman menace.

While the facility itself is bland enough, the hard-top-mounted rocket relays tracking my approach are intimidating even for someone who could probably outfly them. I go straight for the helipad to avoid ugly accidents. We have no radio connection, though technically I have sufficient gear in my belt pack if I wanted to spend an hour untangling the cables, so calling ahead for air clearance isn't really a goer. They know I'm due. I trust to Zephyr's good name and some of the more life-saving connotations of brand recognition as I touch down and wait for the little trolleys with guards and administrators to shuttle down the half-concealed walkway from the main prison house.

I have met Dr Zane Wilson before, I know, because he tells me so, and he seems like a very trustworthy guy. Otherwise I wouldn't have a clue. I nod with seriousness, hell, compassion even, as we walk from the trolley depot and into the guts of the vast machine. Hospital-slick floors chart the path before us.

"Of course we'll still have your virtual profile on record here, your residual self-image, Zephyr," the scientist says. "This shouldn't take more than an hour or so."

It has been a while since I visited the facility. Hardly my favorite place.

You see White Nine isn't like any ordinary prison. It mixes all the best – which is to say *worst* – elements of a prison, a hospital and a cemetery. Deep behind and within the dense metal walls I can hear a powerful thrumming, the sensation of walking through a clockwork universe, vast elemental machines at work, the whole place one incredible device requiring the super-cooling technology of a small city to keep running without error.

White Nine is the actualization of some weird, perverse Foucauldian metaphor. Jeremy Bentham would be cumming in his grave. It is more crypt than prison, the only technical difference being the inmates are still, at least in one sense, alive.

The interview room is so advanced it resembles little more than a cross between a dentist's clinic and a police interrogation room lifted from some 70s cop film. I move instantly to the weird chair and stride up and onto the mechanical platform with a certainty that only an alter ego can possess. Deep down my bowels bubble with inescapable reptilian fear. This goes against millennia of genetic programming, to submit myself to this strange crossover. But there's no denying it keeps the city safer.

The carceral technicians use a rich chemical cocktail to send even the most hardened villains under, the moment they're collected at a crime scene. Once on board an armored, taxpayer-funded flying ambulance just for them, they're whisked to Rikers and quickly entered into neurological life-support and imprisoned in the vault. I am not sure of the legal processes or whether there's been any successful challenges. Even the most ardent libertarians would have a hard time justifying easing up on the sorts of madball goons kept down here. And since the war in Tajikistan, it's been hard to even discuss the topic, given the Government's atrocious record. If they tried the same thing on the supers community, well, let's just say it would be a different story. Even *they* haven't been silly enough to go there, and for the guys who had to invade Iraq three times to get the job done, that's really saying something.

The white coats come in and clip me up, attaching the gayest-looking futuristic helmet to my head you've ever seen. I saw worse in Doc Prendergast's basement, but they were industrial-strength orgasmatrons, whereas this one will only produce a telemetric connection to my pal on ice, the Terraformer. The technicians confirm who I'm meeting and double-check the clearance and then they kind of encourage me to close my eyes, give me a compressed hypo shot to the wrist, and it's straight to la-la land for twenty-odd minutes while they organize their shit and while me and everyone else not crossing their fingers and toes hope that more bad guys don't choose precisely this moment to attack. It wouldn't be the first time White Nine was breached, sad to say. It ain't a perfect solution, just the best one they've come up with yet.

Somewhere a milky voice unnecessarily starts counting backwards from twenty. I follow the numbers with a strange curiosity until it dawns on me that I'm the one talking. My last thought, before the darkness comes and I go rushing down the cybernetic rabbit hole, is that I should really try and get my hands on some of this shit some time.

*

THE ROOM IS as sterile as a virtual construct could ever be.

I snap awake just in time to see a short guy in a black sweater also snuffle his way into consciousness. He's the same guy I recall from the bank episode, collar-length strawberry blonde hair, nervous eyes, a generous allotment of stubble. The techs really didn't spare the special effects budget when they went in for the render job. I've heard they make the heroes even better looking and more cut than in real life to make sure the baddies stay intimidated. Using advanced tech to send my enemies into my sleep with me would do the trick, as far as I'm concerned, with or without the virtual nip-and-tuck.

Zahn's eyes widen as he drinks in my spectral splendor. While I think I can feel the constraints of the real life seat, we're facing each other at a slight angle on simple black office chairs. The white space has no other details unless I wish it.

"Z-Zephyr," he manages to get out.

"Steven Zahn aka the Terraformer," I reply. "You asked for me to come. What is it?"

The fidgety guy breaks protocol straight away, nervously standing, the chair emitting a convincing blackboard squeal as it tips back, its occupant clearly forgetting straight away this is virtual rather than real space. I hope the shrinks were accurate in their lucidity assessment. Virtual world or not, I don't want this guy freaking out on me.

"I'm not the Terraformer, man," Zahn bleats anxiously. "I wouldn't call myself that. It's so lame. I've never dressed up in spandex my whole life."

I can't say the same, so I keep my mouth shut and let the rant wear itself out.

"I asked them for you to come," he says. "You've gotta know. You've gotta understand. And you've gotta get me out of here."

The plea in his eyes makes me momentarily unwell. Last time I was here it was to hear Crescendo's poppycock posturing, fist raised threateningly despite the virtual prison PJs and the lack of soundwaves curdling the air around us. Zahn's desperation is unsettling, but I can be an insensitive prick most of the time and finally I'm somewhere that talent comes in handy.

"Cut the crap, Zahn. You're in here until hell freezes over for that trick you pulled," I tell him.

"They'd give me life for a first offence?"

His eyes bulge. It would be comical if it wasn't his own life we were discussing.

"I haven't even got a lawyer. What's up with that, man? You tell me. How can they do this? I've never even had a bong hit go down on my record."

I have to concede this is true. I viewed his sheet before they let me in here. His assertion and the nervous air of innocence pique my curiosity.

"How do you explain it then?"

"I didn't just call you in here to beg, Zephyr," the smaller guy says.

He resumes his seat, swipes nervously at his virtual turtleneck and claws fingers I know would normally be green with nicotine stains through his wild hair. I eye him a moment longer, the whole passive-aggressive thing in my favor.

"I have information to offer, you know, if like anyone would fucking ask me for it," he says a moment later. "That wasn't me that did that to the bank. I'm no mutie freak. They say I ripped up the earth with my mind? I can't do that. If I could do that, would I be running errands for a second-hand bookstore? Come on, you gotta give me more'n that, Zephyr."

"Then how do you explain it?"

"*Ras Algethi*," he replies.

"That's not an explanation."

Something goes ping in my mind and those years sitting in the branches of the tree watching the stars between the smog from the interstate and the low-flying ships at Newark come back to me, the dog-eared old book I would've flicked through on summer nights with my dad if I'd had one.

"Ras Algethi is a star," I say.

"Yes, a star," Zahn replies and jumps up again, clicking his fingers at me more like a mad and enthusiastic university professor than the residual self-image of a collared super-criminal. For a moment he reminds me of Paragon going lunatic on Oprah's couch, though Zahn chills out far more quickly.

"It's a star, a living star," he says. "An ancient force. A god. A demon."

"You're into the occult and shit?"

"Totally," he says, grinning for an instant before the smile falls from his face like bath tiles in a time-lapse of decay. "Or I was. I don't know. But this is how it happened. Ras Algethi entered me.

"Ras Algethi is the Terraformer."

Zephyr 2.10 "The Most Lethargic And Ardent Admirers"
I WOULD LOVE to say I shoot the shit with Zahn for half the
afternoon and finally bail out of there with a promise in ink on my
sleeve and a fresh Zephyr business card in his hand, but there's none
of that. First the technicians only risk visitor immersion for thirty-
five minutes max. Second, I'm not sure I can go with the creepy new
angle he's giving me.

Once clear of the institution, I call Synergy's cell number.

"Zephyr, what's up?"

"Your man Calloway. He was into the occult and stuff?"

"Big time," she replies.

"OK. What do you have on cultural background for this Steven
Zahn?"

"Who's that?"

"Synergy, babe," I laugh. "If you want me to do all your work,
you're gonna have to think up a suitable bribe."

"It's not my case," she replies, the word *asshole* throbbing in
its absence.

But I know Synergy well enough and she's a cool chick and I
can hear her taking one of those deep breaths I've admired so often
on the chests of her and Seeker and Vulcana, and then she comes
back on the line.

"I'm calling it up now. I'm bringing in Miss Black if I get
what you're suggesting here, that there's an occult connection?"

I have my own suspicions about that and decide to hang ten on
revealing too much else. We detour through some amiable chit-chat
and when Synergy tries to steer me back toward the territory of what
I do or do not know, I play the Zephyr card once more and start
telling her how much I admire her dress sense. Flustered, bemused,
flattered and pissed-off all in the one take, she distracts herself by
reading big extracts from Zahn's background files. In so doing, she
confirms the bookstore story, and in a slow voice, adds details about
signs of occult interest and paraphernalia found at the Terraformer's
nominated address.

"Now tell me how come your own people didn't put this
together?" I ask.

"I guess we were just waiting on your sheer brilliance, Zeph,"
the agent replies in a tired voice. "Maybe now you'll rethink your
career."

It's not a very sincere recruitment so I handball it off with some quip about needing to be seduced, not recruited. If Synergy groans I can't hear it over my own retching. It's hard being me sometimes, especially when I exploit myself for the greater good.

"White Nine scan confirms a paranormal template, though," Synergy says at last. "You've got to consider we had nothing to suggest these cases were parallel. Calloway's genes weren't registered with the FBI."

"Neither were Zahn's."

"No, but we've got the evidence now."

"That's the benefit of capturing rather than shredding them, I guess."

"Hmmm," Synergy purrs softly. "What is it you are saying there exactly, Zephyr? Are you indicating the Insect King was *not* transported off-shore to another dimension?"

I zip my lip too late after hastily landing us all in it.

I won't say anything else. I hardly want to indict Twilight for murder.

*

THE AIR SCREAMS at that sweet spot just below Mach. Presumably my eardrums are adapted to the effects, just like the rest of me, hurling my physiognomy through the air at hundreds upon hundreds of miles per hour. For a constant recharger like me, the real effect is one of borderline orgasm as I suck up the kinetic tension that producing such a slipstream creates.

None of this will distract me from my replacement ringtone, or at least the vibration alert, which could intrude on the thoughts of a dead man. Casting around quickly for shelter, I alight on the SBSCC UK building roof and startle a handful of foreign office workers playing boules and smoking joints. Although I wave my hands across the roofspace for them to relax, within seconds all have "scarpered," as the Brits would say. The call is from Beth and as I answer it, I sashay in the workers' wake and collect a smoldering roach from beneath an exhaust unit.

"I'm glad I caught you," she says.

There's no "How is your day, honey?" so I ask her myself. The response is a stammered garble she eventually uses all her lawyerly ways to escape. I can hear her mentally backtracking to the origin of the call and resuming the path she planned in the first place. A Doberman with curls. No more curve balls from me today – like actually giving a damn.

"What's up?"

"George and Max called," she says. "We're on for dinner."

I groan and she adds, "Hey, these are your parents. I know how you feel, but you know how persuasive they can be. And persistent. Have you told them about Tessa's school? It seems like they know. Georgia insisted on 'bringing the girl'."

I close my eyes and look down, bemused for a moment, refreshed to know I can still love my wife when she dusts off her disrespectful imitation of my mother. It's been a while, and the lack of visitations would be a factor in that. I nod, blow on the roach to keep it alive, and take a healthy belt before answering back.

"Figures. I'm sorry to drag you into it. Their place? And what time?"

When I exhale the smoke in that pained, Mickey Rourke sort of way, it just sounds like regular street-level deflation, the pressures of the world and yadda yadda yadda. Perhaps it is. The joint stub tastes like I'm smoking a shoe, and a wet one at that.

"Dinner's at eight. Do you think you could manage that?"

"I've had a busy day, but sure."

"You can? Miracles happen. I haven't seen anything on the news."

"I'm able to have a busy day without trashing half of downtown, Elisabeth. Sheesh," I say, sucking the end of the butt and flicking it away, disappointment now the predominant flavor in my mouth.

"OK. Tessa's in my office this afternoon monopolizing the photocopier. I guess I'll take charge of getting us both to Queens by eight."

"Sounds swell," I say.

"Joe, don't be late, OK?"

"Sure, sure."

In my own lawyering books that's a "no undertaking" – and nowhere near like a promise.

Beth rings off and I stare around the building top for a while with the phone clutched thoughtfully in hand, trying to determine the presence of a buzz without much luck. I don't know what the bankers are smoking these days, but they obviously need to upgrade their gear.

As I step to the edge of the banister, I see Seeker flash by in an impresario of ghostly vapors, a tiny man in a blue costume, no more than eight inches tall, riding the middle of her back. I shrug at myself and carefully clear my mind of the awful thoughts such a thing sets off. She's a classy lady and I've never quite worked out where her visionary powers begin and end or really how they function at all.

*

THERE IS MUCH ado at home with no-one there to distract me, the time's creeping on, I've downed a six-pack of JD mixers and a bowl of Hang's noodles I picked up in Grant on the way across town, unlikely to disturb my evening meal and more likely to give me the squirts for an hour or two before the old metabolism kicks in and does its thing.

Home alone, I have the freedom to leave the crawlspace door open and I'm smoking one of Beth's cigarettes wearing just a towel and thumbing through my copy of Teenscene and walking in and out from the computer terminal to check email and wincing as Hang's noodles do their thing and the police scanner is on loud when I hear the panicked call from the bank robbery in process.

Normally I might let it go, but it happens to be my bank, and no more than four blocks from home. Grasshopper, Sun Man or even Seeker are likely in the area, going by the afternoon's play-by-play, but on my home turf and with the six-hundred dollars in my savings account, I definitely feel this is a job for Zephyr. It's also five minutes to six o'clock, which means a good time for a live feed during the evening news, but frankly only a total card would consider that a reason to abuse his super-speed powers and change back into costume and head out the window all in under sixty seconds flat. My only hesitation is to roll up the combo of emergency civvies I keep on the shelf in the office to slip into my jacket back-flap as a just-in-case in case this makes me run late for dinner.

I've got two hours, right?

Once safely elevated from the home-front, I bomb the pavement, hitting Mach gently just to let the bad guys know I'm coming. The feed from the scanner cuts out as the ear-piece dangles out-of-place and I'm not too perturbed, knowing the layout well, the bank inside and out. There's just a solitary cruiser blocking the intersection and two black cops frantically trying to hurry all the pedestrians out of there. For only the briefest moment does it occur to me to wonder who hits a bank after office hours, and then the whole front of the building explodes outwards in a storm-front of dust and debris.

I land behind the crouching police officers just as chunks of concrete and marble render smash into the cruiser, breaking glass and causing the siren's ululations to give a heave. The dust cloud rolls over us, and over the cops' coughing, I tell them to keep the area cordoned while I go forward to examine the carnage. I'm so freaking brave, I impress myself, hehe, but no really, these guys just look up at me like I am insane and for just the briefest second I see myself through their eyes and even I am impressed. But I shake my head to clear delusions of grandeur. If they really understood what I can do they would probably admire less and demand more, which is just human nature, really.

The bank's alarms ring through the haze, but I can still hear voices. Particularly there's a female one, loud and insistent, yelling shrilly at person or persons unknown. I still can't see to save a bug, and that's why Eris manages to flatten me with the first concussion wave.

One moment I'm advancing cautiously on the front of the four-floor granite hard-stone I pinch pennies from every second day of the week. The next I'm like a grand prix motorbike rider acting out the stuff everyone secretly watches motorsport waiting just to see, rocketing along on my leather-clad ass with just enough momentum that I'm not able to gracefully get up and start running. While there is no motorcycle chasing me, I hit the side of the same cop car I've just cleared, and glass and more imprecations rain down, so I figure I'm about even as far as that goes. The force of the contact is enough to jolt the vehicle sideways and I'm thrilled the guys sheltering on the other side are quick enough to scramble free, though the looks they shoot me could kill and the visibility has dropped just sufficient to put my stuff-up in the spotlight while continuing to cloud Eris and a handful of other figures moving like ghosts of trench warfare at the edge of the street.

Identifying the villainess is all largely the work of post-game hindsight thanks to the concrete-powder fog cloaking everything. My bodysuit could pass for a mid-life crisis redesign, white instead of my customary black as if that might make me "fresh". The dust just pisses me off though, and I lope back into the confrontation hoping not only for answers, but someone tough enough I can work out my frustrations on.

Looming from the clouds comes a quartet of balaclava-clad clowns, literally, ghoulish masks in place, shotguns and Tek-9 machine-pistols in gloved hands. The first one catches just a glimpse of my fist as I swing at him; and while he's sailing through the air with a broken jaw, I kick the legs from beneath a second goon, grab him by the back of the mask on momentum alone and toss him through the yawning wreck of the front of the bank.

Over it all I can hear the woman's voice.

"Louder, you guys! Come on. Make it crazy!"

There's a handful of people still nearby, crouching behind street furniture, a phone box, a taxi unlucky to be caught in the explosion with its tires now shredded. I'm still working my way in slow motion through the underlings as a burst of 9mm automatic fire resounds. I don't have time to question why the guy fires into the air instead of trying to get a bead on me. He makes retching noises as I karate chop him on the side of the neck and all but put my fist through his ribs.

The fourth guy just runs. I flick open my palm and an agonizing blue spray erupts. He doesn't make the step to the sidewalk, and the only compensation for him is that Eris now makes her own exit from the bank, a vision of the bizarre in her two-tone banded tights. She directs a blast of concussive force straight at me and it feels like I've just been caught out by a bus while crossing the road.

I pull myself from the window display of the H&M across the road. The dust gradually dissipates. Eris is a spritely form amid the flashing blue lights, short black hair jutting out in dreadlocked spikes, long legs wrapped in zebra-stripe stockings, wrestling boots, black shorts and singlet over a white lycra under-suit. There are metallic bits and bobs around her neck and attached to her knees and shoulders, though they serve no obvious purpose. Some fucked-up symbol rests in white between her perky breasts, but I don't recognize the thing as a stylized apple or understand the connection to – or Eris's psychotic obsession with – Greek mythology until I hit Google in the small hours of the morning some days after this crazy, torturous, ridiculous day has ended. All I know is she looks like a cross between a deranged cyclist and a slightly sexy garbage lady and when she looks at me there's a smile no sane person has a right to produce.

Still halfway to standing, I retaliate with a mid-range electrical blast. The girl is quick, motioning downwards to ride a wave of pillowing force that sees her clear of my attack. First I think she can fly, and I run forward, hurling another lightning bolt only to realize her momentum has a definite gravitational arc. Then I run into another wall of force and I am extricating myself from the side of a second, newly-arrived police car before Eris has legged it down the block toward the Subway.

It's not hard to get ahead of her, travelling at the speed I do. There are many more people down the street, drawn to the chaos of the bank explosion like moths to a flame. I'm appalled to see the villainess lob an object like a hard black tennis ball into the middle of the nearest congested knot. That's how she gets below ground, leaving me like a sucker to dive after the concussion grenade. It goes off harming no-one, but it's only later on that selfsame web search that I learn she feeds off the psychic energy generated by strong radiant emotions like fear, in turn powering her kinesis. Her concussion powers are as wild and untamed as she claims and quite genuinely appears to be herself. The Interpol notes available via Wikipedia back up the suggestion she has more than one screw loose.

By the time I get clear of the horrified crowds in fearful paroxysms over their near-death experiences, there's only a few startled rail commuters around who are unable to give me a precise direction in which the strange villainess decamped. I return to the surface in time to walk right into the flash-bulbs of that Irish twit from the Post and then Imogen Davies appears trailing a camera crew, beatific like followers of a strange religion to which I might consider a subscription. I engage the milky-looking honey in a witty banter she seems not to appreciate and I slip her a card at the conclusion of the interview in a none-too-subtle move that lets her know what I am metaphorically wishing I could slip her instead.

If the delectable Miss Davies has any doubts about my latent homosexual tendencies after this then I will be amazed. If it requires her to find me totally repugnant, so be it. First off, I have attracted way more women in my time flaunting my own bastardry than I would care to admit. Second, if I have to burn one pert-breasted, adorably-blushing sweetie to make sure no-one at News Central decides to keep pushing rumors I'm a back-door lock-pick, that's a price I am willing to pay.

It gets dark. The clean-up crews hose down the streets, deterring even the most lethargic and ardent admirers. I'm surprised White Nine doesn't make an appearance until I remember the villainess got away. While I shouldn't be so ready to front the media in the wake of this less-than-stellar accomplishment, there's something mutually magnetic about the cameras so that once they are packed away, I find myself strangely at a loss.

I say strangely because of course I'm meant to be at dinner halfway across Atlantic City. I have the spare clothes in my concealed back-flap, so I bid farewell to the cops packing up the cordons and rocket into the air.

Suffice to say it is some time later before I recall the only loot Eris appeared to take from the bank was a small wooden urn with a metal plaque.

But of course, this is the night everything changes.

Zephyr 2.11 "This Masquerade That Offers No Escape"

LARGE TRACTS OF Queens remains untouched, even if the name itself was consigned to history, along with so much else when the Atlantic City Redevelopment Authority kicked into action. We got a new civic center, pool, library and a 40,000-seat stadium as a result of the rebuild, but the streets are much the same now as when I was growing up. Astoria is the same generic stand-in for any number of urban locations across the country, with its leafy side-streets, corner grocers and many picturesque laundromats-cum-shooting galleries. I shouldn't take for granted the fact Hauser, where the old house stands, is one of the lucky streets with walnuts and elms lining the road – especially now as it gives me great cover from the streetlamps and other prying eyes as I jet down in the dark – with shop-heavy streets beginning just a couple of blocks over on the way to the river and the Hell Gate Bridge (yeah they really call it that, perhaps because of the resident troll, Nigel, who only gets to stay on thanks to my sufferance).

The house is set back from a street lined with darkened parked cars. A warm hospitable glow radiates through the venetians in the front room, and I'm walking up the drive and trying to reach around behind myself to free my hidden clothes and my breath is spilling out of me in plumes and my ribs ache from the long day. When the woman's voice calls my name, Zephyr, I should be more surprised than I am.

I turn and see Frost in the driveway of my childhood home, the air condensing around her like an arctic nimbus in the lamp-light.

"What the fuck are you doing here?"

"I needed to see you," she says, sounding unsure.

"I'm just, you know, doing my rounds. I heard there was a burglary nearby."

"Been a while since you were fighting crime in the old neighborhood, isn't it Joseph –"

"*Hey*," I interrupt. "What the hell is this?"

It's not because I'm feeling sociable that I grab her by her leather-bound wrist and drag her out of view and into the hedges crowding the side windows of my mothers' parlor. The merest glimpse reveals Tessa and Beth inside, all four of them standing around uncomfortably nursing hot drinks. Beth's Beamer sits further up the drive under the shadows of the greenhouse.

Frost has a look on her blue-lipped face like she's just about to make the sort of wisecrack that will tip me into cold-blooded murder, so I give the lady a heroic shake. As icicles bloom across the windowpanes and the violets in the window-box start looking brittle, somewhere upstairs a penny drops and the gentle shake turns into a full-force about-face as I pull the slim villainess in toward me.

"You were at Mys-tech, weren't you?"

"To paraphrase the Oracle: 'but not too clever, hmmm?'"

I shake Frost again and she pulls her arm free only because I allow it. The moonlight is kind to her painfully thin figure, her face framed by long silvery hair somehow Elven rather than freakish. If I had a D&D fetish, she'd be all mine, especially in that corset and boots. Having taken that ride once before (or sure, actually *I* was the ride), I'm not in any hurry to get in the queue again.

"This is serious, lady," I hiss, almost slurring my words in an effort to keep my voice pitched low and even. "What the hell are you doing here?"

"I told you I had to see you."

"Why?" I ask, then snap, "Forget that, tell me how?"

She shrugs like an embarrassed sorority pledge. "Tracer bug?"

"You're kidding me."

"Don't you ever, like, wash that suit?"

"It's leather," I spit back. "Where is it?"

A thousand thoughts tumble kamikaze through my mind as I track back every damned place I've been, all my regular haunts since last Frost took me out for a shakedown.

"Your phone," she says apologetically.

I pull the Enercom gadget free and turn it over. Sure enough the tiny black sticker is barely visible on the underside. I'd peel it off then and there if only dumping the beacon at my childhood home doesn't seem the wisest move.

"So you know everything?" I ask.

"Afraid so, Mister –"

"Hey, enough with that," I snap. "Who else is in on it?"

"Damned if I know, Joe. But if you play ball, we don't have to have things go unpleasantly."

"If you know, the whole world knows," I reply.

"That's not true."

"If they gave this information to a psycho like you, then anybody's game. Fucking hell, Frost. Don't you understand I have a family? Parents?"

"Listen up," she says, the hand on my chest lacking the strength to truly pin me down. "If you want to protect this miserable thing you call a life, you'll start by showing me some respect."

"What, as the mother of my child?"

Her gaze flickers for a moment and straight away I know it didn't take, thank God.

"Christ, that's what you're after," I slowly ope. "You want another bang?"

"Azzurro doesn't know I can access his mainframe. That access could be two-way, if you wanted it, Zephyr. Think about that. Was there any way the Don wasn't gonna try and get some leverage on you while he had you down by rights? No way. But I could erase it all. The whole file."

"You'd still know," I say.

"I can keep a secret."

"For a price."

Frost nods. Over her shoulder I see George checking the oven, Beth glancing at the wristwatch she bought herself on graduation from law school. Tessa stands with Maxine, a proprietary arm around the grand-daughter's shoulders as they look at pictures on the mantel and it occurs to me the old dykes know when they're with one of their own – meaning Tess' dalliance probably isn't a passing infatuation.

"Let's get this over and done with," I reply.

The one hand turns into two, and Frost grabs my face and kisses me quickly, sexy, but a little too much like a small eager dog for my liking. There's something very wrong about how well the villainess knows her way around my costume's upholstery, because she has me bare in her cold-gloved grasp quicker than I can say "shrinkage". Perhaps she senses this is going to be a problem, and presumably going on past experience Frost has a fairly adequate way to rectify it. She goes down on her knees, facilitating a better view of the warm family scene yonder.

You can imagine yes even I find it hard to reconcile standing outside my mothers' house smashing a blowjob from someone who may or may not be a wanted criminal (note to self) in order to save my secret identity. As the villainess lubes me up with her mouth, making small appreciative noises as she does it, I can't help ponder the looming deadline with Twilight that is meant to ameliorate this complex web of issues I've become entangled in by just being me. It is like fifteen years of playing dress-ups has had a cumulative and complicated effect on my life. I'm in Limbo with my wife and very likely facing years of struggle with my headstrong daughter, the ongoing charade with my two mothers, as if having two mothers isn't worrying enough. The present situation just illustrates so well why I need resolution, but I am not sure I am prepared for the severity of the solution. Twilight's own words bade ominously.

"For God's sake, I don't even want any more children," I say, hard not to moan the words.

Frost disengages with a wet noise and stands, leathery fingers cupping my nuts, giving a gentle squeeze I know is rich with metaphor. I get the message. She needn't say anything else, but she can't help herself.

"Having a hard enough time with the one you've got?" Frost strikes a sardonic pose. "Tell me I'm not the one who's got to break it to you that your little girl's queer?"

"Frost, enough. Please."

The witch gives another squeeze and raises her bare inner thigh against my hip. Her mouth rests close to my ear, issuing instructions I am not game to follow until her words become more insistent.

"Spill the seed, if you don't want me spilling the beans."

"That's blackmail, you bitch," I comment unwisely. "Doesn't it trouble you that you can't get me to do this any other way?"

"It's very disappointing," she replies. "I've been thinking about our last time together ever since. You were so good. So big inside me. Hard to believe that a tiny part of you wasn't willing?"

"It's something about the cold. Don't go getting any illusions, woman."

She turns around, her bare nape brushing against me as she fiddles with her costume. We're both peering through the bushes like any average bored suburban couple experimenting in search of an evening's thrills.

"Nice family you've got there," she laughs huskily.

I feel her bare ass against me, a hand guiding me to work like the collared slave I am. The only difference between me and the fellas who died on the pyramids is the amount of lubricant. I glance down long enough to concede I'm not exactly flagging. For a chick who is more likely to be mistaken for the pole than the stripper climbing it, Frost has a comely tail and it's hard not to appreciate the view. I feel my inner caveman taking charge.

"Come on, Zephyr," she moans. "Fill me."

She starts repeating it like a mantra, adding other obscenities that can't help fuelling my arousal, pathetic, pre-programmed male that I am. I am inadvertently caught in what might otherwise be many men's ultimate fantasy, which only underscores just how insane my private life has become. If she'd just ease off on reminding me we'll make "beautiful, powerful children" and that "our children will be the gods of Atlantic City," the going would be a little easier.

I feel the air pressure swell. Somewhere in the aether, a baby thunderstorm brews. By the time I am laboring hard against Frost, her hands against the window-box, the first spats of rain are coming down. I finish inside her and immediately question my own compliance. All I can think is that come midnight, none of this may be relevant, though I think this without any real conviction and that's when I know I have Twilight's answer for sure.

It's a no – which makes this yet another in a long line of bad ideas.

*

FROST DOES HER lady stuff for a few moments. I leave her to it, noting only that as the warm rain comes down in fat droplets they turn into lozenges around the villainess and hit the ground hard, like leakage from a slushy. I have my own confirmation she is not as cold within as she is without, so I don't have to wonder how my prized tadpoles are faring.

While I might have a few problems meeting the villainess's eyes, Frost doesn't have any of the same qualms. In fact her look is downright sultry. For a strange-looking woman she has a way about her. Now her hips see-saw back and forth as she clinches her hard vinyl costume back into place.

"Tell me about the Mys-tech job," I say quietly.

"Why the hell should I?"

"The Mob's hiring lunatics like Infernus, now?"

"He got the job done. Handed you your ass."

"Only because of that madwoman Raveness. You've heard her rep, I'm sure?"

"I think the whole cannibalism thing is probably highly inflated," Frost replies.

I gag at the ease with which she dismisses the slight against her fellow predator. It's a good reminder of the sort of crowd I'm messing with, I tell myself.

"I don't think the Feebs thought so," I say.

"The Feebs? Fuck them. When Don Azzurro wants their opinion, he gives it to 'em."

I don't reply, mulling over whether this is true or not. Hardly a question for my next run-in with Synergy and her prat offsider Vanguard.

"Tell me about Mys-tech," I say again. "What were they after?"

"Retrieving the rightful property of one of the Don's prized employees. Hardly anything illegal at all, actually," she says.

I recall the minidisc provided by Sal Doro and muse that perhaps I should view it some time.

"Nothing else?"

"Nothing you need to know," she says haughtily.

"Those guards, what the hell kind of gear was that?"

"I don't know. I was on sentry duty. But Mys-tech are exploring the, uh, scientific dimensions of the paranormal, if I recall my briefing right."

"You were on guard, huh? Does that mean you saw me coming or did you just tip your pals off?"

Frost comes back in close and strokes my cheek, which I am forced to endure if I want her answer, which for some reason I do. She knows she has me hooked and I resolve that this is the last free ride the bitch is going to blackmail out of me.

"What, set those animals on the father of my children?"

I note she used the plural and grit my teeth as she laughs throatily once more, her signature, and starts to move off.

"I trust you'll do what you said you would with those Mafia files?"

Frost only gives me her best doe-eyed smirk and skips across the rain-slick road to a waiting black Cadillac. I'm relieved to see there is no-one else inside. I mince further up the drive and seek refuge in the greenhouse, changing into civvies and stashing the costume in an old accustomed place, finding some stale cigarettes there and smoking one before it is time to go inside and continue this masquerade that offers no escape.

Zephyr 2.12 "A Hollow Yellow Flame Erupts Into Being"

IF THERE WAS frost on the windows outside, inside the temperature seems even chillier.

George is the real mummy-looking one of my parents, with her barbed-wire grey hair in a neat bun, chopsticks inserted, a loose-necked pullover with a nautical theme to insulate her against the day. Normally one of the kindest women I have ever met, just to be paradoxical, she now looks like I've devoured someone's live young in front of her. Tessa is across the room, in the kitchen, and Beth holds a teacup like she has been caught in the act of secretly sipping her own pee. To complete the scene, Maxine walks in with her spiky, triple-toned ridiculousness of a 'do and slides her arm through George's and eyes me up and down and sniffs the air.

"Hello Joseph. Have you taken up smoking?"

"Bah, that's a disgustin' habit," Georgia brogues. "After the first twenty years it's really not worth it, Joe."

There's no sanctimony like that of the reformed pariah.

"It's just the odd fag," I reply. "Surely that's nothing new in this family."

With silence thus established, I let myself further into the room.

The house is trapped in the 60s, everything a perfect replica or a painstaking preservation. So we cross from faultless Formica and spotless linoleum up a wooden step into a shag-pile living room. There's one of the energy-efficient heaters the powered suit Arsenal devised, mass produced for about a week-and-a-half in the early 90s until the GE lawyers got onto them, the machine sitting snug and lacking ambience in the fireplace. The mantelpiece has pictures mostly of my two mums and their dogs – dogs relegated to the back room for my appearance, my parents knowing how much I hate the damned things, the last few years of high school like a competition between me and them as I wrestled with the irreconcilable conviction my folks were anticipating my departure by replacing me with a more obedient pet. I'd score top marks in chemistry (OK, maybe civics) and the dogs, for managing not to crap all over the laundry for an hour, would get the reward. I ate half a pack of doggy treats once on the suspicion they were getting the better end of the deal.

Suffice to say it wasn't true.

Around the time I got my powers, I became even more secretive than any teenage boy has the right to be. We bumbled along, Maxine, Georgia and I, but even with their high-octane educations they were at a loss how to deal with a teenage boy. The only thing we had in common was a tendency to ogle girls at the Shop-Rite, and society tends to place taboos on a mum and a son cruising together on a Saturday afternoon. Over the years of my adulthood, the situation has only marginally improved.

There's an awkward air not lessened by my appearance. I do the dutiful thing and cross to my wife, trying to take her elbow and ask how her day was. All I get is rugged defiance and a dearth of eye contact.

"What's up?" I whisper with freak loudness.

Elisabeth shrugs me off, uncomfortable with the private moment in what's a sometime gladiatorial space. After a scan of the room to make sure everyone's fitfully engaged, I grab Beth's elbow more serious and hiss, "What?" loudly.

"*They know*," she replies.

"About what?"

"About the girls," Beth says.

"Oh."

I should've guessed, but now I know, I really don't know what to make of it.

"Shit."

It was bound to happen, I want to explain, but the sterile rictus of Beth's face brooks no comment.

I turn and step into a stormfront. Max and George descend like a linguistic wrestling act so that Beth and I are on the ropes in an instant. I've never been caught in a conversation so terrifying I want to pee myself, but now I'd do almost anything to get out of this. They want to spring for the bill for Greenwood Alternative. Tessa's sexuality is an expression of her genetic inheritance. We shouldn't fight it, or make her feel ashamed. The two girls should be allowed to be together and sort it out themselves. Let the grandparents be the ambassadors for the family and smooth things over with Astrid's folks.

They only take pause long enough for deep breaths and that's when I know I should be really afraid as their narrowed eyes turn on Elisabeth and they beg – without a trace of humility, empathy or concern – for Beth not to lock them out of Tessa's life or discredit their viewpoints just because they happen to share the same orientation.

"Our being queer doesn't demerit our perspective," as Maxine puts it.

"We know you've never been comfortable with our lifestyle, but now those chickens are comin' home to roost," George says, even less clement.

Beth looks like she's just taken a mild psychoactive. I'm reeling. There's something in the series of announcements that must be like what it's like to have policemen knock on your door following a fatal car crash, only no-one's died, there's no cops, and there's no one to blame except to shoot the messenger. And this is just what Beth does.

I stagger into the kitchen like a refugee from the Somme and bust Tessa standing tucked into the corner between the retro stove and the kitchen bin, hands to her face, nails digging without punishment into her youthful cheeks.

"Are you alright?" I ask.

She nods, half says something. I don't know what.

"You told them?"

"They knew, dad," she replies. "They know everything."

"Everything?"

I blink, because we've turned a page and no-one told me we'd switched books. There's a brief flashback, second grade, I think, me desperately leafing through a book on cavemen trying to catch up to where it mentions the agrarian revolution.

Tessa nods *sans* hope and you can't quite describe her gesture as rolling her eyes. It's more like they fall away, indicative of absent tears, the expression rare as a flightless bird and more precious.

"What do you mean?" I ask.

The question hangs in the air like a dropped vase, just hovering for a moment before the inevitable pandemonium.

"Oh Jesus, dad. Come on. Everyone's known for years."

The shouting match just behind me strikes fever pitch and I turn, expecting to intervene in a two-on-one. Instead, Georgia watches me from within the cyclonic eye of that tumult with a hand to her greying coiffure. She just nods.

"I'm not sure I know what you're talking about," I say again eventually to Tess.

I try to laugh to keep it light.

"Dad, it's OK," my little darling says. "You're *Zephyr*."

She elbows her tears away and comes out from under the alcove, no taller than my shoulder and with strands of her rich coppery hair caught in the fabric of her sweater, the interstices of the woolen pattern rendered as tiny sheep, I strangely notice in the still of the moment. I'm staring at the sheep, falling right into them, as a breeze ruffles through the kitchen and blows open some notes from one of the manila folders perched on the green tile ledge above the oven-filled antique fireplace.

I glance around for the open window, but there's none.

"It's OK, dad," Tessa says again.

I check her face and there's a brave smile. The other voices have stopped. Beth judders into the room and comes to a complete halt as the papers arrayed across the floor continue in a dance with a life of their own, swirling into a papery dust devil that scoots around and past each of us until it skirts the back door, swans across the face of the fridge and scatters in a hundred sheets above and around my daughter. The papers form a living fountain. Tessa has her hands splayed and her hair's dancing like the singer of an 80s hard pop band. A weird glow lights her face I know only from newsreel footage of my own exultations.

"Shit."

"Joseph, what's this?" Beth demands.

I'm speechless. The papers divest themselves of motion and fall as if from an upper floor window. Tessa gives a retching sob, although she appears to grin, and George passes me in her haste to get alongside the girl and clinch her, arm around the shoulder.

"That's very brave of you, love, coming out like that," she says.

Tessa beams through the emotions.

"I couldn't've done it without you, grandma."

Beth cocks her head like something feline, animatronic.

"You . . . you can do this too?" She looks at Georgia aghast. "And you told *her*?"

"It's OK, mom."

Tessa looks up into George's slightly elevated face, a clear inquiry inscribed thereupon. The older woman curtly nods, fluorescent light catching off her European frames.

"It's OK, mom," Tessa says again. "It's all in the family."

I'm horrified myself, though for different reasons.

"What are you saying?" I hiss.

George has many smiles. Most I have seen many times. But it's not often I've seen the one she reserves for the revelation of wicked secrets. Still with one woolly sleeve around my daughter's shoulders, my birth mother opens her other palm and her fingers splay open like a time-lapse flower in decline. There's a spark and suddenly a hollow yellow flame erupts into being.

"I'm sorry, Joseph. For a long time I had to keep it secret. We were hiding."

And she smiles – and there's that look again.

"You would have known me as *Catchfire*."

I put my fist to my face and consider stuffing it into my mouth. Screw the confessions of a teenage chick-licker. My mother was the hottest superheroine of the 1970s.

*

I WOULD BE lying if I said some time later we had all calmed down. Beth has to be sedated, eagerly sucking down three valium when Maxine offers. Moments previous they were trading verbal blows as fierce as me and Gigantor going for it. Now all Beth can do is find the hard wooden rest of a padded armchair and watch the scene in the kitchen like a traffic accident through the windows of a café.

I remove my jacket and simply fling it behind the door without any pretense to attention and hold up my hands.

"OK, let's back it up a pace here." I swallow with difficulty and do a quick headcount. "Are you telling me you two always knew I was Zephyr?"

Maxine clucks. "Oh, sorry dear."

Georgia only gives a solemn nod. I don't feel nearly lionized enough, nor groveled to, for me to just shrug off this earth-shattering announcement. I stare somewhere between the small blaze that has only just extinguished itself on my mother's hand and the triumphant, I-can't-believe-I've-done-it furrow of my daughter's brow.

"Oh for God's sake, Joseph," Elisabeth snaps. "This isn't about you."

"For once, I have to agree," Maxine says.

"Well hey, maybe you can just shrug off the twenty years we've been keeping it secret, but for me, it's a lot to adjust to," I say.

"If you think it was a long secret for you, you know nothing of what your mother's been through," Max says.

"No, I don't know nothing, *anything*," I growl, "because nobody ever fucking *told* me about it, did they?"

Because I finally can, I let the sparks leap off me. They find the closest metal points to rattle and George jolts back, exclamation in her eyes if nowhere else, the fear just strongly enough etched that I realize maybe it's not the brightest idea to start cutting loose around my loved ones. Besides, my mum might kick my ass.

"You were young, Joe," George says after a moment. "And it was complicated."

"What isn't? You try keeping your identity secret from your parents for twenty years while being one of the country's better-known bloody . . . whatever I am."

"We've always been very proud of you," Max says weakly.

"Don't you understand, this is why we never hounded you about college?" her partner in crime adds.

I shake my head, do a quick inventory of the room. The back door is open now and Tessa's gone through it, followed by her mother.

"And you knew about her?" I ask, thumb in the indicative.

"Your daughter might take after you, Joseph, but she's no fool. D'you not think if she had an inkling she might be queer that a word with her *lesbian grandmothers* might help?"

"Well fuck."

"And stop that swearing in the house," George adds.

I look around. Like a hard drive restoring after a power-out, slowly my brain fills with a catalogue of times and places where I was forced into ridiculous, Seinfeld-esque situations to preserve my precious secret. Now I find it was all for naught. That they knew makes me a laughing stock. As I eye the night-filled space of the open door, I can't believe I have to add my daughter to the lengthening list of those not fooled by daddy's tiresome charade. If anything could belittle my inexplicably limited sense of achievements in this life, this takes the cake.

"And what's the deal with Catchfire?" I ask. "You're, like, American History 101, mom."

"It's complicated."

"We'll tell you about it another time," Maxine adds. "There's things now we'll have to talk about. Including your father."

I groan. Those three words turn my bowels to water, and while often enough I've daydreamed I might like a better explanation for my freak parentage than a family friend who was a sperm donor and later grew apart from them, now I cling to that cover story like a safety blanket clutched in the tight little guy fists of a child who's just wet the bed.

"For fuck's sake," is the best pronouncement I can make.

"Enough of that, Joe," Maxine scolds.

She clucks again and, truly chicken-like, indicates the doorway with a nudge of her head.

"Now's not the time. Your daughter needs you. It's like your wife said: this is about *her* now."

Before I can ask anything about why it's not allowed to be about me, even if for just a few seconds, it really does become about Tessa as Elisabeth appears breathless at the door.

"It's Tessa," she says shortly. "She's gone. She can fly."

Georgia lowers her serious gaze my way and nods her head once. If there's a flicker of a flash in her eye, I've probably imagined it.

"You're the flyer," she says. "Better get after her."

I swear again, inwardly, curbed by my Irish mum's stern face. I have the mask in my back pocket, but the rest of the gear's hidden in the garden shed. If she's a flyer anywhere near my own capacity, inside of twenty seconds and she could be anywhere. With a flagrancy that would be exhilarating if it were for any other reason than to settle a domestic, I jog through the doorway and spring into the air.

Above, the night sky awaits.

Zephyr 2.13 "The Delegated Truth-Breaker"

THE INKY GLOOM is counter-point to my thoughts. Aside from glancing left and right once I've hit the thousand yard-high mark, I can't see a single sign of Tessa. I'm as likely to catch a glimpse of her up here now as I am to win a Grammy. I can tell you I've contemplated the latter a lot more than the former in my life. I, we, they, all of us, simply didn't see this situation coming. This is what I tell myself, lacking conviction even as I flip and swoop and swirl over the river, suspicion like a cowpat sorbet in the back of my throat.

At first I think my mood is worsening the weather. There's a build-up to the east. It's only when I catch the first cloud-muffled flash that I am sure I'm no longer hallucinating. And as I've been at pains to point out on numerous occasions throughout my life and in this narrative, my air-bending powers don't extend to weather control, just the odd creative input on whatever's brewing. I can conjure a rainstorm, but one thing that always remains the same is that I'm stuck at ground zero when it strikes. This little baby brewing in the direction of my destiny has got to have another source. And while I can't put it into words for you, dear reader, or whatever the term was Stan Lee used to say before the Kirlians got him, my internal barometer tells me the air's all wrong. There's nothing natural about the astral whippoorwill fluttering a thousand wings out over the bay, and on a hunch I power in that direction hoping my little girl's trumped her daddy and I'm not walking in on something completely unrelated. If I was Spider-Man, this would all be some malevolent plan by Doc Ock. In real life, it's more likely I'm going to have to admit to my daughter that I'm no closer than she is to knowing the meaning of life or any other tricky metaphysical answers.

As I trash the ionosphere, my mind drifts on gossamer wings toward the various threads of my life that seem to be pulling me in separate directions, if not apart on this cool and blustery night. It's just a few hours till my anointed appointment with arch-magus Twilight and my growling stomach reminds me we just skipped the wholesome family dinner for coffee and a punch-up. Like I've said elsewhere, burning the juice without enough fuel is a bad move for me, and I already feel stretched without all the fancy metaphors to describe my inner distress. Turmoil, frustration, angst – call it what you will, it seems like with so many things in life there is one day or one evening out of the ordinary that comes along every so often, and life-changing and significant events are clustered around them in statistical disarray as if drawn to the *zeitgeist* moment like lightning to a metal rod.

Speaking of which, again comes the flash from the purple thunderhead, vibrant with its pulsing electrical heart against the deeper gloom.

Now my daughter is conducting the orchestra. Is that metaphor too trite? While I momentarily push away the concern, forged over a career nearly two decades long, for the public exposure of her true identity, I'm able to marvel at the sight of my darling girl in full-blown euphoric catharsis suspended within the thunder's heart. But I can only appreciate the imagery of wind-lashed hair and blazing barometric energies for so long. I swing in and dissolve the climactic scene, Tessa floating for all the world to see a mile up in the sky as I grab her by the upper arm.

"Tessa, you can't expose yourself like this," I growl.

The rain breaks around us. For one ungodly moment we are lit by another arc that reverberates across the city, residents undoubtedly scratching their heads at the unexpected change in the weather, and Tessa is a stranger, face prematurely adult, lips full, sensuous and surprised.

"Can't you see?" she yells. "This is one of the only times I'm really able to be *me*."

I shake my head. There's water in my ears.

"That's not my worry, honey. Out like this, you're vulnerable."

"I just want to be *free*, dad."

"Tessa, I have *enemies*. Don't you understand?"

In the movie of this moment I hope I am played by Harrison Ford, though I don't know what they can do about him being such an old guy. Tessa resembles a young, tawny-haired Beverly d'Angelo, though the association this has with the National Lampoon movies is not something I really want to promote so I'll say Jennifer Garner minus a few inches and without the starvation diet.

I realize I am retreating into this cynical/remote/childish mode because the impending confrontation is more than I can really stand. One thing is for sure, though: whatever Twilight has on offer, I'm firm now. I've got too much going on to go running away. Certainly this is without knowing Elisabeth will file for divorce in fourteen hours, throwing the private life I bemoaned so wantonly into a repute so severe I'll eventually wonder what the fuck I was ever complaining about in the first place. Nonetheless, as events pan out and prove to show, in my heart I feel this is the right choice. This one illuminating moment with Tessa is like a lifetime of life lessons and I am desperate not to fail this spot test.

I take her wrist.

"I'm happy for you," I say with rain clattering against my chest and into my mouth. "I didn't think that was something I would ever say, seeing you up here with me, and you know, considering everything else that's happened this week . . . but I am."

"It's not about Astrid, dad," Tessa says.

Her hand goes to my shoulder. I'm aware we are slowly turning about on some centrifugal vector caused by the dissipating weather system.

"It's me. Who I am. And who we are. I'm Zephyr's daughter. I think I've always known that."

"For real?"

She blushes invisibly and nods and laughs and wet hair plasters itself across her face and tickles mine.

"Ever since I first watched cartoons. I thought Zephyr was from the television, come to life. I don't know why I knew I couldn't tell. For years, it was like a dream. Then there were things you said, this hopeless thing you call your attempt at a normal life, and things mom would always say. . . ."

"She knew you knew?"

"I think so. We never . . . talked. Much. About anything."

She looks away, eyes downwind.

"You know how it is."

"Come home with me now, honey," I say. "There's just one more thing I've got to do tonight and then tomorrow, now, it'll be a beautiful day. We can talk until the well runs dry. You know? But now, if a camera catches you, or some passing mask, we're both in danger."

"Alright," she says and nods. "But one thing?"

"Name it."

"You call me *Windsong*."

Tessa laughs, spiraling on the spot as she gathers momentum and then shoots like a pellet from the world's biggest spud gun over and across the rain-dappled towers below us. I check my mask is in place and survey the ground before gently accelerating behind her, my dearest target.

*

I'M REDISCOVERING MYSELF as a hero.

This is the thought that occurs to me as I narrowly avoid crash-landing behind my childhood home on confirmation my daughter Tessa did as instructed and has got herself inside.

Rediscovering my inner hero. It sounds like something Dr Phil might say if he ever did a show specializing in therapy for burn-out masks.

It takes a moment for the lemonade bubbles of my memory to press themselves through the cerebral cortex and then I remember it actually *was* something from a Dr Phil special – so not my over-fertile imagination after all.

Heroes Who Removed Their Masks, I think it was called. I remember now, watching it with Red Monolith, Mastodon and the Evolutionary, wherever he is these days, passing the crack pipe between us and bemoaning the lack of effects. If I recall correctly, the show was notable for an appearance by septuagenarian 1960s badass the Tungsten Terror. It was a sobering moment for us all watching that depleted old chrome-dome motherfucker blubbering into the equally bald shrink's Hugo Boss shoulder-pads and wishing his mother had seen the work he did with disaffected youth in Chicago before the cancer took her.

Oh boy. Depression. Settling in.

As I smoke another contraband cigarette, ankles crossed as I lean against the gardenias in the greenhouse, I'm reflecting yet again on why I do this. The fact I can do a four-second mile and flick lightning from my palms is a pretty compelling reason, and for years, that was enough for me. I have been tempted by the Devil's offer (that should read *Twilight*), mysterious as it may have been, to shed my second life like a bad taste snakeskin and morph into a purer, less complicated form of myself. A new Zephyr for a new life – though I remain uncomfortably vague about what this really means except Twilight's eldritch forces are involved. The news my daughter has not only inherited my family's predilection for eating pussy, but can whip up a mean-ass thunderstorm to boot should give me pause, throwing a celestial spanner into the works somehow and letting me either reconfirm my commitment to disappointing Twilight in about an hour's time, or give this hanging thread dilemma another round of crystalline introspection.

Instead, I'm a blank. The most significant thought I can conjure is that even stale cigarette smoke is pretty good when you need five minutes to think and work on taking that leak that the adrenaline sucked back up into your bladder about an hour before. My stomach rumbles. I'm hungry and all that subliminal advertising and enculturation is starting to have the desired effect as I unconsciously plot routes to Twilight's manse that take in fried chicken outlets. And there's an uncomfortable pressure somewhere above my perineum, if men have those, me being more familiar with it only because of the recommended massage for my wife I dutifully gave her during "our" pregnancy with Tessa, about a million years ago, back when I was a devoted twenty-year-old husband and I was yet to ever sink my dick into any other person on Earth but my dear Beth.

Speaking of the devil, in the cooling night air I watch the porch light flare behind the nimbus of my wife's wild hair as she steps out the back door and casts around for privacy, finding only its surrogate as she remains unknowingly surveilled extracting a cigarette from the sleeve of her crofter's pullover as she wends her way into my parents' copious back yard with its ridiculously compact exotic jungle of hand-reared, multi-grafted plants. I guess back when Max realized she was shacked up with a reformed and on-the-run superhero, she channeled a lot of that rage into her exquisite shrubberies.

Yeah OK, so I'm taking the piss – literally, as well as . . . you know.

The temperature has dropped significantly, though I'm confident Frost has well and truly quit the scene. Pity for her. A hell of a night for updating your Zephyr dossier, with all these family revelations flying thick and fast.

My wife resembles an angel in the subtle light, though the languid motions of her cigarette would be familiar to doormen and freezing office workers the world over, a series of quick jabs and snatched drags, just enough to fend off the nicotine monster before the inviting warmth of inside calls. There's only a small patch of open ground in the yard otherwise dominated by the tiered garden, the greenhouse, the back neighbor's enormous Irish strawberry that looms over all, and a small disused garage that probably contains Catchfire's secret laboratory or her jet-powered motorcycle or whatever kitsch baggage remains from the groovy heyday of afro-clad crime-fighters and kitten-costumed kid-friendly crims. Standing in front of the dilapidated green doors, if it weren't for the darkness, Elisabeth might pass for an overenthusiastic model come hours too early to a photo shoot for some crossover gardening/high fashion/metropolitan living mage. Instead, she looks tired and harassed despite the years being kind, if that's not too sexist and fucked for me to say about a 34-year-old woman who also happens to be my wife, keeping in mind I have strayed about fifteen times in the past five years if you include the TV reporters, who I'm still not really sure should count.

I step from the greenhouse with a deliberate throat-clearing, jettisoning the butt into the gently burbling frog pool. To that truculent hiss I add a wry smile, arms folded as I step, masked still, across the crunchy gravel to where Beth's grappling with her addiction.

"I'm surprised you didn't stay hiding in there," she greets me.

"Why would I do that?"

I have a subtle grin, encouraging relaxation she has the perfect right to ignore.

"I'm not sure it's your night, Joe."

"It's been a hell of a night. I know that much," I say.

"For real," Beth says, reviving a popular aphorism from our old high school days, though I think she does so without any self-awareness, no joke-within-a-joke, no attempt to break down barriers. She looks worried, and I eventually realize, scared.

"Are you . . . OK?"

Beth looks at me like maybe it seems an unusual thing to ask, and it strikes me that way as well, though that feeling just underscores my own sense of failure as a husband that it should come to pass that the simple act of asking after my wife's welfare seems so strange. Nonetheless, the awkwardness lends a genuine concern that not even Beth can shrug off.

"Not really, Joe. Not really."

"It all comes as quite a shock," I say. "For me, I mean. And I'm the one with powers. I can't imagine how you're feeling."

Elisabeth starts to reply, but she halts, lips in a grimace as she shakes her head of unpleasant thoughts like a cheap vodka aftertaste.

"What?"

"No," she says. "It's too soon."

"Too soon for what?"

"Joseph, please. Just this once." She flicks her gaze to me and finishes her cigarette. "Just this once let it go, please. I'm tired. You're right that this has all been too much."

"Going home?"

"Yes."

"Taking Tessa with you?"

Beth sighs and surrenders to her own lack of care, dropping the cigarette butt and grinding it into the designer gravel an admission of so much about her place in the world, our family, her own hopelessness. Perhaps that sounds melodramatic, but consider yourself in the shoes of a woman grappling with a lousy husband, oddball in-laws, a gay daughter who also turns out to be a freak likely to follow her father into a closeted public lifestyle that could bring ruin on the family at any moment if not murder at the hands of some costumed nut-job. Add a hellish career of her own. Stir gently. No wonder she's freaked out.

"I take it you won't be joining us?"

"Well. . . ."

"Christ, Joe. It's going to be hard enough to get Tessa in the car as it is."

"Maybe in future she can fly. . . ?"

"Joseph, don't tell me you endorse this."

"Endorse . . . this?"

"*Windsong.*"

She says the name like her mouth has suddenly become a cat's ass, required to do something unpleasant and vaguely shameful.

"Hmmm yeah, she said that to me too."

I ponder for a moment. Beth watches me at work, a look only somewhat removed from the wonder that eighteenth century people had while watching the first clockwork automaton. Once the gears have moved sufficiently, I join the dots and say as much. Elisabeth only nods gravely.

"I don't want her following me into this lunacy," I say. "Not in this business. There's plenty of . . . *masks* in public life, people with abilities, who aren't punching bags like I am. Hey, if I could sing, this whole thing would've turned down another road, right?"

I grin and gesture as if to trigger what few memories we share of the time I was approached to do a pop album. One of the many times I should be grateful my wife talked me back from the edge. She was the only one who'd heard me in the shower, after all.

"I somehow don't think Tessa wants to be the next Queen Latifah," Beth replies.

"She could do worse."

"Can she sing?"

I blink. "Have you ever heard our daughter sing? Like, in her whole life?"

At some point I failed to notice Beth is crying.

"She used to sing in her stroller," she says mournfully. "Remember? I would go to the park or to get milk . . . Old women would smile at me and say, 'You must be doing something right. Listen to her sing'."

Beth sighs like a gunshot victim, leaning back and accepting death.

"She was like a little bird. So happy."

She caves in, face in the mask of her hands, but when I go to give my husbandly comfort, she pushes me back double-handed, face, despite the weak light, filled with red rage like some Kabuki performer after a few tokes of crack. Until I remind myself I can dodge small arms fire, I'm genuinely afraid. After the surprise of the realization has cooled, I'm still upset, should perhaps remain afraid, wondering what it means when a woman at her weakest won't let me near her.

Tomorrow I will find out.

*

THERE'S ONE PIECE of unfinished business I have to deal with before I can leave. After watching the red tail lights recede, my red-eyed Beth chauffeuring a tearful Tessa back across the borough, I head back into the house.

"So how about that dinner?" I grin, rubbing my hands together.

"Joseph, take off that mask while you're inside the house," George tells me.

"Jesus, mum," I remark. "Do you think that's wise?"

"You never did get used to George's sense of humor," Max warns me, walking in with the demeanor of a woman who has just throttled a pet to death in the next room.

An aura of displeasure mars her smooth round dykey face and I realize she's removed her eyeglasses. She probably isn't looking forward to what's coming next. She's not the only one.

I sigh and reflect, mostly to myself, "Christ, and you wonder why I don't visit more often."

"It's not every day you learn your daughter has super-powers," Maxine says.

"I've known about the gay thing for a while," I lie, shrugging. "It's no big deal by me."

"I should hope not," Max says.

I should've remembered there's no brownie points there. Extreme tolerance was *de rigueur* in our house growing up. People who discriminated against gays or even muties were cunts who should be shot or put into camps, as far as I recall.

George is way too busy making a round of coffees. She looks decidedly uncomfortable and I don't think it's the ridiculous Germaine Greer effect of her oversized sweater and old farmer's wife hairstyle. Max sits at the round kitchen table like a self-conscious homily to the bygone era of happy families. It never occurred to me till now to wonder if in all her badass cultural critiques she ever turned that high-powered torch on her own life and wondered what drive compels her to valorize the look – at least the look – of a time in our history that must have suppressed so much individual creativity, not to mention all the unhappy Jews, queers and niggers. Funny, ironic even, to end up fetishizing the very epoch that repressed you. It was when the first mutants started appearing, lynched side-by-side with the black folks down south.

"So, mom," I shrug, chortle, grin, wince and tightly sigh. "How about *your* super-powers, huh?"

There's silence, apart from the tinkling of the teaspoon.

"You were Catchfire, huh?" I continue. "What happened there? If I know my history, you just kinda disappeared all of a sudden one day, right?"

George turns around. She has the good manners to have a tear in her eye at least, not that she looks any more likely to start talking. Instead, she crosses the room and places her wife's coffee mug in front of her, the one with Garfield holding a copy of Nietzsche's *Ecce Homo*. Then she stands behind her man, so to speak, hands on the shoulders of Max's fashionably postmodern garment, fingers sinking in to the pads.

Silence.

"I think you guys were going to tell me something about my dad?"

I fire off the prompt with all the mendacious swagger of the teenager I once was, only to find in the twenty-odd years since I was in short pants I've developed at least the vestiges of mild empathy for my two mothers. The slow-motion shattering of George's pottery visage is like a knife to my chest. Maxine reaches around and clasps her hand atop her lover's. I'm surprised when it is she who speaks.

"It wasn't an easy series of choices, Joseph. It's late now. I think we should set a time to discuss this in greater detail."

"But not now," I say in monotone.

"No," Max replies. "You keep a secret for half your life, you should take pause before you let it all out."

"At least you admit your . . . guilt," I say, croaking at the end because I can't find a better word before my tongue demands the sentence's end.

"We've nothing to be guilty about, Joseph," Max says. "If your father knew you existed, he wouldn't stop until you were dead."

My eyes crinkle at this announcement, which seems completely nonsensical until I slowly come to understand that neither of them is joking.

"You're kidding me," I softly laugh. "Why? Who is he?"

Max looks up at George and she slowly nods, eyes closing like she's approving an execution. My own eyes remain locked on Max, the delegated truth-breaker in this kitchen sink drama.

"J-John Lennon," she says, looking swiftly away.

"John Lennon," George says quietly. "The Doomsday Man."

Zephyr 2.14 (Coda)

"YOU KNEW THE Beatles?"

It's a sucky thing to say, but hell, this is the *Beatles* we're talking about – the first team of supers who weren't just a government propaganda exercise or a way to sell bonds for the war effort. It didn't matter they were Brits. Or Beatniks. Before mutants started appearing in the 60s or really the 70s, and giving masks a bad name, the Beatles were the guys many of us grew up idolizing whether we were secret parahumans or just ordinary schmucks. John, George, Ringo and Paul – they were too badass to have the sorts of costume names now so synonymous with modern day heroes and their lucrative brand endorsements. Sure, sometimes we knew them as Preacher, Saint George, Wolfman and the Visionary, but they were interchangeable, more like hats they could take on and off, like the made-up names of the people Paul and John used to talk about in their regular Global Address. Records of those counter-cultural monologues used to sell like wildfire, like pop albums even, and characters like Eleanor Rigby and Sergeant Pepper came to serve as stand-ins for a whole generation tackling social and political issues their parents never had even the time and luxury to contemplate. It was a changing world. The transformations my mother went through were proof of that.

And many would say the Beatles were never the same after they went to India, which was followed closely by the death of the Wolfman. It was only later John became known as the Doomsday Man. The biggest change of all. Sure, it's a suck-ass name, but it was the 80s, and a good while after my mother Catchfire had left the crime-fighting scene.

"Are you telling me . . . John Lennon is my dad?"

Their hard, nervous faces soften at the one moment of amazement and wonder to be gained from this otherwise bleak story. I understand there's more to be told and perhaps I am not likely to hear the rest of it any time soon, but for fuck's sake, *John Lennon is my father*?

"He's . . . perhaps not everything you'd expect."

"Well sure, he went to jail for like, fucking genocide or something," I remark. "But isn't he dead?"

"No," George says and sounds sad to be saying it.

"He did ten years, and . . . well, we never really understood how, the authorities declared he'd reformed and they let him go in 1994," Max relates. "We've been keeping under the radar ever since, though how you do that from one of the world's most powerful minds, as I'm sure you can imagine, Joseph, that's not an easy task."

"No," I say, all thoughtful-like, because suddenly here we are, my moms and me almost talking shop. And I have to reflect on all my own adventures in the public eye, my famous battles against Crescendo and Think-Tank and the Ill-Centurion and even Mentor, tucked away in the catacombs of Manhattan, and of course they must have known about each and every one.

Bloody hell.

"And you think he would try to kill me?" I ask sincerely. "Why?"

The graven looks on these two faces tells me they're silently hoping I'll let the matter drop for this evening, giving them the chance to regroup and get their story straight before they let me in on the rest of the deal. I can already clue together that the end of Catchfire's cat-suited career coincided with the time the Beatles came back from India and the failed Summer Rebellion of 1972, Ringo's death at the hands of the original Protector and the official disbanding of the team. It's not a big part of history I ever paid much attention to, except I know when John went off on his Messiah trip and grew his hair and beard long, he dropped out of sight somewhere, back in India, the south of France? I have no idea.

Clearly, George and Maxine not only think he's still alive, they *know* something – and it's tied in to the intense secrecy around George's own powers, and serious enough they were willing to lie to me my whole life and let me prance around old New York dressed like some leather fruitcake none the wiser.

So I tell it like it is.

"Can't say I'm very happy about this. I'll leave you two to get your story together and maybe you can call me when you've got a version of the truth you're actually willing to share with me."

Just to add hubris to insult, I throw one of my Zephyr cards on the table complete with the Enercom phone number.

"What about Tessa and Beth. . . ?" Maxine begins, standing up from the table fast enough to make the antique chair squeal.

"What about them?" I snap. "They'll be fine."

"Won't you tell us if there are any more . . . problems, between Tess and her mother?" George asks.

"Hey, you get to be ringside to my life when you come clean about yours."

It's too hard to resist another patented badass scowl, and electricity pours down my arms to my hand as I snap about, probably more Zoolander than Zephyr as I stalk out the door.

Outside, there has been a gentle rain, perhaps Tessa's weather irruption clearing out. Before either of the old women can chase me through the door, if they are even gonna, I do the crouch thing and rocket skywards, accelerating to a fair height and hitting Mach far above the safe level for the skadillions of houses below. Like a new-fangled missile, I veer abruptly for sweet, non-existent Hoboken and then change tack again, passing over the restored heritage precinct of Newport only a handful of minutes later.

I bounce erratically through mild turbulence, my jaw set, a harder, less ignorant man than I was before, but no less fallible. *Human, all too human*, as the coffee mug says.

Zephyr 3.1 "A Sense Of The Cosmic Inevitable"
I BUZZ AN incoming airship as I flit like a human spark across the short stretch of the Atlantic between the New Hampshire coast and Twilight's private island. The sea is remarkably calm, emphatically alien in its darkness, the hidden depths, things that don't like us lurking there and waiting for their next meal. The whole thing gives me the shivers. Sixty-eight million fricking light globes or whatever and the ocean still chills me to the core. I fancy I must've been a whaler in a past life, coming to a messy end bloated and wrapped in kelp and washed ashore somewhere in Scandinavia just like any other piece of driftwood or Atlantic detritus.

At least someone is awake on Fantasy Island, if not the big guy himself. A spotlight plays across my path and eventually I get the drift it is guiding me to the helipad, as if that were necessary, a big black sexy-looking motherfucker parked like a slumbering Transformer on the flight deck. Yeah, I know they probably don't call them that, but hell, you know I mean where the choppers go sleepy bye-byes.

Is Twilight going to be mad at me? And exactly what would that entail? With him, it's always been a Devil-may-care, Lost Boys kind of one-upmanship urging me to the edge. Many a time I've lead the race, but it's easy to have that sort of devilish attitude when you're up to your armpits in black-as-black sorcery. I'm just a guy from Queens who can throw cars and lightning bolts. For all I know, the thunderbolt that brought me down at the windfarm was also responsible for the semi-permanent hard-on that has made normalcy so hard this last decade. Twilight is a whole other deal.

We're at the northern end of Atlantic City here. The woodlands of Maine beckon yonder. I know Twilight mentioned he owned property up there once. Probably a whole town for all I know. The recycled city that engulfs Boston, DC and Philadelphia in its panoptic wake fritters itself away at the edges, at least up here, going from George Jetson territory one moment to shanty towns and drive-by burger joints amid post-industrial and semi-rural towns peopled like Middle Eastern or should that be Middle Ages warzones, the denizens huddling inside from the lights and the loud noises.

Twilight certainly has the right idea, provided you've got a cool half-billion to back it up. And hey, if your daddy is the head of the most powerful ethnic crime syndicate in America, so what, even if he is dead? To his credit, it was Twilight himself who tried to splash cold water on any fancy feelings I might be harboring, reminding me he's the *anti-hero*. What does it mean, for someone to position themselves like that, apart from they've probably read more post-grad papers on comic books than the comics themselves?

I plop to the ground beside the glistening dew-covered ordnance and walk smoothly into the darkness between the helipad and the main house. Twilight's sanctum, no longer divided by a hellish discus of necrotic energy, is tastefully up-lit by halogens concealed in the grass throwing a green tone across the stone exterior. But it is the double doors to the side of the mansion that open, light within twinkling with promises of esoteric conversation and export-grade brandy. A solitary besuited guard stands at the door, seemingly unarmed, however falsely, and another with an Uzi stands inside. By the time I'm thirty feet away they've both disappeared.

Twilight fills the doorframe, robe hanging open to reveal him mostly naked, Adonisian and corrupt in the knowledge of his own charisma. An insouciant smile plays across his lips, his lantern jaw. I am not smitten for the guy. I hope we have established that. Yet I remain somehow fascinated by his power, the incandescence of his soul, despite how much of it he claims to have bartered away or that he keeps in a jar by his bed or whatever that old quip was. More at question than anything else is why it is that I still consider him a friend and a colleague and supporter – and more than that, why he continues to not only tolerate me, but allege I, with all my faults and human frailty, am a worthy ally? He lifts me up at the same time his very being defines me in terms of my lack, my failure by just being myself compared to him.

"Zephyr," the big man drawls. It's a complete put-on, just like George Bush. "I wasn't sure you were coming."

"Dust off your snifters, Twilight-me-lad," I reply, jaunty despite the hour and the starvation-withered constitution I will soon have cause to decry. "I'm here to celebrate."

The dark angel darling of the occult world draws aside to let me into the rear lounge. Yes, yes, there's all that "going into Twilight's rear" again, I know. God damn the pretenses of literary fiction. But seriously, you've got to wonder about a guy who keeps an eighteen-bedroom mansion, but never lets anyone past the front room. The lounge is set up expressly to meet all his entertaining needs. There's even a bathroom through a door between the nearest floor-to-ceiling bookcases.

"What's going on, big guy?" Twilight asks.

The epithet's a bit too *little buddy* for me, but maybe that's my own Twilight-centric inferiority complex getting the upper hand.

"I'm celebrating my daughter," I say.

"I didn't know you had kids."

"Don't ask and I won't tell, you know how it is."

"So what's she done?"

"Keeping it in the family. I found out today my little girl has powers all her own."

I'm grinning. God knows why.

I add, "She's helped me remember who I am. Do you remember that Dr Phil special on retired masks?"

"Masks?" Twilight blinks. "Who calls us that?"

"Everybody," I reply quickly.

"Hmmm, well you're ringing a bell."

"Reconnecting to your inner hero?"

Twilight makes a face and drops heavily into one of the leather-upholstered chairs. The air smells of brandy and hashish and pussy. He narrows drug-slackened lids.

"What are you telling me?"

I'm about to open up on the whole deal when a splinter of red light catches my attention and I note the medallion Twilight used on the Insect King is sitting in a little cradle on a mahogany pedestal, just a tiny something to brighten up the room perhaps, an unintentional conversation piece as one might do with any ensorcelled cross-dimensional portal.

"Is that the, uh, thing you used on . . . on Creeping Death?"

"Creeping Death?" Twilight doesn't catch what I'm on about until he languidly twists on the divan and shoots a look over his shoulder. "Oh fuck, the bug guy. Yeah."

"Hmmm," I reply, less a word than a subliminal vocalization as I mount the carpeted split-deck step and approach the little dais. "I'm surprised it's just . . . sitting around here. Wouldn't you normally keep this in your sanctum?"

Twilight, standing now, shrugs. He glances at his wrist and reacts for all the world like there's really a watch there.

"It's getting late. I thought we were here to discuss your situation?"

"Hey if it's late, that's because you set the time." I smile to show him I am not trying to yank his chain, though we both know I am talking to him like I've grown a spine for a change.

"Well, if you'd rather discuss Hariss as-Sama, you can, if you like?"

"Is that the guy who wrote *Silence of the Lambs*?"

"No, that's the guy who tried to ingest my psyche, but failed, largely thanks to you," Twilight says with the sternest face possible.

"I thought he was called You-are-we. . . ?"

"He has many names. And aspects. The Arabs knew the names for all the Old Gods because they were masters of the stars, as well as other arcane arts."

"Like math."

"Like mathematics."

The occultist inclines his head in agreement.

"FBI picked up a fine scattering of human DNA at the crime scene," I say. "Do you think your little friend, the bug guy, made it through that . . . lens . . . alive?"

"Probably not."

I stare at Twilight a moment. I don't know why I am surprised he feels little remorse. *I'm an anti-hero* plays over in my mind. And in a rare moment of insight, while I can't see much sympathy for the deceased, I do recognize in the tilt of Twilight's eye some other emotions not oft seen.

"You're . . . not letting on all you know, are you?"

"Knowledge is power," Twilight says and smirks, a shade guiltily.

"More Arab wisdom?"

"Foucault."

"Hey, you too," I say and we're both smirking now at the dumb jest.

"Look, Zephyr, I'll let you in on a little secret."

Twilight looks around, more frat boy now than, well, whatever he is normally: pretend philanthropist-cum-superhuman occult crime syndicate heir?

"I kind of, well, knew about Creeping Death before he showed up downtown."

"You knew Michael Calloway?"

"Was that his name?" Twilight shakes his head. "No. It's what was *inside* Calloway. . . ."

"Ras Algethi."

The big guy was about to say something else before I snapped. Now it's his turn to close his mouth astutely and do the tilting head thing at me, frowning, just a hint of sobriety coming into his features.

"That's right."

"Strikes me that that's an Arab name too. Like our pal."

"Hariss as-Sama," Twilight repeats.

"Yeah."

"Hmmm."

"Co-inky-dink?" I give him a shrewd look. "I don't think so."

"Yeah well, like I said, I knew him."

"As in, alas Horatio, I knew him well?"

"Actually, it's 'Alas, poor Yorick. I knew him, Horatio'," Twilight replies with mild distaste. "Not that I see the relevance."

"We're talking about dead people," I say.

"No. We're talking about gods."

If there's a crackle in the air, it ain't me. The deathly silence that fills the void roils outwards until in the end I just have to cough and give a wry laugh as I pick up the metal object with the tiny red threshold trapped inside. One moment the object terrifies me, the next I have it in the palm of my hand on impulse. Jeez, I'm a crazy guy. It's both lighter and heavier than I expect, and I turn it over, only vaguely recalling the words Twilight used to turn a two-hundred pound human being into a very fine mist.

"Funny. I came here to tell you I've decided to stay complete. Myself. Zephyr. Yet sometimes I still wonder who that person is."

"You're a bag of contradictions, my friend."

"You can say what you're thinking if you like. 'A bag of contradictions and petty foibles,' maybe. That's the polite version. It's the least real friends can do, to tell the truth."

"Fuck Zephyr, you're getting so serious on me," the other super says with casual alarm.

"We must all look pretty pathetic to a guy like you, you know, doing the whole HP Lovecraft thing, piercing the veil and looking beyond."

"I have a different perspective," Twilight says carefully. "There's nothing in that to suggest I . . . value you any less for the fact you haven't . . . what, walked a mile in my shoes?"

"I'm not sure we share the same values when it comes to people we *don't* know, though, do we?"

Twilight shrugs. "Like I said before, I'm not a hero like you are."

"My turn to correct the quote: 'I'm an anti-hero,' you said."

"Not a hero, anti-hero, whatever. The consorting with demons thing isn't just a catchphrase, Zephyr. I'm sorry. Deal with it."

"And consorting with demons, speaking of which, is that what this Hamas al-what's-his-fuck is?"

"Again, it's a matter of perspective."

He stares at me a moment like a failed child actor or something, one hundred per cent spoiled brat. I've pissed on his cookies and now we're in strange new territory. Funny how little it can take to cross that line.

"What?" he barks in the voice probably reserved for the servants. "What are you looking at me like that for? I let him out. Is that what you want to hear? Well I did. It's my fault and you know what? He's still fucking loose. That's what the lens is there for. I've got a problem."

He clears his throat and goes to speak and hangs on a moment like he's struggling to swallow a particularly big loogie, but it's all a charade – stalling for time, to think, to concoct a story, maybe. He's watched too many Matt Damon movies, I think, because his technique sucks and I'm not buying it.

"You can bemoan being human all you want, Zephyr," he finally says in a strained voice. "And by the way, copping out of fulfilling your own potential is just a pathetic waste. I let this motherfucker loose trying to research *your problem* man, so don't get on your high horse with me."

I stare at the pattern in the miniature portal for longer than may be good for my sanity. With an effort of will, I carefully put the item back down on the pedestal. And for the first time I notice what I mistook to be a snow globe beside it now looks to me to be a genuine A-grade crystal ball on the lower shelf of the wall just behind the wooden lectern.

"What's this?" I ask. "Is it what I think it is?"

"*No*, Zephyr," my host answers sternly.

A quick glance assures me Twilight would prefer to rip me limb-from-limb at the moment, but either hospitality or some other rules seem to be getting in the way. My hand, hovering over the pearly-lit globe, slowly retracts.

"OK. Sorry."

"I'm sorry too," Twilight says. "If you want to reconsider, I can give you time to think, but I don't think you'll want to. You seem to have . . . come to a decision."

"I had a confrontation with my family tonight, Twilight," I say in response. "I'm not the sort to run from a fight."

"You're a good man, Zephyr. That's why I keep you around."

The barest smile. I try and reciprocate, but keep seeing a male model in silk pajamas meeting his fate almost literally trying to squeeze through the eye of a needle and winding up little more than a smear on an Atlantic City sidewalk. I think upon what Vanguard and Synergy might call that, and call me amoral ordinarily, compared to Twilight I feel suddenly self-righteous, almost holy, above it all, you know, like Judge Judy.

"You know the saying," Twilight continues. "A good man is hard to find."

"Better to have one handy when you need him, then."

My reply is flat. Twilight nods, that calculating side of him he normally keeps cleverly masked now ousted like the naked, drooling, misshapen freak it really is. But he's lost in his own perspective. For once I am the one with knowledge and therefore the power. I can nod calmly, now that we are so close to the back doors and the final exit.

"I'll see you around," I say, the brandy bottle never even breached let alone broached.

The glass door judders closed behind me and because I feel adrift in this new spiritual winter, I walk rather than power into the air as I might otherwise be inclined.

It's those vital ten seconds that change things forever.

Walking, I linger long enough to see the woman opening the door from within Twilight's sanctum sanctorum. Although the distance from the rear of the house is considerable, the aforementioned display lights do a fine job of catching her in profile, not much more on but a bathrobe and a sleepy smile. And while it's the grass over the edges of the halogen globe that give the side of the building a viridescent aura, there's no mistaking the color of her hair even at a hundred paces.

Cusp.

Her green hair looks wet from the shower. It occurs to me I owe the lady a phone call, but perhaps understandably, this is not the first thing I'm thinking. It's a mix of emotions that will momentarily unravel in a most bizarre way. So instead I stand practically mesmerized, and I can't believe Twilight isn't watching any of this and doing something to stop it, but at the same time there's a sense of the cosmic inevitable as the woman catches sight of me and puts her hand to her mouth and comes across the impeccable grass toward me in her towel, barefoot on the crunching, fresh-mowed shoots, and holds out her hand like a baroness to be admired and greeted.

"Hi. You're Zephyr, aren't you?" She smiles, more beautiful than any vinyl mask could ever hope to conceal. "I'm Holland. I'm here with Twilight."

Zephyr 3.2 "A Good Dream"

IT PAYS TO be sure of your facts in my game, even in the face of the ridiculous.

"Cusp?"

Holland smiles, and I think: *What kind of fucking name is that? Nigeria? Skandia? Jamaica? No, she went herself.*

"Excuse me?"

"You're Cusp."

"Who is?"

"You are."

"Cusp?" She looks at me weird, completely unprepared to find that in real life the hero Zephyr is a blithering madman. "Uh, no. You must have me mixed up with someone else."

"Green hair."

Self-consciously, she raises her hand to the wet strands forming into ringlets at their exposure to the cool night air.

"This? Ha ha, yeah. It's for Twilight. He never really explained." She shrugs. "You know how he is."

"I thought I did."

"Are you . . . OK? Were you . . . leaving?"

I don't say another word, but turn instead and march back toward the house. Perhaps it's rude, but I'm pretty sure of my footing even if I'm not on solid ground as I put my fist through the door and tear the whole thing aside, panes of glass falling like slow-motion rain to shatter on the tasteful stone flags.

The entrance surprises Twilight to say the least. He's standing where I stood before, the Hariss as-Sama medallion in his bare hand. His mouth makes a comic book "O" of surprise and then I charge straight for him, taking out the big blonde anti-hero along with most of the wall behind.

"Zephyr! No, wait!"

Call it insurance, but I land a few solid punches to the side of his head to even up the argument in my favor.

"Remember Tabitha, Queen of Cats?" I yell.

"You're meant to say 'TM' after that," Twilight grins, seemingly unperturbed by my homicidal rage and the steady trickle of blood from his right nostril.

"Commsec Tower, three years ago. You used your astral powers to take control of her body when she was making like a sequel to Die Hard, holding that Afghani delegation hostage in the ballroom."

Twilight bunches under me and throws me off, back into the rear lounge. He picks off books and pieces of wood and plaster, standing in the ruins of what looks like a billiards room.

"What of it?"

"You told me one night we wouldn't be hearing from her again. You maintained the 'spiritual link'," I say, my words echoing as Twilight dully repeats them word-perfect with me.

"Nice to know we finally got our quotes right," he says. "I take it you met Holland?"

"Yes."

"Fucking chick. I told her to wait for me in the sanctum until I was finished."

"What, like you don't have enough rooms to stash her away inside the house?"

I'm so angry I sound like I'm blubbering, all high-pitched and Woody Allen-like. I desperately try to suck down a few calming breaths, ignoring the coruscating electrics across my upper body.

"Get serious, Zephyr. Where do you think all the wops with guns sleep?"

He sighs, makes a little show of cricking his neck, and adds, "Speaking of which."

I roll aside just as submachinegun fire rakes the décor. Books, plaques, ceremonial plates, a rich man's DVD collection – they all dance themselves loose from the shelves as the widescreen plasma explodes and a few of the 9mm slugs actually tear through the sofa and past me. I don't get to take much more than a glance amid the rain of shredded upholstery, but that's enough. With my boots against the back of the heavy leather couch, I give one almighty push and two of the three mooks are erased from the gaping doorway. Without even standing I Taser the third one. He shits his pants and goes down in a smelly pile, Uzi ejaculating the rest of its clip into the ceiling.

Twilight has the initiative. And heavy globes of green fire spring into life in the palms of his hands.

*

ALL THE ENERGY superhumans throw around comes from somewhere: fire is radiant energy, mine's electrical, telekinesis is physical force, and good ol' laser beams are compressed light. Twilight's blasts are mystical energy, in this instance literal hell-fire, sucked through space and time and infinite dimensions to radiate through his fingers like the world's best Hallowe'en decoration – and when it hits it burns like the son of God and sticks to me like a motherfucker. Past experience has taught me to stay on the run, but I've never come up against Twilight in anything other than repressed homoerotic horseplay, so I'm not exactly prepared to dodge as the greenish fire starts flying.

The second throw hits me in the shoulder and spins me around just as I get my momentum. I judder around the room like a smoldering version of my namesake, yowling like a cat in heat – no pun intended.

"Twilight," I growl for no particular reason.

"Zephyr," the big guy responds.

I'm not sure how we're gonna save the friendship.

As I come to a halt brushing bits of charcoalized leather from my arm, I can tell he's holding back, the look in his eye more quizzical than murderous as he takes in the extensive damage to his bachelor pad without focusing on any one thing in particular. Lightning crackles down my sleeves and I'm breathing heavy, aware my metabolism is at the mercy of hours without food and my earlier night's activities. It all just crept up on me so natural and believable – like any other slow-moving plot development – that now I can feel the familiar queasy sinking sensation at the cellular level and the comparative weakness that comes with it.

I say comparative because one man's failure is another's inspiration. I'm down from my best, but that doesn't mean I still couldn't go a few rounds with Dr Nefarious if I need to – the only problem is I know Twilight could beat the old doctor to death with one arm tied behind his back.

"This is fucking ridiculous, Twilight," I gasp at last.

"You're telling me." He motions mock-serenely at the damage. "Is all this really necessary?"

"I think you need to remind yourself about why I'm angry."

I manage to say this with a barely-suppressed rage that seethes through my gritted teeth like venom.

"What, the Cusp thing?"

"Uh-huh."

"Jesus, Zephyr. You're hot. Who cares? You know that."

"I spend all this time introspecting on whether *I'm* the gay one in this relationship and then it turns out you've been, what . . . *possessing* this poor dumb Holland chick and using her to . . . fuck me?"

"I don't see what's gay about that," Twilight replies with a straight face. "Like you say, Holland's a chick. A hot one at that. I really only fancy you when I'm her, if that makes you feel any safer, Zeph."

He says that last line sarcastically, as if I need it explained to me, poor little me with my ass against the wall because of the big bad pervert.

"Twilight, did I give you permission to cast me in your own little version of Being John fucking Malkovich or something?" I try not to bawl the next line, but fail miserably. "That was you in there! You, Twilight! You, in the driver's seat."

"I don't think that makes me gay. I was a *chick*."

"You're missing the point."

"No, maybe you are," he replies. "It's a bit of harmless fun."

"You're my friend, you clown."

"You need to get some perspective on this, pal. You should spend some time as a disincarnated soul, like I have, Zephyr. It might do you a world of good."

"I'm not even going to ask what that is," I say.

"It's the form we exist in within the afterlife," he casually replies. "Sexless, genderless, without a past, no memories. . . ."

"That doesn't stop what you did," I tell him. "You . . . violated me."

"Sheesh, Zeph." The big guy makes a pained face. "Save it for Oprah."

While I am tempted to agree – the strength of my own revulsion raises questions about my tolerance I never thought I'd face, let alone wondering where the depth of feeling I might be unconsciously tapping into at this moment actually comes from – on a whole other level this is a pretty clear-cut instance for me being right and the pervert millionaire in the tattered bathrobe being wrong.

My natural inclinations kick back in and I growl, the whole electrical thing flooding out of me like a mini-stormfront, the irony, this shitty reversal, our dying friendship tasting like sewage in my mouth. I clench my fists and fly right at Twilight, fists blazing, accelerating so hard in the tight space that he can't do much more than express his surprise as I cross his jaw and pile into him. We go straight down the center of the room this time and into the painted oak door in the middle of the far wall, into a hallway, smashing through the plaster and boards, the dry wall, a layer of bricks, topple over a heavy stainless steel twin-door refrigerator and an ethnic woman in a 1960s-style cook's livery, and continue on through forty pounds of kitchenware and about seven thousand dollars of artisan carpentry before hitting a tiled wall with a supporting steel beam. We rebound, Twilight's arms around me now like he never dared before, anger turning the erotics pale, my elbow under his weeping chin, our foreheads colliding, his knee in my thigh and my hand, the only one really free, karate-chopping at the side of his neck that may as well be made of oak itself, and me a greased-up, naked lumberjack for all the good it does me.

If Twilight wanted to force me over and ride me around the room at this point, he probably could, but I believe him when he suggests his attraction is somehow only a function or an extension of whatever kink he derives from astral possession of the poor dumb woman I can hear somewhere close by screaming her box off as Twilight flings me free. And as I fly, agile as a fucking mannequin, I carom off another wall, yet another steel girder concealed within, and pinball into and then through the servants' door to the formal dining room on the other side. Twenty years ago if I'd woken up, shaking to clear my head beneath a three-hundred-year-old chestnut dining table inside some squillionaire's manor, I'd have probably shouted "Awesome" in my best Bill and Ted voice and looked around for one of my buddies to high-five.

But this is a very different scenario.

*

WITH MINUTE GROGGINESS, I clamber to my feet, dazed

enough for a moment to stand there running my fingertips over the smooth grain of the deeply oiled wood.

The moment Twilight's shadow appears in the ruined doorway, I grasp the furniture with two hands and sling it sideways toward him, though it busts into a thousand pieces either side of the gaping entrance rather than crashing into Twilight himself. Seeing the ancient table destroyed sends the big man into a fit of pique the likes the world has never seen, and he throws himself at me, all reticence gone, and those big bare mitts come down on my leather costume like the Harpies of Greek legend, hauling me from the floor and tossing me with embarrassing helplessness across the room and through a double-glazed window. Just like that, I am out of the house, the sound of footsteps running down paths in the dark barely audible over the thumping pulse in my head, and I hardly look as I turn and send a crackling wave of compressed air pressure behind me, at moments of heightened awareness like these practically able to read my surroundings through super-sense and air displacement alone, the Uzi-toting guards just interruptions of blankness in the expanding waves of barometric sensitivity all around me.

Twilight comes through the window ready to repeat his trick, but I roll aside, getting in a karate kick at his ribs that hurls him across the virginal lawn, and after collecting a statue of a nymph doing something unsightly, he comes down hard on the stone edge of a decorative pool and topples into the murky water. I follow his progress with hardened eyes, and sensing vulnerability, unleash crackling hell on him and his watery surrounds. Twilight lights up like a Christmas tree and does the whole Lion King thing, arms in the air as his blonde wig stands on end and he fades slowly back into the water as his own harsh cries cease.

He disappears beneath the lily pads riled by the wavelets of his own demise. I exhale hoarsely, bent double with my hands on my thighs, my hands smoking and my left sleeve pretty much gone, aware but incoherent to the sound of more of Twilight's goons moving in. Only at the last moment do I manage to crouch slightly and expel myself up, just as the harsh language of automatic gunfire punctuates the night, one of the fools mowing down a colleague just as stupid as to present himself on the other side.

I swoop around, collect two of them like a giant bat sweeping out of the dark, and by the time I've turned back from the cliff's edge and the nearby ocean, I see Holland running like a woodland nymph around the side of the mansion and toward the slurping-edged pond where Twilight, completely naked now – him and her almost a matching pair, but for her towel – hauls himself weakly up onto the edge of the masonry.

I alight on the lanced turf where I stood before, figuring I had such success last time perhaps it's a lucky patch. Twilight looks like he's been eat-up and shat out by one of those weird star gods he seems to think so highly of, though its ordinary run-of-the-mill and innocent pond scum clinging to his ardent musculature and not the mucus of some cosmic entity for a change. Holland kneels at his brawny shoulder like she can help, shooting me displeasured looks mixed with equal parts clandestine panic and confusion. I can't help grunting my amusement, but my tongue is a balled-up pair of socks in my mouth, and the words, the anger, the poisoning of her against him, whatever it is, it just won't come.

"You fucking . . . Nancy," I gasp.

"What are you doing this for?" the woman who I knew as Cusp yells at me.

Tears slide down her cheeks, but I'm sensitive to her confusion, the doe-ish look in her eyes, the doubt, and what might even be the submerged unconscious memory of the time she took me in her mouth while another mind kept her repressed within the cavern of her own thoughts.

I shake my head. Twilight gives one more baleful look and then struggles free the rest of the way and steps a few paces from Holland and the pool and actually coughs, almost retches more like it, and then looks again at me more like a man who sees a nuisance than one who has just trounced him on home ground.

And that's the moment when I realize I'm really in trouble.

When he starts to speak, I don't immediately recognize the ancient language of his addled sorcery coming out of him. My ear strains and my mind wants to make sense of it, which is the only excuse I can offer to explain why I stand there like a punch-drunk tequila-swigging hooker and let him get into his whole magic act. At about the point where the manifesting syllables start popping and sizzling in the air like retarded fireworks, the sorcerous glyphs hissing into oblivion as fast as they ever existed, the earth starts to lurch and I'm not as heavily surprised as I might be when the lawn lifts up as the broad, impossibly fucking wide shoulders of some sleeping goliath of the ancient order Twilight has just unshackled from a centuries-long dream.

And it must've been a good dream, because he looks plenty angry.

Zephyr 3.3 "The Earth That One Day Must Entomb Us All"

I THINK THE metaphor "wall of earth" probably gets overused a bit in this memoir, but here I go again because I'm screwed if I can think of any other way to describe how the world just blanks out like an enormous etch-a-sketch as the avalanche of the demon's fist collides into me, not so much actually striking me as just forcing me along at incredible speed into the wall of the house.

Now, I'm tough. I've said that before, or intimated as much. I have a super-charged metabolism, incredible density to my bones, and I know from past experience that the bottom teeth I am soon to spit out will regrow over the course of the next month if I just let them, provided I live that long. However, a collision with quarried sandstone a good yard-and-a-half thick is more than even I can handle. If the fucking thing gave way I might've had a chance, but instead I'm all broken ribs and tooth decay as I crumple in the wake of the beast's withdrawal, the grains of pulverized stone clattering around me as I drop onto the ornamental flagstones bordering the house. Of course, I attempt to right myself. I catch a glimpse of Twilight easing himself into another dressing gown as his surviving flunkies rally around, the green-haired, half-naked lass in their midst with her pretty eyes bulging out at the sight of such maleficent sorcery unveiled seemingly an oversight. Then the elemental – think of it as a giant faceless ape about yay big and yay wide, a rug of inch-high green grass across its shoulders and back rather than silver streaks, and you have half the picture – it grasps me with both its crunching, pebble-filled paws and rams me back into the concavity I've just made.

This time the wall gives. I roll away. Almost lazily, the pain's so intense. The heavy blocks slip apart from higher up and threaten to tumble down on me. Twilight's creature isn't so lucky, though any hope I have that such a simple consequence might do more than just slow him down proves short-lived. It seems to shrug off the tons-heavy stone like a child inconvenienced by a tangle of wool, the weak electrical sting I manage to give it likewise utterly ineffectual.

Getting the hell out of there seems to be a pretty sound strategy. I have no idea if it's now Twilight's intention to kill me for this ultimate insult, though I recall a line I read somewhere that had a lot of resonance, saying most people would rather commit murder in their own home than face disrespect. I imagine that's how our city's favorite anti-hero lawman feels right now, so I stumble back through the cavernous dining room, overturning the display cases like they might somehow slow the thing as it lurches inexpertly in through the chasm it's made in the side of its conjurer's house. I'm rebounding off the walls in my haste to get back through the shortcuts I've created in what's otherwise a maze within the house, and on the other side of the kitchen I slip on whatever putrid messes have escaped the tumbled refrigerator and I'm just about to dive through the gap made earlier when suddenly Twilight's monster, dropping bits of lawn and clods of dirt and leaving a black trail back through the house that – even with me being dragged backwards and clawing at the tiles – I can't help wonder how the fuck they are going to clean, and then the thing lifts me up by my ankle and swings me around in the confined space.

I collect the scullery cupboard with my head and momentarily black out. It's like the joke from that old British TV show where the hippie wakes up from a dream of skinheads bashing him to realize he's just fallen asleep on the toilet, only to then wake up realizing the reprieve was the dream. I couldn't tell you what stupid fantasy I have for those three-odd seconds, but I am screaming like a gutted fish when I come to amid a whorl of plaster and cutlery and shattered glass and kettles and frying pans and electric beaters and cake ingredients. It's only by electrocuting my own foot and basically vaporizing a few pounds of solid earth that I manage to get free, released like from a Herculean discus throw to go careening off yet another kitchen wall and tumble to a standstill huddled like an advert for abuse survivors in the corner of the room. With surprisingly little hesitation, I scuttle through what passes for the creature's legs and jet on into my host's entertainment quarters, tripping over debris and slipping on fallen books and quite accurately named DVD slipcases in my transit.

Barely thinking as I continue on into the room, I whirl and see the thing on my tail, the damage and inevitable erosion destroying any semblance it once had to a giant humanoid, and now just a diseased, decaying, terrifying embodiment of mulch and entropy, a living slab of the earth that must one day entomb us all, an incarnation of that soil come to claim me for its own. I'll have nightmares about this for frigging weeks, but as Johnny-on-the-spot I barely hesitate in grabbing the shiny bauble I glimpsed hours, weeks, years previous, and turn and hurl it straight at the bowel-watering abomination.

On reflex, if you can call it that from a ten-foot compost golem, the creature bats one giant mangled paw at the crystal ball as it flies across the room. The object promptly shatters. A golden swirl of gaseous matter erupts from the collision and pretty much instantly vanishes. I turn back, something that doesn't quite yet register as a coherent thought driving my instincts, like my fingers have received the message before my brain, and they fix around the metallic artefact and my tongue gets in on the act and I'm turning, feet still fairly pointed in completely the wrong direction as I heft Twilight's troublesome red lens up and bawl the same words I heard him chant once earlier, or close enough it seems, something about get-you-the-hell-outta-here, the words imparted in my brain like only magick can, because my earthy friend starts emitting a terrific, high-pitched whistling noise that is three parts shit-straining horror, wild disbelief and complete and starkly total comprehension as the lightest and weakest grains of its body start emigrating to the land of their forefathers via a very unique shortcut. If I wasn't nursing so many injuries I might even be indebted to my old pal Twilight, though at the moment I would settle for seeing the dawn – along with my wife and daughter again – as I hold up the ensorcelled amulet and kind of avert my eyes from the whipping black sandstorm that ensues as the demon demanifests itself through the tiny narrow aperture Twilight created.

For a long while it's all shrill screaming, howling winds and raining grime, with perhaps my own chattering teeth and unconscious mewling thrown in for good measure. Then the wind drops like a switch was flicked and I look up to see Twilight having the inelegance to limp into the room with a wild-eyed and furious look on his face.

"What the fuck have you done?"

"Given your creature . . . a taste of its own medicine," I manage back.

Twilight scans around, only briefly taking in the amulet in my clawed grasp.

"Where's the stone?"

"Huh?"

He clicks his fingers and points to the despoiled shelves where the milk-white pearl of the crystal ball once sat.

"That wasn't a stone."

"Yes it was," he says.

"Uh-uh," I reply. "It broke like a motherfucker."

Twilight's voice is strained. "You . . . *broke* . . . it?"

"I fed it to your pal there."

I motion, though of course there's nothing left of the gruesome creation except a hefty dark patch on the rug. I imagine multi-millionaires like Twilight keep pretty groovy vacuum cleaners. Should be enough. I'm not sure why I was worried.

"That was my . . . heart-stone, Zephyr."

"Jeez," I shrug. "I hope I haven't like *killed* you or anything, pal."

"No." Twilight shakes his head slowly. "No, you've probably just killed yourself."

It's at about this moment – the same moment enormous horns begin curling out of Twilight's forehead and he lets out a scream like a monster in childbirth – that I look down at my palm and realize the swirling red-filled amulet is sizzling white-hot in the palm of my hand.

I immediately drop the thing on the carpet, but it's taken on a life of its own, the heat warping and distorting and erupting in weird liquid molten blotches I soon realize are more than just expanding metals.

It's an eruption of space-time – and I get about three-feet clear before it blows.

*

I'M NOT EXACTLY sure what follows is real. I've been in a lot of crazy situations in my life, not all of them thanks to my adventures as Zephyr, but yeah, mostly, and I think maybe this one takes the cake.

I am not sure what has happened with Twilight. He's screaming, roaring somewhere close by, but everything for the moment is in merciful darkness. I say merciful because, when the darkness fades, a nightmare is revealed.

To be precise, it's my nightmare.

My costume is in strips. Shards of exploded stone are embedded in my arms and up my sides. Something wet, scaled and slithery has my arms twisted above my head, but such is my exhaustion and disorientation it's a while before I'll even come to question how and why I got here.

The landscape is apocalyptic – and completely phantasmal. Sere cliffs, ashen ground, basalt protuberances like something from a Bollywood retelling of the Odyssey, roiling black stormclouds overhead just waiting the arrival of Thor or Zeus, except this god-awful interstitial state is neither Jotunheim nor Hades nor even truly Hell, but an Abyss of my own making.

As much as I can piece it together later, this dreadful realm that escaped when Twilight's amulet collapsed in on itself can only be understood through a direct psychic translation. While the netherworldly dimension spills over into our realm, its epicenter now the smoking ruins of Twilight's mansion, it seems the human senses can only digest and comprehend it via unconscious means. For me, that obviously means dog-headed babies the size of London buses crawling past with lava dribbling from their ends, rose-thorns like botanical spear-heads jutting from every inch of their wrinkled skins, snakes that weep acid, giant bees that more resemble enormous flying porcupines with the heads of rotting eels, darkly intellectual fountains of black ichor leaping from one fissure to the next, collections of bugs and spiders and silverfish that would, like passing clouds, at any moment resemble crabs or octopi or pinwheels or Greco-Roman portraits, enormous stalking creatures roaming the distant countryside with cunts for hands and living skyscrapers for heads, the insides like some baleful gigantic wickerman, lifeforms if not people, beings, *somethings*, living, alive and trapped inside them and yet really just fleshy components of some even greater machine organism, guided on vast leashes by strangely-robed figures, acolytes with hacksaws for arms and gaping black voids where heads should be within their cowls. And all around this incessant heat. And in the center, a king, or God, with golden skin and enormous horns and a bare chest dappled with beads of sweat like the dew of some alien world or the tears of a hundred thousand penitents.

Twilight. The Antichrist.

I am trembling with fear, so terrified that when I realize I am going to shit myself, there's no guilt or shame, just an over-riding need to do so silently, to not attract attention, to not allow any of the dreadful things, most importantly the dreadful golden-skinned thing, be drawn my way because of the noise. And it slides down my thighs like the wet mud it so much resembles, and something of that feculent breeze must carry to where a great number of those weird dog-fly-ant-corpse servitors I glimpsed in the realm behind the red portal now gather at the base of the stone cairn on which Twilight stands writhing, as much a column of living fire as a man, because all at once their heads snap in my direction and I realize what they intend. And there's something in my childhood, just a faded gel slide of a memory of stumbling around in my first pair of jeans with Squeaky McGonagill and Andy Foster behind the old garage on Colonnade Row, a purloined tin can full of one hundred per cent ethanol and the ants dying in their hundreds, dying angrily, Andy with his buck teeth chattering and lenses filling up with steam as he hee-haws how the ants think its water, but the alcohol burns through their gizzards.

As soon as I recognize the memory for what it is I desperately try to disavow it, to unthink it, but deep in my already-loosened bowels I recognize it for what it is: neither a precursor nor memory, neither destined nor avoidable, but an actualization of a deep and inevitable fear.

And the red ants in their thousands boil up out of the ground and around me and are up my legs in seconds and invading my tattered costume, my body, my sanity.

And I think: *fuck being quiet.*

That's when the screaming starts, and I keep on screaming pretty much forever, or at least until I wake up.

Zephyr 3.4 "A Curtain Of Black"

FOR ALL INTENTS and purposes I should be dead. The screaming, my abject hollering, has been going on for so long these fucking ants should've eaten me a hundred times over. Or at least that's what it feels like. Perhaps you can appreciate time sort of loses its meaning when you're being torn apart one tiny pincer-sized bite at a time.

My skull is not much more than a pair of eyes and ears, my tongue nonsensically in place so that I can continue with the black metal vocals, the whole thing's just an illusory scarp anyway, but as its happening, again and over again, likewise you might also be able to appreciate that this cold, clear logic evades me.

I'm just a screaming skull with chalk white bones, my skeleton and the remains of my central nervous system flayed like deli meats over the calcium-heavy stones, when I hear Seeker's voice and feel the slightest of touches and I simply open my eyes – imagine opening your eyes when you think your eyes are already wide open, looking down where ants are crawling every which way but loose between your bones.

And what eyes. Words cannot describe. Seeker is a beautiful piece of work, let me tell you, and sorry to be so crass, between that ass that won't quit and those fantastic boobs that seem to float just as buoyant as that thick dark hair of hers does, suspended interminably on the wind-between-worlds that only she, a creature of this world and the next can feel, and I am humbled and amazed that she would bother rescuing someone as low as I am, someone who spent a handful of years on the same team and never thought of her as much more than a choice hardbody and probably out of my league.

I look into those delicious golden-brown eyes and we both gasp, each with very different reasons. Seeker has always been a wild card, skittish with her sensitivity to the spirit world and the human emotions that come with it. She's a psychic reservoir and her vulnerability in that moment is just as naked and exposed as my own deep and profound feelings of unworthiness and gratitude at her arrival.

"Zephyr!"

"Seeker, I – I don't know . . . I don't know what to say," I gasp the awful cliché.

"Say nothing," she replies. "Let me . . . let me help you up."

I go to move and pain wracks my body, but I'm almost glad to feel it. It has nothing to do with the spectral horrors of death by formication I imagined, and everything to do with the pounding I received courtesy of Twilight and his pet earth demon.

"My God, Zephyr," the beautiful, glowing lady intones, and there's every sense in the world that when she invokes the big guy's name, it's on a very familiar basis.

This is the same lady, contradiction that she is, who earned a name as the team's serial spoilsport at after-battle parties, back in the Sentinels' heyday. Yet now she cares enough to cast her glowing gaze over my shattered ribs and twisted bones, my missing teeth and torn skin, and she neither flinches nor recoils from what she sees, telling me to hold still instead, and then there's another miracle, her hands up, breasts barely restrained and leaving little to the imagination in that white durex skivvy she wears as the rolling warmth of her power washes over me and I am the pilgrim washed by Christ's hand as the otherworldly energy pours through me. The feeling is like nothing I could describe except to say if they ever find a chemical substitute then the whole world's fucked. I feel the bones and sinews knit painlessly together riding a wave of pure sweet warmth. I am mortified, but hopefully alone with the knowledge I also just creamed my leathers, and as a counter-point to this revelation, I know with sudden clarity that I have just experienced what the Christians talk about as the Rapture, though this in inexplicably non-Christian.

I sit up, only to be stilled by Seeker as if I'm still a ruin.

"How did you. . . ?"

"We are no longer on the Earth, but in the Otherrealms where my powers are greater," she replies.

I wriggle out from beneath her hand and we both stand, me shakily, jism oozing down my leg and disappearing from my awareness as I look around over the nightmare Judgement Day scenario that is still at least residually informed by my psychic perceptions in this weird Erehwon.

The skulls form ziggurats, small and great alike, dotting the uneven lunar landscape upon which timeless obelisks and vast albino mountains impose themselves like the enormous slumbering gods they very well might be, the sense of oppression, suppression, repression radiating through the very air enough to chill my soul, let alone kill the urge to wisecrack.

I'm still tentatively holding Seeker's nimble hand and glance down while she remains beholden to her inner wonderment, and for all the cosmic seasickness and disorientation that would be enough to befuddle a mortal lifetime, I find myself wondering on what strange and unexpected new journey I have in no way tacitly decided to embark.

"Look," she says, her lips not moving, and I follow her gaze as directly as if a vast hand turns my jaw.

There across the shattered terrain we can see a writhing column of flame gushing up like an oilfield disaster. Seeker gives my hand a squeeze and lets it go.

"You'll need to distract him while I get the others," she says.

"Him?" I ask.

"Twilight. Or the creature he's become."

"Others?"

"We'll need others," she nods. "Twilight has been overcome by his shadow-self, the part of him he has pledged at some point to become the Being he is."

"He was . . . we were . . . *friends,*" I say and feel I lack conviction.

Seeker fortunately doesn't ask me any curly ones, though I seem to remember she was a reporter in her secret identity, though actually this is just something I gleaned and eventually confirm isn't true at all. Like me, Loren spends ninety per cent of her time "on". Just another instance of me not paying attention.

The fact that I own large chunks of responsibility in this disaster stands pregnant between us. She turns her impossibly fine-featured face away, long lashes downcast as the cosmic breeze I can see but cannot feel plays about her in her hair.

"We will need others," she murmurs. "The Fates are watching us. Someone must die and a new evil be unleashed to replace the old before this evening's over."

"Is this what your God says?"

She turns back with the kind of look that bad-hearted people like me reserve for particularly stupid dogs.

"Which God would that be?"

"Um. . . ?" And I gesture with a finger upward.

Seeker lightly *tsks*.

"Really Zephyr, after all this time, *that's* what you think I'm about?"

"Well, you're like . . . a spiritual warrior, right?"

I'm on shaky ground, quicksand probably, and we both know it.

"A guardian of this world and the next?"

"Maybe that's as apt as any other description you could steal from a movie," she says in a low voice. "There are only two worlds, Zephyr: this world, and every other. The rest is just perception."

Before she can elucidate any further, the spiritual siren gives the merest of laughs, dismissive in its brevity, and launches into the air. By the time I turn to trace her path she's gone.

Leaving me to refocus on the beacon, the morning star.

*

FOR A WHILE I am content to trudge across the horizon toward him. First, because I am in no haste to do this. Second, because I gather Seeker needs some time to collect a few more suicide bombers. Third, well, even though Seeker's radiant shower trick has healed me completely, I feel as wrung out as an old sock left to dry stiff and scratchy at the bottom of a washing machine, fragile enough I might just shatter next time someone plays too rough. And playing rough – well let's just say that between now and day's end, that's looking inevitable.

I'm still pondering some of what Seeker said when the earth begins quietly splitting open around me, the shale-heavy ground birthing skeletal, insectoid shapes that quickly fold out into more of the fly-dog-corpse-headed servitors with which I am now familiar and I must accept are almost certainly a construct of my own deepest thoughts, fears and too much H.P. Lovecraft in high school. For the first time in a mile or so I take to the air just to keep out of immediate grief – and unleash a white-hot coruscating death-ray on the closest two wee beasties. As before, they fry quite nicely, and when I drop beside another, I can punch my fingertips through its desiccated thorax and simply throw the bastard a few dozen yards away to where he tumbles and comes apart on the harsh, sharp ruggedness of this hallucinatory landscape.

"What is the point of this?" I scowl aloud.

Two more of the things buzz in at me with their nictitating wings and I flash-fry them both. They hit the ground like week-old roasts, hardly anything but charcoal in them as they crack open on the pale ground. A sixth creature comes lurching forward and I put my fist through its face with a satisfying explosion of dry meat and scales. And I back-hand another one sneaking up and its head comes clean off and the body just wilts away like a time-lapse flower. Further off, there comes another of them just emerging from its stony womb, and I give it a long dose of the old electrics until it falls back, cooked and jittery, and hardly raising a huff, I look around for more.

And more come. Now a dozen of the fucking things smash their way out of the ground, slightly faster, more menacing than the ones before. Their wing bones, angular over their shoulders, end in diseased-looking spear-points. While I virtually disintegrate the first one to come close enough, the next few mob me as a group charge, and after putting my fist through one's jaw and pushing back the next, it's only by electrifying my whole body that I get breathing space enough to roll free, shoot down the next two I spy and then whip around, blocking a deadly-enough downward thrust from a wing-point and bodily hurling my assailant over a city block yonder. The last three or four lack cohesion and go down easily, but by then I have more than raised a sweat and when the ground starts trembling beneath me like the adumbration of some city-wide disaster, getting airborne seems to be the only option as the world goes dark with the flying things, it's a regular old double-page splash with me throwing enough lightning bolts around to make Zeus happy, though it would be hard to explain the weird targets and how they seem more supple, more co-ordinated each time.

So I fly toward Twilight, a curtain of black serrated winged things behind me.

Zephyr 3.5 "Afterlife 101"

IT OCCURS TO me I am once more in my erstwhile colleague's domain as the sky fills in above me with stone and the wretched flaming column becomes the warm glow of some dungeon-like theatre set. There's a stone throne large enough to fit a small giant and Twilight stands from it looking every inch the demonic messiah he may very well be.

"You continue to fight it, Zephyr."

The words come out of his mouth the moment I land heavily on the flagstones before him. I don't know where the chittering horde of space monkeys goes, but we feel deeply, claustrophobically underground now.

Twilight has no eyeballs. Sheer incandescence ghosts from his orbits as a kind of steam, phosphor burning within him. Gigantic horns stem away from his swollen brow. He still has the mask and the costume. Its grey chest turns imperceptibly black on the way to each of his extremities. The only thing different is the black cloak, which rises behind him now in the form of two enormous dragon's wings. And it's not just the eyes, there's a radiance to his face that makes it kind of hard to look at. I swallow uneasily.

"Minutes ago I was being torn to shreds by carnivorous ants," I reply.

"Just as you expected."

He grins, well, demonically, and makes his dentist proud.

"Right, so I am making all this up," I grunt, gesture around and give an unfortunately effete *harrumph*.

"Not any longer. You're in *my* world now."

"Cute," I say. "Better the devil you know, hey?"

"That might turn out to be less true than you might've thought," Twilight replies.

"My best friend is the Antichrist. Fuck me. I can see the headline now."

"Just because I worship the Devil doesn't make me a bad person."

He delivers the line in a flat monotone and I have to give it to him, in there somewhere there's a bone for me if I wanted to take it. I do, but I don't.

"Afterlife 101 tells me your Satan and mine may not be the same thing," I reply.

"Very good, Zephyr. You're learning. There's hope for you yet."

"What, to survive?"

"No," Twilight explains. "Just to learn something, before I send you on to your next life."

While his response demands something witty, the well's dry – as dry as my mouth. At this moment I would happily drink a cup of my own pee or possibly someone else's. Perhaps it's just as well neither materialize. Despite my complete lack of optimism, I plan to survive this – and this hasn't exactly been my best day as it stands so far.

"You seem to be suggesting the road ends here," I say finally.

"I wouldn't want to disappoint you."

"Is this more of the 'creating the world of my expectations'? Because, you know, if so, I'm happy to be disappointed. I'm not really one of these guys who has to be right no matter what."

A shadow of a smile plays across the face of my friend, at once so familiar and yet so remote, and I'm reminded of yet more lines of spurious logic from the beautiful Seeker, the only one really able to comprehend this place. I'm just fluffing it.

"Problem is, Twilight," I begin again, "we have a mutual problem."

The big guy gestures royally around.

"I don't see any problem. Not for me."

"Actually, yeah," I say. "You're not really Twilight . . . and you're holding on to a friend of mine."

"And that's a problem?"

The demon gives a rich laugh.

"Yeah actually, it is."

I jolt suddenly to the side and unfurl my palm and for the briefest speck there's a glowing white-blue light there and then I explode the air, creating a confusion of whiteness that most mortal eyes, including my own, can't really bear. Fortunately for me I already have my lids clenched and my face turned away. Twilight, or the full demonic force in possession of him, howls like what I imagine people do – crowd and victim – during crucifixions. As the phosphor swirl fades, his glowing eyes remain sightless and it's nothing for me to unleash my most powerful electrical attack yet.

This is not the sort of thing I'd normally do in the real world, with people and buildings and God-knows-who-else lumbering perhaps accidentally into the way. Here, I don't have any compunction to hold back and the lightshow goes from the vigor of its first attack into an ongoing channel of pure energy as I sink every inch of my Being into frying the shit out of my one-time best pal, hero and mentor, hoping that somehow in doing so I will still have the chance to reclaim him in the end. I mean at the end. And if I fail and Twilight dies by my hand – if I have anywhere near half-a-handle on this affair so far – then perhaps in his own next incarnation Twilight might eventually come to understand and forgive.

Problem is, "giving it my all" eventually turns out to be a somewhat less impressive feat than I need it to be. I gasp like a man at the end of an unexpectedly long and probably illicit orgasm and drop gasping to my knees, clouds of steam billowing across the curious scarp that Twilight's demon lover conjured, and the throne, Twilight, pretty much everything is gone, a blackened, sand-blasted stump on an under-lit stage.

The stump twitches. It moves, unfolding slowly as the form of a man who, like a sleeper not wishing to wake, rolls onto his back and gives a mighty groan. He is at rest for no more than two seconds – two seconds during which I judge the arrival of Seeker and a handful of others into our intimate quasi-lit arena. Then the figure sits up, skin blackened, just the glowing white eyes to give the masked face definition. And as the fingers of his fist clench, I'm sure I can see burnt flesh peeling away.

"Twilight?" I call weakly.

The bull-horned figure shakes his head slowly and tuts, but the answer is relatively simple.

"No."

*

I HAVE BUT a second to glance around and work out who my reinforcements are: Seeker, the giant robot Hermes, his accidental nemesis Chamber, Streethawk, and Grasshopper, crouched like we might shoo him away, a young kid who I've never even spoken to before. I am grateful to them, one and all, though still I have too much pride for that to show. Instead, I cast a welcoming grimace toward them. Streethawk waves like we're at a gamers' convention rather than some kind of metaphoric Hell, and of them all, it's Seeker who appears to have the most serious and tactical view of the situation.

She sidesteps around Chamber's lumbering armor while the rest of us are still drinking in the scene and our places in it, the charred form of Twilight thinking through his options before us. Then just as quickly, Seeker rushes straight for our host and flings her arms and hands wide.

"The Light of Truth!" she yells.

The sizzling light-storm isn't anywhere near as brilliant as I expected. My studied flinch turns out quite unnecessary. If I were to guess anything, I'd say we were witness to a lightshow from another dimension, visible to our human eyes only by dint of the souls Seeker would tell us we have within.

The cone of light banishes the image I have superposed upon Twilight. Gone is the char-grilled superhero playboy. In his place stands a slavering, six-armed monstrosity with an obscene nexus of erect cocks where normally one would do the job. Mildly broiled, its skin is more the texture of meat with the skin torn off, and decidedly reptilian towards its head, which is pure Hollywood with its alligator smile, jaguar teeth, four slitted eyes and equine silhouette, the bull's horns notwithstanding.

"So *that's* what you look like, huh?"

Grasshopper yells, "*Imposter!*" and springs forward, God bless him, the first of us to screw our courage to the sticking point or place or whatever it is the Bard wrote, and it's unfortunate for him that the demonoid moves faster than probably Twilight himself, and a damned sight quicker than Grasshopper. It grabs the green-clad hero by the head and gives a sharp twist.

Chamber's particle cannon is too late to stop the murder. The demon leaps away, the wrenched-off head still in its hands as Grasshopper's sinewy body drops to his knees like a pole-axed Jedi.

I acknowledge I'm feeling too remote for these events. It's too many hours strung out on violent emotions. Too many hours with my body in pain. Yet with what little flicker of energy I have left, I fire some sparks the creature's way in a token show for the death of a fellow mask.

Undeterred by the murder of a mere human, the Classical robot Hermes thunders in, grabbing one of the demon's six arms and then smashing his enormous metal fist into the beast's head so many times that I begin to cheer, Chamber firing into the creature's legs, Seeker hovering in the air over the scene like the ghost of a former Sports Illustrated beauty. Streethawk scrambles around behind them on all fours, and while I know he's planning something, I also know he's giving himself a lot of time to do it.

Twilight's shadow-self, or whatever it is we're calling this thing now, headbutts Hermes with sudden ferocity and turns around his grip, snatching up the robot with multiplex arms and hoisting him in the air over his head. The creature yowls like the God of Cats in heat and shimmering energy pours through him and into poor Hermes, the experience sufficiently graphic that even I can sympathize as the robot shudders and judders before the demonoid crouches and hurls the whole weighty effort about thirty yards away. Hermes crashes to the ground and doesn't look in any hurry to start moving. I also note he's no longer silver, but a strangely iridescent gold, from the end of his sculpted toes to the helmet of curls that laminate the back of his head.

"This isn't going so well," I growl loud enough for the troops to hear.

The monster jumps, sailing through the air toward Chamber, and as it jumps, it slaps one and then two pairs of hands together. When those meaty palms collide, the result is an energy blast of some sort. We don't get to find out just how devastating they can be because Chamber motors aside, peppering the creature's ribs with white-hot bolts of his own. When the six-armed killer twirls to give chase, Chamber sickeningly folds in on himself and disappears through the slot in his chest, reappearing just feet away from me and leaving the Twilight-imposter surprisingly bewildered for a creature that has otherwise shown such sophistication so far – or sophistication at least as far as Antichrists go.

"Bright ideas?" Chamber asks.

I give a curt nod, though nothing occurs to me until I actually start speaking.

"With all those cocks, you've gotta think about kicking him in the balls. . . ."

"This is the great Zephyr's strategy?"

I look at the metal-headed techno-hero for a long moment and realize all at once that this is not the same man who has stood shoulder-to-shoulder with me in more than a dozen battles and on strange, alien worlds. The explanation will have to wait for another time.

"That's right."

I clasp my hand on his shoulder like in the days of old it turns out we never shared.

"Take me in there, Tin Man. Close."

And the shuddering blackness overwhelms us.

*

AS PLANNED, WE appear immediately behind and to one side of the hyperventilating horror.

I roll clear like a good old-fashioned action hero and the bastard is big enough that I can basically slide halfway between his legs before bringing my boot up and into the deadly nerve plexus that comes with having the sort of genitalia only Angels – and their Hellish counterparts – dare possess.

For added effect I channel a few more volts through my boot. I am satisfied to see the creature crumple, though I have to move aside or risk the damned thing falling on top of me.

At that moment Streethawk leaps from wherever he's been laying low, a spinning axe kick, I have to give it to him, performed with stunning precision, taking out half of the demonoid's teeth along the left-hand side. The creature rasps and makes a play for the denim-clad hero, but however it is his powers work, Streethawk looks like he's the only one of us who really has the monster's number. Up against six arms and two horns, he weaves like a man with a black belt in Vogue, snapping into a variety of postures that are conveniently just not within reach of the numerous attacks that try and land on him. In-between these, he retaliates with a few low blows of his own, I rabbit punch the sucker from behind, and Chamber finishes the encounter by hauling in a five-ton slab of stone and bringing it down on the fucker's head.

Astonishingly, the Beast goes down. Seeker lands nearby and starts swathing the curled form in her ambient glow, her hands moving over the creature from afar in such a way that I first think the silly tart is trying to heal him. She's got the sort of look one pulls drying hands under the heater in a gas station toilet, calm but vaguely impatient, and I have to pull my eyes away from the spectacle to glean that she's actually talking.

"What?"

"What became of the talisman that began this calamity?"

"Talisman?"

"Twilight pledged part of himself, vouchsafed for demonic power. It would have been something he carefully protected," she says.

"Hmmm, not carefully enough."

"You know it?"

"It was like a crystal ball," I say. "He called it his . . . heart-stone."

"That's right. And where is it now?"

"Ruined," I reply. "It broke. Breaking it is what began all this."

"Only because the borders of the world were forced out of alignment in the first place," Seeker says, and immediately I picture the natty amulet.

With Twilight down for the count, we're no longer in a dungeon. Again, as far as I'm concerned, we're on the set of Terminator Seven and any moment now those fruit bats from Hell are going to start breaking out from the ground.

"What's the matter, Zephyr?" Seeker asks.

"What do you see?"

"Around us? Zephyr, these eyes were born to pierce the Veil. I understand that yours would not be so effective."

I scan the scene some more. Chamber appears to be tending to Hermes – ineffectually, it would seem. Neither of them look concerned about the erratic stack of skulls and white thigh-bones immediately beside them.

I am not sure how else to do it, so I narrow my eyes and clench my ring-piece and grit my teeth and almost mutter that line from the Wizard Of Oz. When I open my eyes we're all in the same positions, but now we are in the ruins of Twilight's mansion.

"Something like this?" I ask Seeker.

I'm surprised to see a warm smile break across her face.

"Something like it. More to the rear, perhaps."

"No," I mutter, scouring the rubble now. "If I imagine it all, let it be to our advantage. It should be around here somewhere. . . ."

A minute passes as I sort through the smoldering books and half-melted DVD cases and priceless furniture reduced to matchsticks and loose snooker balls and then under a slat of wood I retrieve the roiling red lens, the metal frame melted and re-formed in an ugly, distorted shape.

"In here," I say, tiredness washing over me.

"We need assistance."

Seeker calls to Chamber, who drops Hermes' lifeless arm and comes over. After just a moment's parley the suited hero nods and activates his N-space transporter, disappearing in on himself in that unusual way that once seemed so normal.

"Can we do this?" I ask.

Seeker walks over, picking with surprising daintiness through the ruins.

"I think so. Yes."

"And Twilight?"

"As long as yonder creature doesn't wake."

I nod. "My department then."

I look over to where Streethawk sits cross-legged on a block of stone, gaze over his shoulder at where Hermes was laying just seconds before. The one-time silver sentinel is now nowhere to be seen.

"I'll need your help?" I tell him.

"Sure."

"Where did the robot go?"

"Beats me," Streethawk says and shrugs.

It's just a short while later Chamber returns with Miss Black, and of all people, Jocelyn aka Lady Macbeth. I roll my eyes, but Seeker approaches me and places her hand gently on my shoulder.

"I am sorry about Paul. He was a good man."

"Who?"

"Grasshopper," she says.

I slowly sigh.

"It's not like the fucking comics, is it?"

My back's to her now and so I can't see her face, but her voice sounds strange in reply.

"Not always, Zephyr, no. Not always."

Zephyr 3.6 "Off The Hook"

A SHORT WHILE later, working together, the three magickally-inclined women manage to retrieve the elements of Twilight's heart-stone from the Otherrealm within the red lens. In a brief but artful ceremony, they fix it to the intricate crystal lattice of a bag of South African diamonds inadvertently exposed amid the destruction of Twilight's headquarters. Sadly there's nothing else in the safe to grab.

With the restoration done, the women are then able to balance the equation, drawing out from the demonic body a slippery, eel-like appendage Miss Black quickly seals tight in one of the caponic jars she keeps handy for such things. She just as quickly conjures the container out of sight. It's only later that I wonder into exactly whose custody Twilight's shadow-self has now passed, given Annie Black's now working for the Man. But in the heat of the moment we're far too busy congratulating ourselves and watching as the blackened features of the demon soften and retreat once the spilled "extra space" of the Otherrealm retracts back through the Gothic lens, now that Twilight's vouchsafed essence is no longer creating the extra-dimensional equivalent of a Moebius Strip. As the shadow realm passes back over the ruins, crossing the superman's body in the process, it reveals a bruised, half-incinerated and barely conscious Twilight in its wake. To my surprise and enormous delight, our impromptu celebration at this feat sees Seeker jumping into my arms with schoolgirlish abandon and we lock lips for a few seconds more than even I would normally deem appropriate, given the man who passed himself off as a woman and had me go down on him is now waking up and giving me his best graveled stare.

With the crisis over and our triumph slowly becoming normal, I don't think too closely about Seeker's sudden affection despite years of being aloof and generally unattainable. Then again, it's at least a week before I even start to really think about what happened to our little robot pal Hermes – he was flat out one moment and missing the next – and connect it to Seeker's insight that our victory, sealed in the blood of Paul Pyeong the Grasshopper, would only be balanced out by the creation of a new evil.

Hell, it is really weeks before I start making those sorts of connections, and by then Mercury has made his first public appearance and I am deep, deep into the business of working out what the fuck to do with the rest of my life. Because following the party of the century to celebrate this amazing victory, I return home to find the apartment as quiet as a tomb and a letter from my wife, adjoined by all the necessary legal documentation, telling me she and Tessa are staying at the Heart of the City until I've had a chance to clear out my things.

She's divorcing me.

*

I AM AT Café Kong on the corner of Malmo and Trondheim. It is the same location made famous as one of the regular sets for TV's Seinfeld, within the playground for the elites known as Thermopylae, a prefecture constructed in the north of the city.

A woman who is far too good-looking for me walks in off the street and heads unerringly for my table. She's about five-seven, loose darkish hair aswirl beneath a fashionable cap and huge sunglasses, a brown leather Italian leather jacket stopping at her elbows matched by knee-high Aquarius high-heeled boots, laces up the side. She should click as she walks, but she doesn't make a noise. I don't know how Seeker disguises her usual emanations, that glow of hers, but even with the passing disguise I know it's her at once.

"Zephyr."

"I think you'd better call me Joe. Sit down."

I move deeper into the booth and slump, though it is hard to slump further than I already am in my dirty-necked white tee, faded biker jacket and week-old stubble. I have my sunglasses on inside, though I think that's not the reason why all the men and most of the women are glancing our way. We must look like a pair of models, slumming it in Kong's, though I'm the only one who looks like a victim of the Recession.

"I needed to talk to you," Seeker says.

"Couldn't you wait until I was, you know, out and about?"

"But you haven't been 'out and about'," she replies.

I grunt at the truth of the statement. It's a week since we rescued Twilight.

Amazing to think while fifteen people died and ninety-odd will probably never see the outside of a mental institution again, that was really all the collateral damage from Twilight's little toxic waste spill. The majority of the victims came from trawler crews working the strait beyond Newark that evening, the rest just loners I guess no-one will miss. And I imagine the rest came from Twilight's household.

The chaos of the last week obviously had no hold on Beth, but finally convinced her it was time to pull the plug. As the news stations pumped out their insane chatter and the world watched the dubbed "Darkwave panic," my darling wife single-mindedly went ahead with her decision, sharpened in the dark like a prison shiv, something she finally resolved upon at the moment Tessa's grandmother revealed she, too, was a parahuman like me. Only moments later our darling little girl did the same. Too much for Elisabeth. Even the risk of Hell boiling over and consuming the world didn't stall her.

And poor Beth, I have to say too, after the first few years knocking around with me, then getting knocked up herself, all she ever wanted was a normal life. Work, earn, splurge, revel. Didn't have the sense to leave me even when her instincts were screaming for her to do so.

Anyway that's what she said, drunk I think, during last night's five-minute phone call. The night before, something about why I always had to run away, that she shouldn't even speak to me again. That's how we've been traveling so far, five minutes of venom in the evening, regular as clockwork, a drip feed to wean me off the life I once knew and she claims I took for granted.

The night previously, she agrees to split custody of Tessa, saying she knows I would probably be glad to be off the hook, but then accuses me of being lost without the responsibility of caring for someone other than myself.

The cheek. I don't know what she thinks I've been doing all these years.

I hunch down yet further in the seat opposite my gorgeous companion.

"I don't know what you want, Seeker," I eventually mutter.

She orders Earl Grey. I signal half-heartedly for more coffee. It's more likely to make me sprout wings than keep awake, the state I'm in, and getting up six times in the night to piss is just about what I deserve considering all I've been putting myself through.

Waves of self-pity roll off me and I think about Seeker's sensitivity to such things and actually apologize for projecting such a fucked-up mental state.

"Don't worry," she says quietly. "We are . . . together . . . in the everyday world. I'm not much more telepathic here than you are. It's just, Elsewhere, my powers amplify. . . ."

"Like last week," I say.

"Yes."

"I'm sorry for that."

To my astonishment, Seeker, disguised as J-Lo or something, reaches across and takes my hand.

"I'm not."

I stare down at her porcelain knuckles, dusted with the lightest summer tan, the bones in her hand a perfect form, a sculpture Da Vinci would have killed for, though I realize belatedly that however much she pulls back the glow, this resonance, part of her considerable beauty, is a consequence of that – her eternal connection to her Afterlife.

"I'm not sure where you're taking this, Seeker."

"Here you should call me Lo –"

"You're *Seeker*," I hiss, not with malice but insistence, and a few heads rise at neighboring booths and I sink my face into another scalding cup and mutter something unhelpful about my shitty luck. I've got a talent for looking a gift horse in the mouth.

When I lift my weary eyes, the hurt and vulnerability, the sheer virginity of her gaze is too much for me – me who has shed too many tears of my own during the past days. She removes the tinted glasses, bringing in the heavy artillery with every splinter of fragility apparent in that dangerous honey-eyed gaze.

Freshly disintegrated marriage notwithstanding, I could take her home and shag her six different ways. I could spend a week with my face between her legs alone. And then perhaps I would be the piece of shit everything and everyone seems to be telling me I am. And so the only answer is to be an even bigger shit and walk away.

I pull back my hand and something in her gaze resolves, hardens.

"I'll get to the point," she says.

"Good," I reply. "Please do."

"I'm reforming the Sentinels," she says. "I want you on the team."

It's a brand new day. Wifeless, a new future calls. It's still a big leap.

"You're crazy."

"I think this latest fiasco shows we need some greater co-ordination."

I shake my head in wordless thought, the concept ticking over.

"You're crazy."

"I'm deadly serious, Zephyr. I want you to consider my offer. I already have backers willing to support us. We won't have to cosy up to the Government or the Mayor's office."

"Fine," I reply. "I'll think about it. Next time you want to talk, call my cell."

Like a total pimp, I toss a business card on the table and walk.

*

I AM AWARE that three ski-masked gunmen have robbed the van that carries the Skyrail ticket take. What they are going to do with a ton-and-a-half of coins is anyone's guess. I'm not interested. Let the police deal with it for once.

I am at home on the sofa. I haven't got any further than a single cardboard box of my possessions, stacked on the edge of the glass coffee table to suggest I've been fired from a job rather than a marriage. I wave the TV remote with sullen indolence. The police commissioner is on television barely managing not to swear as reporters do their job for a change and ask why Atlantic City's founding fathers didn't build in a better disaster defense system. To the plebs at street level it's a valid question. And it raises again the inevitable specter of Seeker reforming the Sentinels.

I can see they would be . . . useful. I'm just not sure I can bear to be part of all that madness again. But that's not saying much since I'm not sure I can face nightfall at the moment.

Commissioner Journey is replaced on the screen by an advertisement for photocopiers. The ad features British heroine Shade laying on one, and then appearing to pleasure herself. It doesn't make a great deal of sense, but probably sells a lot of photocopiers.

The local news is still doing follow-ups of people affected by the Panic. Randall Hugh Dowling, 34, perceived himself to be a bank clerk trapped on a sentient island of incorrectly filed tax receipts, with casual eternities of painful math interrupted only by the savage violence of sporadic bank robberies, the clown-faced villains pistol-raping the tellers, setting them on fire, forcing them to eat excrement, broken glass, used menstrual pads, bad Korean food. While doctors hope Mr Dowling might be clear for release sometime around 2015, he'll never be able to open so much as a savings account without shitting himself, the TV guy explains.

Also in the news: mysterious disappearances in the Australian outback; a nuclear bomb plot by Finnish separatists foiled; a pro-eugenics protester halted by the Coast Guard off the coast of Old Manhattan with a dingy packed full of explosives; author Orson Scott Card dies faking his own death; a Newfoundland trawler crew renounce fishing after claims of contact with "intelligent fish"; three top UN weapons scientists missing from the Ukraine; calls for mutant gene testing in the National Basketball League; unexplained lights over New Hampshire; Paragon and Jocelyn announce their official engagement; the villain Zero hands himself in to police and requests a fair trial; Queen Bee in yet another lesbian photo scandal; and the villain Grimoire sues Neil Gaiman for copyright.

As I watch the flatscreen, I gently probe my front bottom teeth with two fingers. One part of my thrashing at Twilight's hands Seeker wasn't able to simply reverse with a wash of Otherworldly power. I'm an eight-year-old again, at least as far as my lower front incisors are concerned. The stubs are about halfway through now. Makes eating the steak sandwiches I keep ordering from Gunga Diner mighty hard to chew.

The news washes over me as the phone rings. First it's Doc Prendergast, hoping against hope I was too drunk to remember any new sightings of Hermes when he spoke to me last. The news segues into something vaguely interesting about the history of a missing 1960s government eugenics research team when the Enercom phone rings again and it's Nautilus, calling from LA following a mild quake, just wanting to "you know, catch up," and quickly moving on to asking if I have the number of "that guy, you know, we busted him that time on his first outing as a bad guy, wore a hockey mask and called himself Night Stalker or something – didn't his father work for Warner Brothers"? I hate disappointing old friends so I pretend it's a bad line, and after several minutes' hesitation staring at the phone like a broken facial recognition program, I dunk the stupid thing in a flat, half-empty schooner of lite beer with cigarette butts bobbing in it.

The home phone rings almost straight away and I guiltily look around at the disheveled apartment and slump lower in the chair. I'm wearing a dirty Hawkwind tee-shirt and nothing else. Hell, I live alone now and I wipe my ass properly, so why not? I snatch up the phone and it's only because there's not enough room left in the glass that I relent and answer.

"Daddy?"

The trembling lip and incipient tears sends an electric tingle down my spine that tightens my asshole as I imagine those dreaded next few words, words telling me that finally an old enemy has caught up with my wife and daughter and is about to extract his revenge.

But it's not. Not this time at least. Tessa's hesitation is everything I've otherwise come to associate with my own fucked-up, irrational and completely ordinary home life. There's no plot-driven revenge here, folks, just a fearful, tearful little girl, the same one who used to pretend the fairies were the ones leaving those "I love you dad and mum" notes whenever she could hear Beth and I arguing late at night.

"Tessa. Baby. Are you OK?"

When the howling stops, she explains her mother destroyed her cell and has banned her from calling "that monster you call your father".

"It's like she's making herself hate you so she can't turn back," my nearly fifteen-year-old wise woman tells me.

"I'm not sure it's an act, baby," I explain. "It's been hard for your mother, all these years. You know. The secret."

"But the secret is wonderful, daddy."

Tessa's reply catapults her right back securely into childhood. And her naivety is enough to make me well up. I shake my head to clear the sentiment and only half succeed, sounding like a blubbery mess to her on the other end of the phone.

"I'll be gone from here soon, honey, then you can have your room back. Maybe it'll help make things feel a little more normal."

"That's what mum says," Tessa replies. "She says it wasn't like you were ever there anyway."

I hang my head a moment and when I lift it up, the curious image of snowstorms sweeping across the Hell Gate Bridge catches my attention seconds before the overhyped voice-over starts making sense. Tessa keeps talking, but to my shame it is the flatscreen newscast that wins out.

"Breaking news now from the Queens area, our local affiliate is on the ground and in the air. Do not adjust your sets, viewers. While winter storms are still more than three months away, Weather Department satellites are confirming what you are seeing now courtesy of a live NBN feed. An unusual spike in weather activity. . . ."

"Dad?" Tessa senses my absence again, a sixth sense due her particular upbringing. "What is it?"

"Trouble I think, honey. I've gotta go."

Zephyr 3.7 "The Impromptu Freakshow"

STUPIDLY, I DON'T even wait for her reply. I hang up, still watching open-mouthed as the news cameras hone in on the image of a man blurred to obscurity by the hissing white fog around him, walking down the middle of the bridge. The helicopter can't catch the phenomenon of stalled car windshields shattering as the ghostly character advances. On the ground, a reporter with a borrowed anorak and a ten dollar haircut adjusts himself like the fine upstanding peacock of the species he is before leaping in front of the end of the bridge, oblivious to the waves of unseasonably dressed motorists exiting vehicles around him in a great dystopian rush.

The reporter, quickly rendered anonymous for the white phosphorescence, yells in a well-mannered way, one finger in his ear.

"Eyewitnesses say the man walked out of a downtown tenement just under an hour ago, and temperatures started dropping from that point on. No one's yet been able to identify the man or where he comes from. Rumors that he stepped ashore from an ice floe in Miskatonic Harbor are untrue, the Port Authority says."

I watch the reporter and his invisible flunkies. With nervous enthusiasm, they hurry on to the bridge. The epicenter of the phenomenon is still too distant for the telecast, much to the frustration of its producers. The view switches to the chopper again, an interchangeable female for the scarf-wearing male on the ground, the blonde hair and stylish reading glasses little more than a prop for a piece of lucrative televised theatre.

"Experts estimate the air temperature is below freezing point down on the Hell Gate Bridge."

The woman shouts into the camera, positioned precariously to catch the money shot out the open door. I can't claim to know the girl, but the harness does wonders for her cleavage.

"Contrast this to a forecast for earlier today and twenty-two degrees Celsius."

The camera zooms through the freezing air to disclose the vaguest images of a man – at least something humanoid in shape. It is either the intrusion of the lens or a precipitous moment, for the figure gestures roughly and a sheet of whiteness obscures the view, but not the sound. The chopper's engine noise becomes decidedly intermittent and the cutesy reporter starts shrieking like a wounded baboon.

In a studio somewhere, the best contribution a male anchor can make is to repeat the words "Oh dear" over and over again.

On the bridge, they know what side their bread is buttered on. The male reporter no more than harshly waves and the cameraman shifts to focus through the tense struts of the bridge to catch a view of the ice-bound helicopter falling lazily, heavy all of a sudden as its implausible physics catches up to it, forcing it down and into the river. The few remaining spectators shriek. The wavering camera accidentally catches a shot of the earnest young journo blanching at what he's just witnessed. First draft of history my ass. He clears his throat, nods that he's OK to keep going, and just as he readjusts the concealed knot of his tie, a sheet of snow floods the camera, whiting out the scene like God's own hasty edit.

The erasure is total. It would be embarrassing if it wasn't so morbid as the home broadcasters try and rustle up a signal, a live body to say something. Instead, the silence rules supreme. The image flicks to a studio, the camera focusing in a rush on the man with the useless epithets. They're good, though, these TV news people. Used to thinking on their feet. Suspended in the top right corner of the screen is a little boxed image of their own news chopper dropping like a stone, the NBN brand hazed by static on the vehicle's side, the words "Arctic mystery" emblazoned beneath.

I am perplexed by the persistent buzzing noise in my apartment until the beer glass at my left explodes and my sponsor-endorsed phone starts vibrating around the wet table like a fresh fish with a call-sign all its own. I shake the dripping thing off before reluctantly pressing down on the receiver.

"Zephyr," the voice says.

It's Twilight.

"This is the big one," he says.

"It's Hammer time?"

"Hariss as-Sama, yes."

"You don't have to correct me," comes my arch reply. "I knew who you meant. I was making a pun."

". . . OK."

"I take it you're *in*?"

"Yes. Zephyr," Twilight says, his voice unused to hesitation. "This is . . . a chance for me."

"It is," I reply. "Your last chance, you fucking cross-dresser. Screw this up and next time when I kick your ass, you're history."

I snap the phone shut, victorious in every sense except that I have an ear wet with stale, nicotine-flavored beer.

*

THERE ARE SOME things a guy has to do sometimes, even a super-guy like me, despite the, uh, clarion call to battle, or whatever it is.

The moment the phone is down I hit the fridge, grabbing another one of those god-awful lite beers Beth must've started buying, along with a plastic satchel of slightly suspect-looking pastrami and packet cheese. I crack the beer and take a grimacing slug before making a rough sandwich from the remaining bread crusts. Then I head to the lavatory, take a quick leak, and hit the secret button for my den.

It's depressing to think I'll soon be living out of a motel or something while my wife will continue on in the apartment with a superhero's homemade secret laboratory in the wallspace. Maybe I should do something about it. God knows how I'm going to react if she ends up with another guy. It's a sobering thought, and not the least of it the ongoing risk to my secret identity.

My leather costume has fallen from the peg during my week off and come to rest in a spot of damp I normally conceal with the wastepaper basket. I retrieve the leather leggings and they don't smell good. I haven't even done anything about the shredded sleeves and cum stains, courtesy of Seeker's dose of holy goodness. I would consider it the first orgasm I've had courtesy of that particular superbabe except perhaps my right hand and I wouldn't be being honest.

The costume, then, is a no go. I sigh, moving aside some clutter to expose the museum piece red-and-white suit, the long narrow cape in red with the logo, refined somewhat since those days, cast in white down the middle. It's not like I am capable of putting on much weight, so the dang thing should still fit no matter how far I've let myself go – and a quick glance into the Ikea shaving mirror reminds me of the stubble I really don't have time to remove. So the facts being what they are, with a mouthful of pastrami and cheddar that won't quite go down, I strip off my tee-shirt and start sliding on the double-lycra thickened by waterproofing and flame-retardant chemicals.

The little mirror doesn't have much range, so I can only imagine what my ass looks like in this and marvel at the fact I used to stretch into this get-up for hours every day and even sometimes grabbed late-night supplies from the store when Tessa was little and kept Beth up late with her teething. There's nothing for it now.

The cloak gets caught as I maneuver uncomfortably in the confined space, nearly upending the computer on its card table. I finish the beer for good luck, and I tell myself sincerely, also the energy, and then hit the catch on the secret exit and launch into the night.

It is going dark. The lights of the city make a pretty spectacle with the falling temperature. For miles upon miles, the whole region succumbs to the advancing cold, snowflakes refracting the artificial light. I belt across the city at a fair clip, Queens my old stomping grounds, a faint trill of worry when I think of my parents, though at least I know there's not much chance my wife and child would be in danger there as Queens is the last place Beth would run.

One thing I have to give to the Enercom phones is their watery resilience. The damned thing starts up again as I pour on the speed, the Hell Gate glittering now over the black water, a fleet of choppers in the air suspended like Christmas decorations.

"It's Zephyr," I bawl into the phone, aware I'm doing just under five miles per minute.

Elisabeth's voice is wobbly for all sorts of reasons. I slow, go into freefall and even hold my breath, I'm so desperate for the reply.

"What is it?"

"It's Tessa. She's gone. And she's left a note," Elisabeth says. "'Don't worry. Gone to help dad'."

I alight on the roof of a tenement and watch the barges in the bay and the police boats for one angry moment.

"Jesus."

"And I'm missing a pair of stockings and that Italian designer jacket you bought me," Beth says.

"The one you never wore."

"You know I hate leather."

I nod. *Windsong.*

*

THE POLICE HAVE erected a massive cordon on the other side of the bridge. I lose track after twenty police cars and a number of armored vehicles. The closest buildings are crawling with tactical units, snipers, signalmen. Arc lamps flood the scene and the ice-swept avenue leading onto the bridge, the daunting eternal blackness of the river moving sluggishly beneath. Suddenly its December, the cops in their fur-collared drill jackets accessorized with M-16s.

The cordon bristles with an impromptu gathering of the city's masked heroes. I drop to a space out in the open for safety's sake, turning and burrowing back into the warm press of costumed humanity, eyes scouring the silhouettes for my daughter. Paragon, glowing warmly, and Red Monolith are nearby holding coffees and talking to one of the captains. The moment I am settled I hear reporters yelling as if from some distant dimension, but I ignore the projected sense of their own urgency and then the Commissioner himself walks across the ice in one of those neat Commie-era bearskin caps, a clipboard, thick gloves and a klaxon by his side.

"Zephyr," he growls loud enough for everyone to hear the love.

"Commissioner Journey."

"You want your people to have a crack at this, or do we just give the order to take him down?"

I finish my search of the terrain without any luck and turn back to the man in charge.

"It *is* a him, is it?" I ask. "You have an ID?"

"Reporters were good for something. They fingered a back-room massage parlor in Pierce."

"Queens," I say.

Journey raises one of those thick blonde eyebrows of his.

"You a local boy?"

"Just saying it like it is, Commish."

Journey grunts.

"Our boy, we don't have an ID on him, but a search of the scene reveals five hookers and their receptionist dead. Looks like he'd been in there for at least two days, loaded on crack, JB and some bad mojo. Can't explain the freak weather. Mutant?"

"Bad mojo?" I ask. "Explain."

"You tell me, hero-boy. Detectives said the dead girls had words etched into their skins, body parts missing, scorch marks on the floor. All the hallmarks of –"

"Witchcraft."

"That's right."

"OK, that's all I need to know."

I look around. Paragon and Red Monolith have been joined by Seeker, Darkstorm, Mastodon, Vulcana and Miss Black. Further back among the police and forcing their way through I see Sky Blue, Nocturne and Falconer among a few less familiar faces. No diminutive auburn-haired flyers in short-cut Italian jackets.

"Our guy out there on the bridge is Ras Algethi," I say perhaps too loudly considering the topic, but I've recently watched Kurt Russell in Big Trouble In Little China again and I admit his delivery has rubbed off. "This is the same guy behind the bug invasion and the bank that went walking early last month. We need to put him *down* this time. There's no point waiting for White Nine."

Miss Black pushes her way to the front.

"If you're talking demonic possession, we need to get Jocelyn here, now," she says.

Aware the ex-villainess's fiancé is standing behind my left shoulder, I still manage to give my former teammate a look and say, "I think one potential enemy is enough here, don't you?"

Before Paragon can rile, there's a fresh voice, and a big figure in grey-and-black wades through the impromptu freakshow.

"You needed her last week, Zephyr, and you'll need her now," Twilight says. "We can all throw trucks around and melt tanks, but she's a natural conjurer. There's a chance The Kneeler may bow to her, if the moment's right."

Everyone knows about the tension between Twilight and I – just thankfully not the sordid details. We stare at each other under the floodlights for a long moment and it's me who breaks off contact, shrugging as I turn to review the bridge.

"Well if you want her here, you do that."

Nearby, Darkstorm grunts under his Darth Vader helm.

"We'll go," he says, and he and Paragon disappear together in the swirl of his black cloak.

A new voice, feminine and throaty, pipes up.

"Alright, gentlemen. . . ."

Seeker walks forward, a light in the darkness even without the distinct feeling we're all getting ready for a game of night football.

"It seems we're having a run on wayward spirits in Atlantic City lately," she says aloud to the gathering. "It's time to set an example."

"Let's put the genie back in the fucking bottle, people," I say and clap in keeping with the gridiron theme.

And Seeker and I lead the flyers into the air.

Zephyr 3.8 "Like Atlanteans"

THERE IS A man sitting cross-legged in the middle of the Hell Gate Bridge.

I should say there is an ice statue. In the half-hour he has knelt there, acknowledging the authorities blocking off the bridge from both ends, the ice has gathered with sculptural force. He sits in the middle of a circle also fashioned by the coldness of the air, a complicated sigil in frost drawn across it. I'm not sure he has made it himself, or perhaps simply just willed it into being. The other option is that it's formed of its own volition – an even scarier prospect.

Nocturne should know to set up the head radio system, but whether it's because she's too far behind the cordon or just flaking out again, we're reduced to yelling over the wind and the noise of ice cracking in the river far below. Seeker indicates she wants to open negotiations with our frosty friend, and proprietary feelings notwithstanding, I swing around to offer back-up, drinking in the air currents as they lash across my garish uniform no-one has yet even noticed. Again, my eyes are half-distracted by the crowds, but I can't see Tessa anywhere.

Seeker lands gracefully and crouches for a moment, then advances on where the figurine glistens, unmoving in the middle of the bridge with frozen cars and minibuses pushed up along the sides.

"I am Seeker," she yells loud enough for at least the first of us to hear. "My colleagues and I are this city's guardians. You are not welcome. We call on you to be gone."

Eventually she has to halt. Whether there's power in the magick circle or not, it's not wise to mess with the unknown, especially when you're trying to run cosmic entities out of town. Unfortunately for diplomacy, the crouched figure doesn't move. I can only hope he's succumbed to the elements and in the morning the coroner's office will be using a hacksaw to make way for traffic. But no, there's something menacing and Otherworldly about the way the ice has constrained him, draping the possessed victim in the appearance of long robes and beard.

More heroes arrive on the bridge and in the air around me: Crash Tiger, Devil Betty, and some of the even more rare ones, including a few oddities: Jackanape, Treesinger, Lynx, the newcomer Cipher, Amadeus in his Chancellor armor – a regular hometown showing, in support for Atlantic City. Perhaps the last week's tragedy, courtesy of Twilight, has shown people that action may have staved off the worst of the damage.

For a moment there's a vision of a girl that makes my heart jump, but it isn't Tessa. Against all logic I see Cusp, vinyl bodice packaging the goods as usual, moving around the backdrop. It makes desperate nonsense in my mind, logic the crusher of hopes. When our eyes meet, she glances through and over me. A stranger. I glance at Twilight, but he's elsewhere, snapping instructions to the east flank. I can't fathom it, but this is a mystery for another time.

Sun Man gestures and a little fire cloud billows out from his palm. Chamber warps into view and we can hear his arsenal rotate into readiness. I drop to the ground and find myself beside Mastodon.

"Hey," he grunts, a cigar in the corner of his mouth. "Sorry I wasn't there for you last week, comrade. You know I've got that wrestling gig in Tijuana at the end of every month. . . ?"

"Hey don't mention it," I say. "It's OK, brother."

We clasp forearms like Atlanteans and Mastodon gives a fierce nod, stamps his foot a few times and suddenly inflates beside me to his full nine-foot height. Lynx bounds over the roofs of the cars down one side of the bridge, dislodging ice, and Treesinger . . . well, Treesinger tunes his harp and continues with his quiet vocal warm-ups.

"You think that turkey's gonna have much luck out here with any trees?" I ask the 'Don.

"Well we're on a bridge, Zephyr," he says almost tiredly. "Some of these people just won't ever frigging learn."

The ice guy still doesn't move and I can hear nervous chatter among us good guys. Red Monolith, a hundred feet up in the air, yells, "Hey Zephyr! What gives?" and I have to shrug and console myself that we're biding our time.

And just like that the crouched figure cracks with a sound like audible gunshots, standing stubbornly, the frozen air giving him a wizardly appearance as a staff of ice manifests in his hand and he just as quickly hurls it point blank at Chamber.

The armored guy deflects the missile with his forearm and the particle cannon whirls in reply, but the frozen dude, who they later imaginatively call the "Winter King," actually cartwheels out of the way. And stupidly, Chamber's attack sizzles amid the heroes on the other side, Jackanape tumbling and Cipher diving for it, while Devil Betty slips sideways into that pocket universe of hers and doesn't come back till sometime around dawn.

The colorful hordes around me surge and I fly with them, the city's avengers, and the game as we play it around these parts is well and truly afoot.

*

ALL DOES NOT go according to plan, including the plan, which manifests stillborn and besides, we're comic book heroes, we don't have time for plans. We knock heads together and two plus two always adds up to the location of the bad guy's lair. Or so we must think, because I can't otherwise explain how within ten minutes the bridge is hanging by the thread of its last few remaining tensile steel cables and the police cordon's utterly compromised.

Sky Blue lies dead in the middle of the heaving bridge, burning cars and minivans screeching across the tattered tarmac and plunging into the river to the hissing of giant snakes and vast plumes of steam that erupt as if from the bowels of the very earth itself. There's enough overtones of Ragnarok that I'm about ready for that fat lady to come in singing, but I could only wish this was a Wagnerian opera and not the balls-up it seems to be.

As I crouch for cover behind an upturned police cruiser, its paint effectively sandblasted off by the raging wind, I see a delivery van tip over and accidentally collect up the dead, blue-suited air-controller, and they go careening together off the edge into the blackness below. Another cable snaps, whipping through the air with the fatalism of a guillotine, and in my immediate foreground a figure radiant with an icy aurora tips over police cars and ignores automatic gunfire like they were merely condiments on the Arctic breeze.

Nocturne finally gathers some control over the telepathy thing. In a world first, Commissioner Matthew Journey clears his mental throat and addresses the supers.

The creature doesn't appear affected by our ballistics, he says gravely. *If any of you people have a better idea, now's the time to hear it.*

There's some back-channel chatter I can't quite get my mind around, pun intended, and as I squat there recharging and desperately trying to think through the twisted logic of how to beat on an alien god, I notice a compact figure descend through the dark sky to the rear of a row of police searchlights and then move between huddled cops to the very edge of the damage-strewn stage at the mouth of the bridge.

My little girl looks grown up in her costume, but up close there would be no doubting she's just a teenager.

She wears the purloined leather jacket, black tights and knee-high leather heels. Her emblem is a deliberately punk W slashed haphazardly in spray paint over a rough circle in the middle of her back and while her hair's tied back, it remains wild and aloof and the ferocious wind isn't helping. And if that's not one of my old masks concealing her beautiful pug-nosed face then it must come from one of those Zephyr novelty bags they used to sell at high school fairs a decade ago when this costume was still fashionable.

Tessa takes a moment to assess the scene. Chancellor and Chamber rip into our opponent with their power blasts, Jackanape cartwheels in and realizes his dissembling powers, whatever they are, don't work on something without a human mind, and Vulcana takes a powerful backhander that sees her disappear into the dark. In those few seconds I cross around behind Tessa, I mean Windsong, and I grab her by the upper arm just as she starts to rush forward.

"Dad! What are you doing?"

Against her futile efforts, I drag her back into the shadows at the base of the bridge. Two SWAT officers are triaging a Port Authority worker with a shrapnel wound to his arm that bleeds badly. The scene is too chaotic for ambulances to get through and last I saw, Darkstorm was taking those who would go with him on a shortcut through the shadow realms to Mt Mercy Hospital.

"Tessa, what are you thinking? And keep your voice down."

I can't restrain the deathly growl in my voice and Tessa, eyes wide under her mask, pulls her arm free with difficulty.

"What's going on?" she asks. "I'm here to help."

"We haven't even discussed this," I snap. "Tonight is not the night."

"I came to help!"

"We haven't even talked about how we're going to handle this, Tessa."

"Hey," she replies. "You're the one who needs to keep your voice down. I'm Windsong, OK?"

"Then stop calling me *dad*."

"Why?" she asks. "Can't –"

"Do you want every madman who's ever held a grudge with me or lost out in a punch-up to start taking a number?" I hiss. "This is the kind of thing I'm talking about. We need a strategy – and that's *if* not *when* your mother and I decide you're allowed to start . . . going on missions."

"Hehe, 'going on missions'," she laughs.

"*Windsong*," I growl. "For Christ's sake, it's a *school* night."

"Oh dad. . . ."

"It's Zephyr."

"Our powers are similar. . . ."

"I've never been a weather controller," I say.

For a moment I can't help but feel a little proud.

"You really do that?"

"Yes. And I *can* help here," she replies. "You've got to let me. Hell, everyone's here. I just saw the Crimson Cowl. Crimson Cowl 5, you know, the good one?"

"Jeez, you've really been following this stuff. . . ?"

"Why do you think my grades suck so bad?"

"I thought because you were spending all your time eating pussy," I reply off-handedly and blanch. "Crap, did I just say that? Uh, sorry honey. I meant, you know, teenage girls. . . ."

My hands flail uselessly. I can guess that Tessa is blushing and looking around in that innocent teenage way kids do when wondering how they're going to ditch their parents before they get seen together in the mall car park.

After a few more moments pass, the girl in front of me flicks her hair from her shoulders and pouts, womanly all of a sudden, powerful and unknown.

"I'm not a kid anymore Zephyr. You need to understand that, OK? I want your trust. Give me this chance?"

"You're killing me, honey. I have to say no. *This time*. This time, OK?"

I wait a moment, but there's not a lot of empathy coming back my way.

"This time, Windsong," I tell her, feeling ridiculous using that name. "This is just too big. Let's ease into it. Train for it. I don't even know what you can really do. *You* don't even know what you can really do."

I'm winning. The pout sours.

"So what am I supposed to do?" she asks.

"Watch. Stay in the shadows for God's sake, but watch. Sure. Watch."

Windsong says nothing. I rest a palm on her shoulder, the first time in living memory I have not been hitting on a female super in so doing. The thought of what some of these sleazeballs will make of her is enough to turn my stomach until I remember she's a lesbian, or at least she thinks she is for now. I actually smile.

"You're outfit looks cool," I grin.

"Dad, you look gay, OK? You need your leathers."

I laugh and take to the sky. Next to parenthood, tackling an ancient demon incarnate as the god of winter has got to be a piece of cake.

Zephyr 3.9 "You Know What Nietzsche Said"

THE FROZEN MAN looks up as Twilight and I come down, but there's not a lot he can do. He throws up an igloo wall we smash through before we even register it's there, and Twilight is fractionally ahead of me and so lands the lead blow. With a second attack, a body slam, he sends the possessed occultist flying back into a row of emergency vehicles already pressed tightly together.

While amazing, it's unsurprising the man gets up. He has an alien god as his engine, after all. Waves of ice build up on him like body armor and on the short march back to us, he fends off diving attacks from Red Monolith and Falconer. Then it's Twilight and I, two-on-one, fighting side-by-side deflecting attacks and trying to land a few, the face of the madman up close slack and inanimate beneath the freezing nimbus. The cold is so intense at ground zero I have genuine concerns I can't keep this up. I feel like Amundsen at the South Pole or something, or at least that's what I imagine. Then I manage to put my hand against the bad guy's chest as Twilight twists his forearms away and I channel the power supply of a medium-sized town into the bastard, and to my surprise, he abruptly explodes into a thousand frozen chunks flying backward at a hundred miles per hour.

"Oh fuck."

I look at Twilight and he's equally aghast, though it's worse for him because he's still holding the dead guy's forearms, hands attached. We look at each other for a moment and despite everything else, on the wave of hope this latest development brings, we can't help cracking up in laughter all of a sudden, and I fall to my knees in hysterics as Twilight jabbers something about having disarmed the threat, which of course only makes it worse.

Seeker and Miss Black approach cautiously. I note that behind them comes Paragon and Jocelyn. Between Paragon, Seeker and the searchlights of the police and news choppers, it's as bright as day, and for the sake of decorum, Twilight quickly divests himself of the grisly evidence and I stand, one handy aspect of the old uniform being the cape with which to dry my eyes.

"I wouldn't celebrate just yet," Miss Black says without any certainty.

Seeker also looks around as if hardwired to fear the worst. The bad guy's remains aren't moving, though in time they will defrost into an unpleasant sludge. I catch Jocelyn's eye and she gives me a secretarial grin and says, "Hey there Zephyr. I really missed the old threads. What happened to your suit?"

Fortunately I don't have to answer. Instead, the ice and the snowdrifts and the wind all start circling around us, conspiring to a center-point where a diffident mass takes shape. Within moments it solidifies. It accrues more and more ice with each passing second, elements of debris, tatters of newspaper and Styrofoam and plastic bags and Chinese take-away cartons and cigarette butts and all the city's other rubbish massing into that Herculean form so that it raises two mighty and enormous white ice-encrusted fists to the sky, but from the knees down, it is the grey sludge of a rush hour sidewalk the morning after a good fall.

"What the hell is that?" I gasp.

"An elemental," Twilight says tiredly. "An elemental unrestrained."

"Which means?" Paragon asks, glowing gently.

"A god," Jocelyn says, and I swear she's still smiling, gleeful no doubt to see how us schmucks are gonna deal with this one. "A god on a rampage."

"On a rampage and in his element," Seeker adds.

*

ONCE THE THING has grown to twenty-five feet tall, it grabs a pair of sedans and smashes them together like a gladiator with a sword on shield. Glass rains down on it like confetti, shards sticking to it just to add to the danger. It doesn't even bother to throw the wrecked cars at us.

The heroes spread out. For some reason Twilight remains with me.

"Once it's free of its physical host, there's no telling what it could do," he says.

"Jesus," I sigh, our plight made all the worse knowing we're on a live feed and they might even have mikes strong enough to pick up our deliberations. "Shame we don't have the lens any more, huh?"

"I guess it's probably best that we don't, if you consider what happened last time," Twilight says.

"Yeah."

Cue awkward silence. Motes of ice cartwheel slowly past and I start wishing the snow creature would attack.

"I'm sorry, Zephyr," Twilight suddenly says. "Sorry. And I was wrong."

"Well, Jesus. . . ." I stammer.

I can't look him in the eye. We're nearly three hundred feet into the air by now and of all the things I am worried about right now, radar microphones are prime on my list.

"It's something I'll have to dwell on to truly understand," Twilight continues. "But I want you to know that I will be meditating on it. To understand where I crossed the line."

"That's . . . great, Twilight."

"You know what Nietzsche said," he replies.

"Hmmm, that thing about bank managers being the bane of society?"

"No, I was referring to the 'stare into the abyss,' you know, his 'hunting monsters' kind of stuff."

"Oh."

We stare down at the ice demon for a few seconds. It keeps accumulating snow and ice and it occurs to me if we don't start kicking this thing's tail soon, it's going to be a hundred feet tall. Yet there's still too many things nibbling at me.

"So let me get this straight," I say finally, turning to Twilight. "You agreed to be the Antichrist?"

"Well . . . yeah. To stand in for him. Not *him*, of course. It's not *the* Antichrist."

"Oh sure," I say, clueless.

"I mean, there's no such thing. I agreed to accept an ancient title, a *bane*," Twilight shrugs. "I guess I was young, I didn't really think I was ever gonna get called on it."

"All for the sake of a little power?"

"For the sake of *a lot* of power, believe me," he says.

Sensing my admonishment, Twilight adds, "Hey, not all of us can manage to get struck by lightning."

I grunt and turn slightly away.

"Yeah. Well I learnt a bit more about that too lately."

"Oh?"

"Yeah." I shrug. "I figure the lightning may have been the trigger, but not the cause."

"How's that?"

"Apparently my old man had powers too," I practically mutter.

"Oh yeah? How does that work?"

"Sheesh Twilight, have we got an alien god to beat on or what?"

Twilight shrugs.

"Hey, I was just fucken asking. Trying to show a little brotherly concern."

"Brotherly. Fuck. And this from the guy who –"

The big guy snaps. "We don't talk about that. Not. Any. More."

And I sigh. "OK. Maybe we don't . . . Maybe that's how we do this."

And I sigh again, and now the creature is in a blind range as those with distance attacks open up, ice and steam spewing out of the thing, but ultimately making very little impact as the riven fissures seal themselves almost at once.

"Let's do this, before it does us."

"Not much of a battle cry, but you're on."

*

IT'S A BIG ask. As we throw ourselves at the blizzard beast, it accumulates caped heroes like flies on a peach. Wave after wave of attacks are repelled or outright ignored. At some point, I take one of the creature's fists right in the smacker, and after rebounding from a pylon, find myself in a pool of shadows where the arc lights can't find me.

Vulcana is there. Her arm is off. The blue of her transformed flesh disappears in the conflicting light and she looks like a silent movie star with her short, dark, stylishly-trimmed hair. I can tell she's trying hard not to totally freak.

"You remember that guy who teamed up with the Laughter Boys? Called himself Eliminator?" she asks shakily.

I smile as I come back from the edge of blacking out.

"Crap name."

Vulcana titters. I grin and nod at her arm.

"What are you gonna do about that?"

"Rambo would melt the ends and stick them back together," she replies, tired-sounding rather than panicked now. "I'm not sure that's going to work for me."

"Hurt much?"

"Not like this," she says and gulps. "I'm worried 'bout, you know, when I turn back."

I nod uselessly.

"I'll see what Seeker can do. She's fixed me up before."

After hesitating, I gingerly pat her shoulder. Twice in one day. Vulcana doesn't look up.

I'm glad to return to the fight, though as I stagger back into the open, I watch the raging white beast hammer Twilight into a row of nearby stores approaching the bridge and then it snatches Chancellor from the air. I fear for Amadeus – that is, until a wave of rippling force transforms the creature's arm to slush and the armored figure flits free. I acknowledge green-haired Cipher with a curt nod, and it's a shame he can't fly, because the Winter King's new groove quickly reforms the slush into a massive, twisted fist and brings it down and across. Cipher disappears like last week's newspaper.

I glimpse Cusp. She's actually flying. How the fuck is that even possible?

I channel another blast of electricity into the beast's core. It lumbers over toward a few other heroes who've come too close – Treesinger and Nocturne and Omeganaut and a guy dressed like Robin Hood and a black guy in gold lame and a dude who looks like a giant stack of twigs with arms and legs – and they run away, except the wooden guy, he's called Susurrus apparently, I recall as I watch him get flattened. Another figure comes up beside me who I don't immediately recognize because I don't expect to be shoulder-to-shoulder with a villain. His name is Manticore and last time I heard he moved in the same circles as Frost and Gravitas and Thunderbird, whoring himself out to the Calabrese.

"We need a better strategy," the long-haired mercenary shouts into my ear. "This thing shrugs off surface damage and its core seems all but impervious."

"You blast shit, right?" I snap. "So join in. There's enough to go round."

Manticore shakes his head.

"My attacks are psionic. I can't locate a coherent mind in there."

I glance around. That would explain Nocturne's uselessness and the number of psychic heroes like Miss Black and Seeker hanging back, unable to do much more than shout encouragements. Jackanape keeps making fool rushes in, gesturing wildly and seeming unable to comprehend that his powers, whatever exactly they are – I think I said that already – that they don't hold any sway over the monster. Someone later explains that the barefoot, trench-coated madman can disturb mental activity as well as memories, but it's his super-strength and acrobatics that save him from the clobbering of a lifetime.

So I have to concede Manticore is right. I release another discharge, vaporizing a chunk of icy torso that will refill its freezing lattice within seconds.

"Yeah, this isn't working."

"Someone said this is a demon?" Manticore asks. "I'm not sure what that means."

"It's all relative, or at least that's what I'm learning," I say, then do a double-take. "What the fuck are you here for, anyway? Nobody's paying you."

The guy wears a domino mask and has too much bare chest for my liking. He looks hurt by my suggestion all the same.

"I . . . the city needs help," he says weakly.

And I look up and away.

"Amen to that."

Twilight lands beside us. The left side of his costume is missing, the leg holding on by fibers alone. He only looks better, more majestic for it. Gay, huh?

"What's the plan, man?"

"He's your pal," I say. "Bright ideas?"

"The pregnant chick says we need to immobilize him and dig out the manifestation," Twilight says. "There should be a slug or something, on this side of the Barrier."

I frown, remembering the eerie serpent they dug from the carcass of the demon-god who possessed Twilight, and then I catch myself on.

"Who's pregnant?"

Twilight clicks his fingers and gestures absently. In that direction there's only the few – what I call super-bystanders – able to watch crimes unfold in a single bound, and then the dark suggestion of the retreating police line.

"What, Jocelyn?"

"I thought that was Lady Macbeth? You know, Overlord's squeeze."

Manticore follows Twilight's gaze. "She's called Jocelyn, now."

He catches my look and shrugs, embarrassed.

"So I was watching Oprah? Who cares? I was eating lunch."

"So we need to whittle him down a bit more. . . ."

I actually stroke my chin before the beginnings of a strategy start falling into place. I impress myself as I pass for the closest thing we have to a general. I click my fingers, but it's really just to get into character.

"Sun Man! Chamber! Chancellor! Start blowing up those cars!"

There's a lot of stalled traffic, police cars, even a fire truck that hasn't yet been flung around by the rampaging figure. A good amount of those wrecks now lie to the beast's rear. Dutifully, the three nominated heroes get to work and it's only a moment later that the first of the fuel tanks go up with a loud and satisfying *kaboom*.

"OK," I say, motioning forward and following the direction with my own footsteps. "Bring in the Supermen."

Mastodon, Twilight, Red Monolith and I hit the thing at once. Twilight's fists are ablaze with a familiar viridescent naphtha. The storm demon makes a sizzling noise, steam pissing everywhere, and a sound like kittens being euthanized unwillingly fills the air as we manage to wrench one of its arm loose. Twilight takes the enormous severed limb and prods the beast back with it.

"This is what you're thinking?" he calls.

We have the elemental backing into the car fires and water pours like sweat from its back, pooling and refreezing and melting again on the ruined bridge.

"Keep going!" I yell so all can hear. "There's a thing in there, like a snake."

Quick as a snake itself, the monster snatches out with its one remaining hand – a hand just big enough to grab Red Monolith by his helmeted head.

The crushing noise is like glaciers grinding together as we, the assembled, shriek and focus on the enormous stony wrist, Falconer and Susurrus and Jackanape and Paragon pitching in to do their level best and being rewarded with nothing as Monolith gives a twitch, standing on his booted tip-toes as if that might save his life, and black blood runs in enormous treacle smears down his costume and over his famous yellow side panels.

The monster releases him with the universal disdain such creatures share for the recently dead. Red Monolith's helmet looks like a hammer-smashed snail, mind-numbingly narrow and flat and broken and wrong.

"Oh God, oh God," I mutter, looking around for who would say such a stupid thing.

Twilight drags me out of the way as the thing stomps down, Chamber 'ports in and peppers the creature with superheated light, and Darkstorm vanishes part of the creature's leg into shadowspace.

It's not enough.

The blizzard beast topples over briefly, scrambling, and bats Jackanape away so hard the guy vanishes like he can teleport. Jackanape's later uncovered in the rubble of a record store and spends six weeks in a medically-induced coma.

I can hear the tensile cables of the bridge snapping and collapsing behind us and Lynx, still wet and licking herself from an earlier swim in the freezing waters, yowls and leaps to safety. Then, where the bridge joins the roadway again, there's now just a black chasm, and without thinking, a couple of us gang up on the monster and Twilight comes in with a mint condition '62 Dodge he has somehow acquired and we ram the fucking monster back into that abyss.

As it hits the debris-filled water, the river crackles with sudden ice as it freezes solid and I start to weep.

Zephyr 3.10 "On The Edge Of The Abyss"

THERE'S CHAOS AS we regroup and the alien god scrambles at the jagged bank, its black earth, torn pipes, exposed cabling and shattered concrete an effective ladder for it to slowly work its way up.

Tessa, which is to say Windsong, lands beside me and helps me to my feet. I had no idea I was sitting on the road, head in my hands, with Red Monolith's practically headless corpse just yards away.

"What are you doing?" I ask, mindful of the devastation. "You shouldn't be here."

"Let me help," she replies. "I've seen everything. I can feel what this guy does, we're . . . we're both weather controllers. Everything he does tugs at my mind, my . . . senses."

I stare at her without anything to say for long enough that even my daughter is creeped out. Thankfully, she *is* my daughter, and for some reason not prone to dismiss me outright. She places a tentative hand on my arm, my costume torn to the shoulder.

We don't evade scrutiny for long. Soon Twilight, Seeker, Miss Black, Paragon and frigging Jocelyn are jostling around us, and it soon gets even worse since it appears the FBI field team landed some time back when my dope-smoking friend Monolith was still alive, and Vanguard, silent and grim, and also Synergy arrive, the latter demanding to know what's going on.

"This is . . . Windsong," I say weakly. "She says she knows something about the creature."

With all eyes on her, Tessa doesn't blanch.

"I can feel what he does," Windsong replies. "Controlling the air, the currents. I think I could shut him down – shut down that aspect of him."

The heroes are speechless for a moment. Only Twilight's gaze moves speculatively between Windsong and I. There's a noise in the distance as the earth is torn frozen asunder. As one of the only duly deputized Federal agents present, Synergy seems determined to take charge or at least appear to be doing something. She puts her hand on Windsong's shoulder like she has no idea she's technically dealing with a minor and squeezes encouragingly.

"You know what I do, Zephyr," Synergy says. "If she says she can do this, then with me boosting her, we can maybe give the rest of you a shot."

I look at my darling girl, and sure I'm proud, but damn it, I never expected to be flung into a situation like this – and judging by the panicked look on her face beneath the mask, even she's finding the learning curve more than she can chew.

God bless her, though. She sets her jaw and nods at Synergy and asks, "So you do *what*?"

"I'm Synergy, girl," the agent says in her rich Afro tones, a voice made for condescension. "Come with me and I'll boost anything you can throw at that thing."

It is around this moment Ras Algethi emerges over the lip of the chasm and the head, just a nightmare slushy now of rock and ice and trash, throws open what I take to be its maw and lets loose with a long and guttural howl.

If I spoke Assyrian or maybe Hunnic, perhaps I would know it had just announced its plan to devour us all.

*

THE TWO WOMEN are out in front of the rest of us and I am not sure if anything in my life ever felt so wrong on so many levels. I am imperceptibly cringing, shoulder-to-shoulder with Falconer and Twilight and Manticore, horribly aware that not one of them know my secret connection to Windsong – and what would happen if they found out. Yet I'm almost too worried to keep it quiet. I can't help thinking that without outing myself as Tessa's dad, I don't have a spitball's chance in Hell of protecting my little girl from this weird, dangerous, creepy world and all the gangbanging spandex-worshippers in it.

Not that anyone wears actual spandex anymore. The technical accomplishments of the hero world know no bounds when it comes to the artistry of apparel. You'd almost wonder sometimes that advances in fashion aren't about the most we've got to show with the sixty-something years dudes with hard-ons in masks have been turning up to fights.

I'm being cynical again, here in the middle of our cross-your-fingers-and-save-the-world moment. Mostly I am proud. Proud and a little nauseous. Actually, a lot nauseous. And really the pride is what I know I should be feeling. I'm trying to zoom in on it, but instead I'm just quietly freaking out and hoping Nocturne isn't poking around in my brain right now like I know she can.

"What are they doing?" I hear someone say, the guy is called Jetstar apparently, his high voice rich with suspicion.

"She's a weather controller," I snap.

A few heads turn.

"Haven't heard of her," Falconer opines.

"Nice ass," someone else contributes.

My head snaps around so fast I swear there's a wind. I can't decide between Cipher and Paragon and just as I'm about to glare, I catch Twilight looking right at me with a dangerous glimmer to his grin. Based on past experience, this is not a guy I want armed to the teeth with facts about my private life. It's like trying to have a dinner date with a shark. Makes you wonder what the hell I was thinking with my little confessional bout earlier. What do I tell you? He brings it out in me. The kinky deviant big brother I never had.

"What do you think, Zeph?" Twilight asks with a twinkle. "Cute ass?"

So I look at Windsong's rear. Like all the rest of us at this moment. The city's poised on the edge of the Abyss and we're a line of color-coordinated guys in tight pants, most of us unwittingly checking out a fourteen-year-old girl's butt.

To me she's just a little girl – a curvy little girl, I must admit – more puppy fat than voluptuous. The little girl who has to stand on tip-toe to kiss me goodnight. And as much as my chagrin burns at the stupidity of it all, I know if you turned that big old powerful lens around and focused some of that righteousness on where my own eyes have wandered while on the job these past fifteen years, there's probably a bunch more dads who are proud of their little girls in uniform, fighting the good fight, who'd baseball bat pricks like me into the ground given half the chance.

Truth is – and this is what I fear – I've done a lot worse than look, over the years, though my real straying from Elisabeth only began four or five years back. This is a guy (yes, me, stay with me) who quite literally notched his belt for each female reporter who'd swallowed his jizz. Suddenly, I've got the whole virginal Madonna thing happening, just because now it's my daughter who's pulled on a pair of tights.

I figure it's God's final laugh, the piece of shit.

I close my eyes briefly and listen to the gruesome noise of the thing hauling itself up. The ice-creature finally rights itself over the lip of the destruction-wrought chasm. Windsong has her arms out, hands splayed, and Synergy stands behind her with her hands on the back of my daughter's jacket, her back to us, but a look of intense concentration on her face no doubt. Motes of light candle around them. There's something palpable in the air and in the space before where Tessa gently motions and it's not just the snowflakes.

Manticore's the first to put a finger on it.

"The air's getting drier," he says.

"She's not controlling the weather," Seeker says from nearby. "She's cancelling it."

"This is a creature of the elements, not the weather," floats Jocelyn's arch reply.

"Well watch, then," Seeker says again. "How else do you explain it?"

The creature who should be known as Ras Algethi gives a bellow and starts down the avenue toward us. It's just the two courageous women between us and the beast. Oh, and the rest of the city behind us.

Faintly, we hear Synergy urge Windsong on. My fists ball up and crackle with renewed power and I start forward, others joining me, knowing if something doesn't change fast then we're the last bastion.

But things do change. The air goes from dry to downright sultry, the warmth not just a change in temperature, but now with a feel like the passing of the seasons. And that's exactly what Tessa's done. With her powers boosted beyond all ken thanks to Synergy's assistance, it is more than the weather – there is something sidereal about what my little girl's managed.

It has its effect on the star-god too. Huge sections of the ice and slush making up its current form fall away as hidden seeds and spores within suddenly flower. Weeds and seedlings buried deep inside it spring into sudden life like a hippie's green psychedelia. The costumed crowd gasp, jostling and shaking each other to see the startling effects of the seasonal change as we fast forward in seconds through spring and right into summer.

The few pieces of organic matter keeping the weird simulacra together turn brown now and wither and the hidden junk, the tin cans and pulped pizza cartons and cigarette butts, they all collapse on the street and something hard and brown erupts, or perhaps I should say pours out of the collapsing mass paused in the street. I recall with squinting memory the slug-thing they withdrew in the aftermath of Twilight's mad jaunt and open my hand and throw lightning into the remains. Seeker, Miss Black, Jocelyn walk past me. Windsong collapses into Synergy's arms and I have to do and say nothing now and just join half-a-dozen others in a spastic moment of applause, a show of appreciation for what the teenage girl hero has done.

It's only moments and then the tactical police start leaping from wherever they went to ground, dragging in cordons and rushing across the scene to triangulate new security zones. The first of the ambulances are waved onto the scene and for a moment I gaze out at the bridge, the dozens of silent cars banked right up to the collapsed edge with their windscreens still frosted by the living force that has now gone.

Gone, amazingly, at the hands of my daughter. I must be grinning like a fool. A few of the other masks pause to high five me or nudge my shoulder and I spot Seeker turning at the waist to regard me with a curious look I will never learn to read. I cast about myself, wondering where the woman who may or may not be Cusp has disappeared to, and by then I am right at the edge of the knot of people dealing with the demon's remains.

In some final defense mechanism, the entity has drawn a compelling cocoon around itself. It is chiseled and rectangular and faceted like a gemstone lozenge and an alien glyph marks the center, though later it will turn out it's just Arabic. The capsule stands on its end, Jocelyn claiming to have the monolith in a telekinetic vice, and she calls over her boyfriend Paragon, glowing like a lantern in the midnight fog, and there's just something to the swanky way this bitch is suddenly holding court that I don't like. I can't believe veterans, even young ones like Annie Black, are now treating Jocelyn like she's a fellow "practitioner". Jesus, the PC movement really ass-fucked the magick scene. And so I step across as it just so happens that the serpent's obelisk splits in jagged two down the middle.

There are screams and shouts all around, but I'm the only one with anything like super speed. And while some later say they expected me to rescue the lady, it's my first instinct to dive like a footballer and take down Paragon. He's the one who was for some reason idiotically standing way too close following her call.

I feel something, I'm not sure what, pass through the air above us. I'm moving still, so there's hardly anything to glance at as I twist my neck behind and the air fills with an inconsistent glimmer that disappears with the sparkling shards of the gemstone cocoon that go everywhere as its two brittle halves collapse.

"Jocelyn!" Paragon roars and rolls clear of me.

The lady lies in a heap on the ground and somewhere in the ensuing kerfuffle Paragon breaks loose with the public revelation that she is pregnant – and Paragon's soap opera moment, captured by the hovering E! helicopter, the two lovers holding hands as their lips tremble with happiness and joy at the news, it doesn't occur to anyone that our mysterious opponent has vanished and the rubbery, eel-like thing they excavate from the rubble is desiccated and lifeless and not worth anything except perhaps being put in that half-dollar Museum of the Supernatural they restored inside the Bubble downtown.

Zephyr 3.11 "Beautiful Women Always Have The Meanest Scowls"

IT IS SOMETHING of the patriarch in me, displaced fatherhood perhaps, that eventually makes me stop by where Jocelyn has been treated by the paramedics for her fall. It's the closest she's come to a battle injury.

"Not much more than a scuffed knee and morning sickness," a cute ambulance officer says and smiles and disappears, feeling unnecessarily superfluous I guess in the face of we costumed idiots.

Jocelyn has removed her headpiece, the mask-cum-crown she wore to such great effect on so many occasions. It also kept her hair in place, which now hangs, veiling her seductive expression. I don't know where Paragon's disappeared. Fetching coffee, I hope.

"You know, I always thought you had a great ass in that outfit," she says huskily.

I'd forgotten about the old costume, which is faring about as well as my newer suit thanks to the evening's ruckus, though at least this outfit doesn't have cum stains.

"I'm not sure your fiancé would be so cool with those sentiments, and he happens to be a friend of mine, Paragon."

We eye each other off. Cat-like, her green-eyed gaze slowly travels down my torso and she stands and steps closer and puts her finger into a hole in my costume near my ribs.

"A girl has to have secrets," she says.

"I think you probably have more than your fair share."

Jocelyn pouts, but she has no power over me. Never did. Her old boyfriend, the one Twilight mentioned, had a psychic affinity for machine technology and a complete and utter lack of scruples. He's in White Nine for mass murder. I wouldn't trust Jocelyn as far as I could kick her, and because we're alone, I tell her as much. This is hardly news to the so-called reformed villainess and she only tries to pout more dramatically.

"Do you remember that time you fought the Clockwork King and uncovered our little operation in Siberia?" she drawls.

"How could I forget?" I say. "All that snow was a good reason to redesign the suit."

"Do you remember when Overlord's men brought you down with the sonic cannon?" Jocelyn asks coyly.

I eye the chunks of ice bobbing in the river beyond us with uncertainty.

"Yeah, you guys took me out. For about an hour. Big deal. You're gonna crow over that, after all that's happened here tonight?"

"The mighty Zephyr brought so low, and by some cheap machine knocked out by a half-blind Russian who used to hallucinate most of the time that he was in Fairyland."

The woman gives a laugh, head back, glossy thick fall of gingery blonde hair swaying around her waist like a curtain. With the same theatrical bent she always possessed, she straightens and stares at me, completely fascinated by her own allure.

"I had you for an hour on your own then," she gloats. "I stripped you down, had every inch of you in my mouth. Did you know that? Tell me. Is it our little secret? Always has been?"

I roll my shoulders and think of Snake Plissken.

"Lady, if I notched my belt every time I woke up with some villainess sucking my dick, I wouldn't be able to keep my pants up."

I shrug and look away, the breath uncoiling from my mouth.

"I do sure hope you swallowed, though. Last lady had some pretty crazy designs on my tadpoles."

I add, "By the way, that better be Paragon's baby you're carrying, or God help me I'll be the first one on the phone to Sal Doro."

I walk away leaving her with her mouth opening and closing, little more than bursts of white air coming out.

*

IT IS A night for the ladies. I find Cusp getting hit on by Falconer and Chancellor. Neither male seems deterred by the other, like maybe they have an unspoken agreement where a double-team wouldn't be considered a bad outcome. Sadly for them I am not easily put off myself and I stand a short distance away and *ahem* and fold my arms until they get the clue and sod off. Cusp, looking truly delectable, turns my way and I am sure now there's not a single glimmer of recognition in her crystalline blue eyes.

"How's that working out for you?" I ask with a wan smile.

Her nose does a cute turn at wrinkling as her eyes narrow behind the cat mask.

"What's that?"

"You're bluffing your heart out," I reply. "How did you do that before? The flying thing."

"I can fly," she replies deadpan. "Can't you?"

"Sure. Me, I got hit by lightning during some tomfoolery when I was sixteen. What's your excuse?"

Cusp works those cute lips for a second, but nothing comes out.

"Having trouble remembering?" I take pity on her and ask.

"Um. Yeah."

"Maybe I could help you with that?"

Beautiful women always have the meanest scowls. Hers is a doozy.

"I might not be able to remember what I'm doing here, but I know who you are well enough, Zephyr," she says. "I'm not gonna be another one of your little trophies."

She is so full of it. And herself. I like.

"Trophies?" I step in close.

"Trophies?" More quietly.

We lock eyes. I could kiss her, though she might kick my balls in.

"Your name is Holland," I say. "Until tonight you never had any real powers. I'm not sure what else to tell you. Something's happened, that's for sure."

"I . . . didn't have powers?"

"Something's happened to you though, obviously," I say.

Cusp makes a fist. Darkness congeals around it.

"The name," she asks. "Do you know what it's about?"

"Holland? No. Weird name for a chick. I'd find your parents."

"I meant Cusp," she says.

I watch as the darkened blur slowly fades and pinpricks of light begin shining from across her gloved palm, the whole thing coalescing into a powerful radiance that silhouettes the pair of us standing amid the police cars and wreckage, news choppers whirring overhead.

"Maybe we can talk soon," Cusp says.

She crouches slightly and then lifts, is away and up into the air before I can say another word – if anything would actually occur to me to say. Instead, I'm left with a mouth formed into a curious bow and a tingling in my loins.

Behind me, there's a muted cheer and I turn and see Windsong emerge from the barricade of ambulances with Synergy by her arm.

Zephyr 3.12 (Coda)

"THE GIRL DID good, hey Zeph?" someone asks.

A few elbows nudge me, hands pat my shoulders. My costume is in rags and I am glad for it.

"Yeah," I say weakly. "She was . . . amazing."

They crowd her, and my little girl looks like she's just won every fourteen-year-old's lottery. The heroes of Atlantic City surround her and she is one of them, perhaps the best of them. A shining new hope.

It's Twilight who pulls me back. Once I recognize who he is, I give a patient leer and my uneasiness should be stronger than it is, so I perform as I am accustomed and he ignores it as is his wont.

"Give the girl some room," the big blonde hero says in his deepest voice. "They'll get bored in a few minutes and then you can get her out of here."

"You know?"

"It's a reflection on these idiots that they don't put two-and-two together."

"Probably just as well."

Falconer and Chancellor are there at the front. I can't be entirely sure my daughter isn't flirting with Miss Black, which just weirds me out. Treesinger is plucking his lute and grinning foolishly and the black guy in gold lamé looks my way and winks, setting me with a feeling of deep unease. Manticore is there as well, along with Chamber and Mastodon, who I think is smoking a thick joint behind Paragon spooning standing up with Lady Macbeth and I am reminded for one cold sad moment that Red Monolith will no longer be dancing from foot to impatient foot waiting for Mastodon to finish his deep inhalations, warning him not to "do the Bogart" on that joint.

The other costumes are so distracted by the drama before them they don't clue into the gravid animal noises coming from another of the ambulances near where Windsong and Synergy so recently evacuated. I give Twilight a surprisingly comrade-like pat on the shoulder with a look that suggests "I'll be back, but see you later if I'm not," and then I trot over to the row of ambulances and shoot a curious glance at one of the paramedics, who looks like a woman on a mission as she runs over to some cops nearby to get them to start clearing a path through the debris.

Seeker provides the field hospital a muted radiance as she stands, her face a mask of concern, watching a civilian and three more ambulance officers tending to Constance Da Silva. Better known to the world as the former Sentinel Vulcana, she now thrashes on a blood-stained trolley while others struggle to keep her in place. Vulcana mutters, over and over, words I barely absorb as my eyes remain locked on the jagged stump of her arm.

"I can't hold it, I can't, I can't hold it, oh God. . . ."

And just like that a flush goes through the blue-skinned woman and she's just an ordinary woman, the sweating, dying sort, and the freaked-out ambos stab the dark with their wild eyes and the doctor looks at me and says something he has to repeat to get me to understand.

"This woman needs to get to a hospital five minutes ago."

I nod. "Right."

This is the part where I take the wounded heroine in my arms – I don't know what we do about the severed arm – and fly in desperation to the hospital and where the city's finest surgeons perform the night's real miracle. Except Connie is a weeping, thrashing mess, and there's blood everywhere as a rubber tourniquet comes loose.

"Oh shit . . . shit," the doctor gapes.

"She has to come with me," Seeker says and gently thrusts me aside.

In her hand is some small weird device, like a remote control fashioned by Hobbits. She gestures and perhaps it is telepathy that instructs me to bring the trolley. So I push Connie free of the desperate paramedics as Seeker goes ahead of us, walking toward the end of the ruined street and the river beyond, something like the keyless entry for a sports car in her hand. Blood is thick in my nostrils like off soup.

"This way," Seeker says. "Come on."

There's a subsonic beep and the crowds, attentive now, gasp as an enormous stone castle materializes into wobbly view in a move so implausibly real that only the very dodgiest of 1980s special effects could truly capture it.

"What the fuck?"

Seeker turns.

"Zephyr, we have much to talk about. I'll call you."

With that, she takes the handles of the gurney from my fingers and starts pushing it up a vague slope I eventually realize is a drawbridge, and then Seeker, with Vulcana, is disappearing into the enormous black skull face of the strange ancient castle and after the vaguely intangible wooden bridge has drawn up once more, the whole thing fades like a spectral vision with the dawn.

Dawn, however, is still in fact some time away.

The supers chat animatedly about "Seeker's awesome castle" for a while, circling like we've licensed an open-air nightclub just for freaks, small groups forming and reforming amid the emergency crews and the traumatized paramedics and the tired cops and the surly city council crews arriving in their yellow vehicles to start making head or tail of this mess, the international journalists filing for their prime time slots despite the hour, the autograph hunters back at the cordons calling for their favorite masks like there couldn't be anything more important in the world.

When the cool air does start to glow with the first sign of day, a number of us make arrangements to catch up at the Silver Tower later on, drinks on Amadeus, and while Tessa fields a few invites half-heartedly, I know she is cluing in to the fact that this is the part where reality has to step back in and there's no way on earth she's going to be going with Cipher to the new Terminator series wrap party or the opening of a new restaurant called Crayons across town with Miss Black. And I have to ask myself if it is a school night until I remember we haven't actually worked out the school arrangements yet, with George and Max offering to pay for the fucking Academy, much to Elisabeth's chagrin.

I'm like a statue or something: a grinning, wry, admittedly exhausted homage to dads everywhere in my tattered red-and-white suit, Vulcana's blood dappling my shredded cape as I wait through the lessening crowds until we are nearly alone and Windsong daintily treads my way in her expensive-looking boots. I don't care if the dawn sweepers or the displaced homeless people or Nigel the Troll or the last psychotic fans are watching as I sling an arm around my daughter's shoulder and we walk through the trampled wasteland where an hour or so previous an imaginary castle touched down or where, an hour previous to that, we vanquished the earthly incarnation of a living star, or something like it.

Windsong and I get to the river and I admit it feels not only good to be alive, but there's a resonance of Old New York here as the grey clouds scud across the horizon and the city begins waking up, the smell of rotting garbage and fresh-ground coffee mingling into one heady mix as we inhale the brisk freshness of the breeze that lifts Tessa's hair trailing and coiling like a scarf and my cloak flaps backwards like the flag I guess these things were made to imitate.

"That was one crazy night," I say at long last, it almost being a profane thing to intrude on the meditative silence of daybreak and the weird intimacy of us being in costume together.

"Tell me it's not always going to be like that," Tessa replies.

"No," I say and turn so she knows it's serious. "It won't be. Take it from me, you just got pretty much all the good bits without too much of the shit. I'd consider retirement."

After a moment I let the grin break through and it conjures a levity in Tessa's face I haven't often seen, masked or otherwise, and we briefly hold hands and she squeezes my fingers and I concede she has a hell of a grip for a fourteen-year-old girl.

"I love you, dad."

"Yes, baby. I love you too . . . Windsong."

Tessa gives a giddy laugh, every inch the teenager.

By osmosis, we agree not to discuss all the shit things, not the least being the imminent divorce. Instead, Windsong adjusts her mask and winks at me and punches me in the shoulder and shoots up into the sky and I just stand there, watching for a moment as my daughter ascends in a blurry arc across the city where a bridge once stood, and then I do the crouch thing, and well, for a guy with the power of however many fucking light bulbs it's meant to be, I don't think I'm gonna catch her. Not today. Or at least not if I don't want to spoil the moment.

CONTINUED IN ZEPHYR II

Find Zephyr on Facebook at www.facebook.com/Zephyrseries

73757919R00151

Made in the USA
San Bernardino, CA
09 April 2018